Round The Corner

By

Gilbert Cannan

Round The Corner
by Gilbert Cannan

Copyright © 2023

All Rights reserved.

ISBN: 978-93-59958-58-3
Published by

DOUBLE 9 BOOKS

2/13-B, Ansari Road
Daryaganj, New Delhi – 110002
info@double9books.com
www.double9books.com
Tel. 011-40042856

ABOUT THE AUTHOR

Gilbert Eric Cannan was a British author who lived from June 25, 1884, to June 30, 1955. Though he was born in Manchester and was of Scottish descent, he did not get along with his family. In 1897, he was sent to live with the economist Edwin Cannan in Oxford. He went to Manchester Grammar School and King's College, Cambridge for his education. He wanted to be a lawyer at first, but after a short time as an actor, he switched his focus to writing in 1908. It was as a translator and writer for London publications that Cannan got his start. A lot of his books are based on his own life, and they all fit together into a series called the Lawrie Saga, which is about a figure named Stephen Lawrie. Samuel Butler had a big impact on his writing. In a story in The Times in 1914, novelist Henry James named Cannan as one of four important new writers on the rise, along with D. H. Lawrence, Compton Mackenzie, and Hugh Walpole. He worked as a servant for J. M. Barrie and helped him fight against the Lord Chamberlain's attempts to shut down the theater. In 1909, Cannan started dating Barrie's wife, actress Mary Ansell. Ansell had been an actress herself and felt ignored in her marriage.

CONTENTS

A LITTLE PREFACE

Care I for the limbs, the thews, the stature, bulk and big assemblance of a man? Give me the spirit.

HENRY IV, Part II.

Being of such a strange temper and vision that when I aim my pen at a man I am as likely as not to hit his grandfather, I have in this instance endeavoured to forestall the treachery of my faculties and to go straight for the grandfather, though my interest is centred in the man. In a sense I have written his life as it was long before he was born, when he was nothing more than a growing presentiment. I have found it instructive and entertaining to observe and follow the evolution of the material, moral, and intellectual atmosphere which was to bear on him first of all through his mother's mind, and then through his own senses as soon as his life was separated from hers.

I launch my hero upon the world and leave it to anybody who likes to kill him, and I pray that those who are in process of morally slaughtering their own innocents may take my imaginary child instead, for there is no remedy for the murder of a living soul, but, should it ever happen that my bantling demanded the right to continue his existence and in his turn to become a father, I have only to revive him, give him another name, and let him do his worst.

My conscience has been greatly exercised for some time now over the many errors and literary sins I have committed in the past—sins not against the rules (there are none) but against the persons whom I have forced to live in a mutilated, limited sort of life in the printed page, and those other excellent persons whom I have invited to collaborate in the fun of watching them. Upon these two sets of persons I have too often forced my beliefs without making it clear to them what my beliefs are. And here again I shall often seem to offend, because, honestly, I can neither codify my beliefs nor force them into any existing code. I can, however, give a hint at them by saying that, in my view, we can only accept life with dignity and without injury to our self-respect in perfect freedom—by which I shall be taken to mean Licence. Freedom is a much-abused word, and when you use it to seven men and women out of ten they at once think of a world full of satyrs. When I use the word Freedom, I think of a world full of what Walt Whitman, who had no sense of humour when he took pen in hand, called "superb persons," that is, men and women who are not imprisoned in their own thoughts. Only a man's own mind can make him a slave, and every healthy human being from first to last of conscious life struggles for the freedom of his own mind. We set about it often in strange ways and make dreadful muddles, but the fight itself renders life enjoyable, even if the aim be never attained. Freedom, of course, like everything else, is subject to the limitations of this existence. A man's thoughts, like his life, are bounded by birth and death. When he tries to cast them beyond death they fall cold and lifeless, as will be seen in much imaginative poetry, many spiritualistic theories, and all presentations of Heaven. For reasons quite explicable when we consider the dying belief in a sort of straight-line human progress, men have never been interested in events antecedent to birth. I look forward to the day when they will be as little interested in events after death. A man's father and his son (mother and daughter included) are all the past and future vouchsafed to him, and if he will take the trouble to understand them he will find satisfaction and to spare for what is at present called his thirst for immortality.

I find immortality an admirable word upon which to end my preface, but, in face of the grey tints of this composition, I must protest my optimism, believing human life to be like a river, that, if it be fouled, will run itself clear in time. Only, you must trace the poison to its source and stop it.

I
FRANCIS OBLIGES

One is One and all alone
And ever more shall be so.

OLD SONG.

THERE was once a time, and not so long ago either, when gentle people were so gentle that the males could not (with the countenance of their families) enter upon any profession other than the Army, the Navy, or the Church.

Francis Christopher Folyat was a male member of a gentle family that had done no work for two generations and, unfortunately, had not been clever enough to keep its revenues from dwindling. He was the eldest son and he had two brothers, so that there was one Folyat for each of the three professions, if enough patronage could be collected from their various titled and more or less influential connections. Francis had a snub nose, William had an aquiline nose which his mother adored, and Peter had a nose which betrayed a very remote Jewish infection of the blood of the race.

Parenthetically let it be observed that the name Folyat should be written with two little *f*s—ffolyat, for so the name was spelt by the only really distinguished Folyat, Henry, who had been mixed up in the Gunpowder Plot, so that his name is printed to this day in more than one History of England, and to this day, in spite of its deep-rooted conservatism, the family is proud of that insurgent son. He marks its descent for all to see, and, as it is all so long ago, it is easy to forget that he failed to do that for which certain politicians have become infamous, namely, to blow up the House of Lords and, with it, his cousins, the Baron Folyat and the Viscount Bampfield of his day. He escaped from England, and the French Feuillats, of whom the present representative keeps a newspaper kiosk on the Rue de Rivoli, just outside the Métro station by the Louvre, are his direct descendants. English interest in that branch of the family ceases with the conspirator Henry.

The grandfather of Francis Folyat had a seat in the country and a mansion in London, also a coach and a barouche, an advowson or two, and a vast number of servants; also a large collection of portraits, including a Van Dyck, a Holbein, and a Sir Peter Lely. The father of Francis Folyat left the seat in the country in a dilapidated condition, and only so much else as he could not possibly avoid leaving. However, Baron Folyat and Viscount Bampfield behaved very handsomely and agreed to assist the widow with their patronage. Baron Folyat's magnanimity stopped short at his promise, but Viscount Bampfield was as good as his word, and when the time came for Francis to enter upon a career he procured him a commission in His Majesty's Army. Francis was highly delighted at this, and saw himself stepping into the Duke of Wellington's shoes when that illustrious man should be gathered to that fold where the most illustrious are even as the meanest of God's creatures. He spent a glorious day in the top of his favourite oak-tree in the park planning heroic wars for England and telling the birds that at last they had something to sing about. He had never thought of it before, but, as it had been decided that he was to be a soldier, he flared to the project, saw himself in a red coat charging like Marmion, or dancing at a ball like that described so melodramatically by the wicked poet, Lord Byron, when Belgium's capital had "gathered there her beauty and her chivalry"; more, since it might be his duty to die for England, he fetched up an England worth dying for, a heroic, majestic king, a cause, and a God cursing England's enemies. He thoroughly enjoyed himself and prepared a martial oration in good Ciceronic periods for his mother's benefit, when, as he knew she would, she gave him her blessing and delivered herself of a homily over her soldier-son.

"I will be," he said, "a true Folyat, worthy of the name I bear."

As he entered the house he met his brother William, whom he had always disliked more than any one in the world—he had often prayed to God to make him like William better—and he thought there was a curious look in his eyes. He put it down to envy and liked William less than ever. William sidled up to him and said:

"Mother wishes to see you."

A wish from their mother was a command, always obeyed, as he obeyed it now. She was a very handsome woman. She had been the celebrated Miss Cresitter and she never forgot it. She had been a toast, and queened it accordingly. Her portrait had been painted by an extremely fashionable and very indifferent painter and it hung in her room, the best in the house. She wore a beautiful lace fichu and black lace mittens, and the lines of her face were hard. Her hair was done in ringlets on either side of her face and drawn up into a knot at the back of her head. In front it was parted in the middle and plentifully oiled. The furniture in the room was handsome and ponderous, and there was nowhere an indication of any sort of recognition of the loveliness of the view from the window.

Francis stood, as he had been trained to do in his mother's presence, and waited for her to speak. She was in no hurry and kept him standing, and when she spoke he was startled, as he never failed to be, by the rich tones of her voice. It was a magnificent voice, and she knew it and used it caressingly, lingering on her favourite notes, which she threw cunningly upon the open vowels. Francis was a fine word for her purposes. She might have put a world of affection into her intonation of it, but that seems never to have occurred to her. It never occurred to Francis either.

"Francis," she said, "I have been thinking."

This called for no reply and Francis made none.

"I do not think," she went on, "that you are altogether suitable for the army. You are too gentle. You cannot say 'No.' You are—how shall I say it?—too emotional, too much given to dreams. The life of a soldier is stern and calls for resolution. The Folyats are, and always have been, weak. There have been exceptions it is true, but I have never seen any indication that you are one of them."

Francis was cut to the quick, but he had never in his life doubted the truth of anything his mother said, and, when she pointed out the temptations of a soldier's life, he began to see himself as a feeble will-less wastrel utterly unfitted to wear the king's uniform. Better never to wear it than to disgrace it! It was quite as easy for him to see himself in this light as to dream heroically of warlike deeds and successful prowess. His mother played upon his foible and stripped him mercilessly of red coat, sword, epaulets, cocked hat, and glorious future. He capitulated and agreed that he was incapable of saying "No," and was therefore unfitted to take up the commission so kindly obtained for him by his cousin Bampfield.

Having been robbed of his dream, he did not very much care what the future held for him. His mother explained to him that she had very little money and could leave him less, and that if he would go into the Church his Cousin Bampfield could provide him with a living as soon as he had been ordained. She could not send him to Oxford or Cambridge, since the estate of a gentleman in those universities was costly, but she had made inquiries and found that the University of Dublin, the Irish being notoriously poor, could equip a divinity student with Latin, Greek, Hebrew, theology, and a degree for a modest annual sum.

Francis embraced this plan miserably enough, and began to study the Greek Testament with the vicar. The subject of the commission was never reopened, and his mother was more amiable to him than she had ever been.

A few months later it was announced that William was to stay with Cousin Bampfield, and Francis learned that the commission had been transferred to his detested young brother. He lost his temper, waylaid William, dragged him behind the stables, and thumped his aquiline nose until it swelled and assumed a red and purple hue, and William howled and vowed that if ever he could do his brother a mischief he would. No hint of the combat ever reached their mother, in spite of her distress at the damage to her William's beautiful nose, and the brothers went their ways—William abroad, to stay with his aunt by marriage, the Comtessa di Sangiorgi, and Francis to Dublin, where he lodged with a slatternly Irishwoman, who corrupted his habits and encouraged him in his natural indolence of mind and excessive good-nature.

Of his university life nothing very definite is known. He was in every way unremarkable. He was too simple and direct to achieve notoriety by conflict with his fellow-undergraduates. He recognised that he was in Dublin to procure a degree, and set himself to achieve that purpose with the minimum of trouble. He acquired a taste for the Latin poets, especially Juvenal, Horace, and Lucretius, and he was never weary of reading the fragmentary novel of Petronius Arbiter. He had many acquaintances and few friends, and he devoted much time to the growth and cultivation of a long golden beard, which, together with his snub nose, earned him the nickname of Socrates, or Old Soc. In Ireland he was happier than he ever was again in all his long life, though, with his large capacity for enjoyment, it cannot be said that he was ever genuinely unhappy. In Ireland he found an atmosphere altogether congenial to his temperament, which found its food in Rabelais, Montaigne (Voltaire he would not read as he was going to be a clergyman), and so led him to the conviction that English literature was diverted from its true channel after the death of Henry Fielding. (He once took a chaplaincy in Lisbon because he wished to see and to honour the novelist's grave.) He made friends enough to be asked to spend his vacations away from home, and was glad to have excuses to give to his mother—excuses which he conveyed to her in letters beginning "Dear Madam" and subscribed "Your obedient son."

Nothing occurred to disturb his equable determination to enter the Church, and after he had taken the degree of Bachelor of Divinity he swallowed the Thirty-nine Articles without blinking and proceeded to ordination at the hands of the Bishop of Bath and Wells, shortly after the marriage of Queen Victoria with her cousin Prince Albert, not yet either great or good, and almost within a week of his brother William's departure with his regiment for India.

For a few months he acted as chaplain in his cousin Lord Folyat's household, and was amused to find his position as spiritual adviser and curate of souls gave him a status slightly above that of the butler and, so far as cordiality went, distinctly below that of the huntsman who fed and trained the hounds. He comforted himself with the reflection that his condition was at any rate better than that of Parson Adams, though his deserts were less, and took steps to obtain work independently of his family. This greatly upset madam, his mother, who warned him that he might be jeopardising his chances of the next family living. Within himself he argued that, being by profession a shepherd of souls, he must not waste time in places where there was not one to be found. He did not, however, lay this argument before his mother, but accepted a curacy at one hundred and ten pounds in South Devon, on a pleasant estuary, in a little town that had been a seaport in old days, trading busily with France and the Netherlands, and once familiar ground to Francis Drake and many another Elizabethan adventurer. Here there might or might not be souls for his charge, but there was the sea, and romance, and a heronry, and woods that were a perfect paradise for birds. He went down to the place and wrote his mother a very fine literary description of its natural beauties, which he sent to her by the new penny post and promised that he would stay with her for six days before he entered upon his new life.

He arrived to find her in her great four-poster bed, shrivelled and very little, and looking very old in the shadow of its massive hangings. Her appearance shocked him. He had never seen anybody die, and he had a strange feeling that he was being very unfairly treated, and he realised painfully that in honouring his father's memory and his mother he had enjoyed only a very unsatisfactory relationship. His brother William was in India; Peter was on the high seas, and no word was to be expected from him for three years or more. He was alone, and he felt ashamed of his incapacity to grapple with the situation. His mother, perhaps as a tactful tribute to the profession into which she had forced him, asked him to read the Bible, and automatically he turned to the Book of Ecclesiastes and read her the passage in the last chapter which contains some of the soundest and most neglected advice ever given to mankind. He made no attempt to reconcile it with Christian teaching and his work, but found himself delighting in the spiritual health of the words. His mother said:

"Francis, you must read better than that."

This rather irritated him, though he knew it was selfish and inappropriate at such a time. He replied:

"Mother, I could have wished to come to see you in a red coat. It has been ordered that I should wear a black. I do not think I shall ever be a bishop, but I will do my best to remain a gentleman and to be worthy of the name I bear."

His mother turned the subject and talked to him of material matters, and made him promise to preserve intact the family portraits—twelve in all. Certain articles of furniture and plate he was to keep in trust for his brothers when they should return to England. William, she said, was certain to be a general, and Peter could hardly fail, with so much influence, to become an admiral.

"And I," thought Francis, "am a stranger to ambition."

Suddenly tears came to his eyes and he had a feeling of immense pity, and it was so queer to him that he should have an overflowing emotion in his mother's presence that he was relieved when this colloquy was broken off by the entry of Dr. Fish, the physician from the town five miles away, who still wore a wig and knee-breeches and looked like a sparrow after a dust-bath.

Francis left him with his patient and went into the fruit-garden to enjoy a pipe of tobacco, a luxury which had mastered him in Dublin. He learned there to smoke a clay pipe and bird's-eye tobacco and never changed them for sixty years.

Dr. Fish was rather a long time closeted in the dark room with the great bed, and when he came down Francis met him with an anxious face.

"Die?" said Dr. Fish. "Not a bit of it. She'll live to be a hundred."

But to Francis she was already dead, and in his life thereafter she was a ghost whom he regarded with a friendly eye. Never again did he allow her to meddle in his affairs.

II
THE CURATE MARRIES

She's extremely pretty and loves thee entirely. I have heard her breathe such raptures about thee.

THE OLD BACHELOR.

POTSHAM then was very much what it is now. It is doubtful if fifty houses were built in it in as many years. It had then a repairing dock which provided work for the poor. It has now a jam factory. Then its postmistress, with the aid of a kettle, opened all letters that looked interesting. Only the other day a new resident discovered that his private affairs were common property, and the postmistress was deposed. Then, as now, the church, standing high above the river, was the centre of the somnolent life of the place, and Francis Folyat lived upon an eminence. He liked it.

The little society of the place warmed to the curate when it was found that he was welcomed in the houses of one or two of the county families. When it was discovered that Viscount Bampfield was his first cousin once removed, and that Baron Folyat was half a degree nearer in kinship, he became a romantic figure. When a small girl read in her history book that Henry Folyat was associated with Guy Fawkes, she ran with her thumb between the leaves and showed the passage to her governess, who showed it to her mother, who gave a dinner-party to announce the discovery. Thenceforth the curate was bathed in a golden light.

He became the object of the most flattering attentions. Every woman in the town showed herself a mother to him, and Miss Martha Brett won from him the confession that his full name was Francis ffolyat Christopher ffolyat-Folyat. She hugged this information to her bosom, and gloated over the thought that it was hers and hers alone. She devoured romances, though, being not yet seventeen, she was supposed to confine her attentions to "The Fairchild Family" and Miss Maria Edgeworth. In all innocence Francis lent her the poems of a young man named Shelley who was still regarded as a blasphemous and immoral writer. She could not read them, but did not tell him so, though she distressed him by inviting him to read Mrs. Inchbald aloud to her in the gazebo at the end of the garden, above the wall that was washed by the river when the tide was up and slimed with mud when it was out.

The curate's mind was at that time divided into two compartments, one for literature and the other for religion. He saw no necessity for reconciling the two things and made no attempt to do so. He regarded religion as his work, and literature as an escape from it. Life was extremely pleasant: lazy day succeeded lazy day. The obedient flock was rounded into the church on Sunday and quite often on weekdays, for there was no other place in which two or three could gather together. The only tiny clouds in a fair blue sky were drink and dissent, and in the lower classes an occasional outburst of immorality. Dissent was ignored; drink was attacked by prayer; and immorality was defeated by a hurried marriage where possible, and when that was out of the question it was scarified by threats—sure promises even—of eternal punishment. It was all a matter of routine, and so extremely pleasant that Francis soon ceased to regret that he had stifled ambition with a black coat. His vicar was a man who had taken a small active part in the Tractarian movement, without in the least understanding its spiritual significance. He had been attracted by the notion that the Church existed in spite of Henry VIII, and not because of him, and when his leaders told him to adopt the ideas of the Real Presence in the Sacrament and the sacrificial priesthood of the clergy, he did so without making any attempt to bring them into agreement with the facts of his life or the practice of his profession. He instituted ritual in his services, thus making them more entertaining to his flock, and, as he had never looked for any rejuvenation of the spiritual life of his parish, he was not disappointed by the result. He thought he was a good man: everybody said he was a good man, and perhaps he was.

Francis swallowed both his ideas and his goodness without difficulty, examined the ritual of the services with interest and some enthusiasm, corrected it in one or two points, and as he took nearly all the work of the parish off the vicar's shoulders, there could not possibly be any friction between them. The vicar congratulated himself on having found a jewel of curates, and his wife began to dream dreams of vast preferment obtained through the Folyat influence—a rural deanery, a stall, a bishopric, and— why not?—Canterbury or York.

Francis, on the other hand, gave no thought to the future and drifted drowsily, most keenly enjoying himself in the summer days when he could take a boat, a book, an old long-shoreman and fishing tackle, and go down to the sand-banks at the mouth of the estuary and bathe and fish and lie in the sun with his clay pipe between his teeth, and his golden beard glistening and his blue eyes shining as he thought that the world was very good and the sea almost the best of good things in it. It was not his way to compare

16 | Round The Corner

his lot with others, and it had never occurred to him, except in his official capacity, to criticise life. In that capacity he criticised not so much life as a traditional concept of it.

He was rudely awakened from this drowsy golden age by an event which kept Potsham talking for a generation and a half.

One night when he had been dining at Crabtrees, the house of Miss Martha Brett's aunt, where there had been music and cribbage and a walk down the garden to look at the moonlight on the sea, he returned to his rooms to find them occupied by a man with a white face and quivering lips and legs that would not be still. He was a poor man and a sort of seafaring man, and he looked up and in a rustling voice he said:

"Parson, what sort of man would that man be. . . ?"

Then he stopped and rattled in his throat, and Francis felt a curious nausea as he looked at the man and saw how frightened he was.

"What sort of man?" asked Francis, feeling that the question was almost as meaningless as the man's words.

"She's got a cut in her throat and a lot of blood. . . . I say."

"I say," echoed Francis.

"We'd better go," said the man.

"Yes," said Francis. "Does anybody know?"

"No," replied the man, "I been looking at her three hours."

With that he seemed to gain control of himself, and his legs did not shake any more and his lips set in a thin straight line. He stood up and went to the door and Francis followed him. Very cunningly the man looked at him and said: "You do know how a man could do it?"

"No," said Francis, "unless— —"

However, the man seemed to be satisfied and led the way, and they walked down the little crooked street called the Strand and came to a little tumble-down house by the dock, and there they found the woman even as the man had told. To Francis the adventure seemed to be complete and fantastic, and he felt that he was outside it, that the world had stopped and that it was very cold. Then he felt that it was horrible and intolerable, simply because nothing could happen unless he made it happen, and action had never been asked of him before.

There was a tallow candle in a bottle, but it gave very little light. The moon shone through the window, and its light was very pitiless and grim.

The man folded his arms and said with a sort of insistence: "You do know how a man could do it!"

The cold dead harshness of his voice brought Francis out of his fantasy, and at last he found the word that had been buzzing in his brain ever since he saw the man sitting in his chair: Murder.

"No," he said, and he was astonished at the hardness of his own voice.

He turned heavily, but the man was quicker than he. He saw him dart through the door, run a little way up the street, go into a house, and in an instant there sprang up a crowd of people whispering, murmuring, buzzing, huddling, and crushing round the door of the little dark house. They were a little awed when they saw the curate, but the crowd hummed as new people came running up and the tale was told again. Suddenly Francis felt a hand on his arm, and there was the man clinging to him while the beadle and the policeman were tugging at him to take him away. The man would not let go, but he was very strong, and for some way Francis had to move with him through the crowd. Then at last he wrenched free and watched the three figures cleave into the crowd, part it, and then be swallowed up.

He found himself standing at a place where, between two houses, he could see the water swelling with the tide and a black boat rocking, and over all the light of the moon.

The machinery of the law passed over the murderer and he was hanged, but Francis never told a soul how he had been drawn into the eddy of the crime. His experience produced in him a feeling of profound depression, from which he recovered slowly and painfully to find that human beings had emerged from the landscape as they had never done before. They demanded, a different sort of attention from that which he had always given them, and at first he disliked them heartily. He saw them in their habits, sadly, as they were—eating, drinking, sleeping, gossiping, with very little to vary the monotony save foolish love affairs and mean jealousies and petty quarrels. Nothing that they did, not even their sins, seemed to be worth while. What bothered him most was that he found himself sympathising with the criminal and curiously desirous of defending him against the society which had answered ferocity with ferocity.

That did not last long. He was soon brought up against his ignorance of the world outside and his entire lack of comparative standards, and, as young men will, he thought that at all costs he must escape—that is, move from the circumference of a dizzily spinning world to the centre of it.

First of all he came to the conclusion that he had religious doubts and consulted his vicar, who bowled him over with professional arguments.

Against them he could only set his vivid sensation on that strange night and his keen recollection of the tallow candle in the bottle and the moon shining through the window; and of these he dared not speak. He agreed perfectly that he had set his hand to the noblest service in the world and had no right to look back. But looking forward availed him nothing; the present was bewildering and the past had suddenly become empty. The bung had been removed from the tight barrel of his existence and all the good liquor had leaked away.

However, he did his work neither better nor worse than he had done it before. He christened children and churched women and married couples and read solemn and beautiful words over the dead, and for the first time began to ponder the meaning of these ceremonies. The Church, he said, sanctified birth and death and what lay between them, and he tried to persuade himself that it raised them from brutality, spiritualised them, and made them holy; but then he could not help feeling that there was some discrepancy. The facts remained the same, therefore if they were sacred at all they must be sacred in themselves. All that could be done by mind and Holy Writ, the product of inspired minds, was nobly to interpret the facts, to see to it that men lived nobly—lived nobly and nobly died. He had seen several persons die, had given them the comfort of religion, and now, when he remembered, he was struck principally by the dignity with which death was accepted. It seemed to him that men had religion in themselves, that it was not, could not be grafted on them from without.

"Life," he said to himself, "is a religious thing, or it is something less than life."

He felt that he was moving from the circumference to the centre, and then he realised that he was reaching only the centre of his own thoughts, not the heart of the world. He had advanced in theory but in practice was just as far out of his bearings as ever. He had fed himself chiefly with the writings of ironists and he was hungry for belief—in the nobility of life and death and the unity of all things. The lives of birds he knew and the lives of beasts, but of the lives of men he knew nothing at all. Never had he been to a great city, but he conceived that there also the lives of men must be very much what they were in the somnolent little town on the Devon estuary— they were born, they suffered, and they died. That was all. Surely that was all.

He would not have that. The ironists left it at that. He became positive that the manner of it mattered—to Nature, perhaps, not at all, but to men, and to God through men, vitally. To that end the Holy Bible had been written and the Church founded, and to that end Keble and Pusey had sought to rouse the Church from its indolence and indifference. His vicar was right: he could not turn back, but he must know wherein his work as a priest consisted. If it served any purpose at all, it must be for the sanctification of life by endowing it with a noble interpretation.

Francis had no large conception of the universe. At this young period of his life his notions were still mediæval. He believed the earth to be stationary, Hell to be under his feet, and the Heavenly region to be beyond the blue vault of the sky, and that human life led infallibly to one or the other. A noble life, therefore, was that which led to Heaven, and to this idea, and to the cosmogony it implied, he shaped his ethics and his ideals, never suspecting that he was sacrificing the greater to the less.

When men sit down and think out schemes of life they nearly always make the mistake of leaving women out of them. This is easily understood in the case of young men for whom women hardly exist except as an emotion, a fire that may at any moment flame into their existence and lay it waste like the little foxes in the Bible. Our curate made that mistake. Naturally he had been in love—never out of it; but always he had worshipped from afar, and had thought the objects of his adoration as insensible to it as the stars in the sky to his wonder and delight. He was in love now, but could attach his emotion to no particular young woman. There were at least four, and he never credited them with any design when he met them out walking, or they came to him on parish business or demanded his escort or displayed their gardens to him. He enjoyed his emotions while he was ashamed of them. They were not "noble."

When next he sat—at her suggestion—with Miss Martha Brett in the gazebo, he found himself thinking that she was very charming and pretty with her brown ringlets on either side of her face and her plump little shoulders peeping out of her gown, a modification of the style made popular by the young Queen. She was so demure, so quiet, and her manner of listening to him gave him such a sense of authority. He felt it could never leave him, that he would never again have those appalling moments in church when a gulf opened wide in front of him and he felt that any one of his listeners had more right than he to be talking and calling this black and that white.

She sat by a little table and he sat on the other side of it with a book in his hands, and she let her hand fall on the table so that it lay flat, very white and soft and pink at the finger-tips, and in her wrist was the most delicious little bone. He could see nothing else. He gazed and gazed at it, then with a wrench turned to his book, but his eyes were swimming so that the words swallowed each other up.

Roses nodded in at the window, and the smell of the salt water came up and mingled with the garden scents.

"It is most moving," said Miss Martha.

"Most," stuttered the Curate, and he looked up and saw warmth and mischief in her eyes, and almost imperceptibly she edged her hand a little nearer to him.

Her aunt came in on that, and Francis heaved an immense sigh of relief and went spluttering on with his reading as though he had been caught out in some shameful act.

When he left the house later in the evening he admitted to himself that he was in love, and that Miss Martha was the most beautiful, the most peerless, the most chaste, the most innocent of women, and he called his emotion "gross desire" and tried to strangle it, and suffered horribly. The more he wrestled with it, the more powerful it grew.

He was in love, and love swamped all his thoughts. He took long solitary walks, and he hated all the couples whom he married and envied them. They had passed through torment—Oh! who was the fool who said that love was sweet? The old fleeting devotions had been delicious—if shameful; but this, this was fire in the veins, scalding thoughts, an obsession, a fixed idea.

More to be rid of it than with any hope of success, he called upon Miss Martha's aunt, and, coming straight to the point, blurted out that he hoped she could regard him favourably as a suitor and would grant him permission to ask for her niece's hand in marriage—exactly as Miss Martha's aunt had planned that he should when he first came to Potsham and she had satisfied herself as to his antecedents. He explained that he was not rich but had every hope of being given a family living as soon as one should fall vacant. To his amazement he was informed that Miss Martha was something of an heiress, and would own, when she came of age, thirteen houses in Potsham, subject to leases, and one mortgage, a farm on Dartmoor, and fifty acres in Cornwall. Her niece, the aunt added, had often expressed her great admiration for Mr. Folyat, and, with her eyes gleaming exultation and beatitude, she confessed that she could desire no better thing than to see such coincidence between her own wishes and her niece's affections.

Francis took his leave praying devoutly that he might not meet his Martha, but no sooner had he set foot outside the parlour door than there she stood before him, and he could say nothing and she could say nothing, until suddenly he caught her up in his arms and hugged her and kissed her, set her down on her feet gasping, begged her pardon, and blundered out of the house blushing furiously.

Cousin Bampfield warmly congratulated his kinsman on his betrothal, and, two adjacent livings in Cornwall presently falling vacant, gave him both of them.

There was a splendid wedding and the young couple spent their honeymoon in London, for neither had ever before visited the capital. They saw the Tower of London and Westminster Abbey and St. Paul's Cathedral, but Martha was impressed by nothing so much as her husband's grandfather's town house in Curzon Street. She thought it grand, and was never tired of hearing her husband tell of his gentle family, the Folyats.

III
ST. WITHANS

Not knowing how to find the open air,
But toiling desperately to find it out.

HENRY VI, Part III.

IF Potsham was somnolent, St. Withans, our parson's Cornish living, might well have been the home of the Sleeping Beauty. For a time it was a place of enchantment while the charm and novelty of wedded love were upon Francis and his Martha. They were blissfully happy: the county welcomed them, they had a charming house and garden, a carriage, money in plenty, children, and when they were bored with the country they could escape to the gaiety of Plymouth. After they had been married for five years they exchanged duties for a year with the English chaplain at Hâvre-de-Grace in Normandy, and their fourth child, a daughter, was born there. After that it became a habit with them to go over to the Continent every year for a couple of months.

Their sixth child died in infancy, their seventh only lived to be three years old, but the eighth, ninth, and tenth were as healthy and comely as the first five.

It was a year or so after the birth of the tenth, in 1867, that they began to discover that while their family had grown their income had remained stationary. It was at that moment that for the first time they began to think of what they had done and counted up the number of their offspring, and realised that they had brought nine good lives into the world and had to face the responsibility and, somehow or other, establish them.

These were the names of the young Folyats: Serge, Gertrude, Frederic, Mary, Leedham, Minna, Annette, and James.

Serge had early passed out of his parents' control, though not without expense, for he had been sent into the Navy, from which, at the age of fifteen, he deserted in Labrador and was only saved from court-martial by being bought out of the service, to which end the farm on Dartmoor and a house in Potsham were sold. He was not allowed to come home and, since he refused to stay in America, a situation was found for him in a bank in Kimberley, in South Africa, and his correspondence dwindled and then ceased altogether.

Frederic was at a Lycée in France, and the question of his career was being indefinitely postponed.

The girls were the problem. Gertrude and Mary had suddenly become women and there was no man to ask them in marriage. An occasional Folyat was sent to the Vicarage to be coached for some examination, but they either only flirted or they fell desperately in love with Minna, the beauty of the family, who was only fourteen.

After Serge's escapade the carriage had to be given up, and since Mrs. Folyat could not pay calls or visit at a distance, the county soon forgot her and fewer and fewer distinguished ladies drove up to the Vicarage. On the other hand, Mrs. Folyat's aspirations had offended the ladies on whom the county did not call, and when the carriage was disposed of and replaced by a little wicker donkey-cart they did not conceal their rejoicing, and their tattle did not fail to reach Mrs. Folyat's ears. She was confirmed in her conviction of the vulgarity of trade, and she brooded over the situation without saying anything to Francis. He said nothing to her and they skirted the problem. His anxiety was entirely to make expenditure and income meet, and he rather welcomed than deplored the defection of the county. It meant a garden party the less and two of the servants could be dismissed.

The crisis seemed to be tided over and the financial problem adjusted when they were faced with the fact that Frederic was nineteen, of an age to leave the Lycée, and that a profession must be found for him. Mrs. Folyat decided on the Army, but Francis at once squashed that and, all unconsciously, reproduced his mother's arguments. Frederic was a Folyat and weak. Regimental life would be too dangerous for him. The Church? Frederic, who was not a little Frenchified and rather dreadfully freeminded scornfully rejected the suggestion. . . The Bar? Mrs. Folyat was sure Frederic would look well in a wig and gown, and besides, judges and the law officers of the Crown were always knighted. Frederic saw that this plan would take him to London, and he jumped at it greedily.

Francis went to Plymouth and saw his solicitor, who pointed out that it was a matter of great expense and meant supporting the boy until he was over thirty. Francis felt that the problem was insoluble, gave it up for the time being, and consoled himself with buying a parrot from a drunken sailor and a dog in a fancier's shop by the docks because it was impossible to tell which was its head and which was its tail. He called the dog "Muff" and the parrot "Sailor."

Frederic sulked when he learned that he was not to go to the Bar and went down to the village inn and came home very drunk. When he was reproved, he asked what else there was to do in such a dead-alive hole, and his father found it very difficult to reply. It was painfully forced upon his attention that Frederic also had a mind, and that it worked in a way entirely different from his own. This was distressing, because for many years Francis had done all the thinking necessary for his family, and that no great amount. He had an intolerable sense of being cooped up with an enemy, and what bewildered him most of all was to think that the enemy should be his own son. He could not explain it to his wife, or to himself, for that matter, but there it was, and he was thankful when Frederic chose to absent himself from meals.

At last, after much cogitation, he approached his wife with the suggestion that they should make Frederic a solicitor.

"An attorney!" said Martha, and Francis knew that she was thinking of the common, dusty little man in Plymouth.

Parents who have aspired to make their sons physicians and been forced to stop short at dentistry will understand what torture it was to Martha Folyat, and, in a less degree, to her husband, to descend from the higher to the lower branch of the legal profession—no wig, no gown, no access to the Bench, no prospective knighthood. It was a pill and they swallowed it, putting as brave a face on it as possible, and they were somewhat comforted when they found, upon inquiry, that a family of undoubted gentility in the county had sent their son into a solicitor's office in Lincoln's Inn Fields in London.

Martha's ambition leaped within her, and she suggested that Frederic also should be sent to London where he was more likely, if not to meet, at least to handle the affairs of, the aristocracy. Who knows? Even the Royal Family had legal business, and there was a great case coming on to decide the succession of the collateral Folyats, somewhat complicated by a bigamous old clergyman who for his third wife had taken a negress in Africa. The case would be ripe just about the time Frederic was qualified, and Willie Folyat, a possible heir, was one of Minna's most devoted admirers.

Martha only spoke about a hundredth of her musings, but Francis, mindful of Frederic's recent behaviour and his plentiful lack of character, decided for Plymouth, as being more accessible in case of disaster. (He was surprised to find himself taking account of the difference in expense of the two journeys, having always hitherto had a lordly disregard of money.)

It was settled; the dusty little man in Plymouth accepted Frederic as an articled clerk, and, when he had received his premium, went into the affairs of the family, and presented the horrible truth that such inroads had been made upon capital that the income was reduced by one-third from its original dimensions.

Francis was so relieved at having disposed of Frederic that at first he made light of it and said nothing to his wife. He supposed his difficulties would solve themselves, and this to all appearances they did.

Willie Folyat, the possible heir afore-mentioned, an undergraduate at Oxford, a very worthy and high-souled son of a pious and very poor father, spent two long vacations at the St. Withans Vicarage. Gertrude fell in love with him first, as by prescriptive right, and then, as she seemed to make no progress, Mary considered herself free to lose her heart. To their amazement and dismay, Willie sought an interview with their father and proposed for the hand of the chit, Minna, not yet out of short frocks. He was besottedly in love and prepared for all sacrifices; however, he was refused on the score of Minna's youth, but given to understand that in two years or three he might return with every hope of success. Meanwhile there could be no objection to his writing to Minna if he were discreet.

He vowed eternal constancy with all youth's fervent and curious belief in its possibility, and, by way of proving the breach of his heart, accepted an appointment in a school in Bombay. Then by every mail he addressed the most excellently turned love-letters to Minna, who skimmed through them—being already engaged upon another conquest—and handed them over to her mother, who wept over them, read them to father, and saw herself as the beloved mother-in-law of the Earl of Leedham—the title to which Willie had the remotest possible claim.

All this was very exciting and disturbing, and it set the thoughts of Gertrude and Mary in that direction from which there is no turning back. Gertrude, then Mary, made a long stay in Plymouth, and they returned with new costumes, new accents, new thoughts, and all their talk was of the superiority of town-life over the country. They spent a great deal of money, and the problem of income and expenditure occupied their father's mind to the exclusion of everything else. In Plymouth Gertrude and Mary had met the most delightful young man, a friend of Frederic's, named Herbert Fry. On their entreaty he was invited to stay for a holiday. He came and saw and was conquered—by Minna. He was caught kissing her in the shrubbery, his stay came to an end, and the name given him by the nurse—"a reg'lar Apollyon, my dear"—was found to be appropriate. Minna was furious, and in a gust of spite wrote a most offensive letter to Willie Folyat in Bombay. She told her mother what she had done and robbed her of her most cherished dream. She was found to be conducting a clandestine correspondence with "Apollyon," and Martha let loose the thought which for some time had been lurking at the back of her head, namely, that they must make a change and, if possible, seek life in some city. She skirmished about with it, never suspecting that much the same thought might be in her husband's mind also, and she led him to it by easy stages. Really the girls were getting beyond her; they had said things to her which she would never have dared to say to her aunt when *she* was a girl; and the country certainly was dull for young people, and they had the children to think of, and, of course, parents must make some sacrifices.

Francis looked at her with anxious eyes and muttered something about his duty to his parishioners. He was popular with them, and he liked the peace of the country and the simplicity (also the low cunning) of country people. He liked the figure he cut, with his knee-breeches and black shoes with silver buckles, and silk stockings and tall hat. He had grown used to himself in a back-water and shrank from the prospect of city life. Even Plymouth he found bewildering on his rare visits. On the other hand, there was the perpetual leakage in his finances—Frederic in no way to earn his living for at least four years, and his daughters, like the horse-leech's, crying "Give! give!" and no man apparently desirous of marrying them; and beyond them the long tail of his family, all of whom might grow up and develop minds which thought along lines different from his own. He was not in the least resentful about it, that was not in his nature; but he hated his own helplessness, the impossibility of doing anything to relieve the growing strain. He loathed quarrelling, and his daughters were always quarrelling with each other and their mother, and that, in a house which should have been a model to the country-side, made him profoundly ashamed. He had begun once more to think in an extra-professional way, to see things in a humorous light which by all tradition were sacred. A curious desire to tease had taken possession of him, and he fought it with all his might. Further, if he was to continue the war with circumstances in this place he must admit his wife to his inmost thoughts. He tried, but his new failure was the most bitter of all to bear; but yet he would not admit that she was stupid. Still he clung to old memories, and he told himself that he loved her. He did love her—he loved everything and everybody; but he was not and had not been for many years in love with her. She had never understood love, and she had bullied him. When he argued with her she wept; when he agreed with her she wept also, and protested that he was an angel and far, far too good for her.

He came as directly to the point as she would let him, and one night, after a protracted curtain lecture, he proposed that he should consult his bishop and negotiate an exchange of livings with some clergyman desirous of a country life. His only stipulation was that the new parish should be among the poor, and this, unhappily, broke in upon Martha's dreams of a brilliant social life among rich and more or less "gentle" parishioners. She had mapped out marriages for all her daughters and careers for all her sons, and was drowsing off into a golden slumber when the word "poor" punched into her pillow.

"My dear Frank!" she said.

"I must work," said Francis.

"But, my dear Frank, the poor!"

"It is easier for a rich man to enter the Kingdom of Heaven than for a camel to pass through . . ."

"I am not talking about that."

"If I go to a town, I must go to the poor," said Francis, his old ideals stirring in him.

"But think of the girls."

"I am thinking of the girls. I shall make them work among the poor. It will do them good. It will keep their minds healthy and clear of amorous thoughts."

"How can you be so coarse?"

This came with almost a scream, and Francis smothered what he was going to add and turned over and pretended to be asleep. His wife went on talking indignantly to herself. About five o'clock she woke him up and told him that she had been dreaming of water, which she thought meant riches, and also in her dream she had seen her son Leedham crossing the sea, and Mary had made a great match of it with a tall man who looked like a lord, but Minna had appeared very unhappy.

"I do believe," Martha went on, "that in her heart of hearts Minna really loves Willie Folyat."

"Nonsense," replied Francis, "she is much too young to love anything but herself."

Martha was enraged at this, and harped on the string of her husband's crazy notion of living among the poor. On that point he was immovable, and Martha's light skirmishing was fruitless. Francis turned and looked at her, told her that she wanted a clean night-cap, and went off to sleep.

They had many unhappy days, and it was some weeks before they found an incumbent willing to exchange his living for the two in distant Cornwall. This was the rector of St. Paul's Church, Bide Street, in the darker half of our town on the north bank of the poisoned river, about which we have no pride at all.

Neither Francis nor any member of his family had ever been north of Bristol, and the north of England was to them a place where millionaires grew and factories ground out wealth and a set of ideas associated with the name of Richard Cobden, a Liberal of whom no Churchman could entirely approve. There was a bishop in our town, and he was a person of some celebrity. Also there were two churches which had a certain fame or notoriety for their extreme ritual. Welsh Nonconformists teemed in the town, and the Roman Catholics had a cathedral thirty years old.

Francis visited the place and stayed there two days, during which it rained except for half an hour just before he left. He refused to be depressed by the slums in which his church was situated—a black, stunted Gothic building with a ridiculous little steeple, and a sordid school next door to it—and told himself that it was just what he wanted. There was a fried-fish shop directly opposite the church, a dirty greengrocer's shop next to that, and next again three public-houses. Another row of little shops followed on the other side of a bye-street, and for the rest, there were nothing but squat terraces of blackened red-brick cottages, two stories high, with blue slate roofs. In the street were an incredible number of children in curious nondescript garments, and some of them in rags. Many of the women wore clogs and all of them were sallow. The men were pale and ill-nourished and they walked slouchingly. The street was muddy and littered with refuse, and the air was thick and full of smells.

Francis stayed with the rector and met the caretaker of the school and church, the rector's and the people's wardens, and a few earnest men who examined him with hard, curious eyes. They asked after his family and how many children he had, and one of them whistled when he said he had eight. Francis wanted to like them, but he felt a stranger amongst them and could not be at his ease. They asked how he liked the church, and he told them very well, and the rector's warden, Mr. Parsons, said: "Ah! you should see it at 'Arvest Festival."

Their speech sounded uncouth and harsh after the soft drawl of his Cornish peasants, and it was this that Francis felt as the strongest barrier between them.

The living was worth three hundred and fifty pounds a year, and there were pew-rents, which would bring the stipend up to within a hundred pounds of the joint income of his two livings. Francis ignored that, and calculated that as he would have only one curate, the exchange would be equal, and no doubt his daughters would soon marry, and his sons would quickly earn their living in this money-making town. He was told that there were excellent schools for "them as could afford 'em," and that settled the matter. Everything was as far as possible arranged and he returned to St. Withans, tussling with himself during the long journey and telling himself that he was not sorry to renounce his old life, and that at last he was going to enter upon work, real work.

He had arranged to take on the former rector's old house in Fern Square (there was not so much as a blade of grass growing in it), and when Martha asked him about the town he concentrated on a description of the house in one of the largest and most imposing terraces in the district.

It was arranged that Frederic should finish his articles in Plymouth; and then, on a brilliant spring day, all the furniture, heirlooms, family portraits, and the valuable china inherited at intervals by Mrs. Folyat as her few aged relations one by one departed this life, having gone before, the Folyats set out at seven o'clock in the morning, and at half-past ten the same night reached our town where, at last, their history becomes interesting.

IV
FERN SQUARE

Sir, — I pray you take heed how you put a beast, tired with the heat of the sun and with long travel, among others, which, as I hear say, have divers maladies and diseases.

A PETTY THEFT.

HENCEFORTH we see Francis Folyat in trousers, and his broad-brimmed silk hat, like a bishop's without cords, has been exchanged for the soft round black felt which takes so many inches from a man's stature. Black trousers, elastic-sided boots, a black silk waistcoat on which hung an amethyst cross, a clerical frock-coat, and a round white-linen collar were the daily attire of the new Rector of St. Paul's, Bide Street. On great occasions the black-silk waistcoat was renounced in favour of one of violet silk. All day on Sundays he wore his cassock with a black silk sash round his full stomach, and when he walked to church he wore a biretta, to the solemn awe of the street urchins, who confounded him with the Greek *papa*, a strange figure that haunted the children of the northern district of our town and was reputed to be a wizard.

Francis was in fine middle age. His head was beginning to be bald and his golden beard was rapidly turning white. There were red veins on his round cheeks, but his eyes were those of a boy, bright and blue and merry, and when he laughed they used to close up into little slits and all his bulk would shake until tears were squeezed out of them. He had a great capacity for laughter, but always it seemed that he could not shake it out. It possessed him and set him quivering like a jelly, and there was nothing to be heard but a hoarse chuckle deep down in his chest.

There had been times of great difficulty in the beginning. Martha had come to our town with glowing dreams, and when she saw Fern Square and the house she was to live in they came tumbling down on her romantic head, and she wept many tears and declared that she could not bear the house or the people or the town, and she demanded to be taken away—to Potsham, to Plymouth, anywhere out of the smoke and the rain and the filth and the noise and away from the common, common people. She vowed that she would never attend service in the hideous, squalid little church, and could never have anything to do with the nasty, dirty school. It was impossible. She could not let her children mix with the children of these barbarians. They must find another living or give up the Church altogether. Francis could retire, and devote himself to theological literature.

Francis bore it all with excellent good-humour, and pointed out that he could not even write his own sermons (he had amassed a collection of one hundred and fifty, which he delivered in rotation). By sheer amiability he won his wife over to a more sweet and reasonable temper, and helped her to set her house in order.

When he came to tackle his work he found that his predecessor had been a lazy and unpopular man and that his congregation was never more than a hundred and twenty persons, while the Sunday-school was very meagrely attended. He began by having the church and school cleaned and decorated, and it was quickly noised abroad that the new rector had private means. Further, it soon became clear that a new church was to be added to the little ring of churches which upheld the High Church cause in our town. After much cogitation Francis decided to abolish the pew-rents and to open his church free to all and sundry. He bought new surplices and cassocks for his choir, and new vestments for the clergy and the acolytes whom he intended to appoint. Very soon he found adherents and was given presents of new altar-cloths and sacramental vessels. Altogether his prospects were admirably fair.

Fern Square was a wedge-shaped piece of ground enclosed on one side by six old red-brick houses four stories high, built in an imitation of the Georgian style, with three rooms on each floor except the top, which had four and an attic. The dining-room and the study were on the ground floor, the drawing-room on the first. They were fine rooms, and the Folyats' old furniture made a brave show in it. The house was lit by gas, and the drawing-room window looked across the square upon the deliberate ugliness of a Wesleyan chapel. The parrot had his cage in the dining-room among the family portraits, and the dog lived where he liked. He grew very fat and lost what little intelligence he had ever had, so that it ceased to matter even to himself which was his head and which was his tail.

The Clibran-Bells from next door but one were the first to call. Mr Clibran-Bell was the borough treasurer, a man with a huge red beak of a nose, a little white moustache, and a tremendous manner. He had an unfailing source of pride in his wife, who was really beautiful and had frequently been likened to the Marquise in *Caste*, a play which his daughters were always performing in the cause of charity. Mrs. Folyat flourished the

32 | Round The Corner

Folyats and the Bampfields at Mrs. Clibran-Bell, who countered with the Staffordshire Bentleys, her cousins. The Clibran-Bells all talked mincingly, as though they had eaten olives and could find no polite method of getting rid of the stones. Young George Clibran-Bell was in the head office of the Thomson-Beaton Bank, but, let it be added, the Clibran-Bells knew the manager. There were four girls and young George, and they soon became on terms of great intimacy with Gertrude and Mary Folyat, and they fell into the habit of running in and out of each others' houses.

The bishop's wife called.

Very soon St. Paul's by its ritual attracted a number of extra-parishioners who had previously had to go two or three miles to the other end of our town for their religious satisfaction on a Sunday morning. Francis was encouraged and worked very hard, found some excellent people among his poor, and really tried to make his church a centre for them and a source of help in their all-too-frequent times of trouble. Mrs. Folyat, by dint of custom, overcame her dislike of the common people with their coarse accent and rather uncouth manners, and went so far in her compromise with native custom as to renounce dinner in the evening and take to a heavy mid-day meal, a solid tea, and a betwixt-and-between sort of supper about nine in the evening. On Sunday she kept open house. Acquaintances and personages were fed at half-past one, and the familiars of the house at nine, after evening service.

At first she kept three servants, but when one of them gave notice she did not replace her and was content with two. Even that was found to be over-expensive, and she came down to one and a charwoman, and then, on Sunday evenings, Gertrude and Mary were forced to cook the supper and to wash up the dinner afterwards. They were very disagreeable about it until they found that most of the young women they knew, including the Clibran-Bells, did far more housework and did it as a matter of course. Then it became part of the routine of their existence and they raised no further objection, but Sunday supper became a cold feast, and they never cooked anything but potatoes and perhaps a Welsh rarebit for their father, whom they called "Pa."

Soon everybody, including the parrot, called Francis "Pa," and he sunned himself in his new popularity and had no further misgivings as to the wisdom of the step he had taken. Certainly he seemed to have disposed of the strained relations that had existed in his family in the country. The girls were busy and occupied all day long and every day. The boys seemed to have many friends, desirable and otherwise. Martha had taken to knitting and crochet-work, and she had Mrs. Clibran-Bell and Mrs. Starkey, the solicitor's wife, and Mrs. Tuke, the widow of the man who built the Albert Bridge and was killed on the day it opened, all ready and pleased to listen to her tattle of her husband's ancestry and her own property and her hopes for her children. She had taken to lace caps and had settled down to a style in dress and a general appearance which should last to the Judgment Day. She read *The Family Herald* every week, and every month purchased the threepenny novel published by the same firm. She had and was allowed a feeling of superiority, and enjoyed herself immensely. When Francis came to her with misgivings as to their capacity to live within their income she refused to listen to him, observed that they knew all the best people in the place—and what more could they want? Every Sunday they had a splendid congregation, and if the worse came to the worst they could restore the pew-rents. Francis had a vague, uneasy feeling that the worse had come to the worst, but nothing would induce him to do that. He let the subject drop.

Leedham had been sent to the grammar school, and James attended a dame's school round the corner in the Bury Road. Annette at first accompanied him, but her godmother had stepped in and sent her to a school in Edinburgh. Minna, who all her life had done exactly what she wanted, refused to be educated any more, put up her hair and let down her frocks, and claimed equal rights with her two elder sisters. She enjoyed their privileges and avoided their duties.

After the family had been a year in Fern Square Frederic returned a full-blown solicitor, and after a few weeks' idleness was taken into the office of Mr. Starkey at a nominal salary. He had grown a little moustache, which made the weakness of his chin even more pronounced, and, for some reason best known to himself, he wore a monocle. In Plymouth he had discovered a light tenor voice, and he became very useful to the Clibran-Bells in their amateur theatricals. He joined forces with young George, and together they indulged in all those follies with which young men fortify their uneasy sense of manhood. He had pale straw-coloured hair and a very pale complexion. He had a ready wit and a quick tongue, and soon won a reputation for cleverness. His brother Leedham hated him but always shrank away from Frederic's irony. Leedham had a great respect and admiration for his father, while Frederic regarded him with a contempt which originated, perhaps, in the episode of his intoxication at St. Withans. Mrs. Folyat doted on Frederic, and he never had the slightest difficulty in obtaining money from her. He used to play the buffoon to her, set her laughing until the tears ran, and then, with a sudden turn of sentiment, he would make her cry until she laughed. When he could do neither of these things he would shock her with an audacious jest. Always he would contrive to keep her entertained.

Francis, then, had no anxiety about his family. There was always plenty of fun and merriment in his house, and a constant stream of young people enjoying themselves as though the world had only just come into being and was to go on for ever and ever. If the atmosphere was not altogether pious, they were none the worse for that. They attended church regularly, worked in the Sunday-school, and in many other directions for the parish, and their happiness won the confidence of the poor, who made surprising efforts to please the rector and his family. Best of all, from Francis's point of view, numbers of young men were attracted to the house and from there were drawn off into various activities. Enthusiasm for the High Church cause ran high.

Our town is composed of a number of smaller towns and boroughs, all now under one city council, but at that time many of the boroughs and urban districts maintained their separate entities and had their own councils and their own newspapers. The district in which St. Paul's was situate was still a separate borough, and it had a newspaper called *The Pendle Times and Lower Brighton Gazette*, which published local news and copious police reports. The editor of this sheet was a fanatical Low Churchman whose whole religious force had gone into worship of a certain Calvinistic divine, the Reverend Humphrey Clay, a rigid temperance reformer, Puritan and moralist, who, perceiving the growing laxness of the new industrial population, flung himself with fierce zeal into the task of castigating their immorality and whipping them up into a state of religious fervour. He had pictured their lives—ugly and stunted as they were in fact—as a gay rout of sin, and he strove to counteract this peculiar fiction of his own mind by a religion of appalling dulness. He had a commanding spirit and found many disciples. He substituted the intoxication of conversion for that of alcohol, and drew hundreds to the corrugated-iron church he had built on a piece of waste land opposite a public-house and a theatre. His sermons were printed week by week in *The Pendle News*—half a page of fierce exhortation, while the other half was filled with racing results and advertisements of rat-pits and coursing. When he died twenty thousand men and women followed him to the grim cemetery overlooking the canal, and the streets were lined for two miles. In his obituary, Flynn, the editor, called him "the Sainted Humphrey Clay," and the name stuck. A movement was set on foot to replace his iron church with a stone building to be called the "Humphrey Clay Memorial Church"—none of your old Romish saints was to give his name to it—and a house-to-house canvas was instituted. The factory hands gave their pence, the better class their shillings and pounds, and after many years of unceasing work the fund was completed. The building was erected and consecrated by the bishop just six months after Francis Folyat came to St. Paul's.

Flynn, the editor, scented the presence of the enemy, and began the attack by the publication of the "Literary Remains of Humphrey Clay," containing stern denunciations of Popish mummery and mediæval witchcraft. The wildest stories flew, and very soon Francis was credited with worshipping the Virgin Mary and maintaining a secret shrine in his vestry. Flynn wrote two denunciatory articles, blindly prejudiced and pitifully ignorant. Francis read them and wrote to the editor to invite him to attend service in St. Paul's and see for himself.

Flynn waited for some weeks until Easter Sunday, when he fully expected to see a statue of the Virgin carried round the church. There was, in fact, a procession, and there was incense which stank in the editor's nostrils. His first impression as he entered had been one of disgust, for the whole place was filled with flowers, in the windows, on the pulpit, on the altar, twined about the lectern—daffodils and tulips and hyacinths and violets and lilies. He sat in his pew at the back of the church and saw men and women enter, cross themselves, and curtsey and bow to the East in the central aisle, and his gorge rose at it all. When the organ began to boom and send music whirring up to the roof and flooding the nave and the chancel, and a young man in a purple cassock and a lace surplice appeared bearing the Cross, and behind him two censer-bearers, and behind them again the choir, the curate, the special preacher, and Francis Folyat, in robe, cope and stole, carrying his biretta, he was fain to scream out upon the blasphemy of it all—blasphemy upon the memory of Humphrey Clay. He watched the procession wind round the church, singing the gladdest of Easter hymns, and move up into the chancel, where the choir, still singing in their harsh, untrained voices, filed into their places, and the three priests stood solemnly upon the altar steps and waited for the last notes of the organ to die away. Two acolytes appeared in purple cassocks and little lace surplices and stood below the priests, and the solemn service began.

Flynn rushed away and walked for miles until he was dog-weary. He took his class in Sunday-school in the afternoon in a sort of dream, and in the evening with wide-staring eyes he sat unheedingly through the sombre evening service in the Humphrey Clay Memorial. He saw the whole town, the whole world, imperilled. He saw in Francis an emissary of the great whore of Babylon that sitteth upon many waters, a man bent upon seducing souls from salvation, the very devil quoting Scripture to his ends.

Flynn's sensations were those of a pious young man who for the first time in his life enters a music-hall, with this difference, that for Flynn the abhorred thing had no charm nor peril for himself, only for others—those others whom his hero's life had been given to save.

On the Easter Monday his wife discovered that their charwoman had decamped with a sheet and two blankets, and he laid that sin at the door of the new source of corruption he had discovered, called for strong tea, wrapped a wet towel round his aching head, and wrote the first of his famous series of articles. The following is an abstract under the heading:

"*Non Angli sed Romani:*

The Enemy within our Gates.

There is a church in this town, for so long devoted under the leadership of our great and sainted Humphrey Clay, a church where Sunday after Sunday, and on week-days also, blasphemy is committed, blasphemy and a painted mummery. I have been to this church. With my own eyes I have seen the finger-marks of the painted, scented hand of Rome. In this church I saw three priests—*priests*, not *ministers*—clothed like actors in a theatre. They wore purple and fine linen and they carried funny little hats in their hands. They had decked up two young laymen in purple and silk and fine embroidery, and their feet trod upon rich carpets, with gleaming brass stair-rods. The very air was thick and oppressive with the smell of flowers, and to this was added the fulsome stench of incense, carried by conceited, mincing little boys. No pen, least of all mine, could describe the impiousness of the processions, the bowings, the scrapings, the befouling and vulgarisation of things sacred that happen in this church, this so-called church, which is in reality a booth, a theatre. Why, the very costumes are indecent. The choir-boys do not wear surplices, but little laced shirts or shifts which do not even cover their spinal bulbs. Their behaviour, their demeanour, is an affront to all truly religious-minded persons. Had I not remembered that I was in the House of God I should have spat in the face of the arch-mummer as he passed me and bade him begone to Babylon whence he came. Who is this man? Why should he be suffered to defile the religion which he is supposed to practise? Why should this play-actor be permitted to strut and mow and paw the air in the Holy of Holies? Three times at least I saw him change his costume—in public! And each time he was assisted with a mock solemnity by the valet whom he is pleased to call an acolyte. They say this man is a gentleman, the kinsman of a noble family, a rich man, one who has kept his carriage. Let him not play the priest. Humphrey Clay, of blessed memory, was the son of a carpenter, a working carpenter in this town, but before his Maker he was a gentleman indeed. It is but twelve months since our bishop consecrated the memorial which is the crowning edifice that pinnacles the glorious career of Humphrey Clay. Can that same bishop within his diocese tolerate the splendid memorial to the one and the impious practices of the other man? I say he cannot. Such churches as this have not hitherto been tolerated in our part of the town. Citizens, shall we endure it now?

N.B.—Further articles on the subject will appear until something is done. If those in authority will not move, we shall take the matter into our own hands."

Francis read this effusion and was hurt by it. Since he had thumped his brother William on the nose he had quarrelled with no man and deliberately hurt none. Behind the wild writing he could feel the torment, and he was sorry. He felt that he was to a certain extent to blame because he had invited the man to his church in a challenging spirit, and so had perhaps increased prejudice in him. He tried to write to Flynn but could find nothing to say. As he sifted his thoughts he could only discover that he wished his church to be free. All sorts and conditions of men were free to come and free to stay away. He had once found one of his sidesmen turning a ragged old beggar-woman out, and had reproved him and led the old woman to a pew. She spat on the floor and sat fingering an old clay-pipe, but, to Francis's way of thinking, these things might not be unacceptable to the God he honoured, however distasteful they might be to human creatures. The church, then, was free, and Francis desired only to make it pleasing and attractive to those who came to it, to have it a place of beauty amid so much ugliness. The Saturday before Easter had been one of the happiest he ever remembered—a day of hard work in the church, surrounded with young people all gay and blithe and busy with the flowers and draperies and vestments. One such day, he felt, could do much to redeem the waste and folly of years.

However, it was all odious and disgusting to Flynn, and Francis sighed as he reached out for his tin of bird's-eye and filled his pipe. The parrot scrambled out of its cage, shuffled along the floor and climbed up the back of his chair, perched on his shoulders, and stood combing its beak through his beard.

V
HOSTILITIES

Thou liftest me up above those that rise up against me;
thou hast delivered me from the violent man.

PSALM xviii. 48.

THE dead play a not altogether disproportionate part in the affairs of the living. There are so many more of them. The thought would be desperate but for the reflection that in all probability the most numerous of all are the unborn. The Creator may at any moment get tired of the eternal monotonous repetition of birth and death, but no man or woman will ever believe that. We get joy out of it, and His is the sum of all our joy—the dead, the living, and the unborn.

Humphrey Clay, for all the grimness of his words and works, must have been a joyous man, for his spirit was very powerful and roused many men to action. True, their actions were all ugly, but that came from their stupidity and the squalor of their surroundings. There is no country on the north of our town for thirty miles—only smoked bricks and mortar and tall chimneys and colliery stacks. On the south you must go seven miles before you will find a truly green field, and most of us are quite old before we can make such a pilgrimage, and then clear air and trees and streams and sky and the song of birds are things as separate from our lives as our dreams. They are almost a show to us. Our great holiday is Whitsun-week, and then each church takes its children in wagonettes and char-à-bancs out into the nearest semblance of green country, where they wander and play and laugh and squabble and are fed until they can hardly stand. It is called a "treat," and it gives them a new zest for the streets and their adventurous, strangely independent life.

The Roman Catholic churches organise processions which meet in the centre of the town and wind through the streets, the little girls in white and the little boys in the best they can muster.

In his fourth article Flynn exhorted Francis to be an honest man and take his flock to join them. In the meanwhile there had been appeals to the bishop, who refused to move in the matter, being convinced, from what he had seen, that there was nothing uncanonical in the conduct of the services at St. Paul's. He liked Francis, and if he could not altogether approve of the means, the result was eminently satisfactory. As a result of Flynn's campaign there was hardly ever a seat to be had in St. Paul's on Sundays, and some of the most noted preachers in our town and the surrounding district were glad to appear in the pulpit.

Flynn's paper was doing very well out of it. All sorts of people rushed into the fray and filled his columns for nothing, and when his supporters took to interrupting the services at St. Paul's with vehement protests the other papers took the matter up, and Francis found a sort of greatness thrust upon him. He refused to see reporters, and told one persistent Scotsman that it was Flynn's affair, not his, and that he had no intention of moving against Flynn. He received many letters denouncing him as Anti-Christ, and many more proclaiming him the one Spiritual Hope of the North of England. More than one of his correspondents enclosed poems.

Martha was all in a flutter, and was quite sure that Francis was on the point of being made a bishop. He was invited to preach to the judges when they came on assize, and she had no doubt that that would be the first step. Francis had no such illusions. He was not ambitious for promotion. He took out Sermon No. 112 and delivered it with the full consciousness that it was profoundly dull. Flynn came to hear it, took shorthand notes, and printed an abstract without comment.

This official recognition provoked exasperation, and on the following Sunday as Francis was walking in cassock and biretta to his church he was accosted by a gloomy-faced individual with a sandy complexion, who called him a "spawn of Rome," and when Francis smiled at the grotesqueness of the expression he stooped down and picked up a handful of dung and flung it in his face. Francis went on his way amid the hoots of little boys and the jeering of women.

A few days later the windows of his house were broken and the voice of Flynn in *The Pendle News* rose to a triumphant scream. Two policemen were mounted on guard in Fern Square, and the attentions of the malcontents were transferred to the school in Bide Street. The railings were torn down and the furniture of the doors wrenched away. Roughs and hooligans joined in, and one Sunday all the doors of the church were found to be screwed up, and the congregation stood in the street, while from the church steps Francis read the service and delivered the first extempore sermon of his life. He was trembling with emotion and his voice cracked, and hardly a soul could hear him, and he broke down altogether when the people sang

Rock of Ages, cleft for me,

Let me hide myself in thee. . . .

A few days later the authorities made the mistake of arresting Flynn on a charge of inciting to violence. The prosecution failed, but Flynn had the satisfaction and the bitterness of martyrdom, and he returned to the assault with new frenzy.

Meanwhile at home there had been a new development. Leedham, the third son, the one stolid member of the family, had upset his mother by announcing his intention of leaving school and our town and going out to the Brazils. He had made the acquaintance of a family who had connections out there, and he had been fired by their descriptions of Rio de Janeiro. His real reason was a heartfelt desire to get away from Frederic, but of that he said nothing. He observed, with much justice, that he was not doing any good at school and would probably learn no more if he stayed there another two years. (The school was conducted on the principle of forcing the bright boys and leaving the dull ones to pick up what they could.) Further, he argued that if he had to earn his own living, the sooner he began the better. Through his friends, he said, he could obtain a post in a bank in Rio, and he would rather be in a bank there than in our town.

Francis was inclined to approve, but Martha wept. Like so many mothers, she had no notion of her real relation with her children, and lived in a fantasy in which she was the perfect mother who adored and was adored by them. More than once to Mrs. Clibran-Bell she had said:

"There is nothing that my children do that they do not tell me."

And Mrs. Clibran-Bell, being of much the same type, believed her, and together they glowed with rapture over this miracle of domesticity.

Leedham had very little imagination or capacity of invention, and, like his father, had rather a disconcerting way of accepting the facts of his existence for better, for worse. He knew that he was unhappy at home, felt that he was going to be a great deal more unhappy, and saw nothing but the necessity of getting away.

"Darling Leedham," said his mother, "how can you think of entering upon vulgar commerce!"

"What else am I to do?"

"But think of your name! A Folyat in a bank!—a clerk! And with your Christian name too!"

(The Earldom of Leedham was the title which Minna missed sharing when she jilted Willie Folyat.)

"George Clibran-Bell is in a bank," said Leedham.

"But, darling, how can you leave your mother? How can you think of it?"

"People have to leave their mothers sooner or later."

"But you love your mother?"

"Of course," said Leedham sturdily, "but I want to go."

"You cannot go without your father's consent."

"No."

"Very well, then."

And that seemed to end the interview.

Leedham saw his father first and came straight to the point.

"I want to go to the Brazils."

"I know. Your mother is very much upset by it."

"That's not the point."

Francis agreed.

"The point is, what am I going to be if I stay?"

"You might be a clergyman or—or——"

"I don't want to be a clergyman."

"A doctor, then?"

"Can you afford it?"

"No," said Francis, and the admission brought his opposition tumbling down. They discussed ways and means, and Francis delighted in his boy's practical good sense and independence, though he had a feeling of pity and shame that he had not come to know him better before.

"Thank you, sir," said Leedham. "And please, will you ask mother not to cry over me?"

"You can't expect her not to feel it."

"No, I suppose not. But I want her to be glad too."

"Well," said Francis, "I'm glad and I'm proud of you. I wish— —"

The thought of Frederic came to him and he said no more.

Mrs. Folyat cried in public at every possible opportunity, and she came in for a great deal of sympathy. Frederic, who had always used Leedham as a butt, and thoroughly disliked the idea of losing him, did his best to make him feel a callous brute. But Leedham was excited and exalted at the prospect of adventure, though he had no one on his side but his father and the boy James, who gazed at him with large envious eyes and promoted him to heroic rank.

During his last few weeks Leedham spent many hours in the study with his father, and they had long friendly talks all about nothing, in which they skirmished round the new affection that had sprung up between them.

On his last Sunday night there was a farewell supper. Mabel and Jessie Clibran-Bell were there and Gertrude and Mary and Minna. Frederic was out, and the boy James had been in bed all day with a cold caught in crawling along the roof in his night-gown from his attic-window to the attic of the boy next door. He had been thrashed for doing it—but when the boy next door had laid in a feast of sardines and raspberry jam the temptation was too great, and he scrambled over in the pouring rain, sat for two hours in his wet night-gown and then slept in it.

With Frederic away Leedham could talk, and he bragged of how he would return in ten years and buy a carriage for his mother and re-build his father's church and set James up in life and bring jewels for Minna. (He was fond of Minna.)

"But suppose you marry?" said Mary.

"Not I," said Leedham.

"I expect," remarked Francis, with a chuckle, "he'll marry a Portuguese."

"Frank! How can you!" protested Martha. "The Portuguese are Catholics!"

"Perhaps she'll be rich," threw in Minna.

"And beautiful, with dark languishing eyes," added Mabel Clibran-Bell. And in a few minutes they had created the future Mrs. Leedham and, rather maliciously, endowed her with a furious temper.

Leedham took all the chaff in good part and made himself especially amiable to his mother.

Mary went upstairs with some supper for James and the talk turned on Flynn, and everybody wondered what he would do next.

"I hate that Flynn," said Martha.

"Oh, come!" replied Francis, "he's filled the church. I couldn't have done it without him."

"But it is horrid," said Mabel Clibran-Bell.

"Certainly; but Flynn is getting what he wants and I am getting what I want. Both his people and my people are more enthusiastic than they would be otherwise."

"Father says," put in Jessie Clibran-Bell, "that he is getting libellous."

"Let him," returned Francis.

"Wouldn't you proceed against him?"

"Not I. I don't think the clergy should squabble even in the Law Courts."

"But," said Martha, "it would be a case for Frederic."

Mary returned saying that James was not in his room and nowhere in the house. She had called through the window to the boy next door, but there was such a terrific wind her voice was blown away. There were two chimney-pots blown down in the square.

Mrs. Folyat went white and her lips trembled. They all looked from one to the other. Leedham left the room and they heard the front-door bang, and the wind moaned in the chimney.

Francis rose to his feet and moved towards the door. Mary ran upstairs again, and Gertrude put the parrot's cloth over his cage because he was beginning to scream. Came a ring at the door, and presently Leedham appeared with his hair blown into his eyes and his face very pale and his teeth chattering. He turned to his father and said:

"Come!"

Mrs. Folyat fainted.

Francis turned sick at heart and went out into the passage. The front door was open and the gas was flickering in the wind, so that it was very dark. There were two men holding a little white bundle between them.

The boy James had been blown from the roof and they had found him on the pavement below. He was quite cold, and it was impossible to tell how long he had been there.

The house was full of whisperings and the guests withdrew, stealing away like ghosts. Leedham stayed to look after his mother. They carried the boy upstairs and laid his poor broken body on the bed in Mary's room, and Francis fumbled out and along the street to beg the doctor to come at once. There was nothing to be done. Thinking was no use. Tears seemed foolish. It was only mechanically that Francis turned to his God and said, "Thy Will be done."

The boy was buried in the grim cemetery over by the canal. The parishioners clubbed together and erected a little marble cross above his grave. They wanted to express their sympathy, and the very poor sent pathetic little wreaths of ivy and hideous wax monstrosities and horrible crosses of iron filagree. The beauty and charm of the boy were discovered after he was dead, and for a little while the house in Fern Square was a sort of temple in his honour. His belongings were gathered together and partitioned, and Leedham took with him to Rio de Janeiro his little brother's christening mug and spoon.

Mrs. Folyat was prostrate with grief, and the shock to her nerves made her for a long time a valetudinarian. She was just recovering when there came the crowning act of brutality.

Flynn was silenced for a space, but it was strangely whispered among his followers that in St. Paul's mass was being said and candles lit for the dead.

Francis had encouraged the more devout among his parishioners to use the church for private meditation and prayer. He himself, in his grief, spent many hours there, and this found interpretation in the report that he was instituting the confessional. Flynn did not stop to examine the accuracy or probability of the rumour but hurled thunderbolts. A gang of roughs set on Frederic one day, and he came home with his clothes torn and mucked and his face bloody. Urged by his wife, and much against his own inclination, Francis wrote to Flynn and begged him to confine his attentions to himself. He said:

"I am a priest, but I am proud, and if there is to be suffering as the consequence of my actions I would rather bear it on my own shoulders."

Henceforth Francis was known as the Proud Priest.

One of the most fanatical of Flynn's followers discovered that the boy ames was buried not twenty yards away from the angel-guarded tomb of Humphrey Clay, and this, when bruited, fell like a spark upon the dry minds of the most ignorant members of the faction. On a dark evening in November they went up to the cemetery, overturned the little marble cross, effaced the name James Matthew Folyat, and scattered the wreaths and flowers.

Mrs. Folyat took to her bed. The ringleaders were discovered and arrested, and Francis appeared in court, very pale, obviously near breaking-point, and in a very low voice said that he did not wish to prosecute. There was a wave of sympathy for the unfortunate rector of St. Paul's. Flynn's paper was boycotted of advertisements and he fell into low water. He had ruined himself in the struggle and he had almost drained Francis of courage and faith in human-kind. He clung obstinately to his work, but was dogged by a sense of the futility of it all and, in his worst moments, saw it only as a mechanical sanctification of birth, marriage, and death. Humanity seemed so primitive—just a base struggle for existence and satisfaction in existence, and silly devastating squabbles about forms. He realised dreadfully what a gulf lay between himself and his wife, and he strove desperately to bridge it, only to discover that she was unconscious of any disparity and had a diabolical skill in coating any uncomfortable fact with a romantic fiction so that it became as a pearl upon her shell. He blamed himself for it, and was kind to her and fought against the exasperation which her prattle aroused in him. Having no friend to whom he could turn—all the men he knew deferred to his cloth and treated him as a creature apart—he tried to find sympathy and interest in his daughters and Frederic, his remaining son. They were absorbed in their youth and their dreams and folly, and seemed to be afraid of him. He watched them, but soon found that he was spying upon them. The one thing he had to love was the memory of the boy James, who became ever more radiant to him, and he used to watch the goings out and comings in of the boy next door and think him a splendid fellow, and regret all that he had missed when his own boy was alive.

For many, many days life seemed to stand still. There was dull routine, Sunday succeeded Sunday. Gradually gaiety crept once more into the house in Fern Square, but it seemed to Francis so remote—as remote as the woman upstairs, who complained and complained and yet could babble of fashion and the weather and money and the young men who came courting her daughters.

VI
FREDERIC'S FRIENDS

By my troth, Cony, if there were a thousand
boys, thou would'st spoil them all with taking
their parts.

THE KNIGHT OF THE BURNING PESTLE.

AT the age of twenty-four Frederic was earning twenty-five shillings a week as a managing clerk in Mr. Starkey's office in Hanging Row. He was fairly punctual in the morning, having hired Minna to rout him out of bed at eight o'clock, and he would lounge through the morning until one o'clock when he would disappear for two hours for lunch and coffee and dominoes in a smoky cellar called the Mecca Café. In the afternoon he would work furiously from three to five so as to have something to show for his day, and in the evening he would come to life. A sort of swagger would come into his bearing and a pinkish tinge would come into his pale cheeks and a new light into his blue-green eyes. He had discovered that in winter his light tenor voice could be made to earn about thirty shillings a week, and together with a spotty-faced youth in his office who sang comic songs (with patter) he went up and down our town and district giving "I'll Sing Thee Songs of Araby" and "To Anthea" and "There is a Lady Passing By," and winning much applause which invariably went to his head and made him very drunk. He sang under an assumed name, and no one at home knew what he was doing except Minna, whom he bribed with cigarettes to hold her peace. (She used to lock herself in the bath-room and smoke them out of the window.) When occasionally his mother complained that he was never at home in the evening he used to say that he was rehearsing. At intervals he used to   take part in private theatricals with the spotty-faced youth or other of his friends. The pieces generally given were the farces of Madison Morton, or *The Blind Beggars*, or some amateur musical play. There was a Gentlemen's Musical Society which had a little hall in Oswald Street in the centre of our town. Frederic and the spotty-faced youth were members, though the Society had fallen on evil days and its entertainments had become rather broad. For the most part they were smoking-concerts, not unlike the Caves of Harmony that used to be in London, but the air was purified occasionally by a Ladies' Night, when the lions roared as gently as any sucking dove, and gave innocuous theatrical entertainments to which the members brought their daughters. Frederic became a shining light in the performances, and the members' daughters fell in love with him and wrote him ridiculous letters of admiration, which he gulped down without blinking.

It was at the Gentlemen's Concert Hall that he first met James Lawrie, the dramatic critic of our weekly newspaper who wrote under the name of "Snug," and had some public reputation as a writer of elegant poetry, and an immense fame among journalists and actors and theatrical musicians and painters as a composer of bawdy verses. This man was a Scotsman, a hard drinker, and he was said to know every verse that Robert Burns ever wrote by heart, and also to have many poems that had never been printed. He used to write notices of the little performances in the Gentlemen's Concert Hall, and, as he could be very scathing, the actors used to fawn upon him and flatter him. The spotty-faced youth introduced him to Frederic one night, and the old man—he was not above fifty-five, but he had always been Old Lawrie—shook him warmly by the hand and said:

"I'm proud to meet your father's son, sir."

That rather staggered Frederic, to whom it had never occurred that his father might be admirable. Old Lawrie saw that he was a little taken aback and he scowled and went on:

"Come, come! Not ashamed of your father, are you, heh? My sons are, but then my sons are respectable. That's what's the matter with them, they're respectable and safe. Safe's a good word for a gag. You can bring your lips together on it hard."

"I was at school in France," replied Frederic with a flush of timidity under his paint. He had just come from the dress-rehearsal on the stage, the play being *Still Waters Run Deep*.

"If you like France," said Old Lawrie, "you won't like this cursed hole You'll die in it. I've never been to France myself, but I've read their books They pull everything to bits with their brains. Nothing left. They're a better lot than we are. Got no morals, but who has? We pretend to have 'em. They don't. Know your Burns? It's in print, so I see no reason why I shouldn' speak it:

O Lord! yestreen, Thou ken, wi' Meg—
Thy pardon I sincerely beg,
O may it ne'er be a livin' plague

48 | Round The Corner

To my dishonour,
An' I'll ne'er lift a lawless leg
Again upon her.
Maybe Thou lets the fleshly thorn
Beset thy servant e'en and morn,
Lest he owre high and proud should turn
'Cause he's sae gifted:
If sae, Thy hand maun e'en be borne,
Until Thou lift it.
But, Lord, remember me and mine
Wi' mercies temp'ral and divine
That I for fear and grace may shine
Excell'd by nane,
An' a' the glory shall be Thine,
Amen, Amen.

Old Lawrie was a fine man as he declaimed the verses. His eyes flashed and his voice came big from his chest, and when he had done he turned to Frederic and said:

"That's Burns, and out of Shakespeare there isna a healthier spirit in the world. Burns and Shakespeare—both of 'em poor men and straight from the earth, and 'll give ye all the cultured dandies in the world for a farthing gift. So you're playing at play-acting, young man? That's what nine-tenths the world is for ever doing in its daily life. They ca' me a disgusting old man, but they should hear what I ca' them when my tongue's loosed and my mind's eyes seeing visions. I live in Hell, but I've a Heaven in my brain. . . . Your father's a good man to go his own way with the dirty Lutherans and the filthy Puritans yelping at his heels. You'll not be going in for the professional play-acting?"

"No," said Frederic. "I sing."

Old Lawrie clapped his old silk hat on his head, took his blackthorn stick in his hand and gave a shout of laughter. He patted Frederic on the shoulder, pursed his lips and hummed through them strangely and vaguely as though he were turning over a morsel of music on his tongue, and then he broke into verse and said:

O youth it is a pretty thing,
A wild rose in the bud.

But it must die with the passing Spring
All trampled in the mud.
We've heavy feet in our town,
Rough shod with iron bands.
Virginity goes toppling down
Befouled with loutish hands.
O Spring is smoked in our town,
And life's a dirty scrum,
The angels weep to see God's frown
And we make Hell to hum.

He turned away after this impromptu and joined a bibulous-looking individual with white hair and an enormous face, Joshua Yeo, his editor, and the nearest approach to a friend that he had.

Frederic turned to the spotty-faced youth and found him grinning vacantly.

"Quite balmy," said the spotty-faced youth.

"I think he's splendid," returned Frederic, amazed at his own enthusiasm.

"Wants a new coat," said the spotty-faced youth. "He's worn that ever since I've known him, and it's green with age. He gets fighting roaring blind once a month, and his sons lock him up. I know one of them—Bennett Lawrie—a bee-yooti-ful young man, High-Church and all that. May have been to your governor's show. The old man's a Presbyterian as much as he's anything. He used to be in a bank, same bank that Randolph Caldecott used to be in. But he quarrelled, quarrels with every one."

"Do you think he made that up—about youth and our town?"

"Comes easy to him. When he's drunk he talks blank verse. He was run in once, and he harangued the beak like Mark Antony at Cæsar's funeral."

They were called back to the stage, and Frederic found that he was not nearly so pleased with himself in his part as he had been. He began to think the play foolish and shoddy.

After the rehearsal he had an appointment with the spotty-faced youth to meet two girls on Kersley Moors, a high, dark, treeless common just outside the northern suburbs. From Kersley the road ran into the town past the bishop's palace, and here nightly young men and maidens foregathered and stalked each other and exchanged mysterious greetings, sometimes stopping and talking, sometimes passing and disappearing down the dark lanes that enclosed the bishop's huge garden. The spotty-faced youth, who had been impressed by Frederic's braggadocio of the things that were much better done in France, had introduced him to this exchange and mart of foolish emotions and transitory affections. They went there in search of pleasure and adventure, and they generally found them, though more puny and debased than they were prepared to admit. They went there now only half believing that the girls with whom they had made their assignation would turn up, for they had seemed so superior to the usual quarry. They did not know their names or where they lived. It was enough for them that both the girls were pretty and responsive to such wit as they could produce.

The spotty-faced youth's father was a doctor, and he had three brothers, and on the way he regaled Frederic with tales of their escapades and the narrow squeaks they had had, and the great score it was to have a father who was a man of the world and understood these things. He became so foul-mouthed that Frederic stopped him.

"If you don't shut up I shall go home."

"Right ho!" said the spotty-faced youth. "Only I did think you had a better sense of fun. You didn't seem to mind Old Lawrie talking about Burns and Meg."

"That's different. That's poetry."

"Is it?"

"Yes. Like 'Lucrece' and 'Venus and Adonis.'"

"Well. They're pretty hot."

"Oh! Shut up."

Frederic did not rightly understand why he was so indignant with his companion. He was conscious of a difference between the two things— frank acceptance and fumbling—but he could not put his finger on it, nor could he discover why for the first time in years of folly he should feel a sense of shame. It grew on him as they walked up the Kersley Road and, by the second lamp-post past the bishop's gate, saw the two young women arm-in-arm pacing slowly in front of them.

"Bags I the tall one?" said the spotty-faced youth.

Before Frederic could reply they had come up with the girls and his companion had greeted them with a tag from the pantomime of the last winter.

"We thought you wouldn't come," said the tall girl.

"No fear," said the spotty-faced youth. "Trust me when I've spotted a winner."

Frederic set the pace and they walked briskly up the road to Kersley Church. He hardly said a word, but his companion kept up a running fire of facetious chatter. At the church the tall girl and Haslam (that was the spotty-faced youth's name) walked on and disappeared into the darkness of the moors after arranging to meet again at ten. Frederic was left under the lamp-post with the other girl. She was very little and slight, and she was rather poorly dressed. She looked shyly up at Frederic, and he said:

"You're very pretty."

"I like you better than the other one."

"You see," said Frederic, "I was at school in France."

"Oh! France. Are they very wicked in France?"

"It depends what you mean by wicked. No more than they are here."

"I suppose you won't tell me your name."

"I don't mind," said Frederic, with a sudden flow of honesty. He had so often been Snooks and Jones and Walker. "It's Folyat. Fred Folyat."

"Mine's Lipsett, Annie Lipsett. It's a silly name."

It seemed such a silly name to Frederic that he could find nothing to say, and there came a dead silence between them. She was offended at last and moved away and he had almost lost sight of her in the darkness of the moor when he ran and caught her up. They passed through the posts that filled the entrance to the moor, and Frederic put his arm round her hard little waist. She stopped. He stopped and kissed her and they walked on.

There were lovers (and worse) everywhere, and as they crept slowly forward they heard sighs and silly giggles and voices murmuring. It was very dark and the clouds hung low and the wind was a little cold. They found a place to sit where through trees they could see the lights of the houses. Frederic sat a little away from her and with his cane prodded into the ground.

"I wonder where the others are," said Annie Lipsett.

"Does it matter?"

"No."

They were silent for a little, then Frederic remembered old Lawrie, and he pursed up his lips as the old man had done and crooned a little to himself. Then, suddenly, he asked:

"Are you happy?"

He did not wait for her to reply but went on:

"I'm wondering why we mess about with it. What's the good of it, all? Who are you? I don't know. Who am I? You don't know. We live in a beastly dirty town and we wander about like lost souls. And because we be lost souls we take anything that comes along—you me, I you. Is it good enough? It's all wrong. But what's right? . . . It's fun, I suppose. Fun! . . . But what else is there?"

He took the girl's hand.

"I tell you what. I'm damned sorry for you."

"Of course," said Annie Lipsett. "Of course, you're a gentleman."

And Frederic laughed. He told himself that he was an idiot, and that all *that* was not his affair. He had brought this girl here, just as all the other young men in the place had brought all the other young women, to forget, to escape for a little while, to lose all thought of the beastliness of life down below in the town. It *was* beastly. Everything was so dirty, and everybody was so poor and so tired. . . . He took the girl in his arms and held her very close and whispered silly talk to her, and soon she was sighing and lying and nestling to him.

They were ten minutes late in their return to the lamp-post by the church, and Haslam and the tall girl were very ill at ease and silent. Annie Lipsett clung to Frederic's arm and they walked down to the bishop's palace. There they parted. Frederic kissed her and she clung to him. The tall girl led her away and they vanished into the night.

As they turned their faces homewards Haslam said:

"Gawd! I have had a rummy time. I couldn't touch her without her starting on the crying game. Sha'n't see her again."

"No. I suppose not," said Frederic.

Haslam looked at him.

"Well. You're a caution, you are!"

"I'm a bit of a swine, the same as you," retorted Frederic.

VII
YOUNG WOMEN

*Our own precedent passions do instruct us
What levity is in youth.*

TIMON OF ATHENS.

YOUNG people must for ever be trying to fall in love, and in this ancient sport young women are every bit as active as young men. For the matter of that, the greater part of humanity remain adolescent in this affair, that is, hemmed in by a thick-set hedge of prejudice and unsatisfied emotion and convention and childish theory, so that they are for ever in a state of uneasy curiosity about love, always ready to put salt on its tail, but unable to come within reach of it. For that reason they are always confusing love with being in love, an active state of living which can be permanent with an emotional condition which must be transitory.

Mrs. Folyat had the most beautiful illusions about her household. She was not entirely deceived by them when she came face to face with herself, but in her relations with her husband, her friends and her daughters she always exhibited the most profound faith in them. Though her daughters were grown women she never troubled to discover the state of their minds, but assumed their innocence and purity, and she never referred back to her own state of mind at the same age and the same maiden condition. In short, she burked the difficulty and the responsibility, though she was secretly alarmed at their slowness in finding husbands. She had no notion of their finding any career outside marriage, and took no steps to prepare them even for that.

There was a constant stream of young men passing through the house, and they all seemed to do their best to fall in love with Gertrude and Mary, but they either fell victims to Minna, who played with them and squeezed their young hearts dry between her finger and thumb, or they disappeared and were caught in the toils elsewhere. There were so many young women and so few eligible young men. They flirted, they danced, they paid visits to the theatres, and Gertrude sang and Mary played her violin, but nothing happened. It was very annoying. The Clibran-Bell girls did not marry either, but there was no comfort in that. They had such large noses; and they were not Folyats. They had not the charm of high gentility. . . . Neither Gertrude nor Mary was pretty, but they could be amusing and they seemed to attract attention. Minna was decidedly pretty, with a wide delightful grin and a mocking humour. The most serious and solemn young men were devoted to her. They were always proposing to her, but she always refused them or became engaged to them for about a week. Her betrothals hardly ever seemed to survive the visit to their families. She invariably seemed to see them in caricature, and had amassed quite a large collection of mental pictures of North-country families who received her at high tea and welcomed her with shy effusiveness.

Mrs. Folyat was fonder of Minna than of her other daughters. She was easier to get on with and much less expensive. Mary and Gertrude had acquired the habit of visiting relations in the South much richer than themselves, and every year they demanded an exorbitant outlay on clothes, and they came back rather scornful of life in Fern Square and rather rebellious at having to resume their household duties or work in the church and Sunday-school. Also, for a time, they would assume a lofty tone with the young men of their acquaintance, and they used to prick at Frederic and tell him he was becoming provincial. Minna used to lash them with her tongue, dealing out the wickedest malice with the most urbane good-humour, and deliberately annex any young men whom they brought to the house. She called Gertrude "Mother Bub" and Mary "Mottle-tooth." From their superiority in years they affected to ignore her, but they lost no opportunity of annoying her and upsetting her plans for her own comfort and enjoyment.

The money-cloud had grown darker over Francis. It seemed impossible to make his expenditure acknowledge even a bowing acquaintance with his income. He had credit with the tradespeople but it was abused. Fifty pounds had become a large sum of money to him, because the payment of it meant dislocation of his finances. Frederic was always sending in small bills that were too large for his slender earnings. The girls—Mary and Gertrude were still called "the girls"—were always wanting money. Annette in Edinburgh hardly ever wrote without wanting money, and Mrs. Folyat seemed to have no notion of the decreasing elasticity of his resources. It was perfectly clear to him that a change must be made, and quickly. He went into his accounts, found that he owed three hundred and fifty pounds—nearly a year's stipend—and wrote the figures down on a scrap of paper and laid it before his wife.

"We owe that," he said. "It's a lot of money."

Mrs. Folyat turned the piece of paper round and round in her fingers, and Francis stood above her pulling at his beard.

"It's a big sum," he said.

Mrs. Folyat pulled out her handkerchief and began to whimper, as she always did when Francis was masterful.

"I'm sure," she said, "I'm sure it's not my fault. I'm sure I wish we'd never come to this hateful pace. I don't know why we did."

Francis felt a gust of exasperation.

"We came here," he said, "to marry the girls. They're not married."

Mrs. Folyat saw reproach in what was only a statement of fact, and she protested with some vehemence. The failure of her daughters hurt her. She felt it as keenly as Sarah, the wife of Abraham, felt her barrenness, for she saw life altogether in terms of marriage, romantic marriage. Her own life had fallen into the lines laid down by the fiction with which she refreshed herself—as a girl she had dreamed of a romantic lover—he had come—a parson, a creature of noble birth—and she had married him. She had borne him a truly biblical number of children and looked for them to follow a similar destiny. She had regarded it as a thing that happened automatically, for she was in mind a child, and life was to her a toy presented to her by a beneficent Creator, already wound up and prepared to go indefinitely. When apparently it ran down she could do nothing but weep and make things as uncomfortable as possible for those nearest her. She hated facts, and Francis, her husband, had the most odious habit of plumping them down in front of her.

Always before when they had been presented with any financial difficulty they had sold a house at Potsham, for the reduction of their private income by twenty or thirty pounds had seemed no great matter. But they had already sold five houses, and the loss of one hundred and fifty pounds a year had, as Francis now pointed out, played a considerable part in bringing them to their present quandary. He was loth to sacrifice another house and more income, and nervously proposed that they should raise the required sum by selling some of their valuable china and perhaps a piece or two of Martha's jewellery. She hardly ever wore her jewellery, but she loved to hoard it, and whenever she was particularly pleased with her women friends she used to reward them by displaying the contents of her treasure-drawers, jewels, old lace, silks and brocades and fans, acquired and inherited—things valuable and trumpery all lying higgledy-piggledy.

Her husband's suggestion acted like salt rubbed into the wounds occasioned by his statement of fact. She asked why she should always be the sufferer for the delinquencies of her family, and almost persuaded herself that she was their scapegoat. She went back over the years and raked over the ashes of old resentments and grievances, even going so far as to disinter the sacrifice of her carriage at St. Withans.

"The fact remains," said Francis, "that we owe a large sum of money. I am a clergyman, and my house should be free of the sordid troubles that beset the laity. It is not free of them and I am ashamed."

"Very well, then," said Martha, "Let us sell everything, spend everything—the girls will do that easily enough—and then go into the workhouse."

"Please be reasonable," rejoined Francis. "We must pay our debts and reduce our expenditure. If necessary, the girls must go out and earn what they can."

"The girls!"

"There is no shame in honest work, whatever it may be."

"But they will *never* marry if they work."

"Half the women I marry are working women."

"I won't discuss it. You have never been the same since we came to this hateful place."

"I was thinking chiefly of Mary. She could teach music. And Annette has had a better education than the others. She could . . ."

"What?"

"She could obtain a situation as a governess."

"A governess! Annette! A governess!"

In Mrs. Folyat's eyes to send your daughter out as a governess was a confession of poverty. There could be no glossing it over. Of course the clergy were miserably paid, but Francis had always risen superior to that reproach in public opinion by the general belief in the amplitude of his private means. It could be little short of disaster then to confess to inadequacy. And a governess! Poor Annette! though to be sure when she was a child her godmother had looked at her sadly and observed that she must assuredly be prepared for a convent. She was so plain—a remark which Minna had never ceased to brandish over poor Annette's head whenever their wills clashed. . . .

Francis at length cut short his wife's protestations with a sigh and said:

"My dear, I'm sorry. That's the position. We have to swallow it. We can't give the girls the opportunities they ought to have. We must let them fight their own way. At present anything is better than the sort of life they are leading. We'll sell another house, but that shall be the last. We'll make a fresh start. Be patient with me, my dear."

"And am *I* to tell Mary?"

"No. I'll do that, and I'll find a family for Annette."

Francis went away feeling that there was a great deal to be said for the celibacy of the clergy. Other men, of course, did not see so much of their families, and perhaps, for that reason, could understand them better, be better friends with them, and not so acutely conscious of their irritating peculiarities. The relation between a father and daughter should be a very beautiful thing, and indeed there were moments when the house in Fern Square was a place of happiness and affectionate unity. Only—only, there was the future. Martha growing more and more helpless, and the household duties and responsibilities devolving more and more upon Gertrude and Mary, and they losing their bloom.

Francis had a vague feeling of injustice which was harshly in disaccord with his professional teaching of acceptance—"Whatever is, is right" and "It's all for the best." At any rate there was still abundant laughter in his house, and that was better than the grim smile which was all these Northerners would for the most part allow themselves. The days of violent opposition were gone, but the Puritans still looked askance at the Proud Priest—for the nickname clung—and his family. The grocer with an off-licence round the corner spread tales of the large quantities of beer that were consumed in the parson's house.

Mary took the suggestion very well, and soon she had five pupils, little boys and girls, whom she taught to fumble on the piano and to extract horrible noises from the violin. She went to their houses and enjoyed making new friends. Annette was brought home from Edinburgh at the end of the term and was found a situation with an ironmaster's family named Fender. She had one pupil, a little hunchbacked girl who alternately adored her and bullied her. Annette was very happy. At home she had been so mercilessly teased by Minna that she was glad to get away. The Fenders lived in Burnley, ten miles away, and in summer they moved to a lovely house they had in Westmoreland, high-perched on a hill looking down on Grasmere and Rydal. She read enormous quantities of novels, and devoured the pounds and pounds of sweets and chocolates that were lavished on her pupil. Once a week she wrote dutiful letters to her parents and surreptitiously she began to write a novel in the manner of Mr. James Payn. She wrote three chapters, and then found the labour of writing too exhausting and continued the story mentally in her many idle moments.

At home in Fern Square the conduct of Gertrude had been causing some astonishment and alarm. For five consecutive Sundays she failed to put in an appearance at morning service, and once she neglected her Sunday-school class. When questioned about it—she was a woman in years, but Mrs. Folyat was not the mother to relax her authority until it was wrested from her—she replied that she was making a tour of the High Churches in our town—with a friend. The answer was found satisfactory, but Minna looked into the facts and found that her elder sister had spent every one of those five Sundays in St. Saviour's, where there was a young acolyte who had a beautiful profile and soulful eyes. He wore the most exquisite garments, and his expression was as near monkish as anything you can find in the Church of England. His face was lean and pale, and his whole bearing was mournful in the extreme.

For two Sundays after the inquisition Gertrude went to service in St. Paul's. On the third she disappeared again, and Minna pleaded headache, watched the others go off with their prayer-books and Sunday clothes, and then hurried to St. Saviour's, a little church built on a slag-heap above the Jewish quarter. She crept in just before eleven and found Gertrude sitting far up near the steps of the nave gazing in rapt and religious devotion at the young acolyte as with almost theatrical solemnity he performed his rites. If he was conscious of her he gave no sign. With an almost yearning intensity he crept noiselessly about ministering to the priest. Gertrude's great moment came after the sermon when, the churchwardens and sidesmen moving lugubriously from pew to pew, the acolyte came down to the altar steps and stood with a large brass plate in his hands waiting for the offertory. He stood there proudly with his pale face upturned, his whole soul seeming to be borne aloft on the hymn sung by the congregation. On this occasion it was:

> O God our help in ages past,
> Our hope for years to come;
> Our shelter from the stormy blast,
> And our eternal home.

Minna had come in a mischievous spirit, but even she was impressed. There was a soulfulness in the young man, the look of one hopelessly atoning for all the sins of the world, and, above all, there was artistry in his movements. Everything that he did seemed to be immensely important and pregnant with meaning. When he stooped and the churchwardens and sidesmen laid their little bags in the great brass plate, he did it with the air of one accepting a worthless gift for the grace of the giving. To him at least it did seem to be true that it is more blessed to give than to receive. His humility was so great, so moving, that Minna wished she had put sixpence into the bag instead of a penny.

She could not see Gertrude's face, but she was familiar enough with her back to be able to gauge her feelings. Gertrude had rather a poor figure, with high shoulders and a very short waist. Now her shoulders were higher than ever, and she was leaning forward and her elbows were trembling ever so slightly. Minna smiled and thought maliciously of all she knew about Gertrude, and that was not a little.

Before the service was over she left the church, and was lying in the study with a wet handkerchief over her head and a volume of Tennyson on her knees when the rest of the family came home from St. Paul's and Gertrude from St. Saviour's.

"Where did you go to, my dear?" asked Mrs. Folyat.

"Oh! To St. Benedict's," replied Gertrude. "They have the most lovely altar-cloth I ever saw. But the curate intones very badly."

"As badly as pa?" asked Minna.

"That's impossible," said Francis with a long chuckle.

There was some chatter, circulation of gossip got at the church door, and then with some anxiety Mrs. Folyat looked across the long table at her husband and said:

"Are you going to tell them, Frank?"

Francis had his mouth full and could only say "Hum! Ha!"

"What is it?" Frederic turned a little pale and wondered what was coming. His misdeeds, taken collectively, were very trivial, but he knew from experience that any one of them taken singly, robbed of its context and placed under the scrutiny of other eyes, would assume gigantic proportions.

"Have all the Folkestone Folyats died and left us all their money? Or has uncle William come back from India with a gigantic fortune?" Minna was rushing wildly ahead on all the strangest possibilities when Francis finished his mouthful and cleared his throat.

"No," he said. "I have heard from your brother Serge."

"Serge!" said Mary.

"Serge!" said Gertrude, snatched from her tender dreams.

"Is he rich?" asked Minna.

"I don't know. He talks of coming home."

"Where is he?" This came from Frederic.

"He wrote from Durban in South Africa."

"Oh! Then of course he's a millionaire. Hurrah! He'll buy Frederic a partnership, and me a husband—catch me marrying a poor man—and Mary a genuine Strad, and Gertie a—an acolyte."

Gertrude flushed hotly and looked daggers across the table.

"He merely writes that he is coming home, as though he had only been away a week."

"Some of you children can hardly remember him," said Martha.

Minna said she could just recollect his putting her into a bassinette and letting her go flying down a hill into a pond.

Francis went on:

"He sent your mother some water-colour drawings."

"Any good?" asked Frederic.

"I think they're quite good. But I don't know anything about these things."

"I'll take them to old Lawrie. He'll know," said Frederic.

"Lawrie?" murmured Gertrude.

"Yes. D'you know him?"

"No. No."

Minna winked at Frederic. He had often talked to her about old Lawrie, and she had discovered that the name of the young acolyte at St. Saviour's was Bennett Lawrie, old James' third son.

"I say," said Frederic, "does Serge know we're here?"

"No. The letter was forwarded from St. Withans."

"Don't you think you ought to let him know what he's in for?"

"I can't do that. He gave no address."

"It won't matter to him if he's rich," said Minna, and they all fell to and rummaged their memories for recollections of Serge as a boy. Minna invented lavishly and suddenly she shouted:

"Did he say whether he'd got a wife?"

"I bet it's a blackamoor like old Nicholas Folyat," said Frederic.

"Even if she is black," said Mrs. Folyat solemnly, "if he is married to her she will be my daughter-in-law and I shall receive her."

The conversation took on a broad complexion which is more permissible in the family circle than in the printed page.

That evening Frederic took Serge's drawings with him and sought out old Lawrie in the Arts Club, where always on a Sunday evening there was a gathering of old warriors and choice spirits—Joshua Yeo, Elihu Beecroft, the painter, Peter Maitland, who wrote pantomimes, and Warlock Clynes, the photographer, and B. J. Strutt, the manager of the old theatre, where, as a young man, Henry Irving had been a member of the stock company. They were smoking and drinking and yarning. They had vast stores of anecdotes of the great Bohemians in London. Beecroft had twice had pictures in the Academy, and B. J. Strutt had begun life as a call-boy at the Haymarket Theatre. Old James Lawrie had been to London three times and had shaken hands with J. L. Toole and Helen Faucit, and Clement Scott had sent him a copy of his Ballads, of which he had produced many gross parodies.

The club was simply three rooms in a dark block of offices—a bar, an eating room, and a smoke-room. Frederic was shown in by the grubby boy whom he found at the door reading a penny "blood," and he stood foolishly in the middle of the room realising dreadfully that old Lawrie did not remember who he was.

"Mr. Lawrie. . ." he said.

"Eh?"

"I—I—My name's Folyat. I—I acted. You asked me to—to look you up here some day."

"Eh? Oh, yes. Come and sit down. What'll you have? I can't pay for your drink, but some one will."

Frederic sat down, and the little group of old men were embarrassed by his presence.

"So. . . so you act, do you? Here's B. J. Strutt. Get him to give you a job in his next pantomime."

"I'm—I'm not a pro," said Frederic. "I'm a solicitor." And, as he said it, he felt that it was a small thing to be among these free men who practised the arts. Frederic was a chameleon who took his colour from his surroundings. He had a queer capacity for enthusiasm, which came and went and was altogether beyond his control. He drank a little whiskey and he felt that he was in the company of very wonderful beings. They talked of things and men that were glorious dreams to him, and they spoke of them with such ease and familiarity, like giants playing marbles with the mountains. His own little celebrity, which had been very dear to him, dwindled into nothing, and it was to protect himself that he produced Serge's drawings and began to talk of his brother.

Beecroft took the drawings and looked them through. He had a huge red beard and a glistening bald head and round spectacles that made him look like a benevolent spider. He clapped his hands to his bald pink head and with immense fervour said:

"By God!"

"Are they good?" rasped Lawrie.

"No. Damn bad."

Frederic felt very small.

"I don't know," said B. J. Strutt. "I like that one all yellow in the foreground and blue in the distance. And I like that one with the niggers filing through the orange-trees with the pinky-white house beyond."

"So do I," cried Beecroft. "I like 'em all. The man can't draw, but he can feel colour and big distances and lots and lots of air."

Frederic began to feel better. The old men gathered round the drawings and gave grunts of satisfaction. (They had been very bored all the evening and were glad of something to interest them).

"Where is he?" said Beecroft. "This brother of yours."

"In Africa. He's coming home."

"He's a genius. Do you know that? A genius."

"Be careful, Beecroft," put in Lawrie. "There have been about twenty men of genius—real genius—in forty, or is it sixty?—thousand years."

"A genius," reiterated Beecroft. "We'll give a show. You can ram him down their throats week by week, Yeo."

"It's no good running a genius in this place," growled Lawrie.—He was always discovering poets and seeing them go to ruin.—"They don't want genius. They're so used to imitations."

"At any rate," protested Beecroft, "they haven't had anything like this for years, and I don't think we ought to let 'em off."

"My brother's coming home now. I'll tell him what you said. It's rather funny. I haven't seen him since we were boys, and then he was much older than I."

"We'll have a show," repeated Beecroft. "He's a local man?"

"We weren't born here. But my father's been rector of St. Paul's, Bide Street, for some years now."

"That's good enough. The stinking rotters here like to think they've had a hand in anything produced in the place—if people talk about it enough. Have some more whiskey?"

Frederic was beyond saying "no." The drink went to his head, inflated him, and he offered to sing. Strutt played his accompaniments, and they kept him at it for an hour until he was hoarse, and they shouted the choruses in cracked, beery voices.

It was very late when Frederic left the club, after shaking hands all round and promising tearfully to bring his brother, the genius, as soon as he arrived. He forgot the drawings altogether, and old Lawrie, being the soberest of the party, gathered them together and took them home with him.

VIII
SERGE

It's a queer place, and indeed I don't know the place that isn't.

THE ARAN ISLANDS.

SERGE FOLYAT landed at Plymouth on a wet autumn day and walked to St. Withans rejoicing and declaring in his heart that England was the most beautiful country in the world. He saw no reason to alter his opinion as he walked north until he came to the outcrop of industrialism in the plain of Cheshire.

It took him ten days to walk from St. Withans to our town, and six of them were wet. He loved the soft English rain and the rich green of the countryside and the glorious gold and red of the sodden autumn leaves, and when, for the first time, he saw the black and grey of South Lancashire skies and the dark chimneys rising out of the dense mass of buildings he could be glad of them too. All the same he wondered what strange whimsey could have taken his father out of the soft Southern air into such menacing harshness. However, it did not greatly exercise his mind. He had never troubled to find reasons for his own follies and accepted those of others with as good a grace.

He was a man a little above middle height, tanned and brown, with bright blue eyes like his father's, and a close clipped golden-brown beard, turning grey at the corners of the jawbones. He loved talking, and engaged all whom he met or caught up on the road, and nearly always left them more cheerful than when he encountered them. When he was alone he talked or sang to himself in a very loud voice. He was not looking for adventure and met with none. His clothes he carried in a sack on his back, and he had a great stick in his hand, a pocketful of tobacco, and a calabash pipe. Other possessions he had none. He walked very fast and sometimes covered forty miles in a day.

In the evening of the tenth day he entered the town by the Derby Road and followed his nose and the tramlines until he came to St. Thomas' Church.

There he asked for Fern Square and received no response. He stopped a dismal-looking man and asked him. The stranger gaped at him and said:

"A'm a stranger 'ere, my sen."

His next enquiry provoked a long answer in a language so uncouth that he could make nothing of it. He followed the tram-lines again and wandered vaguely until he came to a cross-road from which he could see the Collegiate Church standing velvety-black against a sooty sky, with a railway bridge and the dome of a station beyond. He saw a tram labelled Pendle and followed it. The road led him under the railway bridge, past a sequestered market and a sort of fair with booths and swing-boats and a cocoa-nut shy and a merry-go-round. He stopped and watched the dirty mournful-looking people taking their pleasure, and the sight rather depressed him. A little farther on he had to pass through the places in which these people lived, and under the factories where they worked. He liked the hum and business of it all, and he liked the slatternly grubby little shops.

There is a place where the road skirts a height, and from the road a public park stretches down to the oily-black river winding through flats. Beyond the river gleam the reservoirs of the mills, steaming under the humid air. Beyond them again are hills covered with houses, and away to right and left a forest of tall chimneys. Over all hangs a pall of mist and smoke, a railing edges the road, and here Serge stood and gazed at the queer degraded beauty of it all. There was hardly a blade of grass in the park, none at all on the flats by the river. Trees and plants were stunted. Down in the park, on the benches, sauntering down the paths, hiding behind the bushes, he could see lovers, and that comforted him.

He moved on singing to himself and swinging his stick, and presently he came to a wide place over against a washing-machine factory. The road here was finely broad, but it was flanked on either side by mean little houses and forlorn little shops. It made the slow ascent of a long hill, and although there was plenty of traffic—trams, cabs, drays, lorries—it looked empty and desolate. There was not a tree in sight.

Serge stopped a man with a sandy moustache and a complexion like a suet-pudding and asked his direction to Fern Square.

"I'll take you there," said the man. "What number?"

"Five," answered Serge.

"Mr. Folyat's." Serge nodded.

"He's a good man is Mr. Folyat, and that kind to the poor, and they don't need to go to his church neither. Him and the Roman priest, Father

Soledano, they does a lot of good, and there's a deal of good needs doing, there is. He gave me a job when I come out o' prison."

"Oh! You've been in prison?"

"A month ago, I come out."

"What for?"

"'Spicious character. The p'leece put a jemmy in my carpenter's bag and found it there. Mr. Folyat 'e spoke for my repu-character, but you can't say nothing agin the p'leece. There it was, and I 'ad to do my six months. Here we are. You look like a sea-faring man."

"Good-night," said Serge.

"Good-night." And the man shambled off.

Serge stood gazing at the door and then he turned and looked over the square at the Wesleyan Chapel. A factory hooter buzzed. From the inside of the house came the wailing of a violin.

Serge knocked at the door Minna opened it and stood peering out at him.

"Hullo!" said Serge. "Which are you? Mary?"

"My father isn't in," replied Minna.

"All the better. You don't remember me, and I've been thinking of you as a baby. I'm Serge."

"Serge!"

He stepped in. Minna rushed away, and he heard her calling all over the house:

"Serge has come! Serge has come!"

There was a pattering of feet on the stairs, a banging of doors, and presently Gertrude, Mary, Mrs. Folyat and Minna came down upon him. He caught his mother up in a great hug and squeezed the breath out of her, and she stood talking and crying while he kissed Gertrude and Mary on the cheek and Minna full on the lips.

Mrs. Folyat led the way to the dining-room, and he sat at the table and they round him, and they devoured him with their eyes. He looked from one to the other. He thought that Gertrude looked sly, Mary plain, but he liked the mischief in Minna's eyes, and she had a wide friendly grin and a dimple in her cheek. His mother was so much older than he had imagined her and he wanted to tease her out of it. She was wearing a white woollen shawl, and she had shoved her spectacles up on to her forehead when Minna broke in upon her reading. The room was dark and rather oppressive and none of the windows were open.

Minna lit the gas and pulled down the blinds.

"Well!" said Mrs. Folyat, "you *have* taken us by surprise."

"I meant to," replied Serge. "I went to St. Withans first. I didn't know you'd gone. I walked on here."

"Walked!" This came from Mary.

"Yes. It's a nice cheerful hole you've come to live in."

"Horrible!" said Minna.

"Dreadful!" capped Mrs. Folyat. "But your father would come. He said his place was among the poor."

Gertrude and Mary exchanged glances, but said nothing. Serge noticed it and tried another topic.

"How's all the children? How many are there?"

"Oh! My dear." Mrs. Folyat felt for her handkerchief.

Minna answered for her.

"Annette's away. She's a governess with some rich vulgar people. James is dead. He fell from the roof. Frederic is out. He always is. We're in. We always are. And that's the lot."

"What about Leedham?"

"I forgot Leedham. He's in Rio, in a bank. Are you rich, Serge?"

Serge felt in his trousers pocket and produced four sovereigns, three shillings and ten coppers. He laid them out neatly on the red baize table-cloth.

"That's all," he said.

Minna laughed and counted out the money. Gertrude and Mary and his mother looked at Serge in dismay.

"I don't know," said Serge. "If this place isn't full of money, there's no excuse for it."

"It's a queer place," said Minna, "and not so much money in it as all that. What you've got would be wealth to most of father's people."

"Your father," put in Mrs. Folyat, "said his place was among the poor. I'm sure he got what he wanted."

Serge felt that she was fishing for his opinion. He gave it.

"I met a man," he said, "who brought me to the door. He said my father was very good to the poor. He was a wretched devil who had just been let out of prison."

"Sam Dimsdale. That's his name." Minna heaped Serge's money up into little piles.

"How's Frederic?" asked Serge.

"Frederic's a solicitor," replied Mrs. Folyat with a little show of pride.

Conversation flagged until Mrs. Folyat asked Gertrude and Mary to get the supper, and then Serge insisted on helping and asked if he might cook an omelette. Mrs. Folyat bade him stay with her.

He sat opposite her and she fixed her spectacles and looked long at him. Then she said:

"You're like your father, but there's a look in you too of my mother. What are you going to do?"

"Do? I don't know. I've spent all my life trying things and leaving them before they left me."

"It was a terrible blow to us, your leaving the Navy like that."

"Was it? It's so long ago now, but I was rather surprised at it myself. I was sick of the water and pretending to defend England's shores when nobody seemed to want to attack them."

"But you were only a boy."

"I sometimes think I shall never be anything else. I can't stand the things men do. They waste such a lot of time over them."

"But you must work."

"I suppose so. But I shall have to ask you to feed me for a little."

"Oh! your father won't say no to you. He never says no to any one."

"There's consistency in that."

"Your father is not the man he was. We have had terrible times, my dear. Too dreadful. The people in this town."

"Why don't the girls get married?" asked Serge.

"My dear," answered his mother, "there are so few men whom one would like to see them marry."

Mary and Gertrude returned, and just then Francis came in. Serge went up to him and kissed him, and Francis said "God bless my soul." When he realised who it was he shook his son warmly by the hand and went on saying: "I'm glad to see you, glad to see you, glad to see you." And he chuckled inside him and made Serge sit down, and stood looking at him, taking him in, and went on:

"Something like a prodigal son, eh, Martha? Only the queer thing is that I feel it is I who ought to say 'I am no more worthy to be called thy father!'"

Martha protested, and they sat down to supper.

Francis sat absolutely silent at the head of the table and Martha prattled and told Serge all the family news, all the deaths, and all the contents of all the wills, especially those by which neither she nor Francis had benefited, and how Willie Folyat had won his case and become Earl of Leedham, and how Minna had been practically engaged to him once and might have been a countess but for her folly.

"I couldn't have borne Willie for a husband. He was so mushy," said Minna.

"You might have left him and got a handsome settlement," suggested Serge.

"Oh, no! The title carries very little money."

"Left him! Serge!" Mrs. Folyat apostrophised him.

Minna winked at Serge and said:

"You're not married, I suppose?"

"No."

They ate cold ham and pickles and Gruyère cheese and captains' biscuits. Francis drank toast and water and Serge disposed of two bottles of beer. He looked round at the family portraits and drank their healths.

"I wonder," he said, "how they like seeing us here?"

"I often sit with them," replied Francis, breaking his silence, "and I fancy they are snobs and like being in a place where they can feel themselves immeasurably superior."

"Some of them," remarked Mrs. Folyat, "are worth at least a hundred pounds."

"I found myself rather liking this place as I walked here," said Serge. "But I found myself wondering what happens to all the suppressed vitality of the people in it. How many people are there? There must be half a million. What do they all do? Their work can't be very satisfying. Do they produce children at an appalling rate? Or is there any artistic outlet? There can't be, or it wouldn't be so ugly. I suppose there's a lot of crime and a lot of mess.

I must have a look at it. Do they have frightful diseases, and isn't it rather a mockery spreading the Gospel of Christ in such a place?"

"Serge!" Mrs. Folyat was unable to follow what he said, but she was hurt at the mention of one whom she had always regarded as her Saviour at the supper-table.

"Have I shocked you, mother? I'm sorry," said Serge. "You're all so different from what I have been thinking you for years and years and I find it difficult to say anything. You're not exactly full of news about yourselves, and my thoughts ran away with me. That's bad."

"You haven't become an infidel I hope." Mrs. Folyat was rather querulous. "You went to church in Africa?"

"I was lay reader to the Bishop of Bloemfontein for six months."

"Ah!"

That reassured Mrs. Folyat, and she turned to her food again. She enjoyed eating, and took very small mouthfuls and nibbled at them in a most genteel fashion. Francis on the other hand ate hurriedly in large gulps and had always finished his plateful before everybody else. Serge suddenly found their methods of eating intensely interesting. He too loved eating— he had revelled in English cooking after his years in Africa—and it was pleasant to find that he had something in common with his father and mother, though, instinctively, he knew that he must not talk about it.

Francis rose from the table and took up pipe and tobacco. Serge produced his calabash and filled it.

"You don't smoke cigarettes?" asked Francis.

"No."

"Frederic does. Beastly habit."

Mary and Minna cleared away the things from the table and Gertrude disappeared upstairs. Francis sat by the fireplace and said nothing. Mrs. Folyat remained in her chair at the end of the table and said nothing either. Serge blew rings and clouds of smoke into the air and stretched his legs. Outside it had begun to rain, and the water gurgled in the gutters.

"How long have you been here?" asked Serge.

For a long time it seemed that he was to receive no answer, but then Mrs. Folyat in a ventriloquial voice, without the smallest expression in her face and without turning her head said to her husband:

"How many years have we been here, Frank?"

"A good many. Nine, ten—more."

"It seems more than that."

Again there was a silence, and Serge glared at the gas-jet until black spots swam in front of his eyes. A gust of indignation swept through him, and he brought his fist down on the table with a bang.

"Look here!" he almost shouted, "this isn't good enough! Aren't you glad to see me? I've come home to you after nearly twenty years, and here you are as silent and gloom-stricken as though I'd risen and confronted you from the grave. . . . Do you remember how I blubbered when I left you at the rectory gate at St. Withans? A boy's grief is a little thing, but it's kept you warm in my thoughts all these years. . . ."

He stopped. He saw that his mother was mopping at her eyes and her hand was fumbling at the tablecloth, and she seemed very old and pitiful to him then, and he knew that he must not hurt her. His father seemed not to have heard him and went on sucking at his pipe, which he smoked with great skill so that the blue smoke only came from the bowl and his mouth at long intervals. He looked all beard and spectacles, impersonal and unexpressive, sitting there by the fireplace, and yet there was humour in his very bulk. Serge felt that he had made an error in tactics, a blunder in manners. These people, his father and mother, were not to be taken by assault. They had ramparts and bulwarks against all comers, perhaps against each other, and their inmost lives were not to be laid bare for the first clamorous belligerent. He realised that his mother's tears were defensive weapons—a shower of Greek fire and boiling pitch. They were very effective, and they drove Serge back blistered and wounded, but also they roused the devil of obstinacy in him and made him resolved to stay in the queer dark house so full of shadows and to fight with all his might against its oppressive atmosphere, and to win his way through to the hearts of the old woman, his mother, and the bulky, silent, bearded man, his father.

He leaned forward and took his mother's hand and fondled it. He squeezed it like a lover, and gave a funny little laugh deep down in his chest.

"I'm sorry," he said.

She gave his hand a convulsive, sudden little pressure, and he began to talk about himself and his adventures. How he had wandered in America and worked his way across to Cape Town and gone up-country hunting elephants; and how he had fought in the Zulu War and taught Dutch girls English on a Boer farm, done anything and everything—prospected for gold, diamonds; cheated and been cheated; thrashed and been thrashed and as he told the smoke came faster from his father's bowl and pipe, and at last he told how he had taken to painting pictures for a living, because he was starving in Kimberley, and how he made enough money to pay his passage home, and came because he wanted to see green England again and the people with whom he had been happy as a boy.

"Did you get the pictures I sent you?"

"Oh, yes," said Francis. "I thought some of them very good."

"I'm glad of that. I don't know much about it, but they said out there the colour was fine. One or two were sent to London and a picture swell there wrote to me about them."

Mrs. Folyat said she thought she would like to finish her book before she went to bed, gathered her shawl about her shoulders, told them not to be late, gave Serge her cheek to kiss, and wandered from the room. Serge opened the door and closed it after her.

Francis laid down his pipe. He grunted once or twice and then leaned forward in his chair and said:

"I don't think I realised before that my children are grown men and women. It makes a difference. One loses the right to interfere, if one ever had any. What are you going to do?"

"If possible I shall become a painter. If it's impossible—there are plenty of other things to do."

"And where will you live?"

"Here. I've got four pounds and a few shillings and the clothes I stand up in and my drawings."

"I'm not a rich man."

"You haven't paid out a penny for me since I was fifteen."

"That's true."

"Give me a couple of years' board and lodging and a hundred a year and I'll pay you back every penny as soon as I can."

"I can't give you a hundred a year."

"How much has Frederic had?"

"Frederic? A good deal. . . . More than I could afford. Your mother's very fond of Frederic."

"Shall I tell you what will happen if you don't take my offer? I shall stay, and go on staying until you suddenly realise that I have been here for years."

"How do you know that?" asked Francis, a little uneasily.

"The house is like that. I'm rather like that myself—sometimes. I suppose it's in the blood. We get into false positions—we're intelligent enough to know that they're false, but we're not strong enough to break away. Isn't it so? It's called good-nature. Doesn't everybody call you a good-natured man? They do me. A damned good sort they call me—men I hate too—but it only means that I'm easy and don't make situations painful by demanding a clear issue."

"Isn't that what you're doing now?"

"Only because we're both good-natured men and there won't be any issue at all if I don't. I've come home. I'm interested. Things are going to happen in the house, and I want to be in at the fun. I may be useful."

"What sort of things?"

"I don't know. Who does? What matters is that they should happen. . . ."

Francis began to chuckle, and Serge threw back his head and laughed, though there was nothing particular to laugh at, and yet it was very strange to him to be sitting opposite a man and trying to get at him and salute his soul, and that man his father. Their conversation seemed to him like two cogged wheels in a machine missing their clutch and whizzing round separately. They went on talking, but finally admitted the futility of it, exchanged tobacco and sat in silence, enjoying it and each other. Francis found company in his eldest son, and it was very pleasant just to sit and look at him, he was so strong and clean and healthy.

Frederic come in very late and found them sitting there and the room full of smoke. Serge rose and took his thin nervous hand in his great paw and said:

"Hello! Frederic. I'm Serge."

"How are you?" returned Frederic. "Going to stay long?"

"About two years."

"The devil you are. I've just been talking to some men about you. I showed them your drawings. One man says you're a genius. What does it feel like?"

"Being a genius? I don't know. But I imagine it's like being an ordinary person—only more so. You look rather washed out."

"Oh! I've been working hard. I'm tired."

"You're very late," said Francis.

"Yes. I didn't think you'd be sitting up. All the women in bed? Where are you to sleep?"

"I don't know."

"Where is he to sleep, pa?"

"I don't know. I can't wake your mother up, and the girls will be asleep."

Serge laughed.

"I don't see anything to laugh at," muttered Frederic. "I don't want you in my bed."

"I'll sleep on the sofa," said Serge. "I was laughing because it was so like the Folyats."

Francis took a book in his hand and rolled out of the room. Serge removed his collar and covered his feet with his coat and lay down on the sofa. Frederic stood tugging at his little golden-red moustache and looked down at him.

"Good-night," he muttered, and went away.

"God!" said Serge. "What a weak chin he has."

IX
INTERIOR

*Polyerges, on the contrary, already illustrates the
lowering tendency of slavery.*

ANTS, BEES AND WASPS.

FREDERIC had omitted to make any mention of the fact that he had lost his brother's drawings, and had brushed the thought of them aside. He had a comfortable memory and a convenient conscience which never worried about his lapses and misdemeanours until they were known or in danger of being known to other people. Then he lived in dread of the application of official morality and indulged in a perfect orgy of self-torment, grinding himself between the upper and nether millstones of his own laxity and the rigid codes with which his upbringing had imbued him. He had had a qualm or two about Serge's drawings, but it was not until his brother appeared on the scene that he began to think their loss might be serious— that is, fraught with unpleasant consequences to himself. He was essentially amiable. Disagreement hurt him, and he would go to any lengths to avoid an unprofitable quarrel. On the other hand if a squabble seemed to lead to immediate gain he would rush at it head down.

In the morning he was out and away while Serge was still in the bathroom splashing and roaring at the top of his voice. He spent the morning in his office writing letters to Beecroft and Strutt telling them that his brother had come home with a stock of drawings better even than those he had shown them, and letters from London men about them. He had no clear purpose in doing this, but was filled with a vague notion that if the first drawings were irreparably lost he was making some amends.

In the lunch interval he went round to the Arts Club and asked the grubby boy if the drawings had been found. The grubby boy made an effort of memory and said that he seemed to recollect Mr. Lawrie going off with something under his arm that night. Yes; it was a big, square thing, because he had put Mr. Lawrie into a cab and it fell on to the floor, and he picked it up and laid it on Mr. Lawrie's knees.

Frederic gave the boy a penny, got Mr. Lawrie's address, and, as soon as he could get away in the evening went down to his house. It was one of a terrace of four stucco houses with Gothic windows. It stood at the corner, and a little bye-street led down one side of it to a slum. It had a little raised lawn, two laurel trees and a privet hedge in front of it, and a wide asphalt path led up to the front door, which lay far back in a huge gloomy porch. The windows looked out on to another row of stucco houses with a shop at the corner which for the time being was a laundry. Opposite the laundry was a public-house. Two streets met a few yards along the road, and in the cleft of them was a large red-brick house with its garden gate gleaming with brass plates. Here lived Dr. Haslam, the father of the spotty-faced youth.

Frederic gave a long tug at the bell and stood looking stupidly at the door, the lower panels of which were scratched and dented with heavy kicks. A large tabby cat came and rubbed herself against his legs.

Presently the latch was drawn and the door was opened about six inches, and in the aperture there appeared a long bony face, incredibly lined and wrinkled, and in it two burning-sorrowful eyes. The mouth of this face opened, and out of it came a toneless mournful voice saying:

"What is it?"

"Is Mr. Lawrie in?" asked Frederic.

"He is. But he's busy. Are ye from the office? We'll be ready in ten minutes."

"I want to see Mr. Lawrie most particularly on a private matter."

"Ye cannot see him."

"I must."

"What name?"

"Folyat. Mr. Frederic Folyat."

"I'll see."

The door was closed to and Frederic, left with the cat, stood trying to quiet the omen at his heart. A very pale young man came through the gate and walked up the asphalt path and came into the porch. He looked at Frederic shyly and stood as far away from him as possible. There was an awkward moment until he said:

"Have you rung?"

"Yes."

"She's a bit slow. She's got rheumatism in her feet. I know you, but you don't know me. I've seen you at your father's church. My name's Bennett Lawrie. I'm in business. It's beastly."

"Do you often go to our church?"

"I go to all the High Churches, when I can get away. I wanted to be a clergyman, but I suppose I never shall be now."

"You'd better come and see us. We have supper on Sundays for anybody who likes to come."

"I'd just love to know your father."

"I want to see *your* father."

"Oh! *My* father!"

The boy shied away on that, and again the door was opened six inches. Bennett pushed it open and disappeared into the dark house leaving Frederic confronted with the gaunt personage who owned the haggard face.

"Will ye come with me now?" she said.

Frederic followed her down a long gloomy passage and into a large dining-room, where at the table, surrounded with papers, sat James Lawrie, cursing, smoking, and writing full tilt. He had a huge cup of strong coffee by his side. His brows were drawn tight over his eyes, and Frederic was most struck by his huge jutting nose. He seemed all nose—a nose and a flying pen. He took no notice of Frederic, but growled:

"The figures—give me the figures!"

The old servant took up a newspaper and read out a series of figures which, as far as Frederic could make out, related to the price of cotton. Lawrie took them down as she read, added a few words after them, gathered and folded his sheets, thrust them into a dirty inky envelope and held them out to the old woman.

"I'll be late if I don't take a cab," she said.

Lawrie fumbled in his waistcoat pocket and produced a florin. She took it and shuffled away. Lawrie gulped down the remainder of his coffee, took up a battered green book and said:

"Now we'll have some poetry."

And he read half a canto of Spenser's "Faërie Queene" in a big rumbling voice, mouthing the archaic words.

Frederic could make little sense of it and sat taking in the room, the heavy mahogany sideboard, the horsehair chairs by the fireplace, the Biblical prints on the walls, the books on either side of the window, and through the window the dismal walled garden with its starved hawthorn trees and the cats playing about on the wall. The windows were closed and the air in the room was thick and smelled of tobacco and food and clothes. It was a dingy dusty room, made more than ever forbidding by a reproduction of Munkaczy's *Christ before Pilate,* which hung over the mantelpiece between the *Crucifixion* of Rubens and a photograph of a little Scotch church and a manse with gloomy hills in the background.

When the reading was finished Frederic said:

"I'm sorry I interrupted you."

"Not at all. I'd finished my work. I'm alone. I'm always alone in this house. Have you ever thought how lonely a man can be in his own house? . . . You've not? You don't think? May be you're wise, though, maybe again, you're only young. Well, I tell you, a man can be very lonely in his own house, but not many are as lonely as I am. Looking at it purely philosophically it's something of an achievement—in a negative sort of way. I mean, not many men can have all that nature has provided for a man and get nothing at all out of it. Nearly all men manage to get some pickings for their vanity, but I don't even get that. I get nothing. . . . So do hundreds of thousands of people. They can't. But the difference between them and me is that they can pretend and I can't. Nature's very wasteful. She produces far more men and women than she wants. Just a few are sound and really alive. The rest are shadows. I'm a shadow. I don't know what you are. A sort of betwixt and between I should say, just looking at you. The real men make loveliness, and the intelligent shadows have a sort of echo of it and have a sort of reflected life through it. The rest wither away and are dead years and years before they die. What I can't stand though is their damned cruelty. I can't expect you to make much of that. I talk like that for hours to old Tibby. She's the most real person in this house, and the rest of us are sticking to her like leeches. She's had no life of her own, hasn't Tibby, and sometimes she will stand and look at me and say, 'You're a wonderful talker, man,' and I'll say, 'I'm nothing else, woman.' Queer people, we are. But we're all queer in this place to go on living in the darkness and mist of it as we do. I've met your father. He's a comfortable man. It must be very pleasant to have a comfortable man in the house."

Frederic did his best to follow him in his harangue, and, though he could make very little of it all, he was interested and wanted him to go on. He had never been in a house like it before. Never had he had such a sensation of empty darkness, and he wanted very much to know what was in the rest of the house besides the boy who had spoken to him on the doorstep and Tibby and the cat. And what did they all do when old Lawrie got drunk?

The boy Bennett came into the room, walked across to the book-shelves by the window, took down a book and went out again without taking the smallest notice of his father.

The old man watched him with a sort of hunger, and he took a piece of paper and tore it up into a thousand pieces and let them flutter down on to the floor at his feet.

Frederic plunged into his own affairs and said:

"Do you remember some drawings I showed you? My brother's come back. I think he wants them. The boy at the club . . ."

"I have them."

"You remember Mr. Beecroft said he was a genius."

"Beecroft's a sot and a fool. But they're good. Things seen and felt. I've given over asking for more than that."

He went to a cupboard and produced the portfolio. Frederic saw it with immense relief, and ceased to take any interest in old Lawrie, or Tibby, or Bennett, or the cat. He was secure against any unpleasantness, and the old man's talk seemed to him now only maundering folly. Before he had been more than half convinced that the world was a miserable place of shadows and shams.

Except for awful moments Frederic had always found life very pleasant and amusing. He had done very much as he pleased and fancied that he had been remarkably successful in dodging consequences. He did not imagine that things could ever be different, and thinking about it always seemed to him to be a ridiculous waste of time.

He took the portfolio and began to tell old Lawrie the little he knew about Serge, and soon worked round to Beecroft's declaration that an exhibition ought to be organised, and the old man, more to humour him and to get rid of him than for any enthusiasm that he had, asked him to bring his brother to the club some Sunday evening. Frederic promised and took his leave.

In the dark passage he met Bennett waiting for him. Bennett was very nervous and took him into a little dark cell of a room at the foot of the stairs and took him by the arm and whispered:

"Did you really mean me to come? Of course I can't ask you to come here. I can't, you know. But I would like to come to your house. You sing don't you, and act? I can sing and act, and I can draw and write verses. Your brother's a painter, isn't he? I should love to come."

Frederic felt irritated. The boy was so horribly in earnest. There was nothing particularly delightful in the house in Fern Square, but if the queer little idiot liked to come of course there was no reason why he shouldn't. He was religious, and therefore, presumably, respectable enough.

"All right," said Frederic gruffly. "Next Sunday."

"Oh! Thanks. Thanks."

The boy took his hand and pressed it violently. He had a cold, hard bony hand, and Frederic had a feeling of repulsion. It seemed unnatural to him for a boy to be so emotional.

He reached home to find Serge entertaining a large party, including all the family, the Clibran-Bell girls, and his cousin, Streeten Folyat, who had suddenly appeared on his way to Westmoreland, where he had bought a sheep-farm. Streeten belonged to a wealthy branch of the family and had already tried nine different professions. He was a man of means, and Mrs. Folyat was making herself very charming to him, and had him sitting between herself and Mary. Serge was at the piano playing and singing absurd little buffoonish songs and teasing Jessie Clibran-Bell, whom for the first time Frederic began to think rather pretty. Minna was reading, and Gertrude was browsing in a corner, nursing the dog.

Minna put down her book as he entered and said:

"Doesn't Frederic look important to-night? You shall have all the centre of the room to yourself."

"I got your drawings, Serge," Frederic spoke in rather a loud voice. He wanted to attract Jessie Clibran-Bell's attention. "I lent them to old Lawrie, the dramatic critic. He showed them to some friends of his, and they say you must have an exhibition. We'll make your fortune, yet. They say Africa's very much in the air just now."

"Are you a painter, Mr. Folyat?" asked Jessie Clibran-Bell.

"One of Frederic's friends says I'm a genius," replied Serge.

"Oh! then you won't stay here. All the geniuses go to London. We had a cousin who wrote books and she went to America and made a lot of money."

"I didn't say I was a genius. I only said one of Frederic's friends said I was a genius. It does not follow that it is true."

"You shall judge for yourself, Jessie," said Frederic.

"How can she judge?" asked Serge. "She doesn't know anything about it."

Jessie went pink and her neck stiffened, and she turned to Frederic. He produced the drawings from the portfolio and placed them round the room, and an impromptu exhibition was held. Serge told them which they ought to admire, and they admired them. On the whole they were puzzled rather than interested. They were soon exhausted as a subject of discussion, and Frederic, having drawn Jessie away from Serge, began to tell her of his experience at old Lawrie's house. Presently his voice drowned all the rest and all in the room were listening.

"I asked young Bennett Lawrie to supper next Sunday," he said.

"He's very beautiful, isn't he, Gertie?" observed Minna pointedly.

"You know him then?" asked Frederic.

"He's an acolyte at St. Saviour's. We've been to St. Saviour's once or twice, haven't we Gertie?"

"Have we?" Gertrude's face was a brilliant Turkey red.

Mrs. Folyat wagged her head.

"I don't think your father will like your filling the house with young men."

"Rubbish, mother," said Serge. "Every house ought to be filled with young men and young women. Houses are quite intolerable unless people are making love in them."

"My dear!"

"They've got to make love somewhere."

Frederic caught Jessie's eye, and with a little swagger he said:

"Yes. But we don't talk about it."

"Good gracious me," said Serge with a laugh, "men and women hardly talk about anything else. If they don't talk they think the more, and that's bad for them."

"I think you are disgusting," said Gertrude, tartly, and left the room.

"Is he a nice young man, this Bennett Lawrie?" asked Mrs. Folyat.

"He's the queerest fish I ever met. His father's quite dotty."

"I'd like to know him," interrupted Serge.

"The boy's as nervous as a cat and as soft as a woman. He nearly cried with gratitude when I asked him to come. They live opposite the Haslams—Basil Haslam's a painter, or going to be one."

"Oh! Minna knows him," said Mary with sudden malice.

There was a gap in the conversation. Frederic asked Jessie if she would accompany him, and so manœuvred Serge away from the piano. He sang a very sentimental love-ditty and gazed with soft eyes at the back of Jessie's neck the while.

When she left he insisted on seeing her home with her sister. It took him twenty-five minutes, and when he returned he found Serge buffooning for his mother and making her laugh till she cried.

"Oh! dear. Oh! dear," she cried. "I haven't laughed so much for years. You'd never think Serge was a grown man, would you, Frederic?"

"Never," replied Frederic with asperity.

"My good brother," said Serge solemnly, "you gave a remarkable description just now of the house of the Lawries—an unhappy, middle-class house. You said it felt like a prison with that raw-boned old Scotswoman for goaler. I've been a free man all my life and I feel about this house exactly what you felt about that. There's fear in it and unfriendliness. I don't understand why, but I will understand before I've done."

The two brothers were standing close together, and Serge had unwittingly raised his voice. Mrs. Folyat came and laid her hand on his arm and said:

"Please, please don't quarrel."

"We're not quarrelling, mother," replied Serge, "Frederic is annoyed with me. He doesn't know why, nor do I. It's those Lawries have upset him. It's all right, mother. You go to bed. I'm a disturbing influence at present. You'll get used to me and I shall become a habit like everything else."

"It isn't fair," said Frederic.

"What isn't fair?"

"It isn't fair to talk to mother like that. She doesn't understand you."

"Of course she doesn't. It isn't any good talking. Go to bed mother."

Frederic led his mother to the door and went out with her. Streeten declared that he must go and Mary saw him to the door.

Turning, Serge found Minna watching him with a broad grin on her face. She was as tall as he, big and fine, and he thought:

"Well, she at least is a handsome woman. Pity she doesn't dress better."

Minna said:

"I'm glad you made Frederic feel small. He's a beast."

"Is he? What kind of a beast?"

"The worst kind. A jealous beast."

"I think I rather like you, Minna."

"Thank you. And the rest of us?"

"I'm prepared to like you all."

"You're quite right about this house, Serge. It is a prison. It's been getting worse and worse ever since James died. It was awful, of course."

"Why don't you marry?"

"How can I? I've no money; can't make any—and I've no intention of marrying a poor man. It isn't so easy to fall in love either—unless you're like Bub."

"Who?"

"Gertrude. She's in love with that young Bennett Lawrie. She goes to his church and looks at him as though he were a beautifully-cooked chop. He is rather like that. I shall call him the mutton-chop when he comes."

"Don't any of the young women get married in these parts. What about the Clibran-Bells?"

"Oh! Jessie is in love with Frederic, always has been ever since he turned up."

"How long's that?"

"A good many years. It was awful when we first came. We arrived at five o'clock in the morning. It was pouring with rain, and we drove in two cabs through the horrible dirty streets. We were all very tired, and Gertrude and Mary had been squabbling in the train. We didn't know anything about towns, and Ma had made us very excited by talking about the rich people we were going to know—and marry. She always used to be talking about marriage. She doesn't do it so much now."

"Why on earth did they come? St. Withans was jolly enough."

"I don't know. I think they lost some money, and Ma got sick of the country and Mother Bub got tired of falling in love with the curates, and they worried pa until he did it."

"Does he always do what mother wants him to?"

"Oh! yes. She's a nagger."

Serge went up to Minna and put his arm round her waist and kissed her. She took his face in her hands and kissed his lips. Then she sighed:

"What a pity you're my brother."

"I fancy a good many women say that to their brothers—when they don't know any other men."

"Have you known a lot of women?"

"A good many."

"I thought so. We seem to exist for you as individuals. To the Frederic sort of man women only seem to exist as a surrounding presence. . . . If I did something dreadful you'd stand by me, wouldn't you?"

"I hope so. But don't do anything dreadful just for the fun of it. It isn't worth it."

Minna gave a little purr of contentment and rubbed her cheek against his and said:

"You're so warm and friendly. I'm glad you came. But I can understand people hating you like poison."

"They do, my dear, they do."

He kissed her again and she ran happily away and upstairs.

X
SUNDAY SUPPER

He for God only.—MILTON.

PURITAN hostility to the proceedings in St. Paul's survived the demise of Flynn and his newspaper and spluttered into activity upon occasion, as when Francis instituted the Litany as a separate Sunday afternoon service or allowed his school-room to be used for musical entertainments organised by the local nigger minstrels—(the annual visit of Moore and Burgess gave birth to numerous amateur troupes)—or when in the jumble sales which were held at intervals he countenanced and even patronised raffles. One pretext was as good as another, but the fundamental grievance was his friendship with Father Soledano, a priest attached to the Roman Catholic Cathedral. The offence was greater in that he had no friend, hardly a kindly acquaintance among the Anglican clergy. They fought shy of him because he had incurred the disapproval of the dean, though their wives occasionally called on Mrs. Folyat because she was still visited by the bishop's wife.

Father Soledano was an Irishman of Spanish extraction, a little ugly man, with a lame leg, stiff bristling hair receding from a knobby, wrinkled forehead, little eyes glowing under bushy brows, a long upper lip and a sensitive mouth, and a chin that looked as though he had to shave it every half hour.

The Roman Catholic Cathedral was about a mile away from St. Paul's, and Father Soledano lived in the priest's house in an asphalt court that lay under its shadow. The surrounding district was inhabited mostly by poor Irish—ignorant, drunken, superstitious, and Jews, whose morality was a reproach to the rest of the dwellers in the slums; and there were French people, and Bavarians, Lithuanians, not a few Poles, and refugees from Russia. All these were swept into the various trades and manufactories—sweated tailoring, sweated shirt-making, sweated jam-making, sweated engineering. And Father Soledano found his work of digging for their souls infinitely amusing. Several of his Catholics lived over in the parish of St. Paul's, and he had sought Francis out on hearing a tale of his kindness to an old woman who, by practising midwifery, supported her daughter-in-law and four children. This old woman was a Catholic, and every penny she could spare was spent in buying images of saints. She had the Virgin, and St. Peter, and St. Anthony of Padua, and a little Saint Catherine of Siena. One day two of the men who had assaulted Frederic and overturned the gravestone of the boy James, made a round of all the Catholic houses they could discover and destroyed all the images. When Francis heard of it he went from house to house and was given a list of all that had been destroyed, and a week later he went round with his chief sidesman carrying a clothes-basket full of saints, and made good every loss. When the aforesaid old woman found herself with a new Virgin, a new Saint Peter, and a new Saint Anthony of Padua and a more beautiful new Saint Catherine of Siena than she had ever thought of in her wildest dreams, she knelt down and began to pray for the soul of the English Father. And Francis knelt down and prayed with her, and all the children gathered round and stared at their grandmother and the portly bearded man kneeling there by the kitchen table, and their mother began to cry, and the old woman began to cry, until Francis lifted her up and kissed her on the cheek. Then he sent the children out to buy bread and jam and cake and they had a lovely tea together.

Francis did not tell the tale to anybody, but it was soon out all over the parish, and there was much indignation. A few of the parishioners left the church and Mrs. Folyat was shocked and affronted. What offended her most was that Francis had carried the images publicly and openly through the streets. Being an inveterate gossip herself, she could not endure being the subject of it, except it were flattering to her vanity.

Father Soledano wrote to Francis and thanked him, and Francis invited him to come and see him. The invitation was accepted, and the two men found that they had many things in common outside their profession, and they had many a long talk about old Dublin days. Soledano was amused by the Anglican's easy-going optimism, and Francis was shocked, interested, and stimulated by the priest's almost cynical pessimism. They never discussed religion. To a certain extent they secretly allied forces in their work of dealing with the moral and economic difficulties of their poor, a certain substratum of whom were ultimately Catholic and Anglican according as they could win the attention and sympathy of the district visitors or the Little Sisters, though they hardly ever attended service either in the Cathedral or in St. Paul's.

Every now and then Soledano would come to supper at Fern Square on Sundays, and it so happened that he was there when Bennett Lawrie appeared for the first time dressed sprucely for the occasion with a new suit and a very high collar and a blue birds-eye tie. The whole family was present, having been to church in full force—Serge read the Lessons—and they had sat down to their meal, having forgotten all about young Lawrie,

Round The Corner | 87

when there came a resounding peal at the bell. The servant was out and Gertrude opened the door to him. His face was utterly tragic, and he could hardly find his voice to ask if Mrs. Folyat were in. Gertrude admitted him, showed him into the dining-room, where several people were talking all at once, and disappeared into the kitchen to fetch him plate, knife, and fork. It was some moments before Frederic recognised him—two gas-jets in glass globes do not give very much light—and Bennett suffered agonies of shyness and began to wish he had never come. He saw Francis open his mouth and insert a large piece of cold beef and his beard wag as he chewed it slowly, and he rather resented it. He had romanticised Francis, and had always pictured him in his vestments very saintly and impressive. The other man, Soledano, sitting between Mrs. Folyat and Minna, looked much more like a saint. . . . Minna gazed at Bennett with mischievous approval, and he thought her very beautiful and cast down his eyes. Frederic said "Hullo" and told his mother who Bennett was, and Mrs. Folyat bade Serge and Mary make room for the young man between them. Gertrude returned with plate, knife and fork. Bennett sat down at the place made for him, and conversation was resumed and flowed on over him. It was chiefly concerned with food, and Mrs. Folyat was very anxious to know what Father Soledano had to eat at the priests' house. He told her they ate very little meat and a great deal of macaroni. Mary tried to talk to Bennett but could get nothing out of him but "Yes" and "No." He liked music but knew nothing about it, and had never been to a concert.

Serge tackled him. The directness of his questions embarrassed Bennett, and the kindliness of his interest moved him so that a lump rose in his throat and he could hardly get out his replies. He had, he said, been born in the town and had hardly ever been away from it; once to Scotland, where his father came from, and once to Westmoreland and once to Derbyshire. His family were so poor, you see, though they had once been quite rich and lived in a big house with a garden. He could just remember the garden. He was nineteen and had been in business since he was sixteen, first of all in a little office where there was only one clerk, and then, by the influence of his uncles, in a great firm of shippers where, if you did not earn very much, you were at any rate safe. His mother was Low Church and his father was a Presbyterian but never went to any place of worship. He had two brothers and two sisters, but they were all older than himself and didn't care about the things he cared for, though one of his brothers sang in the choir at the Church of the Ascension, where they only wore surplices and no cassocks. . . . Timidly he asked Serge if it was true that he was an artist, and Serge laughed and said he was a sort of middle-aged embryo.

"That must be splendid," said Bennett, wistfully. "I draw, but not real things, only dreams and horrible grotesques. We started a family paper once but the others wouldn't do anything, and I had to write it all myself and draw all the pictures, and they laughed at everything I did, and I drew a picture of my mother being carried off by the devil and they burnt it. I write verses about the people in the office, but they don't like them unless they're—you know—rather nasty. We can't smoke in our office and everybody takes snuff. I think I'd like to have been a clergyman."

He suddenly became conscious that Gertrude's eyes were upon him and that she was devouring every word he said. He had recognised her as the young woman who came so often to St. Saviour's, and he had thought about her a great deal. He had tortured himself with the notion that she might have come to see him, had even dreamed lofty romances in which she figured as a mysterious lady of high degree who swept him off in a great carriage with two tremendous horses, and then had been ashamed. It comforted him a little to know that she was the daughter of the Rev. Francis Folyat, and that her attendance at St. Saviour's could therefore only have been prompted by the highest spiritual motives. . . . All the same she was looking at him exactly as she did when he came down to the steps of the nave and stood with the great brass offertory-plate. He was wretchedly nervous, but he imagined the Folyats to be a happy united family, and he basked in the warmth which seemed to pervade their house. He listened to their bantering conversation and was very much afraid of them all except Serge. Frederic seemed to drink a vast quantity of beer, and he remembered stories that he had heard of him in the office. Like everybody else who was interested in church matters, he was familiar with the flying gossip concerning the Folyats, and the ill-natured remarks that were current about the unmarried daughters. He thought Minna more and more beautiful, and Mary devoted, and Gertrude—he could not disentangle Gertrude from all the absurd things he had thought of her before he knew who she was.

Mrs. Folyat began, as she always did in the presence of a newcomer, to talk of the ancestors on the wall, and to tell the lurid stories of the Red Lady, who had known more than was ever written of the Monmouth rebellion, and the Grey Lady who had such a violent temper, that, losing it one day out driving with her husband in a high chariot, she boxed his ears so that he lost his balance and fell out and broke his neck. She rambled on by way of Baron Folyat to Willie, now safely established as Earl of Leedham, and she declared, being thoroughly warmed to her subject, that failing heirs male, and in the event of the extirpation of two other branches of the family—and less likely things had happened—Serge would become heir, or his sons, if he ever had any.

Bennett was much impressed, as it was meant that he should be, and began to talk of his own ancestry. There were Lawries in Elgin as far back as Robert the Bruce, and for hundreds of years there had been Lawries who were lairds or in the ministry. Mrs. Folyat asked him who his mother was, and Bennett replied:

"She was a Miss Smith. She married my father when she was seventeen. People don't seem able to marry so young nowadays."

"It is difficult, isn't it, Gertrude?" asked Minna.

The meal came to an end, and Francis asked Frederic to accompany him to the study to discuss a theatrical entertainment that was in process of organisation in aid of the restoration of the organ. Mary and Minna cleared away and Gertrude helped her mother upstairs, carrying her spectacles, book and knitting-bag. Serge, Bennett, and Father Soledano were left in the dining-room. Serge and Bennett smoked and Father Soledano began to talk. Bennett was unused to drinking beer. Serge had plied him with it rather too generously in the frequent lapses in their conversation, and the fumes of it had gone to his head so that it felt very hot and large, while inside it his brain worked with unwonted swiftness and a hectic clarity. His cheeks were flushed and they burned, but on the whole he found his new sensations very pleasant, and there was a sort of splendour in being treated by these grown men, an artist and a priest, as one of themselves. To Bennett all artists were great artists—he was not his father's son for nothing—and the priesthood was the noblest and most exalted calling possible for man. He lived from Sunday to Sunday. On Monday morning he died and was buried in his office. On Saturday evening came a glorious resurrection, and he rose to exalted heights each Sunday morning when he took the sacrament. He was an emotional creature and had no other outlet.

He sat looking from Serge to Father Soledano and from Father Soledano to Serge as they talked, but took little account of what they said. They were exchanging impressions of the town and speaking of it in a curious critical way that Bennett found difficulty in following. He knew nothing of the machinery of the world. He was poor, and he had accepted it as axiomatic that poor people had to do work that was distasteful to them. He had no notion of what that work resulted in, or who profited by it. You went on working until you had enough to marry, and then you married and went on working until you died. His brothers were both bank-clerks, and he gathered that their work was even duller than his own, which consisted in addressing envelopes and taking messages down into the warehouse where there were rough men who were even poorer than himself. They packed and unpacked bales of cotton-goods which were placed on lorries and carried off to trains, which took them away to the sea and across the sea to Bombay and Calcutta and Shanghai and Yokohama. There were many other processes going on in the office and warehouses, but that seemed to be the general principle — cotton came from America, was bought on the Exchange, spun and woven in the mills near Oldham, brought to the warehouse and dispatched — fully insured — through the complicated machinery of the office. There were five partners in the firm and they were all very rich. One of the employees, the head-clerk, had six hundred a year, but he himself, Bennett, received every week only thirty shillings. Many young men of his age were earning only half that sum, and he was quite ready to admit, without thought or examination, that he was worth no more to his employers. He did not understand the machinery in which he played a part, did not want to understand it, and did not find it sufficiently interesting. Being poor, he had to work, and the nature of the work was not his affair. It absorbed the greater part of his life, but it was outside his work that he was as really alive as he could be.

This visit to Fern Square was perhaps the greatest adventure of his life. He had heard Father Soledano's voice droning on for some time, and now he heard words that interested him.

"The middle classes are beginning to invest their savings in industrial securities. That is going to make things worse than ever for the poor, since it means organised exploitation, dividends to be paid as well as the profits of private enterprise. It seems to me that men are inventing machinery for making money and letting them get out of hand. A machine that no man can control or use for the purposes of good is the most perilous engine of destruction."

"A machine," thought Bennett, and at once there came to his mind the streets surrounding his office where all day long there was the thud of machinery and thousands of men and women being swallowed up in the morning by great black ugly buildings, and spewed out again in the evening, all, he supposed, as weary and listless as he felt himself on every evening except Saturday.

"Isn't that," said Serge, "isn't that what has happened with the Church? . . . You don't mind my discussing it in that way? . . . Hasn't it become a machine which takes everything from men and gives them nothing? I fancy my father's Church doesn't meddle much, or, at any rate, effectually, with politics, but yours is always struggling after the temporal power which it has lost."

"That is because we believe that the Church and State should be one."

"I agree. And so they would be if the Church were really a Church, and the State were really a State. I have never been to your church, but I know that my father's is only an imitation, a fairly good imitation and quite attractive, but it has nothing at all to do with religion as I understand it."

"It depends what you mean by religion."

"I take it to mean the profoundest instinct in a human being, that instinct of life which embraces and should direct all the rest."

"I agree, but it is impossible."

"Why is it impossible?"

Bennett did not hear Father Soledano's reply. The dialogue had been to him like the murmuring of mysterious voices in a dream, bearing no relation to his own actual experience. His own religion was so axiomatic that the possibility of criticism, outside crude condemnation, to which he was hardened and accustomed, had never occurred to him, and yet, now that it had happened, it was as something remote, impious, but menacing and disturbing. That Father Soledano should lend himself to such talk perturbed him not at all, for he had been brought up to believe that anything was possible for the Roman Catholic priesthood. He was conscious of resentment, and told himself that it was because these things were being said in Mr. Folyat's house. He was hurt, and childishly he wished to hand on the pain to some one. He waited until Father Soledano's voice had died down, and then he said, taking no account of his words:

"It isn't for us to inquire into these things. If we believe at all in the authority and the Divine origin of the Church we are bound by its tradition and its—its dogma."

"I beg your pardon," replied Serge. "I forgot that you were there. I don't believe in the authority or the Divine origin of the Church, and I refuse to be bound by its tradition, which has always been, to say the least of it, unhappy in its results, or its dogma, which seems to me unsound and more or less contradictory of the spirit of the New Testament."

"But—but . . ." Bennett pounced on Serge with an air of triumph, brandishing his point before proving it. "But what about morals?"

"That," said Serge, "is exactly where you and I part company. You Christians have only evolved a morality which you apply to the affairs of others and not to your own. You have no standard of goodness—only the wickedness of other people, a Pharisaic standard which would have been repulsive to the Man whom you choose to regard as your Founder. My father's sermons, for instance—and they are like every parson's sermons—

begin by drawing such a frightful picture of human wickedness that when it is over his hearers feel that they are angels of goodness in comparison. It's an old dodge, and I daresay Father Soledano makes use of it too."

"I do," said Father Soledano. "I do."

Bennett gaped at him. He felt that he would burst into tears if this went on any longer, and indeed his eyes were wet and his throat was so dry that he could not speak.

"You like your religion?" asked Serge.

"It is my whole life." Bennett was surprised at the ferocity with which he said this. He was staggered by Serge's answer:

"I am sorry for you. You will be badly hurt when life gobbles you up and gives you other engrossing interests, which you will be ill-equipped to tackle."

"Come, come," said Father Soledano. "It is not fair. It is not fair to come down from the general to the particular like that."

"I protest," answered Serge. "My whole indignation arises from the unkindness and dishonesty of stuffing young people, and ignorant people, with generalisations."

"What else can you give them? They are not conscious of individuality."

"I don't believe that, and even if it were so you ought to leave them free to become conscious—if they can."

"The risk is too great."

"What risk?"

Bennett's mind had been moving swiftly and partly by memory, partly by intuition he came to this:

"People can't do as they like."

Serge stood up suddenly and paced round the room.

"Young idiot!" he said. "They can, and they do. Isn't it your experience, Father, that they do? The trouble is that with all these foolish generalisations buzzing in their heads they are always doing the wrong things, and doing them in the wrong way, shuffling, and sneaking so as to hide away from the bogies you give them." He turned to Bennett and asked: "Has what you do and think on Sunday the slightest bearing on what you do and think on week-days?"

"It keeps me from temptation," said Bennett so earnestly that there was not the smallest hint of priggishness in him.

Round The Corner | 93

Serge took him by the arm and lifted him clean out of his chair and set him down with a jolt on to his feet.

"Keeps you from temptation, does it! How?—By running away from it."

Bennett was very angry. He raised his voice:

"If you had to live in my house you wouldn't talk like that. My father's a drunken beast and my mother doesn't even try to understand us. You'd believe in God if you lived in our house. . ." He came to an end suddenly. Serge patted him kindly on the shoulder.

"That's all right. That's all right. Let's go upstairs and see what a happy home is like, or perhaps you would prefer to go and talk to my father and Father Soledano in the study."

"I'll go with you," said Bennett.

They went upstairs, and Father Soledano joined Francis in the study. In the drawing-room they found Frederic holding forth about the performance in the school-room. The piece chosen was *The Rose and the Ring*, in a musical version.

Gertrude asked Bennett if he could sing. He replied that he could, and Frederic graciously allowed him the use of one of his songs, "On, on, my bark, dash through the foam." Bennett had a light baritone voice with a curious harsh quality in the middle notes, but he loved singing and really let himself go. When he had finished Mrs. Folyat looked up from her *Family Herald* and said:

"Very nice, very nice indeed. Even Frederic does not sing it so well."

Frederic asked Bennett to take a part in *The Rose and the Ring*, and he accepted. Gertrude took him aside to show him his part, and Mary produced her violin and played Mendelssohn's Songs Without Words for half an hour, after which she produced a table and cards and sat playing Bézique with her mother. (Mrs. Folyat declared that she could not sleep without her game. No one else was allowed to play cards on Sunday.)

Serge sat teasing Minna, and time flew.

There came a ring at the bell, and after a little interval a gaunt figure in black stalked into the room, stood by the door, and said:

"Bennett, your mother says you're to come home."

Bennett rose to his feet at once, muttered good-bye, turned the colour of a red peony and slunk out after the old Scotch servant.

94 | Round The Corner

XI
ART AND DRAMA

Each had an upper stream of thought
That made all seem as it was not.

PETER BELL THE THIRD.

LAWRIE, Beecroft and Co. had not a monopoly in culture. Our City Fathers provided us with an art gallery, to which, with praiseworthy regularity they added two Academy pictures every year; the Town-hall had been decorated by a Pre-Raphaelite, and there was a whole network of Free Libraries, all equipped with thousands of books in a uniform binding, and with the smell proper to Free Libraries. In the cold weather they were always very full, in the hot weather they were always very empty; but in the hot weather the accumulated smells of the winter were distilled and concentrated. For music we had two or three series of concerts during the winter months. They were chiefly patronised by Germans and Jews, and the English bragged about them. We had a College of Music, and a School of Art in connection with the municipal technical school. This institution was presided over by a Socialistic disciple of William Morris, who spent a great part of his free time in designing banners for Friendly Societies — Buffaloes, Free Foresters, Hearts of Oak — and cartoons for Labour journals. It was situated in a square which was typical of the town. In the centre of it stood a huge ugly Anglican church, and three sides of it were filled with a Presbyterian chapel, a Wesleyan chapel, a Baptist chapel, a Secular hall, a Maternity Hospital and a Dental Hospital. Down a by-street was the headquarters of the Salvation Army, and down another a larger Roman Catholic church. Quite near was the office in which Bennett Lawrie worked, and all round were slums, public-houses, brothels, a wedge of infamy between the working centre and the outskirts. All round the Anglican church in the centre of the square ran a wide pavement on which were wooden benches. Here at night came hundreds of men, women and boys who had no resting-place. They spent half the night there until they were moved on by the police, when they went to a similar pavement with benches outside the Infirmary, meeting half-way their comrades in misery who had been moved on from that place—a sort of general post. In the day-time the square was always busy, for two main roads met in it, and tram-lines from four directions converged. Near at hand were many cheap shops, and the wives of the clerks came thither to make their daily purchases.

It was to this School of Art that Serge Folyat came as the result of his exhibition, which was an almost unredeemed failure. Beecroft banged the drum and old Lawrie blew the trumpet, but the local school of artists were contemptuous, and declared that the new genius could not draw. Serge quite agreed. He sold ten of his pictures, and went to see the disciple of William Morris and arranged to attend eight classes a week, four in the afternoon and four in the evening.

He found the school very amusing, though at first his position was a little difficult, for most of the students were very young and inclined to look askance at a man with a beard turning grey and his hair growing thin on the top of his head. The classes were very cheap, and he was able to pay for the first term himself and postponed discussion as to future ways and means, reckoning that in three months' time his family would have digested and assimilated him, and added him to the already large number of habits which made their common existence tolerable. He worked very hard both at home and at the school, wrestling with the horrible difficulties of the human body. He had an intuitive feeling that he would never be able to draw hands, and he became very ingenious in concealing them.

The classes at the school were mixed. There were a few serious students of both sexes, a great many who attended from the vanity of talent, and some to whom studying art was an occupation. A little hunchback with a malicious intense face had been there for thirteen years, and an old spinster of fifty-five had spent fifteen years without ever passing an examination or taking a single certificate. She was extremely hopeful, and one of the most cheerful persons in the school. On the whole it was not cheerful. It lacked spirit and enthusiasm. Many of the young men no doubt had a secret conviction that they had a great destiny, but they were rather ashamed of it, and only in rare moments of excitement did they dare to let it appear. Theodore Benskin, the Morrisian principal of the school, had been enthusiastic at twenty-five, but he had stopped there. However, he was a good teacher of a mechanical sort. His business was to turn out draughtsmen rather than artists, and he succeeded. Serge desired to become a draughtsman, and he followed Benskin's directions, though all the while he had a feeling of the grotesque in what he was doing, and was inclined to think that a bushman's drawings on the wall of a cave were of more value than all the finished studies turned out under Benskinian rules. However, he was nettled by the failure of his exhibition, and saw that it was quite useless to take keen pleasure in his work unless by the work he could communicate that pleasure to others. He had no concise theory of art beyond a conviction that unless it could create pleasure there was no excuse for it. As for making money by it, there were a thousand easier ways of doing that, ways that left more leisure and did not induce such profound depression. It was all very well, he thought, to gird, as did almost everybody he met, at the sordidness and grimness of the town in which they lived, but the most miserable of all the people in it were the supposed artists, the men who frequented the Arts Club. They were all men of talent, but none of them ever seemed to have used their gifts to any purpose. They were perpetually cursing the lack of appreciation of their fellow-citizens, but they had never made any really serious attempt to win them or to open up any new way for their minds. When it came to the point their standards were those of the rich men, upon whose caprice they lived. Like everybody else in the town they put up with money as the sole channel of communication between one man and another. Serge used sometimes to try to talk to the waifs and strays on the benches outside the church in the square, but he found them nearly all brutalised and fuddled. They seemed to have no thought beyond the next meal, no programme beyond the next drink. They cadged.

Among the students at the school was a young man whom Serge had marked out from the very first moment. He was short, and had a large head, dark hair, bright eyes, and he was always merry. He had a joke for everyone, and he was always in love with one or other of the girl-students. Benskin was proud of him, for he won all possible prizes and was always solidly working. His name was Basil Haslam, brother of that spotty-faced youth who was Frederic's boon companion. They made acquaintance quickly but did not become friends until they both entered for a competition for a prize, the subject being a sea-piece. Haslam won it, and protested with Benskin that Folyat's was the best, because Folyat knew about the sea and he didn't.

He was delighted when Serge told him that he had been a sailor.

"Ah! That's it," he said. "That's it. I've never been anything. I can just draw but I don't understand about men and how they live."

"That's not very difficult," replied Serge. "They are much the same everywhere. They are all born in the same way, and death has not many variations. What lies in between is largely a matter of eating, drinking, and sleeping." "And loving."

"Just a few get as far as that. Not many."

"But all of them seem to think about getting married."

"That has surprisingly little to do with love. How much love do you get in your own house?"

"Not much. But then they think I'm queer. My father's a doctor. He wanted me to be a doctor, but I've got a hundred-and-fifty of my own, so I can do what I like. I shall go to London as soon as I'm through here. It's no good being a painter here. They all think it's a joke, a sort of excuse for doing nothing."

"I know. They think pictures are produced automatically—like everything else."

"Old Benskin's automatic enough."

"Exactly. He can work just as he can go to sleep, almost without knowing that he's doing it. It's a matter of habit. He's almost forgotten how he used to despise that sort of thing."

"Do you think he ever did?"

"Of course, or his work wouldn't be as good as it is."

"I can't understand people ceasing to be keen."

"I can. You only need to wobble a very little to come down on the wrong side. Then you're done for—in Hell. And after a bit you find that you quite like it, except in awful moments when you realise that after all it is Hell and that you might so easily have been in Heaven."

"I know what you mean. You mean that the whole thing rests with yourself. But it's rotten luck when you're weak and can't help doing the wrong thing though you see the right thing the whole time."

"But we're all like that. We only go to Hell when we do the wrong thing and pretend that it's the right."

"How did you find that out?"

"By a careful study of Hell and its inhabitants."

"Then you don't mean the Hell one's people talk about?"

"No. I mean here and now, the world as it is. I'm not interested in any other."

"Neither am I. Hurray!"

This conversation was the first of many. Haslam used to wait for Serge and walk with him as far as their roads lay together. He was an ambitious young man with his eyes set on the road to London, not so much because he was eager for fame and material rewards as because he was hotly impatient of art which stopped short at Benskin and Beecroft.

"But," Serge would say, "Benskin and Beecroft will both die."

"I know, but there'll be a new Beecroft and a new Benskin by that time."

"That's true. We shall never be rid of them."

"I expect London is crammed full of Benskins and Beecrofts."

"Maybe, but there are more of the other sort there too."

"If I don't reach London by the time I'm twenty-seven I shall throw up the sponge."

"Why twenty-seven?" asked Serge, smiling.

"Oh! if a man hasn't done something by the time he's twenty-seven he never will."

"I'm a good deal more than that. . ."

"But you've done everything. You've made yourself. You're not really any older than I am, and everybody here is so horribly old."

"Yes, they all come to a bad and perfectly respectable end."

Haslam swung his fist in the air and shouted indignantly:

"Respectable! Respectable! Give me a list of any ten men living in respectable suburban villas and I warrant you there'll be more dishonesty and cowardly misdoing in their lives than in ten of the so-called criminal classes. I don't understand it. I do rotten things myself—who doesn't?—but I can't shut my eyes to them when they're done. Take my brother. He's a beastly idiot or an idiotic beast, always getting into scrapes and shuffling out of them. By the time he's thirty he'll still be doing the same things, but he'll have learned how to prevent them coming to the surface. He'll marry, settle down, enjoy a comfortable income, be a pillar of the Church and a smug, hard Pharisee like all the rest, with all his tracks carefully covered up and his conscience having a splendid time going over them."

"I don't think it matters to any man," said Serge, "what his brother is and is not."

"I know what you mean. It isn't worth while letting out at brutes like my brother, but it's a great comfort to be able to do it occasionally."

"Good Lord! My dear, we can't do anything. We must all stew in our own juice. I'd have a lively time of it if I began to worry about my brother Frederic's morals. I have quite enough to do to look after my own."

"That's all very well. I don't mind my brother's morals so much, but what I can't swallow is that he will loathe art. . ."

"Art will survive that. Art is the concern of free men. Men who have made themselves prisoners cannot understand it, and men always hate what they cannot understand, until they realise that the few great principles of the world were founded without any consideration for their vanity. Then they can laugh. The artists, I imagine, are free men, and they write, paint, make music, because more direct action is almost impossible for them in a world made captive by lies, shams, and hypocrisies. When all men and all women are free there will be no art, for there will be no need for it. Life itself will be enough. It will be so splendid."

"I don't believe that." Haslam became suddenly despondent. "If there isn't to be anything but life, what's the good of anything?"

"The answer to that is—everything. The few men who attain freedom must tell the joy of it for the rest and for those who come after them. Spiritual evolution is slow, like every other natural process. Every true artist raises the imaginative level of humanity, but imaginative art is a small thing compared with the imaginative life. It is easier. Some men have to choose between the two. They nearly always choose wrongly."

There was a long silence, Haslam strode along by Serge's side. At last he said:

"You are queer. One moment you make me want to shout with joy, and the next you drag me down to the depths and I want to cry. You seem to believe in such big things, but you don't seem to believe in men at all."

"In most men, not at all."

"And women?"

"Even less in women. They are always seeing things with men's eyes, always appealing to them by their debased instincts. Clever women are even worse. They try to escape the dilemma by appealing to men's intellects. I hate intellect. Fine women are always driving fine men into the arms of fools, or worse. The world is in a mess simply because ninety-nine people out of a hundred make a mess of their love affairs."

"But if there is such a thing as spiritual evolution it must all come right in the end."

"That's no comfort to me. I shan't see it. This world will have been snuffed out millions of years before then. It will have served its purpose, and most of us will have missed our opportunity."

"I hope I shan't."

"I hope you won't."

They parted, and Serge made his way to St. Paul's School, where he had promised to attend the final rehearsal of *The Rose and the Ring*. There he found his father sitting half-way down the room which was lit only with one gas-jet and was empty save for Jessie Clibran-Bell at the piano under the rudely-constructed stage—barrels and planks—and many rows of school desks, which were desks and forms combined, with the desks turned down and the ink-wells removed. On the walls were pictures of elephants, tigers and rhinoceroses, texts, the tonic sol-fa, and two or three oleographs representing Biblical scenes—Elisha and the Bears, Saul Listening to David's Harping, and the Foolish Virgins. The walls themselves were distempered a bleak grey, and were rather dirty. A harmonium stood against the wall opposite the door, and above this was a glass case containing a stuffed squirrel that had lost its fur and one glass eye. Serge asked his father what it might be doing there. Francis disclaimed responsibility for the conduct of the week-day school and surmised that it was used for an object-lesson in natural history.

"Better than nothing," he said, but he did not seem to be at all interested.

Serge plunged with a question:

"I've been thinking a good deal since I came here. Why don't you send my mother away for a time?"

"She wouldn't go."

"Why not go with her?"

"Where to?"

"Anywhere. It doesn't matter."

"Are we very stick-in-the-mud?"

"It isn't that. But why not go away—or leave Fern Square? Minna tells me that neither you nor my mother have been the same since James died. . . . It must have been a shock to you."

"It was."

"You don't mind my mentioning it?"

"Not at all."

Serge waited and hoped for more to come, but nothing did. Francis was in his most taciturn mood; he kept humming and buzzing to himself like a great bee, and fingering the amethyst cross on his waistcoat. Serge took another plunge.

"How much is this living worth?"

"Three hundred."

"How much was St. Withans worth?"

"Six-fifty."

Serge made no comment. Presently he asked:

"Did you know what you were coming to?"

"Perfectly."

"Did my mother?"

"I told her."

"Are you sorry?"

"What's the good?"

Francis dropped his amethyst cross and laid his foot on his right knee and began thrusting his finger inside his elastic-sided boot. It was a very old boot and much worn at the heel. Seeing that made Serge notice for the first time that his father's clothes were shabby, out of shape and dusty. He began to cast back in his memory, and with some difficulty he was able to picture his father and mother as a young man and woman—he in knee-breeches and silk stockings and silver buckles to his shoes, and she in a full gown of flowered silk cut low on her pretty shoulders—walking arm in arm. in the gardens at St. Withans, and then that was blotted out with recollections not so pleasing, his father silent and his mother talking, talking, talking, then crying, then talking again; then meals taken in a cold atmosphere of restraint. He could remember jolly walks with his father, and scenes of great tenderness with his mother, and the last day when he sobbed his heart out and he was driven with his chest away and away until the Vicarage and then the church-tower were lost from sight. He could recognise himself in the small boy in all those memories, but in the man and woman of those days he could not see the taciturn old man—for he was old—sitting by his side, or the foolish old woman in Fern Square with her blankly sorrowful face and her pathetic chatter of "the gentry" and "common people." He found that he had much affection for both, was rather surprised to find it, and was amused to discover himself casting about for some melodramatic event which should account for their listlessness and indifference to each other, their daughters, everything and everybody. Francis was a good man; the ex-convict of that first dismal day had said so. Mrs. Folyat was a good woman; more than one woman in the parish had borne witness to that.—Nothing had happened. They had dodged everything, like so many others. For them (Serge thought) as for so many others, life had always been round the corner—round the corner. The words lilted in his mind like a refrain, and he said aloud:

"Round the corner."

"Eh?" said Francis, startled out of his reverie.

"I should think it over if I were you," replied Serge, "about going away, I mean. To be quite frank with you, I find my mother a little dull."

"Dull? I wouldn't say dull. Not dull. No. We're quiet people, that's all, quiet people. She lived in a very quiet place when she was young. I was curate then. Did I ever tell you about the murder that happened there? I will some day."

A head was thrust through the curtain, hurried whispers were exchanged with Jessie Clibran-Bell and she began to thump out some very indifferent music that would have served admirably for a child's game of musical-chairs.

"Was it a good murder?" asked Serge.

"It was a horrible murder."

The curtain was drawn. It showed some reluctance and had to be assisted by the King. Gertrude was the Fairy Gruffanuff, and Bennett Lawrie was Prince Bulbo, with a tenor song much too high for his light baritone voice.

The entertainment was very indifferent in quality, but it seemed to give great pleasure to the performers, especially to Bennett Lawrie, the Bottom of the company. He acted with extraordinary intensity. He seemed to have hypnotised himself into the belief that he was actually a Prince, so that he was extremely comic and yet very pathetic. His legs were very thin, large at the knees and more than a little bowed, and in his pink tights they looked enormously long—a figure of fun, and yet he was compelling and quixotically heroic. He was right out of the picture, and nothing else in it seemed to exist for him. When he was on the stage nothing else existed for his audience of two. He had naturally the gift of making his personality surge over the footlights into the auditorium, and he seemed to exult in the exercise of his power without in the least caring what he did with it. Serge admired him, but on the whole disliked his exhibition. He whispered to his father:

"Sheer blatant egoism."

"Who?"

"That boy."

"He's very funny. Queer, he never says a word when he comes to the house. He is preternaturally solemn and always looks as though he were on the point of bursting into tears."

"I've seen many young men like that here. I fancy they don't get enough to eat."

Bennett appeared on the stage again, and Francis began to shake with laughter at his antics. A moment later and he was brushing a tear-drop from his nose.

When the rehearsal was over Serge went out and bought a bottle of port at the public-house next door but one to the church, a cake and some biscuits, and took them in to the actors assembled in the green-room—one of the two small class-rooms of the school. He found Gertrude in tears and threatening to throw up her part, Frederic shouting at her, Bennett Lawrie supporting her, and the whole company looking very odd and unreal with the paint thick on their faces or melting down into their collars. Francis was making himself amiable and telling everybody in turn that he had never enjoyed any performance so well.

Minna, wearing an absurd golden wig, said:

"I'm sure Serge didn't like it."

"I was interested," he replied.

And indeed he had found it absorbing to see how much these people, when they were pretending to be some one else, revealed their characters as they rarely did in ordinary life. He was immensely sorry for them all without exactly knowing why. Without knowing why, he excepted Minna. He had a curious faith in Minna. In Gertrude he believed not at all. She was in love with Bennett Lawrie. That much was clear, but she was in love idiotically. In the green-room he heard her covering Bennett with gross flattery which he gulped down fatuously.

XII
ANNETTE

Hurrying wind o'er the heaven's hollow
And the heavy rain to follow.

CHIMES.

ANNETTE in Westmoreland had the small happenings in the household in Fern Square week by week as far as her mother knew them. Every Friday evening Mrs. Folyat used to write five letters: a short one to Annette, a long one to Leedham because he was so far away, one to a friend in Potsham with whom she had corresponded ever since her marriage, and two to elegant relations. She had no power of consecutive thought, and her letters rambled and ambled, a queer mixture of narrative and comment, all things being equal in interest (or the lack of it)—"Just fancy, the verger's son is married, and only eighteen! Did I tell you that Betsy, the new cat, had four kittens in the kitchen drawer? Your pa is very well, but the other day I had to go to the dentist and he made a face over the bill, and I said 'I am your wife. You have to keep me in repair.' He looked so surprised and I was surprised at myself. Was it not a fool thing to say? Frederic is working very hard, but Serge is making a dreadful litter in his room with his brushes and paint. I do hate *untidiness* and *shiftlessness*. You will be quite a stranger here when you come. Mary is getting on very well with her music-lessons. She plays the viola now, not the violin. It is easier to get into an orchestra if you play the viola. I hope you are doing your duty, &c., &c. . . ." The letter always wound up with a common form parental sermon, which Annette always skipped. She did not get many letters, and her mother's regular epistles were a boon to her. She was dreadfully afraid of the   servants at High Beck, and letters gave her a feeling of security against them, for they witnessed to the fact that she had ties with the world outside. Occasionally, when Mrs. Folyat mounted her gentility hobby-horse, she would leave her letters lying open in her room in the certain knowledge that they would be read and discussed below stairs.

She had never seen Serge, for she was born after his departure from St. Withans, but he had always been far more real to her than her other brothers

Round The Corner | 105

and sisters. He was a romantic figure to her, and when he cropped up again in her mother's letters she imagined him to herself as a being handsome beyond all other men and brave and strong. She used to regale her pupil with tales of his adventures, borrowing from Scott or Thackeray when her own invention gave out, and she made him so entrancing that her pupil announced her intention of marrying him when she grew up. She had first of all imagined him richer than anybody had ever been, but after a letter from Minna—a poor correspondent with excellent descriptive powers— telling of Serge's homecoming she then imagined him poorer than anybody had ever been, and she invented a lady with boundless wealth who should marry him, restore the family fortunes, and take her (Annette) away from teaching.

On the whole Annette had little cause to complain. Her employers were stupid but not malicious. It never occurred to them that she might need a change from the society of her pupil. Annette was so young in years— younger still in mind—that they regarded her rather as a companion than as an instructress, and lost all idea of authority, so that Deedy, the child, was always playing her parents off against her governess. Annette used to weep many tears over her ineffectuality, but then, having a sense of humour, she would laugh at the idea of herself, who had never successfully learned anything, being paid to instruct another child in French, English grammar, orthography, arithmetic and algebra. She grew fond of Deedy, and Deedy's parents were affectionate with her, as, being kindly people, they would have been with any strange child staying in their house. They led a very quiet life in Westmoreland. Young people hardly ever came to stay with them, and their house was conducted with the regularity of Mr. Fender's office. Prayers were read by Mr. Fender at eight to the four servants on one side of the room and Annette on the other. Breakfast was at half-past. Lessons were from ten till one. Deedy had to be taken for a walk in the afternoon, generally up the beck, for she had a pool where dwelt a fairy and a hippogriff (inventions of Annette's) and loved to send written messages to them over the little waterfall. At six Deedy was taken to see her mother in the drawing-room, and Annette had a free hour. At seven Deedy was put to bed, and the rest of the day was Annette's unless she were desired to play to Mrs. Fender in the evening.

It was a dull life, but it left much time for dreaming, and sometimes Deedy was very amusing. She had an eager prying curiosity and was much interested in God.

"What's an only begotten son?" she asked one day.

"It means the only one."

"Am I only begotten?"

"Yes."

She thought for a very long time. Then:

"Why didn't God get another one?"

"Oh, Deedy. Hush!"

"Why do you always say 'Hush' when I ask questions?"

Annette laughed.

"Because I don't know the answer."

"Does anybody know? Does your father know?"

"Yes."

"How does he know?"

"Because he's a clergyman."

"Doesn't my father know?"

"Perhaps he does."

"I wish I wasn't only begotten."

"I don't think it makes much difference."

"I wish I had a brother like Serge."

"I've never seen Serge, so, you see, it doesn't really make much difference."

"You've never been only begotten, so you don't know, Miss Folyat."

Annette left it at that. She never knew what Deedy was thinking. She hardly knew what she thought herself, and her notions of other people were axiomatic, based on uncritical acceptance of her mother's assumptions. She regarded herself as a very ordinary person—(at school she had thought herself neither above nor below the general run of girls, and had done the things they did, and talked of the things they talked of, very largely because they did them and talked of them). She felt a little resentfully that Deedy was an extraordinary person, but put it down to her deformity and pitied her. Being very active herself she could imagine no greater misfortune, except perhaps being deaf, like Beethoven, than to be unable to run and jump and swim. She loved swimming, and every morning would go up the beck to Deedy's pool and plunge into the cold water or sit under the little waterfall. And then she would lie in the soft grass and rub her body over with crushed flowers, and laugh for the joy and freedom of it all. And she would come back with her hair lank and wet—there was very little of it, and that thin in texture—and wake Deedy and tell her how the morning was full of song. . . . Often when they sat by the pool in the evening the child would make her talk about the water and how it felt when it kissed her body, and one day Deedy said:

"Swim now."

It was a very hot August day, and Annette had been narrating an adventure of Serge, based on the works of Edward S. Ellis, how he had swum two hundred yards Under water in an American river and surprised and captured an Indian spy. The description of under-water had been singularly vivid, and the beck was in mid-flood and very clamorous. Annette slipped out of her clothes and dived into the pool and lay there floating, her eyes closed and her hair floating out and her white body shimmering mysteriously through the water. Deedy crawled to the edge of the pool and looked down.

"Don't lie still. Swim!"

Annette kicked up a white spume of water and Deedy clapped her hands.

"Now work your arms!"

Annette swam swiftly to the waterfall and sat under it and played with the water with her hands. Then she dived again into the pool and brought up a round pebble which she gave to Deedy as a present from the hippogriff. Deedy flung it back into the water.

"Why, Deedy, you're crying!"

"I hate you. You're ugly."

Annette became conscious that the child was staring at her body. She blushed, hastily snatched up her clothes and ran away behind an elder-bush. All her joy had vanished and her thoughts were filled with the whisperings of the little girls at the school in Edinburgh. It was part of the delight of her life here in Westmoreland that all such griminess had been left behind. She was so hurt in the sudden loss of her joy that she could not think nor make any effort to understand. All her thought was to get away as quickly as possible, to get away from Deedy. She dressed rapidly, wound up her hair, wet as it was, and in absolute silence hurried home with Deedy.

In the house she found two letters waiting her, one from her mother, one from Minna, both announcing the same thing, Gertrude's engagement to Bennett Lawrie. Mrs. Folyat wrote:

"My dear, he is a very earnest and worthy young man and he simply adores Gertrude. He is in business in a very large firm. He is a gentleman.

His grandfather was a Scotch minister, and his grandmother was the daughter of a laird. Gertrude is very happy. They fell in love over some theatricals they did in the school-room. Everybody said he was much better than any professional. Frederic brought him to the house. Frederic has such nice friends. Your father has built a greenhouse out in the back garden. The engagement is not to be announced for a year as it will be some time before they can afford to marry. I hope you are attending to your duties and giving all satisfaction to dear Mrs. Fender . . .

Minna wrote:

"Dear Annette. Fancy! Mother Bub is engaged, and Mottle-tooth is green with envy. He is like a shorn lamb, and Mother Bub will eat him cutlet by cutlet, with little paper frills round them. He's a clerk in an office and his father's a drunkard, and when he stays too late an old Scotch servant comes and fetches him away. He's about thirty-nine years younger than Bub, but she couldn't face the thirties—or is it the forties? Serge is very funny about it. Ma is very excited and romantical. Pa hasn't said a word, and I'm not sure even that he knows. I rather like the Lamb, myself, and he *is* rather beautiful. I suppose if Bub goes off and Mottle-tooth and me, there'll be room for you at home. Someone will have to look after Ma . . ."

Minna's flippancy rather offended Annette. Hardly having been at home for so many years she had many delightful fictions about the house in Fern Square. She regarded its inmates as a united and happy family, and herself as the only outcast. It was Home to her, and she enveloped it with all the unreal emotions roused in vast audiences by Madame Patti with her rendering of the famous song. She was touched by the very thought of love and pictured Gertrude radiant and all the house glowing with the happiness of this new event. The poverty of the young man only made it all the more delightful. The first play she had ever seen was *Caste*, and she often cried when she thought of it. It seemed enviable to her to have Eccles for a father-in-law.

All this made her forget her unhappiness by the water, and she forgot Deedy's prying stare and lived through the next few days in a dream of young love.

On the third day she had a rude awakening. After dinner in the evening she sat playing to Mrs. Fender. Mr. Fender came in and whispered to Mrs. Fender for some time, perhaps half an hour. Then he went out. Mrs. Fender sat silent for some moments, then she said.

"Miss Folyat!"

Annette stopped playing. Mrs. Fender was sitting bolt upright in her chair by the hearth, with a book on her knees. It was a brown book—"Enquire Within Upon Everything." There was a peculiar asperity in her voice and her whole manner was big with disapprobation. She looked very like the Red Queen as she opened her mouth square and said again:

"Miss Folyat! Come here!"

Annette rose and went to her.

"Sit down!"

Annette sat down. Mrs. Fender screwed herself up to a cold anger and went on:

"I am sorry for your father's sake and your mother's."

Annette's heart went down into the pit of her stomach and then up into her throat.

"I must ask you," said Mrs. Fender, "to pack up your trunks this evening and to be ready to catch the first train in the morning. I repeat that I am sorry, but it is necessary."

Annette's brain reeled. She blurted out:

"What is it! What have I done!"

"Done? What have you done? You can ask that? Miss Folyat!"

"I'll go, of course. But tell me what it is that I've done. I haven't stolen anything or—or . . ."

"I cannot tell you what it is. It pains me too deeply to think of it. You—you have polluted the mind of my child who was entrusted to your care."

Annette understood. Deedy had been asking questions. She had been cross-examined, and the gentle art of making mountains out of molehills had been called into play. This sudden presentation of a new aspect of her escapade in swimming in the pool bewildered and crushed her. She could make nothing of it, could hardly grasp what was in the Red Queenish mind, and felt only the futility of saying anything.

"You will pack up your things to-night and be ready to catch the first train in the morning."

"Certainly."

"Have you no words of regret?"

"No."

Annette had no words of any sort. She only wanted to get away, only to get away and cry.

"I have written to your mother," said Mrs. Fender.

"Oh!" Annette gasped and she thought: "How mean! How mean! She will make mother think just the same as she does."

She rushed out of the room, upstairs, and flung herself on her bed and cried. She went on crying until she fell asleep and did not wake again until the early morning. It was raining, and she felt very miserable and began to cry again. She wept all through breakfast, wept as Mrs. Fender put money into her hand and gave her a frigid farewell. She wept because she did not see Deedy, and she wept because she did not want to see Deedy. She wept because she was leaving the beautiful hill and the beloved beck. She wept in the carriage all along the five miles to the station, and the rain came pouring down. The clouds were low on the fells. They almost seemed to reach the water of the lakes. All down the fells were little silver streams, and the water ran and trickled all over the roads. The light was dull and grey. The colour seemed to be washed out of everything. The lakes were black, and dour figures walked the roads.

In the train she had a compartment to herself and she wept until she could weep no more, and then miserably she looked out of the window at the miserable country, drenched and drowned. Soon she came to the sea, and that was so dismal that her sorrow overflowed and nothing but absurd laughter was left, and she laughed, and suddenly her thoughts woke again, and she said to herself that she was going home. Serge was at home, and a lot of people, and they had jolly fun together, and they were all happy because Gertrude was engaged, and because they were all happy no one would be unkind to her.

Blacker and blacker grew the skies as the train rolled southward, and the ascending smoke of thousands of chimneys met the downpouring rain. The smoke meant home to Annette, and she was glad of it. It was rather fun to be sent home suddenly like this. It was like the time when there had been measles at school and she had been sent home in the middle of term.

Soon between one town and another there was no country, no green save that of a football field here and there. Everywhere chimney stacks and the derricks of collieries, and great sidings full of trucks, and miles and miles of wet slate roofs, with here and there a dark church steeple or tower. At last she saw the tower of the Collegiate Church. The rain had ceased. A watery smoky sunbeam stole through the clouds to welcome her.

Her father was at the station to meet her. She threw her arms round his neck and hugged him. He kissed her warmly and said:

"Dear, dear. What a young woman you have grown!"

It came on to rain again, and in the four-wheeled cab Francis peered out of the window and said:

"It was like this when we came here from St. Withans."

"How is Ma?" asked Annette with sudden trepidation.

"It has been a great shock to her," said Francis, "and she has been very unhappy about it. We have agreed to say nothing to the others and to pretend that the little Fender girl is ill."

Annette was immensely relieved. She had been most alarmed at the thought of what Minna would say. She wanted reassuring, and she asked her father again:

"Are you angry with me?"

"I? No, no, my dear. Angry! What's the use? Perhaps you'll be happier at home."

"I think I will. I didn't do anything really. I only bathed without any clothes on."

"It is not a usual practice with governesses."

"I expect I ought never to have been a governess. I often used to feel much younger than Deedy."

"There's something in that, something in that. None of you seem to be properly grown up. I don't know what will happen to you all. . . . I expect your mother will talk to you about your ingratitude and wickedness. She and I don't agree about it."

They reached Fern Square. Mrs. Folyat had taken to her bed to nurse her grief, and also by way of impressing Annette with the awfulness of the thing she had done. Annette went up to her and endured an hour's tearful homily on the sinfulness of the flesh. She sat by her mother's bedside with her hands in her lap and her head bowed, and thought comically of Mrs Fender reading "Enquire Within" and discovering from its pages how to treat wicked governesses.

On the way down the dark stairs she met a man with a beard whom she did not know.

"Hullo!" he said. "Who are you?"

"Annette."

He kissed her.

"I'm Serge. They didn't tell me you were coming home. Anything wrong?"

"I've lost my place."

"Did you like it?"

"Not much."

"Then it doesn't matter."

"Mother's terribly upset about it."

"That doesn't matter. She's always upset. We are a queer lot, and she hasn't the ghost of a notion how to handle us. She's baffled because we're not like people out of a novelette, angels engaged in dodging the wickedness of a horrid world."

Annette's own view of things was rather like that. She had always believed it to be her duty to keep herself unspotted by things temporal, though she had no idea how to set about it. Her mother had said many unjust and unfair things to her. She was feeling rather resentful and was pleased with the audacity of Serge's criticism. All her upbringing had been based on the sanctity of parental authority and the parental person, and she was fearful and fascinated by such defiance of it.

"Come up to my room," said Serge, "and let's have a look at you, and you can tell me about yourself—if you want to."

He took her arm and led her upstairs to the top of the house, where he had a room under a north skylight which served him as bed-room, sanctum, and studio. It was a litter of paper, boots, drawing-boards, drawings, pipes, and cigar-boxes. He put on an old dressing-gown, lit a pipe, and made Annette sit on the bed, and stood and looked at her. She felt very happy and smiled at him.

"You've got the most interesting face of the lot," he said presently, "though that isn't saying much. What's brought you home?"

She told him the whole story.

"I see. Poisoning the little beast's mind with the sight of your body. I see. It's part of the game to pretend that you haven't got such a thing. Sorry, but I find it quite impossible."

Annette's traditional modesty twinged, and she shifted a little uneasily on the bed. Serge marked that and went on:

"Sorry. I won't talk about it if it makes you uneasy. You believe in souls and bodies separate, the soul prisoned in the vile clay, and all that. I don't. I believe that the two things are one and indivisible. If you don't believe that, you are apt to take all the surface happenings of life much too seriously, and you lose all sense of proportion and humour and make the most ridiculous messes for yourself and everybody connected with you. Superficially considered, I am a bad egg, so are you. I'm getting on towards middle-age and can't make my own living, much less prevent other people making theirs, which is what success seems to mean in commercial life. As for you, you've been thrown out of your situation without a character, and it will be extremely difficult for you to find another. Looked at a little more closely and searchingly we are seen to be two wonderful people—all people are wonderful—with immense potentialities for happiness or unhappiness. Does all this bore you?"

"No. Please."

"What I'm really trying to get at is that there are only two kinds of people—the people to whom everything that happens is experience, and the people who turn everything that happens to them into a form of self-indulgence, even the most horrible, even the most painful things. Our father is the first kind of person, our mother is the second. Our father was really shattered by the death of our brother James. Our mother has been feeding herself fat on it ever since. Any love that they may have shared was buried in the grave with James. More briefly, the two kinds of people are those who can love and those who cannot. Gertrude is besotted about young Lawrie, but she is quite incapable of loving him. Minna could love a certain kind of man, one who could swamp her mockery with love. There aren't many of them."

Annette sat listening to him open-mouthed. He took paper and charcoal and did a rough sketch of her, but did not show it her.

"I like that story," he said. "It's the most satisfactory reason I ever heard for getting thrown out of a governess' job. You can't live in a house like this, or a place like this, and live without trouble. You have to fight for your life, or lose it. I'm going to work now. Get out. Go and make Minna talk about Bennett Lawrie. She's amusing."

"Thank you," said Annette.

XIII
IMBROGLIO

Quisque suos patimer manes.

AENEID, vi.

ANNETTE was soon absorbed into the household. Mrs. Folyat never could keep any information to herself, and Gertrude and Mary quickly made Annette feel that she was in disgrace and saddled her with their domestic duties. Mary devoted herself entirely to music, rehearsing for concerts, and practising with amateur quartettes, and Gertrude gave all her time to her betrothed. She met him every day at his office and walked home with him, unless they were going to the theatre. Then they would dine out, Bennett having gone without his mid-day meal in order to have money enough. They had the whole of Sunday together always. He would accompany her to early celebration at St. Paul's, breakfast at Fern Square, go to St. Saviour's morning and evening, and spend the afternoon in the Park, for she had given up her Sunday-school class.

Their engagement was not yet announced, and he had not told his family, nor had Gertrude met any of his relations. Bennett's face had grown more and more melancholy, and Gertrude had not spoken to Minna for weeks because, whenever she brought her lover to the house, Minna persisted in singing:

The pain that is all but a pleasure we'll change

For the pleasure that's all but pain,

And never, oh, never this heart will range

From that old, old love again.

Annette thought Bennett very handsome, and she was greatly impressed by his silence and tragic mien. She told herself that he must be enormously in love with Gertrude since his emotions weighed upon him so heavily, and she thought Minna odious for making fun of him. She was very happy herself. She liked doing the housework and being useful to the others, and though her mother and sister were rather tyrannical with her, she had discovered a warm corner in her father's heart in which to take refuge. Indeed her return had made a great difference to Francis. He sought her company and talked intimately with her and teased her, and showed her a side of himself that was hidden from the others. He would take her for long walks, and to see the queer characters among his poor, and often he would ask her to sit with him in his study while he was working. Sometimes, instead of working he would read aloud to her—Fielding, or Sterne, or the poets, and he would make translations of Italian or French poems, or the odes of Horace for her, and he would tell her that she was being much more use to the world teaching him, who was old enough to learn, than wasting time and her employer's money in pretending to instruct little girls.

Except with her father and occasionally with Serge Annette never went out and knew nothing of what was happening in the town, and had even no clear idea of its geography. She gave no thought to past or future, and was quite content to go on living in the tranquil present. She reverted to her childish belief that her father was the most wonderful man in the world, with Serge a good second, and if she could have spent her life in ministering to them both she would have been more than satisfied. She was rather afraid and shy of other women, but the helplessness of men appealed to her, and she loved repairing their garments, always so sadly in need of it, and she would darn socks that any other woman would have thrown away. Nobody praised her, and nobody took much account of what she did save only the one little servant, Ada, who adored her.

To Annette the most mysterious and awful person in the house was her brother Frederic. She could make nothing of him. He looked very pale and unwell, but became peevish under any comment on his appearance, however sympathetic. He was for the most part very silent when he was at home, though that was not often, but suddenly he would break into the wildest spirits and chatter and talk nonsense and laugh a great deal, and make fun of his mother and then be very affectionate with her, and it would seem that of all her children Frederic had the most affection from his mother. He would flatter her and talk about the great riches he was going to make and the wonderful lady he was going to marry, the daughter of a rich client, of whose estate he would be appointed trustee—when he had his own office. That was always the proviso—when he had his own office, and Annette was given to understand that it would be very soon, and then if there was one man more important than any other in the town, that man would be Frederic. Mrs. Folyat would listen excitedly to all this and shake her ringlets, and say to him:

"My dear, my dear, you must look after the girls."

"Of course," Frederic would respond, "rich husbands all round."

"But they must be gentlemen."

"Gentlemen! Of course."

And if Minna were there, she would say with honey and gall in her voice:

"Is Bennett Lawrie a gentleman?"

Mrs. Folyat would say, frigidly:

"He is very poor, but he is extremely well connected."

Frederic would swagger a little, and say:

"After all, you know, it was I who brought him to the house."

Then Minna:

"We all know that all Frederic's friends are gentlemen—and ladies."

It took Annette a little time to pick up the threads of all the family jokes and allusions, and to disentangle the personalities of the various outlying characters who were used for purposes of fun or bickering, or, occasionally, as a weapon to enforce silence. Not all of these personages came to the house, and some of them seemed only to have a shadowy existence in the family consciousness. There were two or three mysterious and almost mythical young men associated with Minna. Mary's personality seemed to be filled out with a vague widower of mature years, who made mincing machines and was said to propose to her once a fortnight, Gertrude was altogether submerged in Bennett Lawrie, while, whenever Frederic became too obstreperous or offensive it was enough to breathe the name "Annie" to reduce him to a laconic moroseness. This Annie was the more real of all these extra-familiar characters, and Annette was very curious about her. She kept cropping up at the most out of the way moments, as every member of the family found it necessary at one time or another to remind Frederic of her existence. She was never given any surname, nor, apparently, was it known where she lived or how, or what she was to Frederic, or Frederic to her. Annette associated her absurdly with Sister Anne in *Bluebeard*, and from that again jumped to the cloud which was no bigger than a man's hand. For no reason at all she regarded Annie as a figure of disaster and was vaguely sorry for her and pitied her. Her pity became concrete one day when an accident brought her nearer to Annie and gave her the whole story.

The lining of Frederic's office coat had worn to tatters. Going over his wardrobe Annette discovered this and took the coat into Serge's room, which she used when Serge was away at the Art School, and began to mend it. When she had repaired the lining she turned out the pockets, and among other papers—a theatre programme, two pawn-tickets, and a race-card—came on a grubby blotted letter written on cheap notepaper in a large wavering scrawl. Rather idly at first, and with no qualms or scruples—(all families read all letters that come into their hands)—she read it. There was neither address nor date. It was very short.

"DEAR FRED.—You must answer my letter, you must, you must. What am I to do? I can't prevent mother finding out soon, and she can't bear any more, she has had so much to bear. I can't tell her it's you, but it's the thinking I can't stand when you don't write to me. If you could only get me away somewhere, like you said you would. I'm just the same, but I can't write like I used to. It's the work in the house that's so awful, with the lodgers being beastly. Dear Fred, do please write to your

ANNIE."

At first it conveyed nothing to Annette. She was conscious of suffering behind the words and rather stupidly fumbled about in her mind for what it was that Annie's mother must find out soon. Abruptly she came to it and dropped the letter, and hot tears came to her eyes, tears of shame. She had never come face to face with this thing before, and it horrified her, but through the horror of it was the knowledge that Annie was wanting Frederic to write to her, and she thought that she must find Frederic at once and tell him. Then she remembered that she ought not to have read the letter, and she thrust it back into the pocket of the coat and hurried back with it into Frederic's room. That done, she went downstairs, saying to herself:

"I wish I didn't know. I wish I didn't know."

With sudden self-criticism, half humorously, she added:

"But I do know, so it isn't any good wishing. I mustn't tell. I mustn't tell."

Her heart was fluttering as she entered the drawing-room, feeling that everybody must know the secret she had discovered. She was surprised to find her mother in her usual chair nodding over her book and Minna talking in the window-seat with a young gentleman, whom she introduced as Mr. Basil Haslam.

"Mr. Haslam is a friend of Serge's," said Minna, "and Mr. Haslam's brother is a great friend of Frederic's."

"Perhaps he knows," thought Annette.

But no. Basil Haslam bowed politely to Annette and took no further notice of her, and went on with his conversation with Minna. Annette went away and down to her father's study, and there she found Francis and Bennett Lawrie in earnest conclave. Did they know? They gave no sign. Francis was smoking, and tapping on the ground with his foot. Bennett was leaning forward and talking emphatically and waving his long hands rather wildly in the air.

"I can do it," he said. "I know I can. I shall never do any good in business. I must lead men. I must move them, lift them up, show them the way to higher things."

Annette stopped in the doorway, and said:

"Am I in the way?"

"Not at all," returned Francis. "Come in. Mr. Lawrie is being very entertaining. We were discussing the possibility of his taking Orders."

"That would be lovely," said Annette.

Bennett turned to her.

"You think I could do it, don't you?"

It was the first time he or any of the young men who came to the house had spoken to her directly, and Annette felt curiously grateful to him. She stammered:

"I . . . I'm sure you . . . you could."

"It's what I've wanted to do all my life, only I've always thought it impossible. You'll laugh, I know, sir, but I used to preach sermons when I was a boy, just to myself in my bed-room, and I made a little altar when I was sixteen. I never dared talk about it at home. They always laughed at me. I never dared tell them what I wanted to do. They said I must go into an office when I was sixteen, and I went there. . . . You know we, Gertrude and I, thought you would take me as curate as soon as I was ordained, and then when I got a living we could be married."

"I'm much obliged to you for letting me know your plans, but it means time and money. We could send you to a theological college, when you're . . . How old are you?"

"Nineteen," said Bennett, with a hot blush.

"Nineteen. When you're twenty-one. The money is the difficulty. I have very little."

"My uncles are both rich men. I'm sure they would help if you would speak for me, and tell them what you think."

Round The Corner | 119

"Oh! do!" said Annette.

Bennett darted a look of gratitude at her.

"What I think!" Francis smiled. "You haven't given me much time yet. I like you. I like your enthusiasm. I've no doubt you would make a good clergyman, but it is a very poorly paid profession . . ."

"That doesn't matter at all," cried Bennett. "It's the work that matters." And he rushed off into a long tirade which Annette thought very splendid, and Francis punctuated with thin blue puffs of smoke from his pipe.

"On the whole," said Francis, reflectively. "On the whole I think it would be better when I meet your father to say nothing about your relationship with my daughter."

Bennett seemed to be on the point of protesting. Francis hurried on:

"I take it seriously, I assure you. My daughter considers herself engaged to you. She is old enough to know her own mind. On the other hand, I don't think I can give you any official recognition until there is some more immediate prospect of your being able to provide a livelihood for the two of you."

Bennett was embarrassed by all this, and his enthusiasm oozed away and left him blank and expressionless. Fortunately—perhaps deliberately— he had his profile towards Annette, and she found it very beautiful. She had a queer feeling that her father was teasing the young man, and she wanted to defend and help him. His ambition was altogether laudable, and he was in love (so she believed); the two things were interdependent and both must be promoted. Had it been in her power she would have turned Bennett into a clergyman there and then, and handed him over to Gertrude with her blessing.

Gertrude came in just then and shattered Annette's bountiful altruism of desire by saying:

"You here!"

And Annette, who had been inflated by her dreams for Bennett and his fervency, felt at once like Cinderella, and she crept away to the kitchen, taking in her mind the picture of Gertrude embracing her father and Bennett shaking her father's hand.

At once the whole scene became curiously remote, as remote as Minna and Basil Haslam in the drawing-room, as remote as her mother nodding foolishly to the buzz of their whispered conversation, as remote as Deedy Fender and all her old life in Edinburgh and Westmoreland. Real only to her then were the happy days of her childhood in Cornwall, and joyous moments here and there—a wild scamper on Arthur's Seat; a long swim in the Firth of Forth, an affectionate talk with a girl at school, a word of praise from a mistress whom she had adored. Then, like tripping over a stone, she came back to Annie. Annie who was in sore trouble. Annie who wanted only a word from Frederic. . . . She heard Serge's step in the hall, on the stairs, then his big voice saluting Basil Haslam, and then the two of them go upstairs to the studio-bedroom at the top of the house. She heard Gertrude and Bennett come out of the study and go upstairs. They stopped on the landing, and she heard them kiss.

Ada, the servant, was out, and she looked round the kitchen and thought how cosy it was, how much nicer, really, than any other room in the house, except, perhaps, the study. Upstairs Serge laughed. No one else in the house laughed—not like Serge. He was always so happy. No one else was happy like that. Not her father, nor her mother, nor Gertrude, even though Bennett Lawrie loved her so. . . . Bennett Lawrie was a vivid figure to Annette. He was so intense, but he never laughed. She felt that she would like to make him laugh. She began to invent foolish jokes and antics that perhaps might make him laugh, and was so busied with them that without her hearing him Frederic came into the kitchen and stood above her.

"Get me some supper," he said, "I'm devilish hungry."

"Oh! You!"

Annette lit the gas and stood staring at him with her hand above her head, leaning on the gas-bracket. He looked very white and mean and shrivelled, and the skin under his eyes was puffy.

"What are you staring at?" he said. "I'm hungry."

Annette put food in front of him, and he ate wolfishly.

"I'm devilish hungry," he said. "I've been walking miles. I'm tired and hungry. I've walked miles."

"Did you go to see her?" It was out before she was aware.

Frederic dropped his knife into his plate with a clatter.

"What the devil do you mean? Who?"

"Annie."

Frederic gripped her wrist and jumped to his feet and thrust his face close to hers.

"For God's sake!" he said under his breath. "For God's sake! What do you mean? Don't you blab. Don't you blab!"

"You're hurting me."

Round The Corner | 121

"What do you mean?"

"I read her letter. It was in your coat. I was mending it. I didn't mean to. Why don't you write to her."

"What letter? I don't know any letter."

"You do. She wants you to write to her."

"I have written."

"Go on with your supper, then."

"You won't tell any one. Promise you won't tell any one."

"No. All right. I won't tell any one."

"You're a queer one, Annette. You don't seem to mind."

"Mind!"

Annette was astonished to find that she had got beyond being distressed or shocked. She was hardly at all interested in Frederic's state of mind or condition. She felt that something must be done, and she wanted to know exactly what. Annie, whoever or whatever she might be, was unhappy and something must be done to help her. Annette turned to Frederic and said:

"What are you going to do?"

He replied:

"What can I do? Don't look at me like that. I'm not so bad as all that, I'm not."

"But it is wicked."

"I know it is, but you can't help it. I don't know. Everything seems all wrong. You go along quite quietly for months and months, and then suddenly everything's all wrong. It's queer to be talking to you like this. You don't understand the least little bit, though you are such a queer one. But I can talk to you just because you don't understand."

"I do understand," said Annette.

"How could you? You're only a little girl. Annie Lipsett—that's her name. She's going to have a baby. I suppose I ought to marry her. Lots of fellows do get married like that. I can't afford it. I don't love her. That's what's so horrible. I don't love her, and I can't pretend that I do, I can't make myself believe that I do. I was so beastly miserable, that's what it was. Things go wrong, and they stay wrong, and then you want something and clutch at it and miss it. Miss it all the time. It wasn't just a beastly thing, I swear it wasn't. I was so miserable, that's what it was. I'm miserable now, and the worst of it all is that I'm enjoying it. That's the sort of brute I am."

Annette found that she was crying. Large tears welled out of her eyes and trickled down her cheeks into her mouth. The thing was closing in on her from all sides and suffocating her. Her imagination was baffled. She had thought herself bold, and suddenly she was out of her depth. She struck out blindly, and presently found a footing on the hard rock of conventional morality. From a suffering human being, craving sympathy, Annie Lipsett became a wicked woman to be condemned and shunned, a base creature who had enticed and enchained Frederic. Her footing on this rock was very insecure. Soon she was swept off it and flung hurtling down an empty sense of the treachery of her own emotions.

She heard Frederic saying again:

"Don't you tell any one!"

She muttered a reply. Frederic finished his supper and she removed his plate and the empty dish into the scullery. Frederic followed her, She trembled from head to foot, and longed only for him to leave her. He stood plucking at the roller-towel on the door, and he said:

"If any one did to you what I've done to her I should have to horsewhip him. Isn't it odd? I should think it simply absurd if anybody wanted to horsewhip me."

Annette had a sudden gust of rage and through her clenched teeth she threw at him:

"If you don't go away I'll smash a plate in your face."

Frederic laughed nervously.

"You are a queer one," he said. "But we're a queer family, and this is a queer house, isn't it?"

Annette rushed by him, all her nerves tingling and throbbing, and flew upstairs until she came to Serge's room. There she stood gasping, and presently broke out laughing and crying together. Serge gave her water and slapped her hands, and motioned to Basil Haslam to leave the room. Basil went and Annette clung to Serge and began to sob. Her laughter ceased, and when she had done crying Serge laid her on the bed and sat holding her hand for a long time, during which he forbade her to speak. Her head began to ache furiously, and every little sound in the house became explosive and a torment to her. Serge seemed to realise that too, and began to talk to her in a low, soothing voice. He described the bay at Cape Town as the ship heaves and throbs her way out of it with the little fringe of lights on the water's-edge under the mountain, and he told of long days at sea, the whole voyage home to England, the most beautiful country in the world. Something he gave her of what it had been to him to see green fields again and English skies and orchards and red poppies in the corn, and little, comfortable, cool English rivers.

She hardly heard what he said. His voice lulled her, and his presence, the pressure of his hand were infinitely soothing. Soon she fell asleep, and while she slept he did not stir.

She woke happy and smiled at him, peering through the darkness for his kind eyes. She told him then, and because he said nothing she asked him if he did not think it wicked.

"Wicked!" he said. "There's good in it and bad too, just the same as there is in everything and everybody. Their happiness has been theirs, their folly has been theirs. Their unhappiness must be theirs too. You and I can do nothing to alter it. We can only help Frederic if he wants help. We can't help him if we make the blunder of applying an abstract moral formula to what is to him a very concrete, actual, human mess. Keep it to yourself, my dear. You will understand one day."

XIV
WHITE BEARD AND GREY

Maggior dolore e ben la Ricordanza
O nell' amaro inferno amena stanza?

D. G. ROSSETTI

FRANCIS had many moments of doubt as to the wisdom of encouraging and abetting Bennett Lawrie in his desire to enter the Church. To begin with he had no money; he was engaged—Francis supposed it must be called an engagement—to Gertrude, and even supposing it were possible to take the young man as curate as soon as he was ordained, that meant at most eighty pounds a year, and he was already earning more than that. Without influence the prospect of his being granted a living was, to say the least of it, remote. To be sure the rector of St. James, Irlam, had begun life as an itinerant violinist, but then he had a fruity tenor voice which made him very popular with women; also he had married a lady with a snug fortune.

"One must," thought Francis, half apologising to himself. "One must think of these things materially. If I had thought of it materially I should never have. . ."

He broke off the thought and began to tell himself that he ought to encourage the young in high-souled endeavour. Young Lawrie was certainly remarkable, talented, very much in earnest, and, as far as one could see, very much in love. To be sure Gertrude was a good ten years older than he, but that was no bad thing for a young man of an ardent temperament. Certainly from Gertrude's point of view it was better for her to be the wife of a clergyman than the wife of a clerk. But ought one to let these social considerations weigh in the matter? It was very difficult (thought Francis), very difficult. She would be poor in any case. She might have a large family. She was a little woman, rather plain, just the type that produces enormous families. And families—could there be anything more harassing than to have a large family and to have no means of making provision for them?

On that Francis's reflections stopped. They went round and round. It was his business to encourage the production of children (in wedlock), and year in and year out he had faithfully fulfilled his duty, without ever pausing to consider whether he had practised what he preached. Now he saw that he had done so, and was shocked to find himself rather dismayed at the result, and reluctant to face the possibility of his daughter doing the same. For years he had hardly thought about his work. Since the death of his son and the brutal outbreak that followed it, hostilities had ceased (with the exception of an occasional splutter at an Easter vestry meeting) and the work of his church, like his domestic life, had run on automatically. Time had hardly existed for him. His thoughts from disuse had grown sluggish, and it was very very slowly borne in upon him that his children were beginning to claim a separate existence, and that they had every right to do so. When he realised it he was forced painfully to face the fact that he was impotent to help them either with money, or, what is more precious, real sympathy. It was only with an effort that he was able to set aside the grotesqueness of Gertrude's fancy and to force himself to see it with her eyes and to take it seriously. He looked back over the years and caught a glimpse of the wasted opportunities, and though he never indulged in the luxury of self-torment he cried in his heart:

"God forbid that when they are as old as I they should be even as I am."

He was not sufficiently skilled in self-analysis to lay his finger on the weakness that had brought him to such a pass. He thought no ill of his wife. He knew enough of human nature to admit that nothing outside a man's own soul could dishonour him or bring him to harm. Unconsciously he was disloyal to the tenets of his calling in considering his own case. With all others he professed that God moved in a mysterious way and that everything happened for the best according to God's providence. He had long since abandoned all belief in the possibility of a noble collective life here on earth, for he had seen too much not to know that when two or three are gathered together it is not to seek God, but to promote knavery and jealousy. Moments of agony he had had when he had half seen his own scepticism, but the simple devotion of some of his parishioners, craftsmen, and factory hands, and his own great liking for many of his poor had kept him from throwing up his work, and he would say:

"Though I do it ill, yet it might be done worse."

Besides, he could not afford to renounce the stipend. Every year he had made small inroads upon his capital, fifty pounds here and a hundred there to satisfy creditors or sudden demands of charity for larger sums than he could afford to pay out of income.

Well, well—no doubt he was making a mountain out of a molehill, and things were not nearly so bad as they seemed. The house had been much jollier since Serge came back and Annette brought youth and joy into it, and if none of the family seemed to be on the way to brilliant lives, after all there were better things in the world than success, and nothing mattered so much as affection and love. And yet, how small a part love played in human life! How soon it died!

In the end Francis laughed at himself, and told himself that thinking was no use. It neither made good better nor bad worse. Things were what they were and nothing would alter them. Young Lawrie, with his brain stuffed full of illusions, wished to enter into Holy Orders. So be it. He had promised to do all he could to help him: after all it was something to find a young man with thoughts higher than the pleasure next to hand, and the first step seemed to be to see his father.

So Francis Folyat wrote to James Lawrie in his awkward spidery hand — (he could not bear writing letters) — and asked for an interview in order to discuss with him the future of his son Bennett.

James Lawrie replied courteously, appointing a day, and on it Francis walked across Dale Park and over the new Cromwell Bridge and up the shabby-genteel street from the river to the stucco Gothic house.

Tibby opened the door to him and looked him up and down.

"You'll be Mr. Folyat," she said.

"That is my name."

"Our Bennett's been a new lad since he went to your house, Mr. Folyat."

"I'm glad of that."

"It's not all to the good," said Tibby, grumpily, and she turned and led him down the long passage to the dining-room.

She announced:

"The Reverend Mr. Folyat to see you."

James Lawrie was sitting at the table engrossed in a game of dominoes. He looked up at Francis and nodded, and pointed with the stem of his pipe to a chair on the other side of the table. Francis took it, and Tibby left them. Old Lawrie rattled the dice and turned up a six and three. He grunted:

"Can't do it. H'm. H'm. Can't borrow again. No more credit. Will you join me, sir?"

"Gladly," said Francis, and they began to play. They played for an hour in silence, and Francis won three times to his opponent's twice.

"You'll be a college man, sir?" asked old Lawrie.

"Dublin," said Francis, and helped himself to tobacco from the greasy old pouch that lay on the table.

"I've a great reverence for college men, having missed it myself. I had two or three friends in Edinburgh, but I was never there except in their letters. I've never been anywhere except in books, and wherever I go, and whatever I do, and whatever I be, I think there's always the printed page between me and myself. . . . Do you understand that?"

"I don't think so."

"It's like this. There's such a thing as a habit of loneliness, and if it really fastens on a man there's nothing can break through it, not love, not misery, not great joy, nor a wife and bairns, nothing. Living like that, a man gets a clear brain like a searchlight so that he can see all his comings out and his goings in and the play of his thoughts, honest and dishonest, and he prowls about and about his own self like a caged beast. Do you know that?"

"Something like it."

"Nine-tenths of us are condemned to it. My father was a minister up in Galloway. A real hell-fire man he was, but he died of a consumption, hell-fire being nothing against the mists of the place he lived in. Several men from our glen, my uncles among them, had gone to England and made money. They said it was easy, so I came down the first. I had a head stuffed full of poetry and the Bible and Scots righteousness—you need to be a Scot to know what that means—and for years I was desperately lonely. Two of my brothers followed me. They did well, as they call it. They made money and saved and saved, and made more money. They both married rich women. I got lonelier and lonelier, and more and more caught up in the trick of watching myself. I lived with my mother for years. I married to get away from her, and it was an awful day for the woman that married me. I could not let her in to me. . . . Can you make anything of that? You're a younger man than I am. Can you make anything of that? I'm an old white-bearded sinner, and if all my life was to be written they'd say it was an awful tragedy. But it isn't that. It's a fool's comedy. There's no tragedy save in a strong man who can put up a fight against his own weakness. Men like me, and that's most of us, waste our lives in fighting against our own strength. Oh! I tell you there's many a thing a man thinks of in his loneliness, but it's all thought, thought, thought; it never grows into action. One thing a man realises pretty quickly, and that is that there is nothing wrong with the world except the monstrous egoism of men and women. It is easy to realise but almost impossible to fight against. All along the line we refuse to accept the laws and principles that govern the universe because they are so little flattering to our precious vanity. We make laws against nature, organise ourselves into churches or states and nations against her, invent trumpery codes of morality in the blind hope of cheating her. From generation to generation it is one long wasteful and pitifully vain struggle against nature. . . . Look at the result. Look at the places we live in. Look at what we call society. Why we haven't even devised any method of insuring that every man and every woman shall have the bare necessaries of life; in thousands of years we haven't learned to contrive that civilisation shall give the majority of men greater comfort and happiness than they can find in barbarism. We've tried this game of civilisation over and over again, but we have never got beyond the most stupid materialism. You can almost count the really civilised men—men who have been masters of life and lived it at all points and enriched it for all those with whom they came in contact—on two hands. The rest of us are caught up by the habit of loneliness, and we are prisoners all our lives. I know. I don't give a brass farthing for material success or failure. I know the bitterness of spiritual failure. You want to talk to me about my son. I know nothing of him. He knows nothing of me. That is my fault, not his. Now, what have you to say?"

"This is all very interesting," replied Francis, rather at a loss where to begin. "My eldest son would discuss the merits and demerits of civilisation with you better than I, and certainly with more warmth than I can bring to bear on the subject."

He had an uncomfortable feeling that he entirely agreed with old Lawrie, and an equally uncomfortable sense that he would agree also with the opposite side if it were presented, and suddenly candour made him say so. Lawrie chuckled and rode off on his crotchet of loneliness again:

"That is so. That is so. Because of the habit of loneliness there cannot be unity among men. What men think is of no importance, because it has so little relation to what they do or what they are. The opinion of any body of men, even the most intelligent, is generally only the lowest common multiple of their prejudices. Theories are quite useless, so are opinions. When a man is in possession of the truth he acts. When he is not he theorises, or cowers behind his prejudicies, which amounts to the same thing. Look at the people in this town. How many of them are capable of action, how many are there whose days are not spent in superficial employments, first to get bread, and second to escape boredom when their work is done. They muddle through their work, they make a great deal of money for a few people who have no idea what to do with it when they have got it, and, since they are in an intolerable position, they have nothing to support them, and the monstrous system they have drifted into creating, but a hard, conceited pride. That makes them blinder than ever. They can do nothing to make their city beautiful, nothing to remedy the shiftless blundering of their fathers, nothing in the way of art to make amends to the people whose lives they have cramped and ruined in their factories and slums. Their only notion is to get more and more money out of them."

"I never thought of it like that," rejoined Francis. "All the people I meet seem to be very pleasant."

"They don't know they're doing it. They follow their own little rules of expedience and call them the unchanging laws of God. Your Pharisee always imagines he has made things all right by taking God's name in vain, vain indeed, for they beget nothing but vanity. I'm just as bad as they, for I've sold my three sons to them for a wage that begins at ten shillings a week and, in the course of thirty years, will grow into a salary of three hundred pounds a year."

"I have worked for thirty years and more for very little more than that."

"Aye, but you believe that you are working in a holy cause, so that the work itself is enough, and you're content while you can pay your way. All work ought to be in a holy cause and done in a holy spirit. . . . I used to think that when I was a young man. I used to feel it too. I think so now, but I don't feel it any more. These things just go on, and I sit and watch them and do nothing, and I understand why everyone else does nothing either. It's the old men who profit by it all and the young men are never wise enough to overturn it, and they could so easily by refusing to step into the old men's shoes. But we must all grow old."

"The youngest time in all my life," said Francis, "was during the years after I first came here, when I had to fight to do things in my own way in my own church."

"Exactly," said old Lawrie. "That's it. The fighting; the fighting to do things in your own way, in your own life; if you can do it, if you can keep it up, and hold out to the very end."

Francis pounced on that as an opportunity of coming to his mission, and he set forth all that he had to say about Bennett.

Old Lawrie received it in blank astonishment.

"Well, well," he said. "Wants to be a parson, does he? Is it the clothes he's after? He was always a great one for dressing up."

"I think it is more serious with him than that. I think it is very serious."

Old Lawrie thought for a long time and tugged at his beard, while Francis gazed at him and said to himself what a fine face the old fellow had.

"Do you mind," said the old man at length, "do you mind if I read you some poetry?" He took up a scrapbook and put spectacles on his beak-like nose and read in a great voice:

> Two shepherds on the windy fell
> Sat crackin' in the peep o' day.
> They heard the tolling o' the bell
> That marked a soul had passed away.
>
> And white beard to old grey beard said,
> "Another soul has passed away."
> But old grey beard this answer made,
> "The night is flowering into day."
>
> "Nay, nay," said white beard, "that's not true,
> 'Tis day that's sinking into night."
> "Night into day!"—and high words flew.
> They cursed and swore with all their might.
>
> They argued on that windy fell
> And came to blows. . . . The twilight sped.
> The distant tolling of the bell
> Told the great sun a man was dead.

That was the end of the poem.

Francis said:

"Did you write that yourself?"

"I did. I wrote that myself. . . . You wish me to say will I or will I not let my son Bennett go for a parson. Have you a mind for irony? There's irony in this. In the first place I have no money. In the second I cannot say 'Yes' or 'No' to that or any other thing in this house. You must see the boy's mother. I'll send you to her with a note. . . . What are you staring at, man? Have you never seen a prisoner before? When you live in a prison you comply with the regulations. . . . Do you see that scar on my forehead? My eldest son did that when he was a boy of twelve. He's a man now and speaks to me once a month. He comes in here and stands by the door, and he says 'How are you, father?' And I say 'I'm very well,' and then he goes away. He's a man now, and, let me tell you, he has a bath every morning."

He had worked himself up to a great state of excitement, and Francis sat gaping at him like a child at a theatre. Old Lawrie went to the door and bawled:

"Tibby!"

The gaunt old Scotswoman came in, treading noiselessly, like a ghost, and stood (thought Francis) like a gaoleress waiting orders from the chieftain of a Border clan.

Old Lawrie sat at table and wrote a note on a very dirty piece of paper, folded it up into a cocked hat, and with great care wrote on it in a neat, impersonal copperplate hand, "Mrs. James Lawrie." He gave it to Tibby and commanded her to take it and Mr. Folyat to Mrs. Lawrie in the drawing-room. He shook Francis warmly by the hand, thanked him for listening to him so patiently and bowed with extraordinary dignity. Francis followed Tibby, feeling, as he said afterwards, like a captive in a strange land. It was very dark in the passage, and, like the night in Jorrocks, it smelled of cheese. At the drawing-room door Tibby whispered to him:

"Will you wait? She may be asleep."

She pushed the door open stealthily and two cats darted out, and, on seeing Francis, rushed away, one upstairs, the other to the end of the passage, and they both sat rumbling like a kettle on the boil. Tibby moved noiselessly into the room, then turned:

"She's no asleep. Ye may come in."

Francis followed her. Tibby planted herself in front of Mrs. Folyat, gave her the note with this:

"From the master."

(If it had been from the Emperor of Russia she could not have put more reverence into her voice.)

"From the master. This is the gentleman."

With that she materialised out of her ghostliness and stalked out of the room, and Francis, on whom the humour of the whole household was beginning to dawn, found himself inventing her report to the Master:

"The prisoner has been boiled in oil, but made no confession."

Mrs. James Lawrie was a large woman with a big face, surprisingly pink and young looking. She had her hair oiled and parted in the middle and surmounted with a tall lace cap adorned with pale-blue ribbons, and skewered on with white china-headed hat-pins that clearly passed through her head and came out on the other side. Her dress was very tight, and seemed to be stretched to breaking-point in the effort to hold in her flesh. From her attitude, certain details of her dress, and a portrait on the wall, it was clear that she prided herself on her resemblance to Queen Victoria, then alive and enjoying all the lustre and celebrity of her Jubilee.

There was another cat on the sofa by the fireplace. In the window was a wire stand full of palms and india-rubber plants and maiden-hair ferns. The windows were closed. The pictures were religious, or views of various seaside resorts and spas, and five pastel drawings of children, and everywhere, on tables, on the piano, on brackets, on the mantelpiece, was a profusion of knick-knacks, cheap china, china ladies, china babies, china shepherdesses, china stags, china birds, and, on a table near where Francis was standing, among various Eastern trivialities, a large elephant's tooth.

Mrs. Lawrie read her husband's letter without giving any sign that she was aware of her visitor. Then she said:

"Sit down."

She had a peculiar mouth that opened like a trap, the upper lip not moving at all, and the lower dropping and springing back as though she had not full control of it. It fascinated Francis so that he hardly heard what she said:

"You are a High Churchman, Mr. Folyat?"

"Yes."

"I was born a Baptist, Mr. Folyat. On my marriage I became a Low Churchwoman. My husband is a Presbyterian."

"Indeed."

"Yes."

Mrs. Lawrie's lip sprang back so violently that Francis began to think grotesquely that she would never be able to open her mouth again. She contrived it, however. She pressed her forefinger into the middle of her cheek—(exactly like the portrait of Queen Victoria)—and went on:

"Let me tell you, Mr. Folyat, that we are not rich. We are not rich, Mr. Folyat, but I have my pride. Mr. Lawrie's relations have begged me on their knees to allow them to educate my children. I have refused. My children are the children of a poor man, they must do what the children of the poor have to do. They must earn their living, and they must be made safe. I believe in safety. My two eldest sons are in the biggest and safest bank in the town, and, if they behave themselves, they will be there all their lives. My youngest is in a very good position in Messrs. Keith's warehouse, and he, too, if he behaves himself, will be there for the rest of his life. My youngest son is very foolish and volatile. I don't believe he knows his own mind. I doubt very much whether he has a mind to know. I think it best that he should stay where he is. I am glad to know that he has found friends in your house and circle, Mr. Folyat. I do not call, or I would call on Mrs. Folyat."

"Mrs. Folyat would, I am sure, be . . ." Francis dropped the remark as insincere. He added hastily, to cover it up:

"The boy seemed to think that his uncles would help."

"I do not allow Mr. Lawrie's brothers to interfere in my affairs in any way."

"Then . . ."

"That is all, Mr. Folyat."

Francis found himself forced to admiration of this woman. There was a sort of finality about her. He told himself that she was like a very large garden roller, a roller so heavy that no one man could move it. He had a trick of nicknaming people—(Minna had inherited it)—and he ticked her off in his mind as the garden-roller. When he had done that, he found that she was talking about the weather and Mr. Gladstone. When she had told him how she wept at the death of Charles Dickens, Francis thought it time to go. Mrs. Lawrie chatted amiably as she took him to the door, and she stood watching him as he walked down the asphalt path to the little rustic-gate. He turned down towards the bridge and took a long breath, and blew it out again. How good the sky was! How good the air upon one's face! . . . He remembered old Lawrie's verses:

> *The distant tolling of the bell*
> *Told the great sun a man was dead. . . .*

What was dead? Old Lawrie? Hardly. The dead were surely not so mad as that. The woman? "Dead as a doornail," said Francis, and he thought with pity of Bennett Lawrie, young, ardent, groping for life, coming back at night, tired from his dull work in his dull office, to that house.

Almost unconsciously he found himself comparing it with his own house and wondering what that might be like for the young people in it— for Minna, for Annette for Frederic. Not so bad as that, surely not so bad as that. And yet . . . He would not admit to himself that all was not well in his own house.

"How strange," he thought. "How strange, to walk out of the street, an ordinary street, into lives like that! One would never have imagined it. . . . But the boy, Bennett; what's to become of the boy?"

XV
WALKING HOME

He that covereth a transgression seeketh love; but he that repeateth a matter separateth very friends.

PROVERBS XVII.

YOU may walk out of a house and yet carry it with you, just as you may cross the Channel and yet always take England with you among your baggage.

Francis carried James Lawrie's house with him on his back like a snail's shell. He could not get the thought of Bennett out of his head, and the thought of Bennett made him sensitive as he had never been to the squalor through which he had to pass on the way home. Everything in him was disturbed. His comfortable good-nature rather than his religion had made him accept the world as good in essence, and he had always done what he could to alleviate poverty and to comfort distress when they had come knocking at his door, but moral distress such as he had found in old Lawrie and divined in old Lawrie's son he had never looked for and never seen. One thing only in his life had so disturbed him, the episode, years and years ago, of the murder in Potsham, but that he had not grasped so fully; it had been so easy to conventionalise it, to watch the man be swallowed up by the machinery of punishment and forget, to pass on to—what had he passed on to? He was dismayed to find himself thinking of his wooing. Even then he had not taken the trouble to understand what he was doing; and the result? Would it have been different if he had taken the trouble to understand? Old Lawrie seemed to take an immense amount of trouble to understand, and look at the pass to which he had brought himself.

He passed the end of a dismal trough of a street—there were hundreds like it in his parish—and the sight of it led him to the thought of poverty. Perhaps, he told himself, perhaps his disasters and old Lawrie's were due only to the fact that they were poor men, too poor for the responsibilities of wife and children they had taken upon themselves. . . . But that must be nonsense. There would soon be an end of everything if the great processes of the world were to be screwed down to the money standard, if . . . But that was too difficult. He must see old Lawrie again. Quite obviously he must think things out, but he was incapable of doing so alone, and admitted it to himself. He liked walking and resented this intrusion of thought upon his pleasure. He had been a fool and supposed that he must pay for his folly, and only hoped that the price asked would not be more than he could pay. He had a feeling that he was only at the beginning of some stupendous change, and on the whole he was excited by it, until he began to think, and then it all lay so far beyond his grasp that he was depressed. One thing relieved him — the knowledge that he had no regret for the fleshpots and the fat glebes of the two Cornish livings of his early manhood.

Then his thoughts took another turn. After all, what did it matter? He did his work conscientiously, and nothing else was greatly his concern. He was only interested in Bennett Lawrie in so far as he was going to be Gertrude's husband. He had promised to see what could be done towards making the young man a clergyman. He had fulfilled the promise, but apparently nothing could be done. The garden roller had passed over that aspiration and squeezed it out flat as a shadow. So be it. Gertrude's husband would continue in commerce, take an active though lay interest in Church matters, and probably be ten times more prosperous, probably also a more satisfactory husband and father, than if he were to take Orders. There was a great deal to be said for work which took a man away all day and every day from his home, a good deal from both sides. It needed a strong affection to withstand the strain of full community of existence and interest.

Finding himself beginning to think critically of marriage, Francis brought himself up with a start. There had been a time when he had given a great deal of thought to it, his thought had necessarily driven him to attempted discussion with his wife, but on the first hint of what was at the back of his mind she had cried scandal and shame upon him and so scared and wounded him that he had never returned to the subject. He had hoped to break down the wall that had grown up between them, but she put up two bricks for every one he removed. Did she know what she was doing? Did she suffer from it? — He did not know. He would never know. She amused him. He told himself that she was more like Mrs. Nickleby than he had conceived it possible for a woman in real life to be. At any rate she was not hard, armoured against even a joke, like Mrs. Lawrie.

That brought him back to Bennett, and he had a gust of anger against the young man — not a violent gust. Francis never could be violent in anything. His anger turned on himself and twinged his conscience with the realisation that he was giving more thought to Bennett and Bennett's affairs than he had to any of his children. The point of it all was the establishment of Bennett in a career superior to that which had been forced upon him, but then which of his children had been established in a career of any sort? Serge had gone his own way; Leedham had taken things into his own hands; Frederic had a profession, but he (Francis) had no notion how that profession was answering or what prospect it held out. Unfortunately Francis had never been able to take Frederic seriously, and the thought of him was enough to set his mind working in caricature. He thrust aside all that had been troubling him—with considerable relief—and the seed of irony planted in him by his conversation with old Lawrie grew like a magic beanstalk, and he saw himself in the absurd position of having obliged a world hungry for population—(Was it not? Did not everybody agree in saying so?)—with, for one man, a large supply of human beings, produced quite legitimately after due notice given, only to find that one after another the world rejected them, or at any rate refused to provide the males with worthy work or the females with husbands. He was walking along Miller Street as this new perception came to him, between fifty little houses on one side and fifty little houses on the other, and half-way down the street the door of a house opened and Frederic came out and stopped him. He had no hat on and he was a little nervous. He said:

"Have you had a letter?"

"Several. You don't write letters to me."

"No. It's from Mrs. Lipsett. She lives here. She said she'd written to you about me. You'd better come and see her. She lives here."

"Friends of yours?"

"Not exactly friends. I've only known her a fortnight. It's about her daughter."

"Oh!"

Francis turned and followed Frederic into the house, and down a narrow little passage into the kitchen at the back. This was a little dark room looking into a backyard. Both kitchen and yard were full of washing, for it was Monday. The remnants of a meal were on the table, walled in with piles of damp linen. From the cellar door just outside the kitchen came clouds of steam.

Mrs. Lipsett was a little, faded woman, very thin, very untidy. She was sitting in a hard Windsor chair gazing into the fire, as though she were hypnotised by it. She did not look up as the father and son entered. Frederic placed a chair for his father, introduced him to Mrs. Lipsett, and without worrying as to whether she heard him or not hurried away and shut the door. Mrs. Lipsett turned to Francis and said:

"My husband left me with five children and went off with a theatre woman. He takes young girls and trains them for the dancing. He's a rich man now, but I don't have a penny from him. It's hard work making a living with the lodgers, and you can't do it when there's illness."

"No, I suppose not. I'm very sorry," replied Francis uneasily. "If I can do anything. . ."

"*Do* anything!" Mrs. Lipsett was scornful. "As if you could. I've worked my fingers to the bone. Two of the girls are in a shop. It wouldn't have been so bad if it had been them, though it would have been bad enough. But Annie's stayed at home helping me, and I don't see what's to be done. I don't see what's to be done. He's owned up to it. There's that much to be said for him. But that doesn't help much, does it?"

"Who? . . . I don't know. . . . I'm in the dark . . ."

"You've not had my letter . . . !"

"Letter?"

"Yes. That tells you."

"Tells me what?"

"What you ought to know."

"About whom? About what?"

"Him."

"Your husband?"

"No. Him and her."

Francis had learned patience in dealing with his parishioners, who were incapable of a direct statement. Mrs. Lipsett had no intention of being mysterious. It only showed that she could not bring herself to the point of open discussion of her affairs with a stranger. She had flung a certain amount of anger into her letter, all the anger she was capable of feeling, and she was not equal to the task of whipping it up again now that she was in the presence of the man to whom she had written in her first desire to injure Frederic. She made an effort and went on:

"I can't have it in the house. I can't lose my lodgers. It would frighten the lodgers."

"What would?"

Mrs. Lipsett looked desperate.

"Don't you know?"

"No, I don't," replied Francis, rather petulantly.

Mrs. Lipsett had risen to her feet. Now she sank back again into her chair and began to cry. Francis preferred that to her incoherence.

"My good woman," he said. "You seem to be in some trouble. If I can give you any consolation . . ."

"I am in trouble," moaned Mrs. Lipsett. "I'm always in trouble. I've never been out of trouble since I was born. Some people are like that you know."

These reflections cheered her up perceptibly, and she asked Francis if he would mind if she began to cook the first floor's tea.

Francis began to feel exasperated.

"My good woman," he said, "will you kindly explain what my son has to do with all this, and why he has brought me here?"

Mrs. Lipsett had moved to the table and taken up an armful of linen.

"Didn't he tell you?"

"No."

Mrs. Lipsett dropped her linen, ran to the door and screamed "Annie!"

A voice answered her.

"Come here!"

Mrs. Lipsett turned to Francis, folded her arms and with her lips tight pressed she worried out her words:

"Not told you, hasn't he? Leaving me to make a nice fool of myself! I've heard of you, Mr. Folyat! That innocent you are that you don't know you're born yet. . . ."

Annie came in and cut short anything else she might have to say.

"Yes, mother?"

"Isn't Mr. Folyat with you?"

"No. I thought he was here with you."

"Sloped, has he? Sloped!—This is Mr. Folyat's father."

"Good evening," said Annie.

An awkward silence came on the three of them, and all three thought of Frederic with varying degrees of wrath.

"My daughter . . ." began Mrs. Lipsett.

"Mother!"

"Tell him yourself then."

Annie blushed.

"I can't."

Mrs. Lipsett dropped into the vernacular.

"Eh! I am vexed!"

Francis took his hat and rose with some dignity.

"I am sorry," he said, "but as neither of you seem disposed to enlighten me . . ."

Annie stood between him and the door. She blurted out:

"It's Fred, Mr. Folyat. It wasn't fair of him to leave you alone with mother like that. We saw you going by and he said he'd go and tell you. I suppose he didn't. He's like that. He means well."

"Means well!" This from Mrs. Lipsett.

"Please, mother!" Annie went on. "Fred ought to have told you, Mr. Folyat. I'm as much to blame as he is. I suppose I'm very wicked, but there's some things you can't help. We didn't think, I suppose. But it's come to that, that we've got to think. I'm going to be a mother in three months, and Fred wants to help as much as he can."

Francis sat down again.

"Frederic!"

"Yes. The beauty! Ain't you proud of him?"

Frederic! Francis was not so much shocked as amazed. He was only too accustomed to irregularity, large and small, but he had always regarded the victims of it as creatures of another clay. Automatically by their offence they passed from one compartment of his mind to another. Where possible they were given benefit of clergy, but only as one finds a home for a stray dog. . . .

Mrs. Lipsett said:

"I say he ought to marry her."

Francis did not hear her. He was still trying to grasp the fact, but once more he found himself confronted with the difficulty that he could not take Frederic seriously. That Frederic should be, regularly or irregularly, on the point of becoming a father struck him as comic and grotesque, and yet (he said to himself) it was only to be expected that in course of time the fate that had overtaken himself should overtake his son also. But also a man was usually given time to get accustomed to the idea. In the ordinary course a man introduced a young woman to his father and mother—(with a pang he thought of Mrs. Folyat's reception of this event!)—they were engaged, married, and as bluntly as possible the Church service announced the probable consequences. Everything went smoothly and one hoped for the best. But Frederic, the buffoon, the play-actor, had dispensed with all this; had, by a sort of conjuring trick, inveigled him into a strange house, and left him with a very cool and collected young woman with a strong accent and an angry mother whose speech was of the broadest, and without a word of marriage, he was told—he was told—what was he told? With a start Francis realised that he was not in the least angry, as he ought to have been, as he had every right to be, and that he was thinking of the thing without the least reference to morality. He could not fit the formula he used for ordinary offenders to the case of his son, and, being honest, though slow and sluggish of mind, he admitted to himself that his one desire was to avoid having his wife know. He looked from the young woman to her mother and saw what a serious matter it was to them and gave up his unprofitable attempt to see the thing in connection with Frederic—(who threw it all out of perspective)—and, with a very real feeling for the two women, he said:

"I'm sorry. What do you want me to do?"

"You're not angry?"

Francis fell back with some relief on formula:

"I am deeply pained and grieved. . ." But then the new little conscience there was developing in him cried out on his insincerity and he was silent.

Mrs. Lipsett repeated:

"I say he ought to marry her. I say . . ."

"He doesn't want to marry me," said Annie. "He says he knows he couldn't make me happy."

"What's right is right," said Mrs. Lipsett. "Can he afford to marry her, Mr. Folyat? Can you make him marry her?"

"Can I?" thought Francis; and his mind flew to the idea of this young woman being presented to his wife as her first daughter-in-law. Then he said to himself:

"It is not I who am to be considered, but these two women. Frederic is least of all to be considered."

He did his best to think of Frederic as a husband, but it was quite hopeless. Frederic was more than ever elusive. It was impossible to conceive him in any responsible position. That made Francis see that it was quite useless to stay any longer. He could only go on repeating that he was sorry. He saw no method of coercing Frederic into marriage (or anything else). The most he could do was to be parentally angry, and he saw the futility of that. If necessary, in the cause of good morals, he could turn Frederic out of doors, but that would necessitate a scene and explanations, and from that he shrank. Only one thing was now clear—that there was nothing to be gained by further discussion with Mrs. Lipsett and her daughter. He rose to his feet again and said:

"I am sorry, very sorry, extremely sorry. I will see my son. I will do what I can. I promise you that everything that can be done will be done."

"Promises," said Mrs. Lipsett, "are like pie-crusts—made to be broken."

"Not mine," returned Francis, as he bowed himself out.

Annie took him to the door and said:

"I only want to get away, sir. I only want to get away."

Francis looked into her eager face. She was almost very pretty, and her eagerness was very touching. He was moved and a lump came into his throat, and tears filled his eyes, and he said:

"God bless you, my dear. You shall."

She bowed her head as he passed out, and as he heard the latch click he said to himself:

"Surely she has suffered enough."

And he felt a purely masculine anger against Frederic, anger which oozed and trickled away on the instant, for, as he turned up the street, he saw his son waiting for him at the corner. As he walked up the street he called Frederic poltroon, scoundrel, blackguard, lecher, debauchee, wastrel, but none of these words could revive his anger. As he came face to face with his son he found another word—play-actor, and if he had sympathy for Annie, the betrayed, he had pity for Frederic, her betrayer. She could suffer, had suffered. Frederic could feel nothing at all.

"After all," thought Francis, "he is my son. I have had my share in making him what he is."

He looked clean through Frederic and made no sign of recognition, but passed on with his heavy rolling stride. Frederic fell in by his side like a terrier trying to attract the attention of a Newfoundland.

"I wonder what they've said to him. I suppose he's devilish angry."

And he fell to counting up his income and his debts, and wondering exactly how cheaply he could live in lodgings.

They walked for about half a mile in that fashion and it was Frederic who broke the silence.

"I didn't mean to leave you like that. I meant to have it all out in one grand scene. I didn't jib at it. I'm not a coward. Only suddenly it seemed to me so absurdly melodramatic. I couldn't stand it so I cleared out . . ."

"I don't think any explanation is necessary," replied Francis in a curious toneless voice.

"By George! He *is* angry!" thought Frederic.

"I only want to know one thing," said Francis. "Did you seduce the young woman with a promise of marriage?"

Frederic stole a glance at his father. It was such an odd question coming from him!

"There was never anything said of marriage from beginning to end. There never is in these cases. It's so casual, you know. It seems to me jolly unfair that it should have the same result as when you are in dead earnest . . ."

"Silence."

"Sorry."

They walked on for a quarter of a mile.

"Does anybody know?"

"Only our two selves, Annie and her mother—oh! and Annette."

"Annette!"

Francis was really angry. The thing had touched his new affection, the treasure of his life, and by that test he saw it in its ugliness and sordidness. For the first time he was wholly human. His one thought was to protect Annette.

"Are you going to marry this girl?" he asked.

"No."

"Are you going to provide for her?"

"I'll do my best."

"After this do you expect me to allow you to stay in my house?"

"I'll clear out if you like."

"I do like."

"Very well then. Only you lose the right to interfere in the matter, or in my affairs in any way."

"I never have interfered in your affairs."

"No. . . . You'll let me come and see my mother?"

That brought Francis up short. (Frederic knew it would.) Frederic was his mother's favourite. His absence from the house or presence in it made an extraordinary difference to her mood. Lately she had grown very jealous of Annette. . . . Francis fumbled for some means of withdrawing the decree of banishment, and he said a little pompously:

"The young woman told me that she was only anxious to get away. I must help her to do that."

"I can't let you do that."

"I must."

"I'm not going to have you interfering . . ."

"You will not marry her. I can conceive of no greater misfortune befalling her than marriage with . . ."

"I quite agree," said Frederic.

"All the same I must see that she is not . . ."

"In short, you are going to connive at her immorality."

"I refuse to discuss the matter with you any further."

"I'm glad of that. I'll leave it in your hands and neither of us will say a word about it to anybody."

"No," said Francis, profoundly ashamed.

Frederic began to hum, and they walked on until they came to the Park.

Frederic said:

"I had a sort of feeling you'd take it like that. You never let us know much of what you're thinking and all that. I suppose you think I'm an infernal scoundrel. I'm not that. You can't despise me half as much as I despise myself, but what I most despise is the way I've let you take the thing out of my hands. I'm very grateful."

"If there is one thing in the world I don't want," said Francis, "it is gratitude from you."

"I knew I should say the wrong thing," replied Frederic, more to himself than to his father. They were passing the little muddy pond inhabited by a few grimy ducks and a black swan, and Frederic stopped and amused himself by throwing bits of paper to the birds, who for some moments were excited by the hope that they were bread. Francis passed on, relieved to find himself once more alone. The nervous irritation caused in him by Frederic's presence at his side had exhausted him. Victory lay with Frederic, but he felt no resentment about that. Hundreds of times in his life the words *Judgment is Mine, saith the Lord* had been on his lips—(one of his sermons had them for text)—but now he seemed to see them in a new light and for the first time to read a real meaning into them.

He was very tired. He felt as though he had been engaged in a long, long fight with shadows, no tangible enemy, but only an evil presence.

As he passed the children's playground he saw some of his choir boys playing tipcat. He turned in through the little gate and stood watching them. They were entirely engrossed in their game, keenly excited about it, and they did not notice him. Their cheeks were aglow and their eyes were sparkling with their healthy activity, and he began to be interested in their play. An exceptionally good shot from one of the boys made him cry out "Bravo!" At once they became self-conscious and uneasy. He tried to talk to them for a little but they assumed an unnatural spryness, and he knew that he had spoiled their game.

He went away unhappier than ever, hurried home to Fern Square and went straight to his study. There he sat in silence and suffered under the tyranny of his thoughts, which went round and round in a silly circle and would not be controlled. With tragic whimsicality he began to run the events of the day together, to merge the Lipsett and the Lawrie households, and he began to think what Mrs. Lawrie would have made of Frederic. She would not have relieved Frederic of the consequences of his folly; she would have pushed him into the morass, forced him down to the common Lipsett level or left him to drown with his paramour. The use of the word paramour struck Francis as particularly absurd, and he smiled. His dislike of Mrs. Lawrie swamped everything else. Decidedly any course of action which could seem right to her must seem wrong to him. The impression left on his mind by Mrs. Lawrie and her dark room was one of grinding effort to make life as like death as possible. To Francis life was—what? The joy of boys at play, health physical and spiritual, the struggle to reach and maintain health; colour and light and sweetness; all things that for want of any other outlet he had expressed, or sought to express, in the services in his Church. . . . The first consequence of it all had been that his wife was a querulous old woman before her time. He had faced that long ago. The second tangible consequence was this affair of Frederic's, and this also he had faced, and the worst that was demanded of him was that he should for the first time deliberately withhold a fact, a new development in his life, from his wife. There was an extraordinary ironic justice about it all. The sins of the fathers are visited upon the children for the castigation of the fathers. . . . Francis found himself on the verge of reflections so unclerical that he flung himself back, and to save himself from further thought took down his Bible. He was familiar with almost every word of it, but now to his dismay he found himself finding in it practical wisdom bearing on the brief life of man here below rather than prophesy and gorgeous promises of the life to come which should be everlasting. It was amazingly comforting to read the book in this (to him) new fashion and to let himself be excited by its call to action. He wearied a little of the savagery and dark pessimism of the Old-Testament, and turning to the Gospels found in them one stirring principle of active love, and hatred only for hypocrisy and fraud and slovenliness.

"Verily I say unto you, whosoever shall not receive the Kingdom of God as a little child shall in no wise enter therein."

He put down the Bible and took up "Tom Jones," and remembered an Irishman, a student in Dublin, who had shocked him by maintaining that Tom Jones had certainly entered into the Kingdom of God and was rewarded with an angel, to wit Sophia Western. Curiously that seemed to Francis to be something more than a profane joke.

"All the same," he said, "it is a long stride from Tom Jones to Frederic."

With that he fell to thinking of the student in Dublin and the men of old days, and wondered what might have become of them all and if they had fared better or worse than himself.

XVI
MRS. FOLYAT DISSECTED

If you had married a conscientious Bishop and made him *live in a pig-stye—à la bonne heure!*

JOHN RUSKIN

FROM being a governess with extremely small wages Annette became a servant with no wages at all. A few months after her return to her father's house, Ada, the cook-general, married (beneath her) and she was replaced by a gnomish child of sixteen who wore short dresses and had her hair done up at the back in a tight little bun. She talked an entirely unintelligible language and delighted the Folyat family on the day after her arrival by saying to Annette, who happened to be in the kitchen:

"Eeh! Annie,"—never a "Miss" from a North-country girl—"Eeh! Annie, will ye whack t' pots on t' table while I wash me 'ead?"

Annette obliged, and "whacking the pots on the table" became the family euphemism for getting a meal ready.

Gertrude and Mary had gradually retired from active service—Mary with better excuse than Gertrude—and the whole administration of the household devolved on Annette. Nothing was said to her about it, no arrangement was made; it just happened, and nobody noticed that it had happened. From early morning when she prepared tea for her mother, to late at night when she boiled her chocolate, Annette was cooking, washing up, dusting, making the beds, &c., and her only excursions, except to church or the schools, were to the shops to buy the wherewithal to cook, wash-up, dust, &c. Nobody ever thanked her: for many weeks nobody remarked that she was doing so much, and then Serge found her dragging a heavy coal-scuttle up the stairs to his studio, relieved her of it and questioned her. After that, when he was at home, he did what he could to assist her in the heavy work.

As for Mrs. Folyat, she was a very lily, in that she toiled not neither did she spin. When she thought of it, she resented the decline and fall of her kitchen from cook-housemaid and parlourmaid to the sixteen-year-old hobgoblin, but, resentment being rather an active state of mind, she avoided it by giving no thought to the matter.

If Mrs. James Lawrie could be likened to a garden roller, Mrs. Folyat could most nearly be said to resemble a mill-stone. She was of the great and ignoble army of people who are neither good nor bad, renounce their potentialities in either direction, and drag all those to whom they cling—for cling they must if they are to remain above ground—down to the lowest depths of impotence, than which there is no worse state. She made herself comfortable with fiction and preferred everything to truth. An amazing capacity she had for compelling others to acquiesce in her self-deceptions by tickling their sentimentality so that it rose in them like a flood of treacle and slopped over their imagination and critical faculty. Had it ever occurred to her to exercise this power in print she might have become an enormously successful novelist. She was to all appearances much loved, and all her acquaintances and many of those whom she called her friends always spoke of her as "dear Mrs. Folyat." She was never unhappy, but, on the other hand, she was never happy. In all material matters she was a furious optimist. She liked eating and sleeping and gossiping and going to the theatre and reading. If she could indulge in all these seemingly harmless pleasures to the extent of her appetite it seemed to her that all was well with the world.

When she married Francis, ambition was stirred in her and satisfied. Through the long years at St. Withans she bore him children with great regularity and also with the indifference of an automaton. She regarded herself as a perfect wife because she was faithful, and as a perfect mother for no other reason than that she was a mother. When her children offended her she chastised them, when they pleased her she kissed and fondled them. On the whole she brought them up on the principle of Rabelais' Abbé: *Fais ce que vouldras.* On that principle also she conducted her own life, but, unhappily, she never wanted anything much.

She believed herself to be a Christian. She was so familiar with the Bible that it had absolutely no meaning for her. Her memory was astonishing, so that she did not need to read the book. Her childhood had been spent in an atmosphere of great piety, and she had absorbed the whole Scripture from Genesis to Revelation, through the pores of her skin rather than through her brains. What most nearly penetrated her consciousness was, curiously enough, the prophecies of the end of the world: *There shall be wars and rumours of wars*, and every now and then she indulged herself in the luxury of terror, reading signs in everything. She was extremely superstitious and would never walk under a ladder, nor sit thirteen at a table, and when a mirror was broken in the house or salt was spilt or knives were crossed, she would see in the next disaster, great or small, the infallible consequence. She was delighted when she met a hunchback in the street, for that portended luck; alarmed on an encounter with a cross-eyed woman, for that boded no good. Her mind was like a dusty empty room, the door of which was sealed with cobwebs, showing that she had not for many years passed out nor had any entered in. She was romantic and picturesque, loving the romance of fiction, and entirely oblivious of the romance of fact. Only twice in her life did she deliver herself of utterances the least philosophical, and as, being what she was, her sincerity must remain suspect, neither can be taken as giving a clue to the inward workings of her mind. These are they:

(1) Long after Gertrude was married and had lived through her little tragi-comedy she said:

"All men are beasts. I married the best of them, and he's a beast."

(2) When one of her grandchildren—(this being a digression we may skirmish up and down the alleys of time)—beset by philosophic doubt, wanted to know what was going to happen to the world she made this pronunciamento:

"The world will go on getting worse and worse until the end of everything comes, just as the Bible tells you. There shall be wars and rumours of wars, . . . &c."

At the back of her mind during all her adult life was the belief in the proximity of the end of the world, and in her inevitable translation to divine regions, where, with her husband, she would live an untroubled and unsexed life of uninterrupted habit. She took her husband with her, partly because he was a clergyman and had a prescriptive right to a heavenly mansion, but chiefly because, after so many years, she was unable to conceive of an existence without him. It was all very hazy, but it was towards this future that she turned when she said her prayers morning and evening. This she did as mechanically as she dressed and undressed, between which two operations she devoted herself to her public duties as rector's wife—Bible classes, mothers' meetings, and mission work—and to the cultivation of the nearest approach to a passion in her existence, gentility. She spent many solitary hours in the drawing-room because she could not sit with Francis in his study, as she disliked the smell of tobacco and detested his allegiance to a clay pipe. She was hardly ever known to stoop to enter the kitchen.

Withal her authority was never questioned, and she obtained from her family, their friends and acquaintances, the homage and service she expected.

She was a match-maker, and no combination of male and female was too grotesque for her. She was delighted with Gertrude's engagement. Bennett Lawrie's personality lent itself to sentimental heroics, and she was more than a little in love with him herself—as a little girl is in love with the first-comer. Minna's plurality in affairs of the heart baffled and annoyed her, for in love she always looked for constancy. She had marked down Streeten Folyat for Mary, though, beyond sending a brace of grouse every August, he showed little sign of desiring the more acquaintance of his cousins. . . . Annette and Serge she left unmated, of Serge she was afraid, and of Annette she took little account. But for Frederic she had planned many famous weddings and had laid countless traps for him. He never saw her scheming, but, going his own way, he ever evaded her until, having failed in her higher flights, she came to look nearer home. The Clibran-Bells had inherited money, and there was only one life between them and a large fortune, so that all the girls would possess some three hundred a year, while George would eventually be a man of large means, for the money came through Mrs. Clibran-Bell and avoided Mr. Clibran-Bell altogether. This sudden and unexpected outcrop of wealth occasioned great excitement in Fern Square, and the Clibran-Bells added another servant to their two. They also made a gift of two new altar-cloths and a chalice to the church. One of the altar-cloths was worked by Jessie Clibran-Bell with embroidery and appliqué. She was an accomplished needlewoman, had many little talents, and she was intelligent and pious. She was the eldest of the family and the most nearly beautiful. Her nose was straight and like her mother's, whereas her sisters had unfortunately gone to their father for their noses and got them of an unwomanly hugeness. Mrs. Folyat selected Jessie for Frederic, and soon perceived, what had escaped her before, that she was in love with him.

Jessie was two years older than Frederic. She was just a little austere in temperament, singularly pure and innocent in mind. The wave of religious fervour which follows on confirmation had endured with her, and she had secretly aspired to become a nun until the advent of Frederic. Then, having escaped the wasteful expenditure of affection upon folly that fills the adolescence of most young women, she suffered a tremendous upheaval. Living with a prying, curious family, she thrust her emotion away and tried to cover it, and affected a frivolity which was entirely foreign to her. Alternately she avoided and sought Frederic's company, as first one and then the other procedure seemed to her the less conspicuous. Her labours were all in vain, for Minna knew her condition almost as soon as she did herself, and made no secret of it. As time went on Jessie grew accustomed to the presence of love in her life, realised that it would be impossible for her to take any other husband than Frederic, and resigned herself with truly Christian fortitude and patience to wait until that happened which she desired should happen. She had never enjoyed any confidence with her mother, whom she had been brought up to regard as the most beautiful lady in the world, the "very pinnacle of human virtue." (The phrase was her father's, often on his lips, and Minna always referred to Mrs. Clibran-Bell as "The Pinnacle.")

It may be ennobling and purifying to idealise your womenkind, but if your womenkind accept the position they are rather apt to believe, with disastrous results, that it is more blessed to receive than to give. Certain it is that if Robert Clibran-Bell had an ideal, he never had a wife, and that his children never had a mother.

Jessie Clibran-Bell in her simplicity believed that the Folyats had all that she had lacked. She was devoted to Francis, and when Mrs. Folyat played her sentimentalist's game with her she was entirely deceived, saw in Mrs. Folyat a perfect hen of a mother and crept under her wing. All this took some time, and it was not until the change in the Clibran-Bell fortunes that Mrs. Folyat made room for Jessie. She made her snug and warm, and, in sheer gratitude, without making any actual confession, Jessie laid bare her feelings. Mrs. Folyat kissed her and gave her to understand that though Frederic was her favourite child and a paragon among men, yet he was unworthy of such profound, such patient, such unselfish devotion. The more she abused Frederic the more warmly did Jessie's fondness flow. They both enjoyed themselves thoroughly, and often met in conclave in the Folyat drawing-room. So absorbed did Mrs. Folyat become in the pursuit of this new intrigue that she lost interest in Gertrude's affair and devoted herself to the snaring of Frederic.

XVII
FREDERIC SNARED

There is a special providence in the fall of a sparrow.
                                        HAMLET

THE snaring of men is the tamest sport in the world. It is so ridiculously easy. Let but the female cast a favourable eye upon the male and he is hers—for as long as she is clever enough to keep him. Whether a prize so easily won is worth the keeping is a matter for every woman to decide for herself. Generally the matter is settled by the advent of children, or by economic complications, or by fear of public opinion. Desire waits upon vanity and vanity is the destroyer of love. Unhappily passion is so exceedingly rare that there would be neither marriage nor giving in marriage if men and women did not hoodwink themselves and each other. Quite clearly the world would be the better without the hoodwinking and the marriages resulting from it, but, these being in the majority, and the ignoble art of hoodwinking being passed on from generation to generation, and commended by eminent divines and popular writers, and since women insist on getting married in all circumstances and at whatever cost of degradation and disappointment, there is nothing to be done but to grin and bear it and applaud every active protest that is made against it.

These were the sentiments roused in Serge Folyat when it was announced that Frederic had entered upon an indefinite engagement to marry Jessie Clibran-Bell.

Quite other and not at all philosophical were the sentiments of Frederic's father when the announcement was made to him exactly a week after his visit to Miller Street, to the house of Mrs. Lipsett. He was shocked and outraged, but as the announcement was made to him by his wife—in their bedroom—and she seemed to take an extraordinary pleasure in it, he was silent. Mrs. Folyat declared herself entirely taken by surprise. She had made Frederic take her and Jessie to the pantomime, and on the way home Jessie had stolen her hand into hers and said:

"I am so happy."

And Frederic had added:

"Yes. Isn't she?"

And then she knew! And Frederic was so proud and happy too. And so brave and manly! He could not think of marrying Jessie until he was making three hundred a year. And didn't Francis think it was time they set Frederic up in a practice by himself?

Francis groaned inwardly.

It would be delightful (continued Mrs. Folyat) to have Frederic settled. Of course he would only have a small establishment to begin with, but when he had made his position, he would be able to live in the best suburbs on the south of the town and his sons would go to public schools. Jessie was such a dear girl, as Francis would find when he knew her better, and she was so devotedly attached to Frederic, and Frederic was so very much in love, so chivalrous and attentive. Nothing better could be wished for. Francis must really consider the possibility of providing Frederic with an office of his own.

"I'll think it over," said Francis. "If you don't mind, I would like to sleep."

Mrs. Folyat continued her monologue for a quarter of an hour and lulled herself to sleep with the sound of her own voice.

Francis lay on his back staring into the darkness. His first impulse was to go up to Frederic's room and have it out with him there and then, but he could hardly do that without waking the woman sleeping at his side. Also he had made it a rule never to act in any difficulty without sleeping on it, or, at any rate, if sleep visited him not, without a night's cogitation. The trouble was that this new complication seemed to him so hideous that he hated to think of it. In the cause of morality, also for the sake of Jessie Clibran-Bell, he ought to denounce Frederic and fling him out neck and crop. But common sense bade him pause. What would be the result? A great deal of wretchedness and misery in two houses, and in all probability Frederic's utter ruin.

Already he was an accessory after the fact of Frederic's first dishonour. Could he become an aider and abettor of the second? Or, rather, having swallowed the first could he reasonably strain at the second? . . . He condemned himself for his weakness in palliating such an offence for the sake of peace. Then, rebounding from self-condemnation—(no man can keep it up for very long)—he told himself that it was not for the sake of peace but to save that poor girl from a drudging life with a man out of her own class. Then, in justice, he was forced to admit that the truth lay between the two.

His final conclusion, just as dawn began to outline the window, was that the world must be much less or more simple than he had thought. The effort of deciding which the world was entirely exhausted him, and sleep came at last.

In the morning he had a letter from his brother William, the first for fifteen years, announcing his return from India and settlement at Sydenham, near the Crystal Palace, where he would be glad to see Francis, his wife, or any of his children. How many were there? He, William, had two.

Francis handed it over to his wife just as Frederic came down.

"Aren't you going to congratulate Frederic, my dear?" asked Mrs. Folyat.

Frederic looked across at his father with malicious defiance in his eyes. Francis opened another letter and ignored the question. Mrs. Folyat returned to the charge.

"My dear, Frederic is to be congratulated."

"I am as delighted," replied Francis, "as Frederic is himself."

Frederic viciously sliced off the top of an egg. Mrs. Folyat seemed to be satisfied. She read William's letter.

"That will be very nice," she said. "Gertrude could stay with them on her way back from the Folkestone Folyats."

Frederic went to the door and bawled peevishly to Annette to bring his coffee.

"Annette," observed Francis, "is not a servant."

"I know," returned Frederic, "but I can't be late."

Annette appeared with Frederic's coffee. He gave her no thanks, and she returned to cook breakfast for Serge, Minna, and Gertrude. (Mary was away on a visit.)

"I think," said Francis, "I think Annette might be the first to stay with William."

"Annette!" Mrs. Folyat swept her out of consideration. "Annette! She has no clothes."

Frederic gulped down his coffee and hurried away.

"It will be time," said Mrs. Folyat, "it will be time to think of Annette when Gertrude and Mary and Minna are married."

"And suppose they never marry?"

"Of course they will marry."

Serge came down in Frederic's dressing-gown, and shortly afterwards Minna and Gertrude followed him.

"Any news?" asked Minna.

"My dear . . ."

Mrs. Folyat wriggled with excitement.

"My dear. What do you think? Frederic took me and Jessie to the pantomime last night; I thought it vulgar and most unsuitable for children. And what do you think? Frederic and Jessie are engaged."

"How clever of you, ma," said Minna.

"I! I was entirely taken by surprise."

Minna grinned:

"So was Wellington when he found he had won the battle of Waterloo."

Francis gathered up his letters and the daily paper, a Conservative organ, together with the *Church Times*, and turned to Serge.

"If you can give me a moment or two," he said, "I should like your opinion on a matter of some importance."

"Delighted," answered Serge.

Five minutes later Serge knocked at the study door, went in, and found his father at his desk writing a letter. Francis laid down his pen and turned.

"I want your opinion as a man of the world. I find myself in a situation with which I am not competent to deal, and yet I must deal with it."

"My experience is," said Serge, "that most problems solve themselves."

"This is a moral problem."

"Moral problems crumble away under the pressure of time more easily than any others."

Francis was not encouraged. However, he went on:

"Frederic . . ."

"Ah! I thought it must be about Frederic."

"Frederic has proposed to and been accepted by Jessie Clibran-Bell."

"A very estimable young woman, though she has no sense of humour."

"Frederic is also entangled . . ."

"With the daughter of a lodging-house keeper."

"You knew that?"

"Yes. I knew that."

"You can imagine then what pain and sorrow this must have caused me."

"Yes. It is always distressing to find fiction overturned by facts."

"You do not condemn Frederic?"

"It is surely one of the first principles of religion to condemn nobody."

"True. True. But one must not encourage immorality."

"Nothing encourages immorality so much as condemnation and prohibition."

"Is that how men of the world think of it?"

"I don't know. It is how I think of it."

Francis combed his fingers through his beard.

"Then . . . Then, what am I to do?"

"It seems to me that the difficulty has already solved itself. Miss Clibran-Bell is in love with Frederic. She will probably make him a good wife. Frederic could not possibly marry the other girl. It would destroy all her chances of marrying a man whom she could love, honour and respect . . ."

"But he has destroyed her chances."

"Not at all. She will be a soberer, a better and a more sympathetic woman after this experience, if she is helped through it and treated with decent human feeling . . . Frederic is finished as far as she is concerned."

"I told Frederic he must leave my house. I went back on it."

"That was just as well. It would have made my mother very unhappy and caused a bitter scandal in your parish. These things are nobody's affair until they are everybody's affair. The only sane course to pursue is to see that they do not become everybody's affair!"

"What do you suggest?"

"Do what you can for the girl and leave Frederic alone. No man can trifle with his emotions with impunity. That is natural law, Divine law if you like, infinitely more searching than your law of crime and punishment. The trouble with you people is that you think moral laws are a human invention. They're not. They are an inherent principle of the universe, and we are as subject to them as we are to the weather. This thing is Frederic's affair and his only. You and I know perfectly well that he won't look after the girl if he is left to himself, therefore you and I must interfere, for purely humane reasons, as you do with your parishioners, and as I do with any human trouble that I happen to come across. You can give the girl a few pounds to take her down into the country. She'll be much better there, and you can allow her, say, ten shillings a week until she gets work or marries."

"I was just writing to her," said Francis. "I wasn't sure whether it's right."

"Perhaps it isn't," replied Serge. "But at least it is practical."

"I am glad to have talked it over with you. Should I say anything to Frederic?"

"No. If you want to hurt him—though I don't see why you should—you will do so far more by simply ignoring him and taking the affair out of his hands."

"Thank you. I'll write to the young woman."

"If you like I'll find a place in the country for her."

"That will be good of you. Thank you."

This conversation with Serge relieved Francis enormously. He was like a man who, after long hesitation at a cross-road had followed one way for a mile or two, and then needed reassuring. He had already written half his letter to Annie Lipsett. He thoroughly enjoyed completing it.

Serge left him at it and found his mother waiting for him by the dining-room door. She said she wanted to speak to him, drew him into the room, and began to cross-examine him as to what his business might have been with Francis. He told her it was nothing of any importance, and then with a great deal of hesitation she came to her business.

"Don't you think Jessie is just the very wife for Frederic, Serge?"

"The usual remark that she is far too good for him seems to be peculiarly appropriate."

"Serge, does Frederic ever talk to you about himself?"

"Only in his more light-hearted moments."

There was a moment's hesitation on Mrs. Folyat's part. Then:

"Serge, there is an odious woman pursuing Frederic. She is threatening him. Has he told you?"

"No. But I know."

"Oh! Serge, please, please, can't you save him from her clutches? I have been so wretched about it. Don't let him marry her!"

"That," said Serge with gusto, "that he shall not do if I can help it."

"Oh! Serge, thank you. . . . Don't let Frederic know I told you, and don't say anything to your father. It would upset him so dreadfully."

"No. I won't say anything to either."

"Oh! Serge. I shall be grateful to you as long as I live. Why does Heaven allow such creatures . . . . ?"

"I must get to my work," said Serge. He kissed his mother and patted her shoulder, and stayed with her until she had dried her eyes and looked up at him with a watery smile.

Later in the morning, hearing Annette in the next room, he called to her, and when she came he asked her:

"Does mother read father's letters?"

"She reads any letters she can find. I don't think she can help it," said Annette, blushing for her own lapse.

"Wicked old woman," chuckled Serge. "Would you like a day in the country, one Saturday, Annette?"

"I should love it more than anything."

"You shall have it. You're the only person in this house who deserves well of the world, and to taste the sweetness of things. Possibly you're the only person who can."

"I would like," said Annette, "I would like to go to a river."

"So you shall, the very best river we can find."

"You're very good to me, Serge."

Annette was too busy to stay talking. Serge turned to his work and she strode away.

As Francis had promised, so it was done. Serge found rooms for Annie Lipsett in a not too dull village. Her mother's lodgers were told that she was run down and going away for a change, and would be away for three months. They received the intelligence with about as much interest as though they had been told that the ceilings needed whitewashing—as they did—and Annie went away. The only condition that had been made was that she should not write to Frederic. Her mother shed a great many tears, but promised to come and see her once a week and to be near her when her time came.

Frederic was received with open arms by his prospective father, mother and sisters-in-law. The Clibran-Bells and the Folyats joined in rejoicing over him, and he found himself doomed to slavery. He affected the attitude of the devoted swain, and every minute of his day, outside his working hours, was given to Jessie, her mother, her sisters, her father, her brother, her cat. He went nowhere alone with her. He went nowhere without her. . . . They were to be married as soon as he was earning three hundred a year. He looked ahead and saw no prospect of it. He became very envious of people who were happy.

XVIII
EXCURSION

Enter these enchanted woods,
You who dare!

THE WOODS OF WESTERMAIN

MRS. FOLYAT had her way—as when did she not?—and it was Gertrude, equipped cap-à-pie with new clothes, who went to stay with her uncle William at Sydenham, near the Crystal Palace. Therefore she was not of the party which grew out of Serge's promise to take Annette into the country on a Saturday. Annette had been unable to keep this entrancing project to herself. Minna had half suggested, half demanded, that she should be of the party. To square the number Serge had asked Basil Haslam, and Minna out of coquetry had invited Herbert Fry, Frederic's quondam Plymouth comrade, who had turned up on legal business, which, moving slowly, had kept him many weeks, so that, to while away the tedious hours, he had resumed relations with her. He was still "Apollyon," had an air of great prosperity, flattered Mrs. Folyat up to the eyes, so that he was altogether in her good graces, and she entertained hopes of his carrying Minna back with him to London. (He had told Frederic, but not Mrs. Folyat nor Minna that he was married.) To pair with either Haslam or Fry, as the case might be, Mary was included, and, in compassion for his forlornness in the absence of his "old, old love," Bennett Lawrie.

Serge paid. Annette made up a great basket of provisions which Bennett Lawrie and Basil Haslam carried between them.

Less than an hour's journey took them to a great river where they hired two boats—a double-sculler and a dinghy. Basil Haslam tried to manœuvre Minna into the dinghy, but could not detach her from her "Apollyon," and was forced to relinquish the little boat to Serge and Annette, who jumped into it while the rest were arguing, pushed off, and rowed away up stream, leaving them to follow in the bigger boat.

"Our party," said Serge, as he sent the little boat skimming over the water, while Annette dipped her fingers over the side and let the water gurgle up her arm.

"But I'm glad the others came," answered Annette. "That boy Lawrie looks so pale."

Serge made her take the rudder lines and taught her how to steer.

"How red your hands are getting," he said.

"It's the housework."

"What a shame!"

"Oh! I like it."

"Better than governessing?"

"Oh! much, much better. It's home, you see. And, of course, there's you. I often sit in your room when you're not there, and sometimes I look at the things. It must be wonderful to be able to—to draw."

"Now, why?"

"I don't quite know, only when you come to beautiful places like this it makes you want to—want to . . ."

"Well?"

"I don't quite know. . . . It's like growing . . ."

"That's quite good. I'd like to know what you think of me, Annette?"

"You're very puzzling. Sometimes I think you don't take anything seriously, but then I think it is because you are so different."

"How different?"

"Not like Frederic."

Out of the bank near them scuttled a vole, and along and into a hole under the roots of a willow. Annette watched him eagerly, and then returned to Serge, and said:

"Don't let's talk about Frederic. I am so happy."

Serge began to sing. He had very fine deep notes, but his voice failed him in the upper register, and whenever it cracked he laughed, and when he laughed Annette had to join in. He could never remember any song through to the end, and he invented the most absurd words. Then over a long stretch, as he rowed, he sang a melancholy canoe-song in a minor key that he had heard on the Zambesi. He sang it over and over again.

"I like that," said Annette. "Do you know, often when I'm in the kitchen I think I'm in a boat sailing away and away. It's like dreaming, only it goes on and on . . ."

"That's love."

"Is it? . . . That's nonsense. I'm not in love."

"Not *in* love, my dear. But it's love all the same! Your little soul growing and expanding, trying to find an outlet, a channel that will lead it to warmth and the sun . . ."

"You make me feel unhappy when you talk like that."

"You're wiser than I am, Annette. You accept things where I think about them."

"We mustn't lose the others."

"We shan't lose them. They'll have to come on until they find us. If I thought that Fry was rowing I'd take him ten miles, but I'm pretty sure he isn't."

"You don't like him."

"No. Do you?"

"No. But he's very pleasant."

"You can admire what you don't like?"

"I like to admire people. When I'm working it's pleasant to remember the things they do and say, and the way they say them."

"So you're a pleased and uncritical audience of the doings in Fern Square?"

Annette dodged the question. She gave a long sigh, and said:

"I am enjoying myself; but I like best being alone with you. It's such a glorious day."

And then she began to tell him some of the stories she composed about him for Deedy Fender's benefit. When she had done she added:

"Of course, I never imagined anything like you."

"Are you disappointed?"

"Oh! no."

They came to a great wood growing down to the water's edge. Serge ran the boat into the bank and moored her. He filled his pipe and began to smoke, then lay back with his head on the little seat in the bows. Annette sat with her hands in her lap, and they basked in the hot sun and felt that it was very good. The birds were very merry in the trees. In the trees the wind whispered songs gathered from the sea only twenty miles away. Over all blazed the sun. Flies danced above the water. All was harmony and peace.

Round the bend of the river came the other boat. Bennett Lawrie and Basil Haslam were rowing. Mary was steering, and on each side of her were Minna and Herbert Fry.

Fry called out:

"You've led us a nice dance. It is an hour past lunch time."

Serge grinned and shouted pleasantly:

"All the better for eating, my dear."

The big boat bumped into the dinghy and moored alongside. The luncheon-basket was hauled out, and on the grass under the trees a cloth was spread. They sat round it, and for some time were silent until their hunger began to be appeased.

"At half-past three," said Serge, "I am going to bathe. Will you join me, Basil?"

Haslam assented.

"What about you, Lawrie?"

"I would like to, only I can't swim."

"You can bob up and down in the shallows."

"I don't think I will," said Bennett miserably.

"Some one," commented Minna, "must stay and look after us. You can't leave three sisters alone."

"Fry will protect you from each other," said Serge.

"Delighted," rejoined Herbert Fry, with a gallant glance at Minna.

Mary said:

"This pie is perfectly delicious, Annette. You certainly make pastry better than any of us."

"Mary's first remark to-day," said Minna, maliciously.

Mary, who had been most amiably disposed, relapsed into silence, then, feeling that she was damping the general cheerfulness, she made another effort and turned to Herbert Fry, and asked him:

"I suppose you find our town very dull after London."

Herbert Fry replied:

"Of course, you know, London is the only place to live in."

"It obviously isn't that," said Serge, "since there are millions of people who don't live in it, don't want to live in it, have never been there, and also many millions who have never heard of it."

Minna was startled.

"Hullo, Serge! You going to defend our horrid, dirty town?"

"It doesn't need me to do that. It is quite satisfied with itself. There is really something admirable about its hard, conceited pride. We don't really belong to it, being parasitic. If we did, we should be like the rest, blinding ourselves with a tragic vanity."

"Whether I'm a parasite or not," rejoined Minna, "I'm going to get out of it as soon as I can."

"So am I," said Haslam. "I'm going to London at the end of the year. I've only been there once, but it is a fine place, and no mistake."

"I've been there twice," said Minna. "Mary's been three times. Annette never. Have you been, Bennett?"

Bennett was rather taken aback at being drawn into the conversation. He was rather shy of Minna.

"No," he said. "I've never been to London. My father has been. I don't suppose I shall ever go. It's such a long way. It must be a wonderful place. I've read a lot about it."

"I don't think they have nearly such good music as we have here . . ." Mary had waited very patiently to produce the remark which had been in her mind when she first spoke. She did so with such a flourish that she brought the conversation to an end. Serge wound it up with:

"We didn't come into the country to talk of towns."

"No," said Minna. "We came to have lunch, and a very good lunch it has been."

She rose to her feet with a whimsical right-and-left glance at Haslam and Fry, as though she were hazarding which to take with her. Both sprang up together as she moved away, but Haslam was the quicker and reached her side first. They disappeared into the woods, and Fry returned sulkily to the rest of the party. Annette began to gather the plates, knives and forks to take them down to the water.

"Shall I help you?" said Serge.

"No, thank you. I think Bennett might, as he's the youngest."

Annette had been feeling very sorry for Bennett. He seemed so solitary, so much out of his element, so unable to cope with grown men like Serge and Basil and the lordly Londoner, Fry. He accepted her invitation with obvious relief, took her burden, and carried it down to the water's edge, under a willow trailing its leaves in the water.

Herbert Fry offered his escort to Mary, and she acquiesced, bridling.

Serge was left alone. He lay on his back and gazed up at the sky—blue, serene, cheering, and comforting. His body relaxed, and he gave himself up to the sweetness of the day's mood, not without a final drowsy reflection:

"If such a moment of contentment as this is the highest good, and, since it can be procured at the cost of a little physical labour rewarded by a solid meal, what's the good of all the rest? The answer to that is that one cannot live alone. What a day for love-making!" He laughed. "Everything leads back to that."

He thought of Herbert Fry fobbed off with Mary, and he chuckled. Then he thought of Bennett Lawrie and Annette together by the water. He raised himself up. He could not see them, but he could hear their voices.

"What a day!" he said again, and added "for love-making."

Down by the river Annette and Bennett were at first very shy of each other. In silence she handed him the plates, and he dipped them in the water and handed them back to her and she dried them; then the forks, and when they came to the knives, Bennett thought:

"Why can't I say something?"

And Annette thought:

"Why can't I say something?"

She looked out along the shining river, slow-moving under its green banks; never a house, never a boat in sight, and Bennett was bending down entirely engrossed in his occupation. It was his air of complete absorption in everything he did and said (though he never did and never said anything remarkable) that interested her and made her want to know more of him.

At last, when they had finished, very timidly she asked him:

"Are you going to be a clergyman?" "I'm afraid not."

"Oh! I'm sorry!" She remembered very vividly his earnestness in her father's study.

Round The Corner | 165

"It costs too much money, you know. And my mother doesn't believe in me. It wouldn't be any good if she did, because there isn't any money."

Annette could only say again:

"I'm sorry."

Instead of moving away, she sat down on the bank, and Bennett knelt quite near her. Seeking to explain away her desire to stay, she said:

"It's so lovely here."

"It's not so beautiful as Scotland."

"Or Westmoreland."

"Have you been to Scotland?"

"I was at school in Edinburgh."

"My father comes from Scotland."

They exchanged the histories of their respective fathers. His was a mournful tale of a gradual descent into poverty, and he ended:

"I suppose I shall be a clerk all my life, unless I run away and become an actor."

"An actor?"

"Yes. I should go to London. I might starve in the beginning, but I'd be a great man in the end. I'd play Shakespeare. Don't you love Shakespeare?"

"I've never read any of his plays."

"I'd like to read you some. I know some of the speeches by heart."

And he delivered himself of the oration of Henry V before Harfleur. When that was done he plunged into the address of Othello to the most potent, grave, and reverend signiors, warmed to the words, lost himself, and came to a triumphant close with: "This was the only witchcraft that I used."

"Who was she?"

"Desdemona. And in the end he smothered her because a beast called Iago told lies about her."

"You do recite well."

"I couldn't recite badly to you."

"But what will . . . ?"

She was going to ask what Gertrude would do while he starved in London, but she could not force Gertrude's name to her lips and she broke off the question, and covered her awkwardness by throwing a twig into the water and watching it float down the stream. Bennett seemed to know what she was going to say, for he became suddenly embarrassed and his excited confidence oozed from him. He threw her back on herself by asking:

"What are you going to do?"

"I—I don't know. Just go on."

"I couldn't do that. Anything's better than just going on."

"But it's different for you. You're a man."

"Yes," said Bennett, pleased by the reflection that, after all, he was a man. "Yes, I suppose it is more difficult for a woman. But I shan't run away. I shall just go on and on being a clerk all the rest of my life."

He was appealing to her for pity; in vain. Annette said, cheerfully:

"There must be thousands of men who are clerks, and they can't all be so wretched."

"Some people don't mind, and the rest get used to it. I'm not like that. I want to do things. It isn't enough just to earn your living. A navvy can do that. A horse does that, or a pony down in a mine."

"What else can you do?"

"You can fight against darkness, and ugliness, and cruelty, and everything that makes life horrible and ugly and terrifying for children."

"Oh! for children!"

"Yes. You don't know what my childhood has been like . . ." And he drew a rapid picture of the loneliness of an imaginative child in a dark unhappy house where no love was. "Even now I'm often afraid of the dark stairs up to the attic where I sleep."

"Please, please," said Annette, "don't talk of it any more. It has all been so dark, and it is so lovely here."

"It's odd, but I've never talked like that to . . ."

He, like Annette, could not force Gertrude's name to his lips.

She began to gather the knives and forks. Then she stopped and looked at him. Their eyes met for a second, then his turned away.

"Well?" he said.

Annette was a little troubled as she gave him her answer:

"I do so want you to be happy."

Round The Corner | 167

She left him on that and returned to Serge. He was asleep, lying on one side with his hand over his face. Noiselessly she began to re-pack the basket. When she had done that she stole away into the woods, and caught up by their happy mystery, their joy in the warm air, and the sun she ran down the first path she came to until she reached a little place full of bracken. She flung herself down on the carpet of dead leaves and looked along under the bracken stalks—the tiny forest under the great—and watched the gleeful play of light and green shadow. It was good to be alive and sweet to be alone.

By the river sat Bennett in an attitude of utter dejection. He tried to tell himself, as so often he had told himself, that he loved Gertrude with a love that should defy death itself, but the idea woke no echo in his heart. It melted not as was its habit. (It had melted for so many, besides Gertrude, with the sick sweet longing of a boy.) The image of Gertrude was cold. It glowed not with its old brilliance of colour. He felt curiously hollow; nothing in either head or heart until he came to Annette's last words. She wanted him to be happy. He would be. He would be. The words set him stirring in a new way, discovered for him a new direction, and stiffened him up for the journey with a sternness that he had never known before. He was half afraid of himself and yet proud. He felt curiously detached, independent, and strong to face all that had weighed on him so crushingly. . . . He noticed then that Annette had left him, and he went in search of her. He found Serge just waking up, and felt a sudden alarm.

"Annette?" he said.

"I thought she was with you."

"So she was. But she left me only a few minutes ago."

"Better find her then. She can't be gone far. I'm going to bathe. No sign of the others?"

"I haven't seen them."

"All right. I'm going to bathe."

In a few seconds Serge had stripped and ran swiftly across the grass, took a great leap head-foremost over a bramble-bush and splashed into the water. Bennett stood envying him. Serge looked so strong, and he moved so beautifully and easily.

He thought Annette must have gone to look for Minna, and walked slowly into the woods. He had only gone a few yards when he half turned back. He wanted to be alone. He half wanted to go and bathe with Serge, but vanity forbade that, for he was ashamed that he could not swim. He took

168 | Round The Corner

Serge's prowess as a reproach to himself. That stung him into moving, and he wandered down the path between the bracken until he came to a rowan-tree in all the glory of its red berries. He stopped and plucked a handful, thinking he would give them to Annette. He passed on until he came to a little clearing full of wild flowers and heather. These seemed to him more beautiful than the berries. He flung them away and filled his hands with heather and wild flowers.

Looking up he could see the river shining through the trees and rich green woods and blue hills beyond. He moved towards the river.

Presently he heard voices behind a hazel-tree and, peeping, he saw Haslam and Minna sitting hand in hand, he murmuring, she smiling. Then suddenly Haslam caught Minna to him and they kissed.

Bennett stole away, his heart fluttering. What he had seen sent a great emotion rushing through him, but soon it withered and became disgust. He felt a strange futile anger against the couple, an anger so absurd that it mocked him. He had idealised the whole of the Folyat family, and to see Minna like that degraded her. He did not see her in any ridiculous aspect. His conception of love was too boyishly lofty for that, and yet beneath his anger and his feeling of outrage was the sense of the ridiculous, which must accompany any intrusion into the private affairs of another.

Bennett had plenty of imagination, but he had not trained it to run in harness with his observation. His imagination had, so far, only coloured and inflamed the theories he had imbibed during his education concerning human nature, and, as these theories nowhere met the facts, he was perpetually being shocked by his observations. Having, as yet, no experience, his theories remained unassailed. He believed that he loved Gertrude Folyat with a pure and ennobling love, as a man should love a woman; as, in fact, a man may love the Venus de Milo, a creature of stone. A woman, according to Bennett's docile acceptance of trite theory, must be a goddess of beauty, purity, and chastity, with never a worldly desire or thought. The woman of his love, in fine, must be the Virgin Mother.

That Gertrude was ten years his senior made it all the easier for him to raise her to this exalted position in his idea. Having achieved this with her, without any reference to her wishes or desires, he had manufactured a halo for each of her sisters as her attendant saints. He had never kissed Gertrude except as a devout person kisses Saint Peter's toe. He had dreamed of kisses, and had, with unholy joy, conceived a horror of himself as a terrible and immoral young man, so that his vanity also was implicated in this catastrophe of Minna's downfall. What, at bottom, troubled him most of all was the obvious truth that Minna kissed Basil Haslam because she liked it.

Bennett had such a tussle with his reflections and emotions—he was not far from calling them "the devil"—that he broke into a sweat, and to seek air and coolness for his eyes he made straight for the bank of the river. He had advanced only a few yards when he heard a voice singing:

> *Bury me deeply when I am dead,*
> *With, a stone at my feet and a cross at my head;*
> *And bury me deep that I ne'er may return*
> *To the scene of my true love—the brown Scottish burn.*

And he heard a splashing of water and, hiding behind the huge trunk of a beech, he looked and saw Annette swinging on the branch of a chestnut tree, her feet dangling to the water and kicking and splashing. She was naked. Her hair was wet and hung limp down to her shoulders. She was as happy as a bird.

Bennett stood rooted. His heart, his whole being melted, and turned away reflections, troubled emotions, all power of thought. He gazed and gazed, and knew that she was beautiful, swinging there under the great leaves of the chestnut. Curiously he thought that she was not so very unlike a boy. He was fascinated. Up and down she swung her branch, scrambled to her feet and dived. . . . The spell was broken. Bennett covered his face with his hands as he realised what he had done. From the extreme of heat he turned very cold and shivered. He found that he had let his heather and wild flowers fall, picked them up, and rushed away, blindly. He lost himself and wandered for a long time before he found again the grassy plot where they had lunched. At the same moment Minna and Basil Haslam returned. Fry, Mary, and Serge were sitting, and Annette was busy boiling the kettle for tea. Entirely oblivious of every one else Bennett went straight up to Annette and held out the wild flowers and heather.

"I brought you these," he said, without looking at her.

"The poor flowers are dead," replied Annette, "but the heather is lovely. Thank you."

"Thank you," echoed Bennett.

Annette's hair was still down her back and wet. She caught him gazing at it.

"I had such a lovely swim," she said.

"The woods," said Bennett, "are very beautiful."

Annette was really grateful to him for giving her the flowers. No one had ever done as much for her before. She said:

"If you like you can row me home in the little boat."

Bennett was filled with alarm and he gazed miserably at her. He longed to accept, but he was terrified. He was roused from his dilemma by Basil Haslam, who, overhearing Annette's remark, called out:

"The dinghy's mine and Minna's."

This he said for the benefit of Herbert Fry, who turned and looked, dog-like, upward at Minna.

A large chuckle escaped Serge.

In the evening, as they turned westward under a glorious sunset, Bennett elected to sit in the bows of the bigger boat. Fry and Serge rowed, and Annette and Minna sat in the stern. Bennett dreamed vaguely. His blood ran warmly through his veins, his brain glowed, and the wind and the water sang to him. He was satisfied as he had never been. When he thought of Minna and Haslam it was with a drowsy, delicious envy. To be together, gently gliding down the river with the evening shadows chasing each other under the trees. To be together—in a little boat—he and Annette . . . Annette . . . Annette . . .

In her lap Annette fingered the heather and wild flowers that Bennett had given her and smiled softly to herself. Serge saw her smile, and said:

"Happy?"

"Oh! yes."

To Bennett her voice sounded distant and very lovely, and it seemed to him that she was speaking to him, for him.

Presently they passed the little boat nestling by the bank under a plane-tree. Mary called out:

"You'll be late."

There came no reply.

They were late. It was half-past twelve before Minna reached home. The household was asleep and Serge had stayed up for her. He said:

"Hardly wise to be so late."

"We missed the train."

"Two or three. Just as well you didn't miss the last."

Minna smiled.

"Why?"

"I don't think you ought to use Haslam as a decoy for Fry. He's too good for it."

"I think you're a beast, Serge."

"Am I? We shall see."

"Fry's married. Frederic told me."

"I don't think that makes a ha'porth of difference—to you or to him."

"It isn't your affair."

"I agree."

"And, anyhow, you're quite wrong. Good-night."

"Good-night."

XIX
GERTRUDE

Nous mettons l'infini dans l'amour. Ce n'est pas la faute des femmes.

ANATOLE FRANCE.

UPON a day Bennett Lawrie escaped early from his office, leaving his day's work to be finished by a co-junior clerk on a promise to do as much for him when he should require it. He was feeling very tired, having had only a walk and two cigarettes for dinner, a practice so common among junior clerks that they have a name for it—Flag Hash. Twice during Gertrude's absence he had taken Annette and her mother to the theatre—three dress-circle seats at five shillings—a heavy drain upon his income, which was now one pound fifteen shillings a week, paid monthly. His mother knew nothing of the advance of five shillings a week that he had obtained on the third application with the plea that he was engaged to be married. That helped a little, but, even so, his position was serious, and at moments made him feel very sick at heart. He had been making efforts to save money when Mrs. Folyat's expression of regret that she had not been to the theatre plunged him into the rash offer to pay for seats. He had no thought but that she would pay for two of them at least. But no; Mrs. Folyat regarded it as the feminine privilege to enjoy entertainment at the expense of the masculine pocket.

Further cause had Bennett for anxiety in that his correspondence with Gertrude had dwindled from the devoted daily letter to an effusion with great difficulty squeezed out twice a week. That her letter had come at longer and longer intervals comforted him not at all. He had never asked testimony of devotion from his betrothed; it was enough that she should so far stoop as to be engaged to him. . . . Also, as he walked to the station through the dark railway arches, through Town Hall Square with its statues of John Bright, the late Bishop, the Prince Consort, and a local philanthropic sweater, past the Infirmary, he was dogged by an unhappy realisation that it gave him no pleasure to be going to meet Gertrude. She had written him a romantic little note:

"Dear, I am coming back to you. I have no thought but for you. I shall arrive by the 5.45. Yours, G. F."

Bennett rehearsed the meeting. He would greet her warmly and with dignity. He would kiss her hand; not her cheek. He would then silently convey that he was fully aware of his delinquences, but asked no pardon for them. Scoundrel as he had shown himself, he would have her "pass on and thank God she was rid of a knave." . . . However, he reflected that upon former occasions his most eloquent silence had conveyed nothing at all to Gertrude, and he began to rehearse the scene from another standpoint. He would say; "You bade me come. I have come. In spite of what has happened, in spite of my sins of thought and deed, I will be loyal. I will keep my troth." That was better, but not altogether appropriate from a station platform. He was still rehearsing when the train came in. He stood by the engine thinking that there he would be sure not to miss his quarry. There was a considerable crowd to meet the train, for in those days a journey from London was an important affair, and travellers were welcomed by their nearest and dearest, glad that they had escaped the perils of the way, hopeful that they had not succumbed to its fatigues, and mindful of the presents that would be in bag or trunk. . . . Bennett Lawrie thought not at all of presents. He was only bothered because he had not yet discovered the right mode of address.

The image of Gertrude that he had always chivalrously borne upon his mind, and what he was pleased to call his heart, bore very little resemblance to her features and figure. It happened that in London she had bought a new hat of a new fashion, so that in the throng he did not recognise her. She saw his blank eyes upon her and petulantly walked past him without giving a sign. She also had been rehearsing their meeting, but she had solved all difficulties by relying upon the dog-like devotion that he had always given her. He would, she had thought, come forward with his sad eyes glowing, take her by the hand and with that solemn dignity of his stoop, kiss, and, if he lingered long enough over it, be kissed in return. He would take her baggage, and carry it, as he always carried her parcels or her umbrella, as though it were a Divine trust, and they would take a four-wheeled cab. By that time one or other would have found the correct words or the inevitable gesture of love, and all would be as it had been.

Absence may make the heart grow fonder, but, where the heart is not very deeply implicated, absence sometimes has the effect of driving love out altogether. Lovers like to vow that they will never change, but they vow the impossible, wherein lies half their pleasure. As Gertrude Folyat had gone farther and farther away from her boy-lover, she had seen him dwindling in stature, but with a microscopic clarity. Having a very human dislike of seeing things as they were presented to her she pumped up a sea of sentiment, dived into it and saw blurred the newly-revealed figure. That sufficed until in the gaieties of Folkestone—she never questioned the gaiety of what was presented to her for pleasure—and the excitement and opulence of life at Sydenham, near the Crystal Palace, she was able to forget him altogether. It had been in a sudden dread that he might be injured and morose when she next saw him that on the eve of her departure she had written to bid him come to meet her. She thought that would please him. As soon as she had done so she regretted it. It seemed to place him in the stronger position which she had always striven to reserve for herself. Her visits had shaken her resignation to marriage with him, for she had been staying with snobs and was ashamed that he should be only a clerk, but all the same she wished to cling to him to avoid solicitude and the horrible possibility which had begun to shadow her of no marriage at all. She told herself that she loved Bennett, and the thought of love was quite enough for her. She never doubted that the thing itself was hers. She was not very intelligent.

It gave her a curious pleasure to ignore Bennett's presence on the station platform. She had never thought of being angry with him, but when anger took possession of her she welcomed and fed it, for it solved her problem. She would overwhelm him with her displeasure and enslave him with a tender reconciliation.

She drove home alone in a four-wheeled cab to Fern Square and enjoyed an extremely pleasant evening with her mother talking about the William Folyats and the Folkestone Folyats, their friends and their refined manner of living. The house in Fern Square struck her as dingy and undistinguished, and she did not trouble to conceal her impression. She had brought a present for each member of her family, except Minna, and, being rather warmly received, complained that no one had come to meet her.

"We thought Bennett darling would be there," said Minna.

"Was he not?" asked Mrs. Folyat.

Bennett arrived to answer the question. He too had found in anger the solvent of his qualms. He was one of those people who suffer cold tortures in sudden glimpses of their dead selves, and as he had paced up and down the station long after the crowd to meet the London train had dispersed he saw himself in his old relation with his betrothed, callow, docile, sheep-like; in a word, unfledged. The day on the river with Serge and Annette—(the rest counted for nothing in his memory of it)—had wrought a greater change in him that he knew. The shrill resentment at his old self that suddenly swept through and took possession of him was his first intimation of it. It was rather more than he could bear, and he shifted the burden of his animosity from himself to Gertrude. If she had not come by the train, well and good. She might perhaps have been kept in London, though a telegram could have saved him from the discomfort of a long wait at the station. He had risked incurring the displeasure of his senior at the office to please her. If she had come and had not looked out for him, that was not lightly to be borne. His anger was just. She should be made to feel that he was not—so he phrased it—"dirt beneath her feet." He resolved that he would not go to Fern Square until she wrote to him.

This resolve oozed away almost as soon as it was made. He had no money to pay for an evening's entertainment, and, if he did not go to Fern Square he must perforce go home and spend the evening with his mother and sisters.

The hobgoblin opened the door to him.

"Has Miss Gertrude returned?" he asked.

"Oopstairs," said the hobgoblin, and she shuffled away to the kitchen, leaving him to close the door.

He went upstairs to find the whole family assembled, with the exception of Frederic, who was at the Clibran-Bells. They all seemed so jolly that he felt that he had done wrong in coming and wished he had adhered to his first resolve. He felt that he was intruding, and by sheer force of the numbers present his old part of the humble, devoted and grateful lover was pressed upon him. In no other rôle could he find room in the company. Once again circumstances had played into Gertrude's hands and she became, what to her family she had always been, the romantic mistress of an unhappy lowly lover.

Before very long their own skill in the playing of these parts and the general feeling of the family had driven them out of the room into the peace and solitude of the study. There silence fell upon them and they stole uneasy glances at each other. Gertrude sat in her father's great chair, Bennett stood with his back against the mantelpiece under the portrait of Gertrude's paternal grandmother.

"I went to meet you," said Bennett at length.

"I didn't see you."

"If you had looked for me you must have seen me. I am tall enough."

There was considerable irritation behind his words.

"Am I then," said Gertrude, "am I so very short that you could not see me?"

"I waited," returned Bennett. "You didn't."

"I did. I waited quite five minutes."

"I waited half an hour."

Gertrude took her courage in both hands and said:

"If you had cared for me, you would have seen me."

"I waited," mumbled Bennett, obstinately.

They were silent again. Gertrude began to feel uneasy. They had quarrelled before, but always when she had touched on his affection for her his opposition had been broken. She could not take his stubbornness seriously even now. A little maliciously she was thinking:

"After all he is ten years younger than I am."

Unhappily for her, Bennett, with more malice, was thinking:

"After all, she is ten years older than I am."

For the first time he had become dimly aware that the advantage lay with himself. He said:

"I left the office earlier than I had any right to do to meet you. You could not have looked for me."

"Why will you go on arguing about it?"

"I've no wish to argue."

He only wished to avoid silence, to avoid facing what was irresistibly being borne in upon him, that all his relations with this woman had been a phantasm, a thing of the mists of yesterday. It was a hateful shock to all his theories, to all his ideals of constancy and single-minded devotion. He had worshipped this woman, set her—(at her own suggestion, though he did not know it)—on a pedestal, and lo! a day had come when she was no longer there. The pedestal remained, but the goddess was spirited away. He was very unhappy.

Gertrude was exasperated. She could have slapped him with infinite pleasure. She tapped with her foot on the ground.

"You are being too ridiculous," she said.

"Am I ever anything else?" returned Bennett, with a sudden plunge into self-torment.

Pat came the reply:

"Never!"

Bennett felt savage, turned on her and cried:

"Now I know what you think of me."

Gertrude was sorely tempted to let him think so, but she had in mind the difficulty of confessing to the women upstairs, her mother and three sisters, her return to unplighted maidenhood. She could not face that. She began to mop at her eyes, ate her words humbly, and declared that he had made her utterly miserable. She had so looked forward to seeing him again. It had made her so happy to be with him in the study once more, like old times, and all he could do was to snarl and growl; and if he was going to be like that before, what would he be like after. . . . Bennett pacified her as best he could, abused himself, said that he was not worthy to touch the hem of her garment, and, just as she was prepared for the final redeeming sinking into tenderness, amazed her—(himself too)—by announcing that he must go and help Annette prepare the supper.

He left her gasping. She hated him in that moment. Never, never, would she forgive him. All the same she followed him. He was almost as aghast at his conduct as she, and it was a relief to him to see her enter the kitchen before he had time to explain his entry to Annette. He stood and smiled weakly—a little vacantly—and, with a forced joviality, he said: "We—we've come to help you with the supper." Gertrude took his arm and said, "Yes, she had come to show Annette how to make a real Indian curry as Uncle William had it done, according to a native recipe, at Sydenham." Annette explained that she was not making a curry, and had not the ingredients for it, but she said how glad she would be of their help, as she was rather late. Bennett and Gertrude selected activities which were necessarily separate. Bennett chose to help at the oven. Gertrude took the heaped-up tray into the dining-room.

Bennett was filled with an extraordinary elation as he saw her go. He had asserted himself more forcibly than he had intended, and, so far as he could see, with a success beyond all anticipation. It went to his head, he brandished a piece of bread on the end of a toasting-fork and chanted to himself:

"I shall be twenty next March, twenty-one next year, twenty-two the year after—twenty-nine in . . . But there. How old are you Annette?"

"Nineteen."

"Have you been confirmed?"

"Of course. Ages ago. At school."

"I wasn't confirmed until I was sixteen. It made a great change in my life."

"You must be very glad to have Gertrude back again."

"I am." He let the toasting-fork drop against the grate. Annette rushed at him:

"You mustn't burn it. It's for pa's toast-and-water. It must never be burned."

The tricksy spirit which is ever lying in wait for the moment when a man is swollen with vanity pounced on Bennett, and out of buffoonery and high spirits he dodged Annette and held the toasting-fork out of her reach. She clutched at it; he dodged again. In her eagerness she tripped and lunged against him. His arm went round her shoulder and he caught her arm. . . . They stood like that for a second and then he found that he could not let her go. His hand gripped tight and hurt her, but she too had passed from laughing excitement to another strange and melting emotion. . . .

She could see the door; he could not. She saw Gertrude, and wrenched away. He followed her, and in a curious strangled voice that he hardly knew for his own he cried:

"Annette . . . I . . ."

But Annette had rushed out of the kitchen and he was alone with Gertrude. He picked up the toasting-fork and held the bread before the glowing coals.

"What are you doing?" asked Gertrude.

"Making toast for your father's toast-and-water."

"So I see. And what was Annette doing?"

"Annette was showing me how to make it."

Gertrude drew herself up heroically, and with what she took for dramatic intensity she said:

"Bennett, do you love me?"

"No," said he, startled into truth.

Gertrude sat down with emphatic suddenness. His answer had crumpled her up, but also it acted boomerang-fashion, flew back and knocked the wind out of Bennett. (In a world of liars truth always acts like that.) He was the first to recover and he approached Gertrude with contrition.

"I'm sorry," he said. "I don't feel myself to-night. Queer things going on inside me and outside. It isn't quite true what I said just now. I do love you. I do, really. But love isn't what I thought it was. I don't know what it is, but it isn't what I thought it was."

Miserably enough Gertrude murmured:

"Are you in love with Annette?"

Hotly and indignantly he answered:

"No, I am not."

"But you . . ."

"I was not making love to Annette. It was an accident."

Gertrude jumped at the occasion for magnanimity and said:

"I believe you."

"Thank you." His heart leaped within him, and privately to his own innermost conscience he whispered delightedly:

"I am in love with Annette; in love, in love, in love with Annette."

This new idea, the admission of the new fact, so absorbed him that he became oblivious of Gertrude. He had not even any regret for the months of folly through which she had dragged him. He was ashamed, not because he had turned from Gertrude, but because he had desired Annette.

True love can never tolerate secrecy. The true lover must cry his emotion from the house-tops, for a new glory has come to the world and it is well that all men should know of it.

A prophet of those days has said: "The woman should not venture to hope for or think for perfectness in him she would love, but *he* should believe the maiden to be purity and perfection absolute and unqualified." — The shadow of that prophet had been on Gertrude and Bennett, unknown to them, and they had gone to the God of Love and asked him to make up the prescription, with this result, that with one little word of truth he had kicked down the slender props of their castle in Spain and brought him to the reality of himself, her to emptiness. She suffered most, for she had a highly developed instinct of possession, lived altogether in her possessions, and was left like a dismantled hulk when any of them were taken from her.

She wept copiously, and Bennett tried to comfort her. He kissed her, and found a sort of pleasure in the salt savour of her tears. He soothed her at last, and with more common sense than he had anticipated she said only:

"You won't let anybody know just yet."

She drew the trumpery little engagement-ring he had given her—(she had not worn it at Folkestone or Sydenham)—from her finger and laid it on the table. He took it up, and after a moment's hesitation, restored it to its place.

"I want you," he said, returning to the old romantic mood that had served them so well in the past, "I want you always to be my friend."

"Always. Always." replied Gertrude with no less fervour, and she took his hand and pressed it against her cheek and kissed it.

She was smiling and cheerful when Annette returned. Bennett took another slice of bread and toasted it a beautiful brown, perfect for the toast-and-water of Annette's father.

XX
EDUCATION

As the great end of human society is to become wiser and better, this ought, therefore, to be the principal view of every man, in every station of life.

THE BACHELOR'S CLUB

BENNETT LAWRIE'S education began at the age of six, when, with his sister, Phœbe, he was every morning taken by Tibby to a little dame's school where he learned the alphabet, the multiplication table, writing, and the stories of the Bible. He was also allowed to draw and taught to embroider little mats with rough silk and to make balls with pieces of wool. In five years he made a great many balls, but he was not allowed to play with them, for they were given to the poor.

When he was ten he passed from this establishment to Wellington House, where there were no girls, but a great many rough boys who frightened him. Among them were his two elder brothers, who afforded him no protection but rather supplied the others with material for teasing. Bennett could not understand that small boys should fight merely out of bluster and cockiness. He only wanted to fight when rage mastered him, and then he was out to kill. He only had one fight at that school and that was enough, for he cut open his adversary's eye and tore the lobe of his ear away from his scalp. Thereafter he suffered from collective rather than individual bullying.

He learned arithmetic as far as fractions, algebra as far as surds, the first, second and third books of Euclid, English composition and literature, French grammar, composition and easy translations, Latin grammar, composition and easy translations, Scripture (the books of Samuel, Kings, and the Acts of the Apostles in rotation), geography, history (Tudor and Stuarts alternatively), elocution and dancing. Without being in the least interested in anything, he had no difficulty in memorising for the purposes of each day the tasks that were set before him. He was said to be intelligent, industrious and eager in his work and generally satisfactory in his conduct.

At the end of each year he found himself with a prize, though he knew not how or why, and his mother became quite amiable to him. There remained one member of her husband's family with whom she had not (as yet) quarrelled, namely Bennett's Aunt Louisa, an ex-governess who had retired upon receipt of a legacy and taken up her residence in our town in order to be near her brothers, James the failure, whom she loved, and Keith the successful merchant, whom she both feared and disliked. This gentle lady offered to pay Bennett's fees, twelve guineas a year, at the Grammar School, and thither accordingly he repaired with a brand new handbag and a quaking heart to find himself one of five hundred boys, of all shapes and sizes and classes and nationalities and religions—the town in little. In his first term he was in the Lower Third Form, and sat between the son of a cab-driver and the son of a millionaire mill-owner.

It does not matter very much what the young are taught, but it does matter enormously who teaches them. The curriculum of the Grammar School was the curriculum of Wellington House administered in larger and more unpleasant doses. Games were not compulsory, and only one hour per week was allowed for them. What the parents wanted and what they got was a good, hard, thorough grounding and no nonsense. There may have been an ideal in the place once upon a time—(it was founded by a Bishop)—but that ideal had produced no offspring, and there were no little ideals to grow up with Bennett's generation. Science had been added to the available subjects to be crammed into the boys' heads, for the voice of Huxley was loud in the land; but though Bennett devoted two hours a week to physics and chemistry, he never got beyond a vague notion that light and heat were not all they seemed, and a jocular idea that chemistry meant making a bad smell.

He was moved up regularly once a year, but he learned no history beyond George III, he devoted four terms to the study of the Acts of the Apostles, he dropped Latin in favour of German; having learned by heart the rivers and capitals of Germany, France, Italy and Spain, and drawn maps of all of them, he left geography behind, and having studied the Tudors and the Stuarts until he was sick of them, he was suddenly, by promotion, switched away from England, and directed to apply himself to the Thirty Years' and the Seven Years' Wars in Germany. Having partially grasped what they were about he was promoted into the middle of the French Revolution. Robespierre was not beheaded when he left school, and he never connected the upheaval in France with the rise of Napoleon.

His instruction in languages was entirely grammarian, and he had no notion but that the works of Corneille, Racine, Goethe and Schiller and Gustav Freytag might have been written expressly to be annotated by the various Masters and Bachelors of Arts whose names appeared on the title-pages of his text-books. He drew skeletons, profiles of girls and caricatures in the margins, and beyond cramming enough of the notes and the dictionary to satisfy his masters he took no further interest in them. He was never asked to do so.

His career and mental development were exactly those of ninety-five per cent. of the boys who passed through the institution, except that he suffered more from fear. Fear was the directing force of the machinery. The High Master was a bearded man with a huge voice, with which he bullied his assistants. The senior members of the staff bullied the junior members, and, without being given any standard of right and wrong, the boys were punished, punished, punished: detentions, impositions, enforced drills, thrashings. The school was enormously successful, and everybody was immensely satisfied with it, though there was never a boy grown man who could look back with pleasure on the years spent in its toils. There were periodical attempts made to pump up the spirit of loyalty—*esprit de corps*—but they always flagged under the general listlessness. The boys understood that they attended day after day to be educated, a process which they regarded as extremely unpleasant, as indeed it was, and only tolerable in that its end was always in sight. The clever boys who were kept until they were nineteen and stuffed for Oxford and Cambridge and the professions were pitied rather than admired. There was nothing admirable in Oxford and Cambridge to those who knew nothing of them, save the second and third-class men who were so poor as to be glad of the miserable pittance granted them for the instruction of generations of Bennett Lawries and the sons of cab-drivers and millionaire mill-owners.

After his first term in the Fifth Form Mrs. Lawrie quarrelled with Bennett's aunt Louisa. Her subsidy was withdrawn, and Bennett left school with a mind untrained except in memory, and stored only with a curious litter of knowledge absolutely unrelated to the facts of his existence.

Education, like charity, should begin at home. Bennett had spent eleven years in being educated, but he had been taught nothing at all of the place in which he lived. He had not been told why it was, what it was, nor for what purpose it existed and grew and expanded. He knew nothing of its history except that it had once had a Latin name and had been occupied by the Romans, and that Oliver Cromwell had passed through or near it with his Roundheads. Everything that was told him was presented to him in such a desiccated form that his gorge rose at it and he could swallow it only with an effort. In a city of Puritans it seemed meet and right that education, like religion and life, should be made as unpleasant as possible.

The only real education that Bennett ever got was in his daily walk to and fro over the two miles that separated his home from the school. He could cover the distance in three ways: either he could go through slums and under factories and engineering shops along the low ground, or he could take the high ground behind the Albert Station and soon come to suburbs and the streets where the middle classes gathered, or he could pass through the Jews' quarter down by the Assize Courts and the gaol. Most often he chose the third way. The mysterious, large-headed, thick-featured creatures with their oily, beady eyes exercised a strange fascination over him. He liked their Kosher shops, their bills written in weird characters, the women with their hard stiff wigs, the men with their queer gnarled legs and their feet loosely hinged at the ankles. He always looked at their feet, because a boy at school had once pointed out to him how the Jews always wore their boots down on the outside edge of the sole. He never knew why the Jews were there in such large numbers, but they interested him. They were romantic. All the cleverest boys at school were Jews. They seemed to learn everything with an extraordinary facility. . . . Almost his only friend at school was a Jew named Kraus, whose father and mother were in Roumania, and at intervals they would send him over a hamper containing queer fishes and black olives and rose-leaf jam, and then Bennett would go home with Kraus and have an orgy. Once Kraus gave him some unleavened bread, and Bennett kept it as a curiosity, and frightened himself with pretending that the tragedy of the Passover was come again, and that the angels would not mark his house because he was not a Jew and had no right to the bread.

Kraus had an aunt who was a musician and a singer. She sang so sweetly that Bennett was moved to tears and fell violently in love with her, though he would not admit it to himself, for all thought of love disgusted him. It was Kraus who revealed to Bennett the mystery of his birth, and in the filthiest way possible explained to him the process by which he had his being. It took Bennett some time to recover from the despair into which the revelation threw him, but it never occurred to him to doubt the truth of his friend's statements. The filthiness was in the world and not in Kraus. They became more intimate, and their talk was almost always dirty, though innocent. It was a swaggering pose, their way of equalising matters with the bawdiness of the world that lay before them.

Bennett had no corrective. No grown person ever held out a hand to save him from his dark thoughts and uneasy desires when they came to him, nor troubled to enquire into what pitfalls he might be tumbling. Instructed by Kraus he went the way of all flesh and lost his peace of mind and the bloom of his boyhood. All around him he saw darkness and ugliness, but never any beauty. The one place in his daily walks that his imagination fastened on was the gaol, and he dreamed of prisoners and policemen and arrestments.

His friendship with Kraus lasted for three years, during which Bennett fell in and out of love (with absurd chivalry and nobility) with his sisters' friends. The rupture came when one day Kraus filled the whole of their walk home with an account—largely invented—of an adventure with a loose factory girl whom he had encountered in the street seeking whom she might devour. A black abyss yawned at Bennett's feet, his brain whirled, and he said:

"You'll go to Hell."

Kraus replied with an obscene jingle which they had often chanted together, and offered to call for Bennett that night.

"I don't ever want to see you again," said Bennett, and he washed his hands of Kraus. Thereafter for the short remaining period of his term at school he avoided the Jewish quarter and took the high road through the most respectable-seeming middle-class streets.

The hours of the school were five, three in the morning and two in the afternoon, with three-quarters of an hour for lunch. This was not provided eatably in the school-building, and as, for most of the boys, the mid-day meal was the most serious of the day, they went, according to their means, to the various restaurants in the locality. Bennett was allowed sixpence a day, and used to repair to one of three or four cheap eating-houses, all in cellars. Here he saw men and youths of the type with which his future life would be spent—warehousemen and clerks, all scraping as much off their food allowance as they could to pay for beer and betting and billiards and tobacco. They were all dull and timid and white-faced, foul-mouthed very many of them, and the conditions under which their food was placed before them were so uninviting that they hurried through their meals as quickly as possible. On the whole Bennett envied them because they were not at school and were independent and doing work for which they were paid. . . Very often he felt too timid or too listless to eat, and he saved the sixpence for his own purposes. When he did that he found it very hard to keep awake during the two hours in the afternoon, and very often he had his homework increased by a long imposition.

In the holidays he was required to read one of the romances of Sir Walter Scott with a view to examination on them when the school re-opened. This begot in him a loathing for Sir Walter from which he never recovered. He was always being examined—every term, every midterm; in some subjects, once a week. As information had been forced into him piecemeal, so piecemeal it was pumped out of him. . . . Perhaps this is a wise provision. Perhaps, having fed their little boys' minds with bran for weeks on end, it is merciful of the pedagogues at the end of term to administer an emetic. Every term the examinations cleaned Bennett out, and by regular repetition of this process he was no further on at the end of five years than he was at the beginning. They even tried to rob him of his delight in Shakespeare by making him learn the stupid hotch-potch of the notes of some Cambridge pundit instead of helping him to discover the glory of the verses and confirming him in his taste for it.

Nothing was ever done to help him to understand the processes of his own existence, or to direct the forces stirring in him, or to pick his way through the whirling maze of divers emotions in which every now and then he lost himself. He was affectionate; no appeal was made to his affections. He was romantic; no food was forthcoming for his hunger. Spiritually and emotionally he was starved; mentally he was grossly and unsuitably fed. His was the average condition of the average boy in the most touching, perhaps the most beautiful period of the average man's life.

He was told that he must be confirmed. Like the minister who prepared him, he understood nothing of the significance of the ceremony, but contact with one or two religiously minded young men released the pent-up emotion in him and it rushed out in such a flood that he was like to drown. He clutched at the first cause that came to hand, turned to the first manly and inspiring personality that he encountered, the rector of St. Saviour's, and he embraced the High Church creed and all its tenets, prejudices, and shibboleths.

Only an accident had saved him from the worst consequences of his education.

XXI
MRS. ENTWISTLE'S HEART

God's rarest blessing is, after all, a good woman.

RICHARD FEVEREL.

WITH the best intentions in the world Francis could not overcome the inevitable dislike with which Frederic's mere presence inspired him. He could not bring himself to speak more than three words to him or to make any inquiry into his affairs. Frederic also suffered under the constraint of the secret they shared, and relieved the situation by absenting himself as much as possible from the house. His fiancée made that easy by her extensive demands upon his time and he became more a member of her family than of his own.

Francis kept his word with Annie Lipsett, and every week sent her ten shillings, and, knowing that his wife opened his letters, got her to write, when she had anything to say, to Serge. His conscience was very uneasy about the whole affair, but he knew that if he did not do what he was doing no one else would, and he could not bring himself to righteous acceptance of the conclusions of his premises, that, after all, the girl had brought it on herself, and, like hundreds of others, must fight through the consequences alone and unaided.

"If I knew the hundreds of others," he said to himself, "I could not possibly help them all. I could not afford it. . . . Can I afford to help this young woman? . . . I cannot, but I must."

He submitted to this moral imperative, but he could not away with the idea that he was encouraging immorality. That idea became fixed, an obsession. It worried him so much that he decided to go and see the young woman and make quite sure as to the state of her mind, to demonstrate if necessary that though things were being made comfortable and easy for her in this world she could not hope to escape the punishment for her sin in the next.

Accordingly one Saturday he resolved to take the ten shillings himself instead of sending them by post. Annie Lipsett was staying in a farm labourer's cottage near a village some fifteen miles away to the south. It was a keen autumn day when Francis walked along the lanes between hedges aflame with hips and haws and red blackberry leaves, and green with holly berries, and he asked himself why he did not devote every Saturday afternoon to a walk in the country. The cold air filled his lungs and the wind blew in his beard and brought the colour to his round cheeks. The trees were burning with colour, the sun shone scarcely warm through the soft mist that lay over the country-side. . . . Decidedly, he must often take such walks and bring Annette. How she would love the orchards, glowing with red apples and plums, and yellow with pears, and the cows and the green fields and the little rivers. Annette would love them all. They would make a habit of it, every Saturday, and they would see all the seasons come and live and pass.

As he approached the cottage where Annie Lipsett was staying he felt less interested in the state of her mind and more concerned to see herself and discover how she was keeping in health. Health, he thought, was most important, perhaps more important than anything else. "Grant us in health and wealth long to live." He recited the words aloud, and his mind commented that wealth meant well-being, not a fine house and raiment and a substantial account at the bankers. That struck him with all the force of an original discovery, and he began to think that his life was not perhaps such a complete failure as he had grown used to thinking it. His arrival at the gate of the cottage cut short his speculations, and he wrenched himself back to the problem immediately before him, the bringing of this sinful soul to repentance. Yes; he must make her see that her sins would only be forgiven her on condition of full repentance. He felt fully convinced of it in that moment, and did his best to make himself feel miserable in spite of the invitation to happiness extended to him by the little grass path leading up to the door of the white cottage, and the Michaelmas daisies and autumn lilies and purple asters growing in the borders and the heavily laden fruit trees in the tiny orchard.

He walked up the grass path and knocked at the low oaken door. In the house he heard a bustling and a rustling, and presently the door was opened to him by the woman of the house. She was enormously fat, red-faced and comely. She said:

"Tha can coom in. Annie be oot in't fields gatherin' noots. Tha'll be Mr. Folyat. Tha's a gradely mon. Coom in."

Francis followed her into the little low oak-beamed room, spick and span and clean as a new pin. There was a picture of Queen Victoria on the walls, five texts, and a grocer's almanac, horribly reproducing in oleographic colour a pre-Raphaelite picture of Christ knocking at a door. The woman, Mrs. Entwistle, brewed a pot of tea and chattered:

"She be that well, tha'd think she were going to make no more fuss than a beast. Eeh! The way t' bloom 'ave coom to her cheeks and 't light to 'er eyes ye'd say a woman was all t' better for carryin'. . . ."

Francis began to take the same delight in the enormous woman that had come to him from the sights of his walk. She was so sane and comfortable.

"Eeh," she said, "It was a good thing to get 'er away from 'er mother. I never could do wi' them stringy little women. A 'ard time? 'Course she's 'ad a 'ard time. So's everybody, but you don't want the world to go grizzlin about it."

Annie came in. She was very pretty, with a new soft pride in her eyes. She was very big. She took Francis's hand and clung to it, and with eyes and voice together she said:

"Thank you."

"Glad to see you, my dear," said he. "Glad to see you looking so well."

She sat down. They had tea, and when they had done Francis intimated that he wished to speak to Annie alone. Mrs. Entwistle took down a yoke from the wall and went off to fetch water from the well. Francis hugged his knee and read several times over a text which ran: "Beloved now are we, the sons of God." It was so illuminated that it was difficult to read: *we* looked like *me*, and *sons* like *guns*. Then he asked if he might smoke.

"Surely," said Annie.

Francis lit his pipe and the tobacco tasted very good.

"You have been happy here," he said.

"Oh, yes. Very happy."

"I've brought you your ten shillings."

"Thank you."

He gave her the coin and she put it in a little purse. Francis found himself at a standstill. He forced himself to speak. He was alarmed at the quiescence of his conscience under the influence of Mrs. Entwistle and the garden and the radiant thankfulness in Annie's face. Her gratitude to him made it very difficult for him to perform what he conceived to be his duty. A humorous gleam shot through his brain, and he began to think himself a little absurd; but he pricked his conscience and it stifled the gleam. He looked very serious as he said:

"I suppose—I hope you realise that you have no right to be happy. You are bringing a child into the world in sin . . ."

He could not go on. He saw that he had hurt the girl to the quick.

"I'm sorry," he said hurriedly. "It is very difficult. I only wanted to be sure that you realised, that you knew, that—that . . ."

With bowed head and with her hands in her lap, Annie said in a low voice:

"I do know all that, sir. I thought that myself, sir, when I first come. Every night I cried because I was so wicked, and I thought I should never be forgiven, and mother had said such awful things to me. But Mr. Folyat came . . ."

"Frederic?"

"No, sir, Mr. Serge. He comes every Saturday. He paints all the afternoon and then comes here in the evening. Sometimes he walks a great many miles. He come and said I must never have any thought in my head that wasn't happy, that I must never for a single instant let myself be afraid, for the sake of the child. He said everything that happened to me happened to the child too. And I've tried and I have been happy, so I know it's true. He says: 'What's done is done, and people aren't wicked all the time or good all the time.' I don't understand everything he says, but I always feel better when he comes, and I don't think of anything but it. I want it to love me . . ."

"Of course, of course," said Francis. "It is very important for you to be well, but you must not imagine . . ."

"I couldn't take money from you, sir, if you thought me wicked. I have been wicked, but I'm not wicked any longer. I couldn't do—what I did, ever again. I couldn't be so silly . . ."

Francis thought to himself: "I must make her appreciate the peril through which her soul has passed. . . . She seems to be leaving her soul out of consideration altogether. I must make her see that she has a soul and can only find true happiness in its salvation through . . ." Once more he drew back from the contemplation of difficulties which he felt were too intricate for him. He said:

"My dear, be sure I think no ill of you. I only desired, my only thought was . . . is . . . has been to secure you as far as possible from the temporal consequences of your—er—betrayal." He breathed heavily. Then he fell back on his natural candour and added: "I came meaning to say a great deal, but I find that I have nothing to say. I find it quite impossible to take a professional view of your situation. You must forgive me. I cannot help feeling that I have been guilty of an impertinence."

Annie still hung her head and plucked at her fingers. She looked at the clock and said:

"Mr. Serge ought to be here now, sir. He's generally here before this. There aren't many gentlemen like Mr. Serge, are there, sir?"

"I hardly know," replied Francis. "I hardly know, but my experience of the world has been very limited. . . . Do you tend the garden yourself?"

"Yes, sir. I help Mrs. Entwistle. I've learned such a lot about the garden since I've been here."

"I had a garden, once, in my old living." He described the garden at St. Withans, and the exercise of visualising the lawns and borders and the orchard under the church-tower and waking the faint echo of his old joy in it won him back to greater confidence. He talked of flowers and bees and birds until there came a knock at the door, when, with joyful alacrity, Annie hurried to open it. Serge came in with paint-box and sketch-book strapped together and slung over his shoulder. He nodded to his father and sat down by the table. Annie brewed him fresh tea and he said:

"Jolly place this?"

"Delightful," replied Francis.

"Don't you think she's looking well?"

"Very. I should hardly have known her again."

"She's in good hands. Mrs. Entwistle has taken her to her heart—me too, and if you come often enough she'll find room for you. It's delightfully warm and comfortable and roomy. I never knew such a heart. You meet all sorts of delightful people in it, all the nicest people in the Bible, and hundreds of children, and everybody loves everybody else. Don't they Annie?"

Annie blushed:

"That's only Mr. Serge's nonsense, Mr. Folyat. He goes on talking like that until Mrs. Entwistle shakes with laughter so that the chair you're sitting in creaks. . . . Have you had a good day, Mr. Serge?"

"You shall tell me." Serge produced his sketches and Annie looked at them.

"That's a lovely one," she said.

"May I see it?" asked Francis.

She handed him a sheet of paper on which was a drawing of a baby in an apple-tree with the wind blowing in its hair and bringing new wonder into its starry eyes.

"Mr. Serge does me one every week," said Annie simply. "I keep them all."

Francis held it up close to his face and peered over the top of it at Serge. Very solemnly he returned the drawing to Annie. . . . A moment or two later he leaned forward and said:

"I can remember you when you were like that, Serge. It's a long time ago, and so many things have happened since then. You were very big and strong, and you used to laugh a great deal. . . . I remember your being ill, and then, when you were a little older, I remember your asking me all sorts of questions that I couldn't answer. And then, quite suddenly, you weren't a baby any longer and then you became a boy . . ."

"And then I went away. That is the whole history of any father and any son. Queer, isn't it? . . . And then we never met again until we came across each other in Mrs. Entwistle's heart."

Annie looked puzzled. There were several moments of silence, warm and comforting and, to Francis, very sweet. Serge laughed.

"After this," he said, "we may expect to hear that Mrs. Entwistle has been caught up into Heaven. As a matter of fact she lives there all the time, because, though you wouldn't think it to look at her, she is a sort of a fairy."

"I should like to be back before dark," said Francis.

"Three minutes," answered Serge, "and I'll go with you." He turned to Annie. "I've found work for you as soon as you're ready. A friend of mine has a farm six miles away. He lives with his sister and he wants an assistant housekeeper."

Annie had never taken her eyes from him since he had come into the room. Her eyes now filled with tears, and her hands made a touching little gesture, almost imperceptible, of gratitude towards him. Serge went on:

"He's not a rich man, but he'll pay you enough, so that you can feel independent and always be putting by a little."

Annie found her voice but she remained inarticulate. Francis was curiously relieved when Serge rose to go. He held out his hand to her. She took it in both hers and said:

"I know. I must have made you very unhappy. You have been very good to me."

"Not at all. Not at all," said Francis huskily. She turned to Serge:

"You'll come again? It won't be long now."

"Next Saturday."

"It might be before then."

"I'll come on Monday."

"Thank you."

Francis found his way out into the garden. Through the window he saw Serge take the girl into his arms and kiss her. More than ever he felt that he had been impertinent.

The sun was setting and the mist had almost cleared as Serge joined him. In the west the sky was crimson, straked with indigo clouds. Serge took his father's arm and said:

"We owe a good deal to that young woman, you and I."

"Yes," replied Francis doubtfully. "It seemed to me that she is more than a little in love with you."

"I hope so."

"Isn't that a little dangerous?" Francis felt very bold in making this excursion into psychology, but the pressure of Serge's hand on his arm reassured him.

"My dear father," came the reply, "for thirty years you have been paid for teaching people that the only safety of our little existence here on earth lies in love. I can imagine nothing more awful and disappointing than for a woman to go through the process of childbirth without being in love. It is dreadful enough to live from moment to moment without being in love, but to pass through a great natural crisis without it would be devastating. If she weren't in love with me I couldn't have touched her heart. I could only have appealed to her intelligence, which would have been quite useless. It seemed to me vitally important that she should be made happy, so that through happiness she could understand and feel she was doing no injury to any one, but was performing the ultimate service which a woman is privileged to perform for only a few human beings, namely, the gift of life. She has understood and felt that."

"But she is in love with you!"

"Why this terror of love? Love, like everything else, becomes a bad thing if it is used selfishly. I ask nothing of her. She knows that. She will love her child the more because of her love for me, and by her greater love she will win the love of the child. . . ."

"But . . ." said Francis.

"What now?"

Francis made full and frank confession of how he had come with a desire to make the young woman understand and feel her sinfulness. Serge pressed his arm affectionately.

"My dear father," he said, "a flower may be impregnated by a very disreputable bee, but it remains a beautiful flower for all that."

"A flower," said Francis, "has no soul."

"In the presence of love," replied Serge, "argument is quite futile. The tragedy of the world, it seems to me, is this, that with such a power of love and friendship and affection as is in us, there should be so little of them."

"I at least have won a little of them to-day," said Francis, and timidly with his arm he pressed Serge's hand.

"That's all right," said Serge.

The night came down as they walked and hung out her most brilliant canopy of stars, and, as in a peaceful lake, their light was mirrored in the soul of Francis Folyat.

XXII
LOVE

Let us roll all our strength and all
Our sweetness up into one ball
And tear our pleasures with rough strife
Through the iron gates of life.

ANDREW MARVELL

WITH consummate skill Gertrude invented contrivances to conceal the change that had come about in her affairs and feelings, but, as she never deceived herself, she deceived no one else either. However, everybody pretended to be deceived, and painlessly her engagement with Bennett Lawrie was allowed to fade out of existence. He came less and less to the house until the transformation in his status was complete, and then he came more and more.

Gertrude grew restless, her unease infected her mother, who had begun to tire of Fern Square and to think it and its neighbourhood squalid. The Clibran-Bells had left Fern Square and gone to a more expensive and more modern house in the select neighbourhood of Burdley Park. Little hints were thrown out, but nothing definite was said to Francis, until he expressed a desire to enlarge his greenhouse in the back garden and return to his old pastime of gardening. He had tired of reading. He could not bring himself to tackle new books, and the old had lost the potency of their appeal. His parish work was organised into a comfortable routine, so that he had plenty of leisure, and he disliked being left alone with tobacco and his thoughts. Gradually he had fallen into a nearer companionship with his wife, reading and discussing her foolish books with her and every evening playing three games of bezique and allowing her to win. He wanted some new form of activity, and one day, the post bringing a seedsman's catalogue, he found what he wanted. He would grow ferns and bulbs and fuchsias and geraniums and cactuses and have a very pleasant refuge from any malign stroke that fate might be keeping in store for him.

Near the Clibran-Bells Gertrude found a house with a large conservatory, and, all leaping to the prospect of a change, the decision was come to, the remainder of the Fern Square lease disposed of, and the household was moved. The new house was one room smaller than the old. Serge took a studio at the top of a huge caravanserai of offices near the Town Hall Square and arranged to live there. He had painted a portrait of Mrs. Clibran-Bell which had brought him a commission or two, and he regarded himself as sufficiently opulent to pay the not very exorbitant rent.

The removal took place in March, and a very pleasant house-warming was held. Gertrude sent out the invitations and expressly did not invite Bennett Lawrie. He turned up all the same, more silent, melancholy and romantical than ever. He sat in a corner and spoke to nobody, and looked so entirely dejected that at last Minna took pity on him, smiled her sweetest, and said:

"Why do you always play the skeleton at the feast? Are you really thinking of death or only of what there is for supper?"

"I didn't know I looked like that," answered Bennett with an effort. "I was feeling rather happy listening to you all."

"Looking on," said Minna, "is a dreadfully bad habit. Whenever I do it, I always find myself wondering who is going to be married to whom, or, at any rate, who is in love with whom, and how it is all going to turn out. That is too horribly depressing. It is much better to be an airy trifler. Why don't you try a little airy trifling?"

"You can't do it alone."

"That is *quite* good. . . . Now then—one—two—three—hop."

"I really couldn't trifle with you, Minna."

This was true. The memory of the day by the river was much too vivid. Bennett was nothing if not rigidly monogamous. Minna did not know that. This new game, which had never occurred to her before, amused her. She went on:

"But you're doing it quite nicely."

Bennett dropped back into the darkest gloom. He began to feel angry with her and said savagely:

"Am I?"

"Indeed you are. And as you ain't going to be a little clergyman, it doesn't matter."

"It does. It always matters."

"It only matters if—shall I say it?"

"You generally say what you feel inclined to say."

"It only matters if our little gentleman is in love."

Bennett scowled. Minna went on with her banter until Annette came into the room with a tray bearing lemonade and claret. Bennett sprang up and hurried to meet her. Minna laughed and nodded to Basil Haslam to come and take Bennett's seat. When he had done so, she said:

"Have you ever noticed my little sister, Annette?"

"Not particularly. Why?"

"She is over there, by that young Lawrie."

"Young idiot."

"What do you think of her?"

"She is looking quite pretty. Has she done her hair differently?"

"No, nothing is different."

"Excitement, perhaps."

"Per—haps."

Basil turned to Minna. He was not interested in Annette.

"Minna, you look . . ."

"Ta, ta, ta . . . Are we to have it all over again?"

"Yes. Every time I see you. It's not long before I go away now. Will you come with me? I can do better with you than without."

"You don't know. You have never lived with me. I should hate being really poor in a house of my own."

"I'd make you rich with love."

"And feed me with it and clothe me, and feed and clothe an enormous family?"

"We shouldn't have an enormous family at once. I'll make you rich before there are . . ."

Minna tapped his hand with amused affection, got up and left him. She went and stood near Bennett and Annette and she heard him say:

"Thank you for wearing them."

She saw then that Annette was wearing two little red roses in her bosom.

"It was kind of you to send them," said Annette.

"I hardly dared," said Bennett. "I didn't know if I might. I never see you now."

Annette looked up at him between fear and delight. His mournful eyes met hers, and with a small envy Minna saw that they were entirely oblivious of everybody in the room. Annette's lips pouted. A little sigh escaped her. She turned and hurried away.

Basil Haslam came up, took Minna rather roughly by the arm and dragged her away to sit on the stairs. In her heart she was pleased by his masterfulness, but superficially she was irritated, and they sat quarrelling.

The party engaged two rooms, one for cards and one for music. The room in which Bennett stood began to fill as Mary produced her violin. Annette returned from the kitchen with biscuits, sandwiches, cakes and a trifle, and when she had disposed them on the table she turned to Bennett and said:

"Come."

He followed her.

She led the way into the little back garden, where, in a plot of grimy grass, grew a sycamore-tree. At the end of the garden was a decayed old summer-house of rustic wood. Bennett's heart thumped as they approached it. They entered and stood for a moment in the darkness, glad of it. Tears came to his eyes. He could not see her. His hands groped in the darkness and soon found hers, warm, trembling. Very gently he drew her to him and kissed her forehead and her hair many times. Closer and closer she pressed to him, her hand went up to his shoulder. He felt enormous strength come to him; the faintest little cry came from her and their lips met.

For each it was the first kiss of the beloved, a greater joy than either had dreamed of, and therefore almost more pain than joy. Holding her to him, Bennett murmured:

"Annette, love, I love you."

And she gave little crooning sounds and was the first to kiss again.

Presently they crept back to the house and stole into the rooms again, Bennett looking more miserable and feeling more aloof than ever. Minna saw that Annette's roses were crushed, so that one of them had lost its petals. Annette's lips were red and her eyes shone with a new light. Bennett sought Minna and stood in silence by her side. Minna turned to him and said tartly:

"Annette is looking quite pretty to-night, isn't she?"

"Is she?" Bennett's voice quavered.

"I should advise you, as a friend, to make yourself very amiable to Ma."

"I have always," said Bennett, "had a great respect for Mrs. Folyat."

"Bah!" answered Minna. "You take yourself much too seriously. You'll never learn the wisdom of running away."

"I ran away from you."

"Of course you did; because I never take you seriously."

Bennett said with asperity:

"You never take anything seriously. Some day you'll have to."

"Pooh!" Minna tossed her head and laughed. "I shall always know when to run away."

Feeling that the remark was idiotic and inappropriate Bennett closed with:

"The world is very beautiful."

"Great heavens! We shall have you writing poetry next!"

Bennett went very red. He had already written much poetry, as Minna well knew, for she had purloined and read many of his effusions to Gertrude. She wondered if it would be going too far to quote, decided that it would, and mentally adapted certain verses to meet the new circumstances.

Bennett was called away to take a hand at whist—he was a fair player— and to pass out of the room he had to go by Annette. He avoided looking at her, but she followed him with her eyes, and, turning, met Minna's gaze, curious and mischievous. Minna saw her expression harden into pride and defiance, and it was Minna who looked away.

The party was very late in breaking up, and as Bennett was putting on his overcoat Annette came and helped him. He turned to her and they smiled at each other. She said:

"Serge is going to make a picture of me. I begin to-morrow, at his studio."

"I'll write to you—then, if I may."

Annette was called away by her mother, very peevish and anxious to go to bed. She caught Bennett's hand, pressed it to her bosom and ran away.

"Good night," he murmured, and when he was out in the street, walking home, he whispered to himself:

"Good night, my love."

With the two crushed roses in her hand Annette slept like a child, hardly stirring all night, smiling. She had prayed to God, as usual, for her father and mother, and had particularly begged Him to bless her love.

Bennett on the other hand had suffered from a violent reaction. He hardly slept, or, when he did so, it was to dream feverishly, seeing himself in ignominious positions with no clothes on, in church, for instance, or at his office. His thoughts flopped like frogs in a pond; his emotions whirled, rushed in a flood up to the memory of that moment of ecstasy, but were driven back by other memories, the Jew, Kraus, Annette by the river, Minna and Haslam. He wanted so terribly to understand, but he could not. He longed for nothing but to be with Annette, to give her all her desire, to rescue her, fly with her. . . . He fell asleep. In a chariot with swift horses he drove along a wild, dismal road. Clothed all in brightness he found Annette under a gallow's tree. Three bodies hung on it and swung in the wind, but she was singing a beautiful song. She mounted into the chariot, and away they sped, so fast, so fast, that presently they soared, and then down they came with the air rushing in their ears. Soon the road caught them again. There were hedges on either side of it now. They grew and grew, taller, taller, taller. It was very dark. Soon he saw that they were in a church. The chariot vanished. Annette vanished. He was alone in a dark empty church, and with a bitter cry he exclaimed . . . He awoke, shivering. He had thrown the bed-clothes off and torn his night-dress from his body. He was so unhappy that he began to cry. Utterly exhausted he fell asleep.

He was late in the morning, dull and dead. The monotonous day's work in the office soothed him. It was not until he left that he thought again of Annette and remembered that he had not written to her as he promised. He went round to Serge's studio and found him smoking and surveying the rough beginnings of a charcoal drawing of Annette.

"Hullo! sir," said Serge. "Anything wrong? You look as though you'd seen a whole car-load of ghosts."

"I didn't sleep well," answered Bennett. "Sometimes I don't."

"That's nonsense at your age. How old are you?"

"Nearly twenty."

They talked for a little, but Bennett hardly heard what Serge was saying. He went away soon and made no response to Serge's invitation to come again. When he reached home he locked himself into the dining-room—his father was out—and wrote to Annette. He made no sort of opening, but plunged directly:

"I do not know what to write. I love you. I hate myself. I cannot even tell you how much or why. Something in me is entirely changed, something of me is gone altogether Nothing exists but you. Everything else is hard and cruel and dark. I dreamed of you last night. I dreamed I had lost you. Have I? I went to look for you to-day. Oh! Annette, I can't write any more."

He did not sign it. He hurried it into an envelope when there came a knocking at the door. The letter was shuffled into his pocket and he went to the door and called:

"Who is it?"

In a very soft voice came:

"Tibby."

He opened to her. She had his night-shirt in her hand. She closed the door and said:

"You've torn your shift."

"Yes. I tore it in my sleep."

"Poor laddie," she said. "If I could do aught to help ye I would. Ye're a poor solitary body. . . . It's this house and the misery that's not of your making."

Bennett looked at her and the kindness in her eyes made him burst into tears. She patted his shoulders, went away into the kitchen and came back with a glass of milk and some biscuits. She saw that he ate and drank, and Bennett said:

"Thank you. I feel better . . . Tibby, why don't people understand what they are?"

"God knows," said she. "It's all a great mystery. There's a deal of unkindness, and a little kindness in the world. It's not given to us to understand."

"Tibby—" he paused. "Tibby, would you love me whatever I did?"

"Surely. You're one of my bairns."

Bennett kissed her. Then he went and posted his letter.

Annette came to meet him next day as he left his office. They had a long walk and were altogether happy, laughing and discovering little jokes that they could share—odd names on the shop-fronts, queer folk in the streets, strange advertisements on the placards. He left her near her home. He had so loved being alone with her that he had no wish to see her with her family. Also he was afraid of Minna. She spoiled everything.

Only one evening a week could Annette give to him, but they had Saturday afternoon and Sundays. She knew very little of the town, and, though he had little pride in it, it was a delight to him to show her such beauties as it had—the Zoological Gardens, the Art Gallery, the Reference Library, the School, the College, Humphrey Bodham's Hospital, the parks, the elegant southern suburbs. They shared it all, and sharing made everything beautiful. Always he found her more wonderful. Her simple trust in him strengthened him, dissipated the mists and dark shadows of his mind, made him, what he had never been, a boy. He could laugh with her.

All the rest of his life seemed small and unimportant. Often at home he sang aloud and talked to himself until his mother rebuked him. Then he would atone by performing all sorts of little services for her. In the office he felt that the silly day's work could be done in ten minutes—nine o'clock, work till a quarter past, send the whole world whizzing round, and then away to Annette. . . . But Annette's days were long and laborious, and the presiding powers at the office demanded his attendance from nine till five. He found his work easier and quite interesting. He began dimly to perceive a purpose in its processes. Talk with one or two of the elder men enlightened him. A great deal of what they said seemed absurd to him. The world did not exist for business. It existed for Annette. He had a trembling desire to tell them so . . . One man told him that though immense fortunes had been made in the cotton trade, they were a mere trifle compared with the misery that had been created in the making of them. "But that," said the man gloomily, "is the way of the world. It's happened so often that nobody worries when it happens again. All business is dirty business. A man must live, though I can never understand why." . . . Such pessimism seemed utterly absurd to Bennett. He did not want to understand why. He had only a general desire to be pleasant to everybody, and became so willing and busy and obliging that his superiors began to reverse their opinion of him. They had thought him conceited, reserved, and, at bottom, stupid. One of the senior clerks went out of his way to speak a few encouraging words to him. Such a thing had never happened before, and Bennett rushed away to Annette to tell her that the ball was at his feet, and he would quickly make his fortune, and then he would call for her one day, and they would be married by the bishop and for ever and ever they would live in a delicious dream. They were always making plans, and living in them, in a future that was so near the present as to be almost indistinguishable from it. There was no past. They ignored obstacles and impediments, lived in and for each other, and it seemed that it had always been so.

They hardly ever kissed each other in those young days. When they did so they set stirring in each other forces that instinctively they felt to be dangerous. What they had was so very precious, just the few hours every week of unclouded happiness. Always—wet or fine—they were out of doors, wandering blindly, oblivious of all else save each other. They would take meals in their pockets the more to be independent.

As the result of one long walk in the rain Annette fell ill and was in bed for a fortnight. She filled all Bennett's thoughts. He dared not write to her, and only once was he bold enough to go and make enquiries of Minna. The outside world began to close in upon him and to insist that he should bring his image of his beloved into some more proportionate relation with it. Much of the glamour left her, but she was not the less precious to him. Rather more; but in a new way, a simpler way, more easy to grasp. His intelligence began to play about her, to appreciate her directness—(how marvellous that was compared with everything else that he had had!)—her honesty, her confiding loyalty, her skill in bending to his mood, and discarding everything that might interfere with their happiness. . . . Days of gold and summer sun, young, green days, all warm and busy with new life. . . . Then, one evening as he sat by the window of his attic, looking across the miles of roofs in the direction where she lay, she began to appear to him in yet another way. He harked back to the night of their first kiss, and he felt again the warmth of her body in its triumphant surrender. He was half terrified by the new flood of warmth that ran through him, and he put his hands over his eyes as if to shut out what he was seeing. He became wholly afraid and ran downstairs to seek company.

He turned to his religion and scourged himself with the most naïvely terrible thoughts of hell and damnation. This only had the effect of a bellows on hot iron: his imagination became white hot, and not Annette, but Woman obsessed him. Against that he could only set Annette and her love: the only pure threads of his life. He was sick and lean for love of her when he saw her again.

She was white and large-eyed. Her mother was present. He could only press her hand. How their two hands trembled as they touched!

Her first excursion was to Serge's studio, where the portrait had been left unfinished. Bennett met her there, and, after the sitting, they had a long silent walk, arm in arm.

"I thought of you all the time," said she.

"And I of you . . ." He was troubled. "Oh! Annette!"

He took her hand and, in the street as they were, kissed it over and over again.

She went away to the sea and Serge with her. She liked being with Serge, but even to him she could not declare herself. Under the warm sun with the strong air blowing over salt from the sea she quickly became well again, but all her longing was to get back. She was uneasy. When she had last seen Bennett she had felt that some of the glamour and delight had gone from him. He had changed. She must change with him. He had gone on. Gone deeper. She must go with him. She had never been trained to think. She never reasoned any difficulty out. All her perception of her circumstances came to her in flashes. . . . It was not long before she had caught Bennett up. She was not afraid, but only glad to be with him once more. She was proud of the new horizon that had opened to her. When health came back to her she was a woman.

One evening as she sat with Serge on the sands gazing at the moon peeping above the sea and silvering the waves she said:

"Serge, tell me, have you ever been in love?"

"Often."

"Happily?"

"Happily and unhappily. It doesn't matter much. The great thing is to love."

"What is love?"

"A great thing, but not the be-all and end-all of existence as so many people try to believe. The greatest things lie beyond it."

"Then you must go through it to get at them."

"Exactly. Most people stick in the middle, or remain shivering on the wrong side."

"Like Frederic?"

"Like Frederic."

"I used to hate Frederic, but now I'm only sorry for him."

"What's come to you?"

She shivered.

"It's very cold. Can I go home to-morrow?"

"If you like. Do you want to?"

"I must."

She returned to the house in Burdley Park next morning, but it was some days before she informed Bennett of her arrival. He came hot-foot as soon as he had her letter, and there was an air of dogged determination about him and the embarrassment of one who has a vital topic to approach.

He had made a compromise between his mental torment and his religious scruples and come to the idea of marriage, and the idea had taken complete possession of him so that he saw nothing else. The vision of the future to which it led was sufficiently entrancing to make him unwilling to look elsewhere. He did try to contemplate the future without that step, but it stretched intolerably blank. He needed action. The upheaval that had taken place in him had set him growing mentally and spiritually; in his office, in his house, he was hurt at every turn, bumping into corners where none had been before. He saw in marriage perfect freedom. It was an illusion, but he was wholly deceived by it. He saw it as a summit of achievement from which he could defy all that he had suffered all his life. He said to Annette:

"Annette, I love you. I want you to marry me. We shall be very poor, but we shall have each other, and nothing else matters."

This he said to convince himself. Annette did not need convincing. She believed.

"No," she said, "nothing else matters."

He had hardly expected such instant compliance. For a moment it shook the firmness of his conviction and blurred his vision of the free future. He told himself that their present existence was intolerable and must not be suffered to continue.

Excitedly they made their plans. They believed that it was their affair and theirs only. They saw the outside world as harsh and menacing and devoid of understanding, were seared by it, and used their fears to fortify their resolve.

"Another month," said Bennett, "and we shall be man and wife."

"I love you," said Annette. It was the first time the words had passed her lips.

When Bennett had paid the expenses of the ceremony in an out-of-the-way church and the price of the ring and their wedding-dinner in a restaurant near his office he had exactly thirty-shillings left until the end of the month. Annette returned to her home until he should have found a lodging for her, and he engaged himself to break the news to his mother at the first fitting moment; fixed, in his own mind, at that when he should next receive his monthly salary of seven pounds.

He anticipated a storm, but, being still borne up by the excitement and the adventure of what they had done, they felt secure against all wrath. Hardly could they understand that there should be wrath. How could their love meet with anything but love?

XXIII
BENNETT TELLS HIS MOTHER

Then would I speak, and not fear.

JOB

AFTER a week's search Bennett found lodgings as far removed as possible from his family in a little pink-brick street that was one of a network woven by a speculative builder over a tract of marshy ground that for years had been unclaimed and used by the neighbourhood for a rubbish heap. In a tiny little house he hired two rooms on the first floor for twelve shillings a week. His landlady was a large German woman who, by threateningly demanding references, inveigled him into paying two weeks' rent in advance. He had to borrow ten shillings to do that. He was terrified of the German but proud of the two rooms, the first place that he had ever been able to call his own. The wall-paper and paint were hideous, but he told himself that that could soon be altered—should be altered before Annette saw the rooms. By neglecting all other engagements he found time in the evenings to hang what he thought a pretty paper and to paint the woodwork apple-green, paint and paper being bought with more borrowed money. This manual activity soothed him greatly, and he felt very proud of himself, whistled and sang all the time as he toiled. He was so busy that for a fortnight he hardly saw Annette, and when he did snatch a moment with her he was exceedingly mysterious, and would not tell her what he was up to, except that it was for her, a beautiful surprise.

"Where is it?" asked she.

"You wouldn't know if I told you. I'll take you there."

"Next week? Is it to be next week?"

"As soon as it is ready. . . . You're not sorry?"

"Of course not."

As the end of the month drew near Bennett realised that it was not going to be so easy as he had thought to break the surprising and splendid news to his mother. He knew so little about her, and had always had great difficulty in talking to her even about the most impersonal matters. There had been differences between them before, many trifling, and one serious, over his secession to the High Church fold. All these differences now rose up and stood like a thick-set hedge between him and her. . . . As long as he remembered her she had been always sitting in the middle of the dark drawing-room waiting and watching for the landmarks of the day—dinner at one, his brothers' return from the bank, his own return from his office, tea, supper, the hour for sleep—as time bore her evenly past them. For years now his only long conversations with her had been at the end of the month when he gave her his earnings and received his dole for spending. It made him ashamed and unhappy to know that he disliked her, but he could not explain it away, and he had never made any attempt to understand why she was as she was—cold and hard and unresponding. If he took sides at all in the antagonism of drawing-room and dining-room his leaning was towards his father, but that was because the only intimacy in the house lay between Tibby and old Lawrie. There was more warmth in the dining-room than in the drawing-room, though, outwardly, it was his father who was disgraced and deposed, his father whom Bennett had been taught to contemn. . . . The only link that bound him to his mother was money. He would use the monthly conversation about money as an opening for his declaration of independence. He had not looked upon it as that: had not contemplated a rupture and open breach between himself and his mother, though he had heard muttered warnings in the depths of his soul.

When he returned home with seven pounds in his pocket, he hesitated for a long time outside the drawing-room door with every nerve in his body throbbing. His suffering was too great and he decided that he would tell his father first. After all, his father was the head of the family. . . . He walked gropingly down the dark passage to the dining-room only to find his father out and Tibby working for dear life at a column of cotton-prices. He knew what that meant. There would be no telling his father. His father was "plang" (the family euphemism), and, as she had often done before, Tibby was finishing his work.

She looked up at him and scowled. The work was never easy for her, she had to supply the gaps of her ignorance with guesses and was always in dread of guessing awry. Bennett sat down in the horsehair chair by the fireplace, under the blue-eyed portrait of his grandfather, the Scots minister, and rattled the money in his pocket. Tibby went on working. Much of Bennett's terror vanished and he broke into the scratching of her pen:

"Tibby."

"Eh?"

"You said once you'd love me whatever I did."

"Aye. What have you been doing?"

"I'm married."

"Losh!"

Tibby dropped her pen and turned sorrowful eyes of wonder upon him. Bennett jingled the money in his pocket.

"I'm married," he said. "I'm very happy."

"Och! The foolishness of men! Married! Laddie, ye'll never have a son as young as yourself."

"I'm married," said Bennett, "and I'm going to be very happy, and I don't care what . . ."

"Have you told your mother?"

"No."

"Better tell her at once. You'll break your neck over it. I'll finish this and then I'll think it out. . . . Married! Losh!"

She turned to her work again, and the pen scratched and spluttered. Bennett reached the door when she called to him:

"Laddie."

He turned.

"If ye love the lassie, ye've no call to be afeard. There's always a way. There's no way where no love is."

"I love her," said Bennett unconsciously dramatic and absurd. "I love her as my life."

"God bless ye."

Fortified by her benison and also by having once told his immense secret Bennett passed swiftly to the drawing-room. He found his mother sitting in her chair in the middle of the room with a cat in her lap. He stooped and kissed her.

"I've got some news for you!"

"Sit down. You don't come and talk to me as often as you might."

There was an unusual geniality in her voice that made it easy for him to go on.

"I've had a rise."

"That's good. They must be pleased with you. How much?"

"Five shillings a week."

"That's very good. You shall have a shilling a week more for your pocket-money. I'm glad you're doing so well. You can keep five shillings for yourself this month."

"That isn't all my news."

"What else?"

"I want to keep it all."

"Nonsense. You can't do that."

"I must. You see. I haven't told you everything. You see . . . I shall want my money now. I'm—what I wanted to tell you is that—that . . ." He gave a little nervous giggle that exasperated his mother and set her tapping with her foot on the floor. "I'm—you see—I'm married."

Her mouth dropped. Her hands waved weakly in the air. She got up and went and stood for a long time—it seemed a very long time—by the window. Without turning she said:

"Who is the woman?"

"Her name is Annette. Annette Folyat."

"I might have known it. . . Will you ask your father to come here?"

"Father's out." Bennett felt that his cause was lost. Only in the most desperate cases was his father's presence over requested in the drawing-room.

"Tibby then." She went to the door and with extraordinary power of the lungs shouted for the old servant.

Tibby came shuffling. She was dressed to go out, in bonnet and shawl, and had an envelope in her hand.

"I'm in haste," she said.

"Tibby, what's to be done? Bennett has married one of the daughters of that High Church popery priest. What am I to do?"

"What can you do?"

"It can't go on. It's miserable folly. It's ruin. It's beggary. . . . Where were you married? When?" She pounced on Bennett.

"A fortnight ago. At St. Barnabas; banns and everything. We signed the register. I forbid you to interfere."

"Silence."

"I will not be silent. I have taken my own life into my own hands. I am going to have my own money and my own house. I shall leave your house to-night, and I shall not enter it again until you ask me and my wife together."

"That's right, laddie," said Tibby quietly.

Mrs. Lawrie opened her mouth to rend Tibby, who added:

"I canna thole a man that winnot stand by his own doings."

Mrs. Lawrie turned to Bennett and said:

"May you never have a child to hurt you as you have hurt me this day."

The wild frenzy that had possessed Bennett oozed away, and weakly he asked:

"Am I to go?"

"Go. . . . As you've made your bed, so you must lie on it."

A little unsteadily Bennett walked upstairs to his attic and began to pack his belongings. He laid them all out on the bed, books, clothes, small pieces of furniture, and they seemed to him very little. In possession of his secret he had felt very large and important; now he felt very small indeed.

Downstairs in the drawing-room his mother sat writing a letter to Francis, denouncing him and all his works and his daughters, who were a snare to youth and guilelessness. Tibby had tried to reason with her, but she was beyond reason. She had been hurt and wished to hurt. Carefully, laboriously, she had toiled to insure her children against all risks and perils of the world. Brick by brick she had built a prison for each of them which should last as long as life, and, at the first touch, the walls that hemmed in and secured her youngest born had come toppling down, and all around herself she saw the abomination of desolation. She hated life, and her enemy had proved too strong for her.

XXIV
ANNETTE TELLS HER FATHER

*You have stores of patience, only now and then
fits of desperation*

DIANA OF THE CROSSWAYS

FRANCIS received Mrs. Lawrie's incoherent offensive letter, gulped down its unpalatable statement of fact, burned it, and rushed to his greenhouse to think it over and to master the anger that was rising in him. . . . He blamed himself for not having seen what was in the air and tried to remember incidents and conversations which should have given him the hint. He recollected several, quite enough to set him scourging himself for his blind neglect, until he began to ask himself what he could have done supposing he had seen and realised. Quite clearly he could not have forbidden Bennett the house. Interference was always dangerous where the emotions were concerned.

Most painful of all was the thought that Annette should not have had trust enough in him to seek his advice and comfort if she were in trouble. She must have suffered, he told himself, to make such a plunge into poverty and the responsibility of marriage. It must have been a tremendous flood of feeling that had swept her into it. . . . It was so pitiful: a mere child: children both of them.

In a second he found himself thinking the worst of it—a scrambled marriage of necessity. He put that from him. Of course not. Annette had been well and happy—except for her illness—extraordinarily happy, and so gentle and sympathetic and thoughtful, so blithe and busy. No wickedness there, no hypocritical covering up of dark gnawing secrets. Only the most absurd, pitiful romantic folly, reckless defiance of all the laws of prudence.

If his thoughts of Annette were gentle and indulgent, he found it hard to extend his kindliness to Bennett. Young men would be young men, but they should leave young women alone. (Francis, still regarded young women as generically and fundamentally different from young men. To him young women who took any active part in the affairs of love were abnormal and unmaidenly. What exactly young men were to do with their ardour or where to present it, he did not know, and he was unconscious of any discrepancy in his thoughts.) The personal factor entered into his contemplation of this side of the pother. He told himself that Bennett had treated him very badly, had accepted his hospitality for years, received his indulgence in his affairs with Gertrude, his—to be sure, unsuccessful—assistance in the furtherance of his clerical ambitions, and then, secretly, with cunning and deceitfulness, he had played upon Annette's young and innocent affections. There was an easy satisfaction in thus angrily vilifying Bennett, but it did not last long, for it led to a conception of Annette which did not sort with her nature as he knew it. She had always been curiously self-reliant and, quite clearly, fully cognisant of the facts of her existence and the purposes of her womanhood. Still he was reluctant to relinquish Bennett from the talons of his wrath. He was going to take Annette away, and could give no guarantee of his ability to provide for her and make her secure against the devastating influences of the hard struggle for daily bread. With his instinct for justice he asked himself what else they had to offer Annette, and, further, what they had given her from day to day ever since her return—drudgery, unending toil, a monotonous, trivial, and unrewarded activity. That brought him hotly near the heart of the mystery, but he turned his back on it, only to find himself most vividly remembering his visit to the house of the Lawries, and finding in that the explanation of Bennett's share in the preposterous marriage. He had wondered then what would become of Bennett. Now he was answered. . . . Presumably Mrs. Lawrie had not been misinformed. Obviously not. Her vituperation came from a fury of despair, a hopelessness in the face of a new turn of fate, which he felt to be so degrading that he desired to avoid it. Clearly there was nothing to be done. If it was salutary by a heavy use of the tongue to lacerate Annette and bring her to a sense of the seriousness of the thing she had done, he would—but he reflected that his wife would do all that and more than was necessary in that kind. For himself then there was nothing to be done and nothing to be said. If they found it impossible—as was more than likely—to live on Bennett's income, something must be done to help them. Both families must contribute. . . For a moment he thought fantastically that the solution might be to ignore their marriage altogether, and keep Annette at home until Bennett could afford to keep her. He knew that for folly. If passion had so far blinded their reason that they had rushed into an insoluble compact, to thwart and repress it would be to invite unimagined disaster.

"It is beyond me," he said. "Did these things happen when I was young? The world seems to be changing. I am too old to change with it."

His last reflection was that, having swallowed Frederic's disaster, he could not logically strain at Annette's. He was wounded. Time would heal his wounds. Above all he must not be reduced to such an ignoble frenzy of bewilderment as Mrs. Lawrie. Then he felt sorry for the "garden-roller."

"It must be," he said, "very distressing to come on a hard stone in the middle of a soft lawn."

That restored his humour. He took twelve little pots and began filling them with earth and fibre for his bulbs.

Annette came into the greenhouse. Francis suppressed a desire to run away. He did not look at her, but pretended to be absorbed in his work. Annette asked if she might help him.

"I think," he said, "I think you had better close the door."

Annette closed the door and stood with her back against it. Francis stole a glance at her. She was excited but there was no fear in her, only a sort of shy obstinacy. She said:

"How you love your greenhouse! You have been so much happier since we came here."

"I have. And you?"

"I'm not altogether happy, because I want to go away."

"My dear!"

"Yes. You can't be quite happy when you're going away from things and people you've loved and grown used to, can you?"

"I suppose not."

"Father . . ." Francis trembled. His affections were touched. In his thoughts he had not realised the poignancy of his loss. It was going to be very painful; more painful almost than anything that had ever happened to him. He could not bear her hesitation, and he hastened the calamity.

"I know," he said.

"You know?"

"Yes. I have had a letter from—his mother. She is very angry."

"And you . . . Are you angry?"

"Oh! my dear, dear child . . ."

Then Annette was in his arms and they were crying together, and she was saying:

"Dear, dear father . . . I didn't mean . . . I didn't know it was going to be like this. I didn't think, I didn't think of anything but him. I haven't thought of anything but him for a long time. . . ."

"But such a wedding . . . no cake, no presents, nobody to cry over you . . ."

"Only you, father."

"I'm an old fool. I ought to be very angry with you. . . . But I'm not. I ought to be predicting the most horrible and miserable future for you. . . . But I can't. . . . It's much too serious. . . . I think you ought to tell your mother. It will hurt her less if it comes from you than if it comes from me. I'll tell the others. . . . There's nothing to be said. I believe that you love each other. I will pray for your happiness. . . ."

"He's ready for me," said Annette. . . . "I wanted to go to him to-night, but I'll wait until to-morrow if you like."

Francis pondered that for a moment.

"No," he said. "No, I think it would be best if you told your mother now and went away at once. It will save many tears. We shall have the night to get used to the idea. . . . It's a new idea; rather a difficult one to digest—our little Annette a married woman."

She told him then that Bennett was coming for her to the end of the street.

"And your belongings?" asked Francis.

"I was going to carry them."

"Could you? I never thought they were so little. . . . Don't brides usually have trousseaux?"

"I'm to have nothing that brides usually have. I don't want anything."

Francis filled the twelfth little pot, and very deliberately squeezed the mould down with his thumbs.

"I think," he said, "I think that while you are talking to your mother I will walk along and see my—my son-in-law."

"Yes. . . . Yes. Bennett will be glad to see you."

"Will he?" said Francis dubiously.

They left the greenhouse. He watched Annette run upstairs, took his hat and stick and walked up the street. At the corner he saw a lean figure, standing under a lamp-post. It was Bennett. He was seized by a sudden fierce desire to hurt him and he gripped his stick more tightly and sawed with it up and down. He was walking rather faster than he knew and caught up with Bennett before the sudden mood had passed. His stick swung in the air, and Bennett was roused from his dreams of bliss by a sudden thwack across his loins. He was more startled than hurt, for he had not heard any approach.

"Ooh!" he cried, then recognised his assailant. "Mr. Folyat!"

Francis breathed heavily and raised his stick again. To feel Bennett's flesh yielding under his blow had given him an intense and peculiar satisfaction, a pleasure so unwonted that his senses craved more of it. His mind however had shot ahead of his mood and he dropped his stick and said:

"I beg your pardon. . . . That was not what I intended. My intentions are frequently belied by my performances. . . . Did I hurt you?"

"You did." Bennett rubbed his thigh ruefully, then stooped and restored his stick to Francis. They stared at each other by the light of the lamp-post and at length Francis said:

"Annette is telling her mother. She has just told me. I propose to stay with you until she comes. We should—a—we should know each other better."

"I told my mother yesterday, I left her house last night."

"It was foolish of you to quarrel."

Francis laid his hand on Bennett's arm and turned with him down the street. They passed up and down on the side opposite the house, Francis explaining as best he could how and why he had come to strike his son-in-law. He was very frank, and pointed out those elements of Bennett's conduct of which, as a gentleman, he could not approve, but made it clear that they should not stand in the way of a friendly acceptance of the inevitable.

Upstairs in the drawing-room Annette had found her mother alone with Serge. Mrs. Folyat was knitting a never-ending woollen vest, and Serge was unwinding a skein for her round the back of a chair. Annette told her news. Serge went on winding the skein. Mrs. Folyat dropped her knitting, took off her spectacles, put them on again, pushed them up to her forehead and looked Annette up and down. Then very slowly, as though she was groping for her words, she said:

"I am thinking only of your father. This will bring his white hairs in sorrow to the grave."

"I have told father," said Annette

Mrs. Folyat was too far gone in sentimentality—forged sentiment—to feel anything. She had chosen what she thought the most appropriate and effective method of attack, only to find it parried. She clutched blindly at the first seemingly fit words that came to her mind, those which had already been used by Mrs. Lawrie:

"As you have made your bed, so you must lie on it."

Serge rose and said:

"That is no reason why you should try to make it more uncomfortable, mother."

Mrs. Folyat hardly heard him. She had begun to think (the specially ordained scourge of the sentimentalist) what people would say of her; not what they would say of Annette: she was incapable of seeing the affair from Annette's point of view. One of her darling fictions, that of her perfect motherhood, was menaced. She was a she-lioness to protect it: her fictions were to her what her children might have been. With incisive and bitter sarcasm she assailed Annette for the space of two minutes. She predicted that Bennett would take to drink, that he would desert her, that there would be a scandal, and she (Mrs. Folyat) would never be able to hold up her head again. When she could find no more baneful prognostications to throw at her offending daughter's head, she took refuge in tears and began to declare that she wished that she were dead, since all the love she had lavished on her children was to be returned with such ingratitude. They were all ungrateful, all, all—except dear Frederic—and she wished she had never had a daughter. . . . Annette bore it all meekly, though she was very near breaking down. It had all seemed so simple to her: she loved, she was obeying her love, and all this made it so complicated. . . . Serge's blood boiled, but he said nothing. He saw that Annette was in an impregnable position, not to be undermined.

Very quietly Annette said:

"I am going to-night, mother. I told father I would stay until to-morrow, but he said I had better go to-night."

Mrs. Folyat covered her face with her handkerchief. Tears she knew were unanswerable, but she did not anticipate that Annette would make no attempt to carry the discussion farther. When she removed her handkerchief Annette was gone and Serge was sitting quietly unwinding her skein of wool.

"Serge! Serge!" she said.

"Yes, mother."

"Has she gone?"

"Yes, mother."

He turned and looked at her, and under his steady gaze she was silenced. She brought her spectacles down on to her nose, took up her knitting and went on with it. Every now and then she sniffed.

Serge wound the new skein of wool into a ball and placed it in the basket by her side. He waited for a moment to see if she had anything to say. She only sniffed. Every line in her figure expressed a perfect wallowing in self-pity. He left her to it.

In the street Francis, still clinging to Bennett's arm, ended his homily thus:

"Marriage, of course, is a blessed condition, and man was not meant to live alone. You will get into difficulties; everybody does. You will look for help; everybody does.—But don't let it become a habit."

He had a great deal more to say, but just as, for the fourteenth time, they came opposite the house, the door opened and Serge and Annette came out, he carrying her luggage, a small trunk. In her hands she had two hats of straw, very high in the crown and very small in the brim. Bennett left his father-in-law and rushed over to her.

"Excuse me," he said to Serge, and took Annette's trunk from him. Annette laid her hand in his arm and they walked off up the street in the direction of a cab-rank in the main Burdley Road.

Francis joined Serge and they followed close behind.

"And to think," said Francis, "that Annette should be the first to go, and that she should go like this! . . . What do you, make of it, Serge?"

"It would be funny," replied Serge, "if it were not so pathetic."

"Just . . . just what I have been feeling. Look at them! They look as if they were going off to an evening's merry-making."

"They have forgotten us already."

That was true. The lovers walked fast, hailed a cab on the rank, and had climbed in to it and were off by the time Serge and Francis came up with them. Serge bawled to the driver, the cab stopped, and Annette, conscience-stricken, jumped down and came quickly to her father. Francis drew a ring from his finger, a gold ring set with an emerald, and said:

"I couldn't let you go without my present."

"I'm not going far, father."

"No, my dear, but it is for ever."

Serge went to Bennett in the cab, shook hands with him, and said:

"You're doing a bigger thing than you know."

Bennett wrung Serge's hand, and could find no better expression of his very real emotion than this:

"You're my brother now, you know."

Annette came up, kissed Serge, and was promised her finished portrait for a wedding present.

"That's two!" she said.

"Good-bye, Annette!"

"Good-bye. Good-bye."

She mounted into the cab again, and its iron wheels went clattering over the cobble-stones.

"I wonder," said Francis, turning homeward, "I wonder if he heard a word of all that I said to him."

"Did you say much?" asked Serge.

"I struck him."

Serge laughed.

"It was most extraordinary. An uncontrollable impulse. It needed some explanation, for I meant only to assure him that, in spite of his burglarious entry into it, I accepted him as a member of my family. Do you approve, Serge?"

"I believe in Annette. I would rather be Annette than Gertrude or Mary or Minna."

"So would I. I wonder why?"

"You won't agree with me, but I detest all this repression of emotion in the name of virtue. It is nothing but cowardice. You can't destroy emotion by suppressing it. It only goes bad. . . . I'm only thankful to see Annette out of your house and away fighting for her own hand."

"Theoretically I cannot applaud Annette, but, frankly, I must confess that I am excited and curiously uplifted by her open defiance of . . ."

"My dear father, you are a sentimentalist yearning over love's young dream. Annette knew that—instinctively. She knew that you would expect her to live on love's young dream indefinitely, until the bloom was gone from her youth and the edge from her appetite. She knew that she could not trust you. Still less my mother. She took the law into her own hands, and I admire her for it."

Francis walked on for some moments in silence. At the gate he said:

"I have reason to respect your opinions, Serge, but I heartily dislike them. . . . Will you come and help me in the greenhouse? I should be obliged if you will stay with me to-night until your mother is in bed and asleep. It will be so bad for her to talk."

Mary saw her mother to bed and then came to say good-night to her father. She wore an expression of intense gloom as she pecked at his cheek. She patted his shoulder as though to tell him to be a little man and bear it.

Minna came.

"I shall be the next, pa."

"Not another elopement, my dear."

"No, pa. . . I want to send a piece of my wedding-cake to Annette. Will you give me away, Serge?"

"With all my heart."

Minna kissed her father and pulled his beard as she used to do when she was a little girl.

At the door of the greenhouse she turned:

"I shall have Gertrude and Mary for my bridesmaids. Won't they be pleased? . . ."

"Go to bed," said Francis.

"We gave Ma some hot gin and water to make her sleep," said Minna, and she winked at Serge. She went away light-heartedly, humming the Dead March in Saul.

Gertrude did not appear.

At half-past twelve Serge went up to his mother's room, peeped in, saw her sleeping, gently closed the door, and tip-toed away. He told his father.

"Thank God, for that," said Francis. "I was afraid she . . ."

He took up the lamp and began slowly to move when there came a peremptory ring at the front-door bell. The lamp in his hand rattled, and he went to open the door. He saw a policeman standing on the door-step. He was so startled and alarmed that he could find nothing to say.

"Anything wrong, constable?" asked Serge.

"The Reverend Mr. Folyat?"

"My name," answered Francis. "Anything wrong?"

"We've got a gentleman at the station; gave us your name for bail, Mr. Folyat."

"A gentleman?"

"Yessir. Drunk and obscene language."

"Have a drink, constable?" said Serge.

"Well, sir . . ."

They went into the study. The constable was refreshed, and told how an old man in a rusty green coat and a battered silk hat had been brought into the station and for many hours had refused to give his name or any information about himself. He was not known to the police. The arrest took place early in the afternoon. At eleven o'clock he had asked for bail, referred the police to Mr. Folyat and given his name, but no address. His name was James Lawrie.

"Good gracious!" exclaimed Francis. "Mr. Lawrie! Dear me! Poor gentleman. . . . Will you come with me, Serge?"

They went out as quietly as they could. With his hand on the knob of the front door Serge heard his mother calling from the landing:

"Serge! Francis! Frank!"

He closed the door and ran after his father and the constable, who were already some way up the street.

At the police-station they were kept for some time in the waiting-room until, escorted by a brawny officer, old Lawrie appeared before them. He was clearly only just roused from sleep. He looked extremely disreputable, with his hat hanging over one eye and his bushy white hair sticking out under the hat. His white beard was filthy with mud and blood. He stood blinking at the light and peering at Francis. After a moment or two he recognised him, removed his hat, and stood with bowed head.

"This is Mr. Folyat," said the inspector.

"Aye."

"Mr. Folyat will go bail for you. You must give your address, age, and occupation."

Old Lawrie mumbled so inarticulately that Francis was appealed to. He gave the address, age, and occupation of Bennett's father.

After a formality or two they were shown out politely, and old Lawrie was bidden to attend in court the next morning.

He said:

"Aye."

Out in the street he shook himself like a wet dog. Francis said kindly:

"I am sorry indeed to meet you again in such unfortunate circumstances, Mr. Lawrie."

"Blethers!" said the old man. "One prison is like unto another. Man. I've made a philosophical discovery of the first magnitude. The dirty soul of man was written on the walls of my cell. . . . When last we met—as they say in the plays—you were kind enough to listen to some verses of mine. What d'ye think of this?"

He took a deep breath, and blew out his chest.

"I composed it as I lay on the hard board in my cell. I wrote it on the wall among the rest, for the benefit and better understanding of my successors:

This place is but a room in Hell,

Damned for the punishment of thieves

Who steal their brothers' booty; for 'tis sure

The small thief starves on what the big thief leaves.

What d'ye think of it?"

"Admirable!" said Serge.

Old Lawrie turned to him:

"And who may you be? You've a bonny voice."

"My son," said Francis, glad to say something, for it had just occurred to him that this old lunatic was the father of his new son-in-law. He was infinitely relieved when Serge said in a whisper:

"I'll take him home. It's on my way."

They parted company as they came into the Burdley Road. Francis watched Serge and the shambling figure of the old man disappear into the darkness, and then, ruefully enough, walked home. It would be difficult, he thought, to persuade his wife to make light of old Lawrie's foibles.

"I shall never be able," he said to himself, "to make her see that Annette has married the son and not the father."

Indeed, when he told his wife of that night's adventure—and she kept him at it until half-past four in the morning—it became very clear to him that not Annette's secrecy nor her highhandedness nor her want of faith in her parents was one-half so bitter to her as the fact that Bennett was, with natural inadvertence, his father's son.

XXV
LAWRIEAN PHILOSOPHY

I now mean to be serious—it is time.

DON JUAN.

MEANWHILE Serge and old Lawrie became so interested in each other that they walked far into the night. It was Serge who opened the conversation:

"I gather that you will be charged with drunkenness and obscene language."

"Aye. When I'm fou I'm mighty full o' poetry. The exact words were 'bloody symbol.' The man probably thought I was referring to his vices. I told him he was a symbol of Society's hypocritical endeavour to suppress the consequences of its own villainy. My drunkenness is one of those consequences. It is the direct outcome of the habit of loneliness. . . . Did I talk to you about that before? . . . No. It would be your father. Have you ever been to prison?"

Serge regretted that he had never had that experience.

"It was a dirty cell they put me in, but it was shining with the truth, the blackguardly truth of all humanity. Man, I found there what I've been seeking these thirty years. . . . I wonder now if ye'll understand me. I would like to know what ye make of life, or if ye make anything of it at all."

"It seems to me simple enough," replied Serge. "A man is born. Two things lie before him, love and death."

"That's it. That's it. Now mark what I'm going to tell you. On the walls of my cell were drawings and writings—horrible drawings of women, lewd verses, and hysterical outbursts in the name of Jesus Christ. They were conventional, I admit, but that only makes it all the worse. It means that men are imprisoned in their own minds, debarred from woman on the one hand and from God on the other. You may tell me that my cell has been occupied only by lowest types, but if the Prince of Wales were to be incarcerated in it he would in time add to the collection of bawdy rhymes, and if he were followed by the Archbishop of Canterbury there would be one more such inscription as: 'Christ died to save me and the magistrate.' Some men are reduced to filthiness, some to hysteria, some to both. For the superficial and trivial purposes of existence such as the day's work, marriage, family duties, the so-called pleasures of society, they contrive to cover up their deplorable condition. Within themselves they are reduced to the most devastating loneliness. In their day-to-day prison of Society they do not write their thoughts on the walls (except for an occasional jubilant outburst over the successful issue of an amorous adventure), and it has remained for me to find in an actual acknowledged prison the frank revelation of the state of the human mind. . . . It has always been so. . . . Britons never shall be slaves indeed! They never have been, never will be, anything else."

Serge quoted:

"L'inconvénient du règne de l'opinion, c'est qu'elle se mêle à ce dont elle n'a que faire; par exemple, la vie privée. De là la tristesse de l'Amérique et de l'Angleterre."

"Aye," said the old man. "And what would the man that wrote that say if he could see our town and all the other towns, the rusty links in the world-wide thing the men of our time are so pleased to call industrialism? Men make everything in their own image. If you want to know what men are look at their towns, look at their houses, look at their books, their art. . . . At first, being human, ye'll be dazzled and pleased by the conceit and egoism that have gone to the making of them, but soon beneath the conceit and the egoism ye'll find nothing but fear—fear of death, fear of love; appeals to Jesus Christ from the one, abuse of women by way of escape from the other. Fools and blind! There's no escape. There's no good life but in the honest meeting of the one and the other. . . ."

"And women?" asked Serge.

"Their minds reflect only the minds of men. I think now that all the trouble, all the distress, and all the muddle come from the arrogance of men, who have always preferred the reflection of life in the flattering mirror of their minds to life itself. They have dropped the bone for the shadow, when they might have had both. They could have admired the shadow and eaten the bone; but, in the folly of their arrogance, they have thrown both away. . . . They must be almost as great a trial to God as they are to themselves. God is very merciful, since, though they will not love, yet He allows them to die. The mistake is understandable. A man's eyes, all his senses, assure him that he is the centre of the universe. Quite obviously his senses lie, but it is often difficult to see the obvious. There cannot be more than one centre of the universe, and, if a man will only reflect for a moment, he will see that all his neighbours, his dog, the tree in his garden—if he has a garden—every star in the sky, must be victims of the same delusion. Unhappily, though man has lived on this world for thousands of years, he has not yet made the small mental effort necessary for the slight correction of his senses. It has taken him thousands of years to discover that this earth on which he has his dwelling is not the centre of the solar system. That was a shock to his vanity, and his endeavour since then has been to prove his own all-importance in the scheme of things. He has turned to and pigeon-holed his knowledge and called it science. He has become increasingly adventurous and busy, simply because of the restlessness that has come over him on being confronted with his mistakes. He has discovered the whole habitable globe and proceeded to defile it. In my lifetime he has blundered into the discovery of steam-power, electricity, and they talk of oil as a generator of more power. I have seen many changes, but always it has come back to the same thing. The principles of life are few and simple. Every discovery puts a girdle round the earth, every invention that liberates man in body and mind makes the command sound clearly and more loud: 'Thou shalt love and thou shalt die. . . .' With every discovery however the egoism of mankind waxes more and more fat and they stop their ears to the command. They insist that they are the crowning achievement and purpose of creation—the old delusion, you observe, of being the centre of the universe. Those who are most strongly obsessed by this delusion thrust those in whom the conviction is not so strong away from their path or down under their feet. They thrust and fight their way to the centres of human organisation, which they mistake for the centre of the universe, the point at which their centre-hood can be most openly declared for all men to see. They thrust and fight their way to power, only to find themselves powerless, for, in spite of themselves, in spite of the lies with which they are fed and feed themselves, men do obey the laws of love and death. . . . But in such a way, such a halting, mean, decrepit, stealthy way!"

Here the old fellow paused, and Serge said:

"You have come to my contention that good and bad, for men and women, lie wholly in the use or the abuse of things."

But old Lawrie was so intent on his own thoughts that he seemed not to hear Serge. They came to the bridge under the Collegiate Church and leaned against the parapet. Oily black the river ran under the dark walls of warehouses and mills. The lights of the windows and the street lamps shone and flickered in the greasy depths of the tainted water.

"Yon river," said old Lawrie, "is like the life of a man. I know not where it rises, but it comes pure and sweet from the hill-side, meandering and murmuring through meadows, growing wider and ever wider in its irresistible and purposeful progress to the sea. In the towns and cities of men it becomes poisoned and poisonous, but, tainted as it is, it hastens onward to its goal. . . . I beg your pardon if I have obscured my meaning with parable. What I see, and what much bitter experience has taught me, is that there is evil enough lying in wait for men without their adding to the sum of it by mental and moral confusion. Say their place in the creation is the highest, say that in them life finds its keenest expression, should not their glory be the glory of service rather than the vain-glory of servitude? Why must they always be demanding applause for the work they do so ill? Is there any work that men have ever done—outside the arts—that could not have been done better? . . . I say there is none. And I have found the answer to all these questions only to-day, in my prison-cell. To a man diseased with egoism—and how many men are not?—love and death are hurtful things, for they are not flattering to his vanity. In the reflection of life in which men strive to live (for in that reflection their vanity can have free play, exactly as it can and always does when a man scans his features in a glass) love and death are not seen. All human codes of conduct and of morals, all dealings between man and man, are cut to fit the reflection and not life itself. . . . What, then, is human life?—what are the depths that sustain the yeasty turbulence of man's knavery and folly and dirtiness and hysteria? . . . A man is kin and comrade with all things living, from the great sun to the motes dancing in the sun's rays. He is a part of that radiance which rises from the centre of the universe and courses through the veins of every stone and every tree and every living thing. . . . Aye, such a power of life in a man, and such a comical small thing as he makes of himself! . . . Such a comical, small thing as I've made of myself! . . . Rapacity made this town what it is. Think what it might have been, what all towns might have been, if love had made them! . . . There'll come a time when Society will no longer be a prison walled off with fear of love and fear of death. The poets have not lived and sung for nothing. They'll cleanse the walls of the filth and the cry of bitter anguish; and when man has done with discovering the world and playing at conquerors and king o' the castle, he will come to the most glorious day of all when he shall know himself, what he is:

> *Great Nature spoke, with air benign:*
> *'Go on, ye human race!*
> *This lower world I you resign,*
> *Be fruitful and increase.*
> *The liquid fire of strong desire,*
> *I've poured in every bosom;*

Here, on this hand, does Mankind stand,
And there is Beauty's blossom.'

That's Robert Burns for ye! . . . Good night."

He walked away abruptly, and Serge only remembered then that he had intended to inform the old man of the fate that had befallen his son. More than ever he felt that Bennett and Annette were, in the main principle of their action, right, though they might be wrong in the details of their manner of doing it. The world would exact a heavy penalty of them. The world would be wrong.

Old Lawrie awoke next morning to find his wife standing by his bedside holding out a letter. It was from Mrs. Folyat and was extremely offensive. Old Lawrie read it:

"There's no doubt," he said, "that he's a son of mine."

He handed the letter back to his wife, turned over on his side and went to sleep again.

XXVI
MINNA'S CHOICE

It is always difficult to get rid of a woman at the end of a tragedy.

CHARLES LAMB.

THERE was no competition for the mantle of Annette. In the Burdley Park house the Folyats began to realise that they were increasingly uncomfortable. Annette's powers of organisation had not been great, but she had acquired considerable skill in preventing the consequences of her mistakes and laches being generally felt. . . . When she left there was a sort of domestic collapse. No meals were ever punctual, nor were they tolerably cooked. Mrs. Folyat's temper suffered, and she lashed her three remaining daughters with shrill sarcasm. . . . Mary had a sudden influx of new pupils and absented herself all day long. Gertrude arranged for a round of visits, and Minna became extremely zealous in church work, while Mrs. Folyat simmered in her indignation against the world in general, Annette in particular, and especially against love, that laughing enemy of public opinion. Not Annette's duplicity, not her secrecy, not her defiance of parental authority so rankled in her mother's mind as the black-and-white fact before all the vulgar, prying world that Bennett's father was not respectable. The unlucky Bennett had inserted an advertisement of the marriage—he read it many times himself: *Lawrie—Folyat. On the 28th Sept., Edward Bennett, youngest son of James Lawrie, to Annette, youngest daughter of the Rev. Francis Folyat;* for it was the first time he had seen words of his own in print. Lower down on the same page was a short paragraph describing his father's appearance in the police court, where, surely, the magistrate had seldom had such an entertaining quarter of an hour. Old Lawrie pursued the argument begun overnight with the policeman (Serge had the third movement of it) and closed it with variations on an idea borrowed from Ruskin, that, Society being responsible for every crime and misdemeanour committed by its individual members, lots should be cast in each case as to which citizen of a certain district should bear the brunt of it. This, he said, would at any rate promote a feeling of responsibility towards one's neighbour, and would in time lead each man to love his neighbour as himself. When that came about there would be neither crime nor misdemeanour.

"Till then," said the magistrate, "I must administer the law as it stands. I am not a philosopher, but it seems to me that the condition you aspire to does obtain. Men do love their neighbours as themselves: that is, very little." (Laughter.)

James Lawrie, cotton-broker and journalist, was fined ten shillings and costs.

The Lawrie family read the report and pretended that they had not done so. The Folyat family read it, and Mrs. Folyat, by continually explaining it away, forced it on the attention of many people who would otherwise never have heard of it. . . . She never forgave Annette. She declared that they, as a family, were utterly disgraced, would never hold up their heads again, that no one would ever call, that there was nothing to be done except for Francis to retire and them all to go and live in some place where no one had ever heard of them before. It was a splendid opportunity for her talent for inventing evils and calling monsters from the vasty deep, and she wasted no moment of it. With her own foolish tongue she set so many scandals going that, for a time, the clerical ladies were chary of calling. The scandals reached the bishop's palace and were inquired into. The bishop's wife, a kindly lady, laid them by calling, and, more, by sending, as she had not done for some years, an invitation to her garden-party. This so elated Mrs. Folyat that she forgot her gloom and tears and set Mary to work on her best black silk gown.

No member of the family, except Francis and Serge, visited Annette in her lodgings in the house of the German woman.

For the benefit of his mother and his fiancée, Frederic vowed that, when next he met Bennett Lawrie, he would horsewhip him.

"At least," said Mrs. Folyat for Serge's benefit, "I have one son who is a man."

They might refuse to visit Annette, but they could not forget her. Now that she was gone, they realised her more nearly than they had ever done when the whole burden of their comfortable existence rested upon her shoulders. Mrs. Folyat grew more and more querulous as the household fell into worse and worse confusion. She demanded an extra servant; Francis said they could not afford it. She dismissed the hobgoblin, now a fully developed gnome, and, one after another, engaged a series of incompetent, untidy, and immoral females. At last, when one of them corrupted the washerwoman—

the washing was done at home in those days on a Monday and Tuesday—and drew her into a wholesale conspiracy of theft, Mrs. Folyat, in despair, sent for Minna and implored her to take the burden of housekeeping off her hands. With a fair show of grace Minna set to, but it was not long before she went to see Annette. Annette was delighted. The days without Bennett were very long, and in their two rooms there was not enough work to occupy her hands for the morning; also, very frequently, she had no money at all and could not go out into the town. She thought, too, that Mina's coming was a sign that her mother was on the point of relenting. Annette never doubted that she loved her mother, and her disapproval often weighed heavily on her spirit.

With a child's pride in a new toy she displayed her two rooms and Bennett's handiwork on the walls and wood and the bulrushes he had painted in oils on the bathroom window.

"What an awful street you live in," said Minna.

"Is it?" Annette had never considered it æsthetically. It was the place she lived in, the scene of her honeymoon. She had filled it with romance and held it holy.

"Ma says," remarked Minna, settling herself largely in Bennett's wicker-chair so that she seemed to overflow it and fill the room,—"Ma says that she is quite sure Bennett will take to drink."

"I don't believe Ma could have said anything so odious."

"Then you don't know Ma."

Minna took stock of the room, and she was divided between pity and contempt for her sister—pity that she should live in such a poor place, contempt that she should be satisfied and pleased with it, and she thought with a shudder of the day when the scales should fall from the lovers' eyes and they should see themselves as they were, in that place, as it was. Minna had so often opened her heart to love only to expel it on finding it ridiculous that she could not conceive of any affection as permanently seated. She was like an inept gardener, who might plant spring flowers in his borders and deem it natural and inevitable that summer and autumn should be empty of all save weeds. She had cultivated a taste for falling in love, and always lost patience with it before she came to love.

She had come to ask Annette how she had contrived the more or less smooth-running of household affairs in Fern Square and Burdley Park, but found herself instead pondering marriage as here represented and also as applied to herself. She asked Annette what she did all day long. Annette told her: she sewed, mended, thought of Bennett, went out to buy his supper.

Round The Corner | 231

"A little different from home?" suggested Minna.

"Of course," replied Annette, "I'd like more people. It's hard to make it go all the day round when there's only one. But then, I read. I usedn't to be able to do that."

"How did you manage at home? I can't."

"I don't think I managed at all. Bennett says I'm an awfully bad manager. There were such a lot of things to do that they had to be done."

"How did you make the servant work?"

"I didn't. I did it all myself. If she did anything I generally had to do it all over again. She lit the fires in the morning and cleaned the boots and all the nasty work. I think in their own homes they leave all the rest undone."

Minna rose from her seat and demanded to be shown the bedroom. This was very ugly. She made a wry face.

"Do you like it?—being married, I mean."

Annette smiled. Musingly she said:

"What a silly question!"

Minna returned to Burdley Park little enlightened but uneasy and troubled. She went to the kitchen and worked, as she thought, very hard, and scolded the servant and lashed herself into a state of anger with things in general. By the evening she was entirely miserable. She sat down in her bedroom and wrote to Basil Haslam:

"I am miserable. Things are getting worse and worse. You have often scolded me for not taking things seriously enough. You little know me. Do men ever know women? Do they ever take women seriously? Don't they always fall back on the woman's instinct which they have invented as an excuse for their own silence and reticence? . . .

"I have been to see Annette. Poor child! It has upset me. I should like to see you—to-morrow, if possible. Can you come?

"Yours, M."

She also wrote to Herbert Fry, on a sudden mischievous impulse which she did not take the trouble to understand, she enjoyed it so thoroughly:

"I am going to be married, and I hope to come to London. This place isn't fit to live in, certainly not to be married in."

Her pen scrawled triumphantly as she added:

"Kind regards to Mrs. Fry.

"Yours, M."

She sent the letter to Mr. Fry's office address in London Wall. She did not know where he lived.

Basil Haslam came next day bursting with sympathy and high hope. Minna received him, for the sake of effect, in the kitchen. Like Charlotte, she was cutting bread and butter. She had sent the servant out on an errand.

Basil came in very quietly, and made Minna think of a young inexperienced doctor cultivating a bedside manner. However, she repressed her desire to tease him and said:

"I have learned my lesson."

"What lesson?"

"Something about a stalled ox."

She scraped the butter very thin on the bread by way of heightening her own sensation of a chastening poverty.

"We shall be very poor," she said.

"Oh, Minna! I will make you rich."

"I suppose there is a lot of money in London."

"Will you come to London with me?"

"Didn't I say so in my letter?"

Basil was always literal. He took out her letter and read it again.

"Stupid," said Minna. "I meant it if I didn't say it."

She laid down the knife and the loaf and submitted to her lover's embraces.

Basil could not contain his delight:

"There's my one-fifty a year. I can make three hundred the first year, five hundred the next, a thousand the next . . ."

"A thousand!"

"We'll live in a studio first of all. Then we'll live in a house and give dinner to the dealers and editors. And then we'll live in a house with a studio and the dealers and editors shall give dinner to us."

Round The Corner | 233

"That will be fun," said Minna.

Together they carried the tea-tray upstairs and broke the news of their engagement to Mrs. Folyat. Frederic and Jessie Clibran-Bell were there. They had been conspiring with Mrs. Folyat to bring about a speedy wedding. With the assistance of Mr. Clibran-Bell Frederic had been taking work on his own account and had made fifty pounds in a year. Herbert Fry had assisted him by letting him act as his agent—on condition that he had Frederic's agency work in London—and now there was talk of his setting up in an office of his own, if his father could guarantee him one year's expenses.

Mrs. Folyat set all this before Basil and Minna, and excitedly they planned a double wedding in two months' time.

Mrs. Folyat saw in this project the chance of wiping out the stain of Annette's offence.

Francis was approached that very night. He was for waiting. They could sell no more of their Potsham houses, or there would be no provision for their old age. (He had already begun to think dimly of retirement to the softer south and a garden.) Mrs. Folyat, however, had set her heart on the plan. She wheedled, cajoled, coaxed, scolded, suggested scheme after scheme, until Francis agreed to sell his life-insurance policy, but on condition that the proceeds were divided equally between his children with the exception of Leedham, who was married to a wealthy Portuguese widow, ten years his senior, in Rio . . . Mrs. Folyat pounced on that, and next morning saw to it that he began to take the necessary steps.

Twelve hundred pounds were raised by this means. Serge disapproved and disclaimed his share, so that the rest had two hundred and forty pounds each.

Frederic took an office near Serge's studio, engaged two clerks, and was regarded as sufficiently established to enter into the state of matrimony.

There was an entertaining wedding. Bennett and Annette were invited and formally taken back into the fold. Basil and Minna Haslam went to London to spend their honeymoon in the studio they had taken in Chelsea. Frederic and Jessie Folyat took a house next door but one to James Lawrie's. There were many tears shed over the brides, and after Mrs. Folyat had delivered herself of a sort of funeral oration *à la* Bossuet, Minna whispered to Serge:

"Ma always did love a theatrical performance."

"'Your son's your son till he gets him a wife,'" said Mrs. Folyat to Frederic, and then to Minna she completed the tag, "'Your daughter's your daughter the rest of your life.'"

It was a very exciting and a very happy day in the Folyat household. Mrs. Folyat chattered all the evening. Mary and Gertrude said not a word and went silently off to bed, so that Francis was compelled to escort his wife to her room and perform the innumerable little services she required.

"Doesn't the house feel empty?" she said.

Francis mumbled.

"I'm sure Annette is going to have a baby."

"M-m-m-m."

"I thought I was never going to be a grandmother."

"You always were impatient," said Francis in an unexpectedly loud voice.

That was criticism, which she could not abide. Francis rued his precipitancy. He was very unhappy about Frederic, but, he asked himself, what could he do? What could he do? There was no doubt that Jessie loved Frederic, but did not that, in itself, the more dangerously expose her to his folly and weak selfishness?

He hardly heard his wife's words as she went maundering on. In the darkness he prayed that all might be, as he tried to believe, for the best.

XXVII
GERTRUDE MAKES THE BEST OF IT

De quels ravissements nous privent nos intempérances.

JOUBERT.

WHEN Annette's baby—a boy—was born, Gertrude was the first to go and see it. She took with her a woollen bonnet and a horn spoon.

Having become capitalists with the enormous sum that had come to Annette, they had left their lodgings for a little house in a row of little houses each of seven rooms and a scullery. They had a little maid, who opened the door to Gertrude. She was a tiny wizened creature but very voluble. Gertrude was not a yard inside the house when she had a full description of the baby, its layette, Annette's condition and appearance, and the devotion of Bennett, who, she said, "never had no eyes for nothink 'cept 'is ugly little wife."

Gertrude was shown upstairs, to find Annette sitting up chattering to an enormously fat woman, who was introduced to her as Mrs. Entwistle. They were talking about Serge, of whom the fat woman expressed the most glowing admiration.

The baby, a very little one, ugly and blotched, was handed to Gertrude, and she was properly ecstatic over it. Mrs. Entwistle said:

"Eeh! Ow I did 'ave to slap 'is little buttocks to make 'im cry!"

"Slap?" said Gertrude, rather horrified.

"Eeh! Miss, didn't ye know that? Well, I never. Sometimes you 'ave to fair leather into 'em."

Gertrude held the baby in her arms and hugged him close to her breast. She was feeling very mournful, and envy tugged at her heart. She said:

"It's a very little house you live in."

"Isn't it? But we love it. It's just big enough for the three of us."

"How—how is Bennett?"

"Oh! He's very well, and he gets more money now, though still very little. I'm afraid we shall never have very much as long as he remains in business, and if he left it I suppose we should have nothing. But we don't think about it—much."

"You must be very happy."

Very mournfully Gertrude said this. She was disappointed. She had fancied that when she held Annette's baby in her arms she would feel all kinds of beautiful and exalted emotions. It was certainly pleasant to feel its warmth, and to hold it, so helpless as it was, gave her a genial sense of protection, but she was wanting, hoping for more than that. And when Annette replied that she was very happy—she looked it too—Gertrude realised painfully that she was brutally indifferent.

The starving cannot rejoice with the well-fed.

Gertrude felt her life trickling away through her fingers: worst of all, though she was not conscious of it, her desire for life was ebbing away from her. All the bitterness, all the hunger, all the hard envy in her heart she translated into one word: "Old." She said to herself: "I am getting old." . . . Having come to a concise and rounded thought she was pricked by it into revolt, and she said gently, at first, to Annette:

"I envy you. I remember you when you were a little girl. I have always thought of you as little, so that I have hardly known you. . . . And I must have always seemed to you beyond your reach. Now it is you who are beyond mine. Isn't it funny?"

She gave the child to Annette, watched it blindly wriggling against its mother's breast, and tears trickled down her nose on to the counterpane. Annette was so engrossed in her boy that she did not notice it, and Gertrude was at once ashamed of her tears, brushed them away, and angrily, in her heart, accused Annette of selfishness. She would have been so grateful only for a little pressure of the hand, a little smile, something that would bid her come into the circle of warmth, so radiant with the joy of the child. She was too timid, too much taken up with pity for herself, to force her way in. She dared not assume that she would be welcome, for she was too conscious of her own awkwardness.

She let slip the opportunity as she had spoiled so many. The conflict in her soul left her bruised and sore, and she almost hated Annette—Annette who had lied and cheated to take her lover. She turned from her thwarted emotion to sentimentality, raked over the ashes of the past, and artificially reconstructed the ruses and stratagems that she supposed Annette had used to capture Bennett during her absence. . . . With effusive cordiality

Round The Corner | 237

she kissed Annette and the baby and promised often to come and see it. A little awkwardly—she was not always tactful—Annette explained that Bennett's sister was to be the baby's Godmother. That gave Gertrude the handle she was seeking, and she persuaded herself that she had deliberately been slighted.

She went away almost without another word. On her way home she was thrust by her fancied injuries into contemplating her future. As people always do when they contemplate the future, she lost sight of the infinite gradations which led from the point at which she stood to the point on which her eyes were fixed, so that all her forward life was presented to her mental vision as acid, cold, bitterly assailing her without clemency. All her desire was to escape that future, and to evade the phantoms conjured up by her own mind—a mind very similar to her mother's and also infected by it—and to do so in a way that should, if ever so slightly, prick Annette's conscience . . .

Ideas are too often the gaolers of our souls, which, seeking health and freedom, groping out of prison, take counsel of the first-comer, an idea whom we have fee'd with prejudice and cowardice to stand guard over us. Gertrude, seeking freedom from her home, from her own folly, from herself, accosted the first-comer, Marriage, who, with a false smile, opened a door and clapped her into another cell. This, being larger than the other, she took for a place wide open to the winds of Heaven, and passed from querulous fear of the future to excitement in the immediate view. To be sure, she only saw four walls, but there was more light on them, more air and mystery between her and them. . . . Above all, nowhere in her cell could she see the figure of her sister Mary, whom she had begun to detest, nervously and irritably. . . . Mrs. Folyat had grown more and more incapable. The work of the house was divided between Gertrude and Mary. Between the two there was a grim struggle as to which of the two should make herself the less indispensable to her mother. It was very certain, as both knew in their inmost hearts, that if one of them were to be left, that one would remain for ever, with nothing to do save to turn the hour-glass when the sands ran out. Mary, being the weaker of the two, was the more good-natured, and it was for Mary that Mrs. Folyat most often called when she dropped her knitting-needle, or mislaid her spectacles, or lost her book by sitting on it, or wished to play Patience at some inappropriate hour. Everybody said Mrs. Folyat was a dear old lady. She liked the character, clung to it and abused it. Either Gertrude or Mary must be gobbled up by her selfishness. Both Gertrude and Mary believed that their mother was a dear old lady. They dreamed not that they were in revolt against her, but fancied—as it seemed more heroical to do—that they were at grips in a fearful struggle with life. They were both very near hysteria, Gertrude, after her visit to Annette, being the nearer.

There came to live near the town at this time Mrs. Bradby-Folyat, an aunt of the Folkestone Folyats, an old lady of much wealth, whose estate was continually being augmented by legacies bequeathed by irascible Bradbys and Folyats who were sickened by the attentions of their legacy-hunting poorer relations. Mrs. Bradby-Folyat left her relations alone, and the harvest of her wisdom was great. . . . Being a lady of strong character and almost masculine intelligence she had a great fondness for the weak and almost idiotic Streeten Folyat, who long ago had abandoned his sheep-farm in Westmoreland and wandered from one profession to another, shedding in each a portion of his patrimony. Between journalism and market-gardening he spent several months with his aunt at Boynton and amused himself in the town in Frederic's company. Occasionally he visited the house in Burdley Park. . . . Then he bought a small fleet of fishing-smacks at Scarborough, sold them after ten months at a heavy loss and returned to Boynton. His income had dwindled to four hundred. He bought houses in our town and was quickly embroiled in a law-suit—his idleness made him quarrelsome— and placed the case in Frederic's hands. By sheer luck Frederic won the case and delighted the old lady at Boynton, who insisted on considering that he had saved Streeten from ruin. She invited Frederic and his wife to stay with her, and entrusted him with the management of her estate. Frederic was almost delirious at this access of fortune, and calculated that if the old lady lived for another ten years he would make at least six thousand pounds. He was in debt—he could not amuse himself with Streeten for nothing—and he borrowed money from a friendly moneylender whose rate of interest per cent. *per mensem* seemed reasonable and low.

When Frederic was not at Boynton Streeten was at Frederic's house, and when Streeten was at Frederic's house there also was Gertrude. Streeten was amazingly vain, a fop, and as eager to scan his features in the glass as a little boy just on the verge of adolescence, who is beginning to feel that the eyes of the world are upon him. Such men, when no mirror is near, will turn to the nearest woman. If in her he can see the faintest reflection of himself, pat he will fall in love with it. . . . There were not many mirrors in Frederic's house. Streeten turned to Jessie but saw only Frederic, to Gertrude then, and he saw himself enlarged, heightened, dazzling. It was the most bewildering reflection of himself that he had ever seen, and at once he was prostrate before it.

Almost before he could realise what had happened he was picked up, thrust into a frock-coat and silk hat, taken to church, married to Gertrude, and packed off for a honeymoon to Ilfracombe. He was very bored and savage. He wanted to be at Boynton or amusing himself with Frederic.

It is one thing to steal glances at your own reflection when you think no one is looking, quite another to be married to it, though the mirror tell its tale never so constantly.

It were too cruel, it were indecent, to write of Gertrude's honeymoon.

XXVIII
MOTHER AND DAUGHTER

Life . . . is like love. All reason is against it, and all healthy instinct for it.

EREWHON REVISITED.

ON hearing of the capture of Streeten, celebrated in the most jubilant strain by Mrs. Folyat, with a magnificently unjust comparison of her new son-in-law with Bennett Lawrie, Minna wrote this letter to Mary:

"Mother Bub loves cutting her lamb up into chops. Did she fix him with an eye? You know how she can bore into the back of a man's neck. I'm almost sorry I missed the fun. I suppose she'll be better off than any of us. We're beastly poor, the studio's always in a mess and we can't get it straight. London is amusing but awfully big and callous. It makes you feel that it never cares whether you're there or not, and the river is almost the most human thing in it. Nobody seems to want Basil's work. I suppose there are thousands of Basils all wanting to do the same thing, and I suppose each Basil has a *me* wanting a great deal to eat and more pleasure and fun than is good for her, and not caring particularly how much of his soul he has to sell to give it her. The Folyats have a certain charm, but we're all selfish— except, of course, dear old Ma, who always would have it that we got our wickedness from Pa. Mother Bub has the charm of a basilisk, or a fly-paper. I hope she will come to London, as it will be nice to borrow money from her.

Dearest love, Mottle dear,

M.

P.S.—Basil has just sold a drawing. Sausages and mashed for supper! Also beer!

P.P.S.—Did Bennett go to the wedding? How grateful he must have been to Streeten for stepping into his shoes.

P.P.P.S.—I wouldn't get married if I were you. And to think I might have been a Countess! Willie Folyat lives in London—the Hearl of Leedham, if you please. I hear he's turned out a horrid little prig. I knew he would, I felt it in my bones. I have such clever bones.

M. H."

Mary was magnanimous and kept the letter to herself. She was essentially good-natured and bore no malice. She was amused by Minna's spite and did not believe a word she said. To her Gertrude was happy; she was married, therefore she loved her husband and her husband loved her. It was impossible for Mary to take a detached view, to tell black from white, good from bad. She was mentally short-sighted and her pleasures lay entirely in sentiment. She loved music as she loved nothing else in the world, but her pleasure in it was the pleasure of rhythm. Harmony touched her not at all. She had a sort of nervous sensitiveness which made her extremely shy and unresponsive. A kind of island existence was hers, and the island on which she dwelt was in a perpetual fog. Every sound that reached her from without—and little else but sound did reach her—was blurred. Voices more easily moved her than actions or the expressions of a person's face. She had always loved her father because of his soft, gentle voice, and when Serge was in the house she was animated and more quickly interested in what was going on around her.

She accepted her defeat by Gertrude docilely enough, gave up the majority of her pupils and much of her chamber-music and took up the reins of the household. With only her father and mother to provide for, it was fairly easy, and the expenses were so much reduced that she was able to pay more wages and to procure a better class of maid. Mrs. Folyat took a dislike to the maid, and all her service had to be performed by Mary herself.

Serge had fallen into the habit of taking supper with his family—his father and mother and Mary—nearly every Sunday evening, and he was exasperated by the petty attentions which his mother was continually demanding. He had tried many a time to find a way to the heart of this curious, stupid, yet gentle and kindly sister of his, but he had always found it impossible to set her thoughts moving. She seemed to have almost lost the capacity of thinking, and she had so little sense of humour that any blunt statement of fact hurt her as a direct attack. She showed in many ways that she was fond of him, but it was as a dog is fond, with a mute uncomprehending sympathy.

Serge fell back on action. Whenever his mother, in the metallic tones of her querulous mood, asked Mary to fetch her book from the other end of the house, or to unravel her knitting when she had dropped a stitch, or to read to her because her eyes ached, Serge bustlingly and rather ostentatiously forestalled his sister. There was never any sign that he had produced any effect on mother or daughter.

This went on for months. Existence in the house in Burdley Park passed smoothly and placidly, and Francis seemed to be happy, as he had never been, busy with his parish and greenhouse. He was silent for days together, except that every now and then he would hum tunelessly to himself, booming like a bumble-bee. He had every small joy that he asked of the world and was content. He liked the new generation of his parishioners better than the old, they were not so dour, and everything seemed to him to be going well and happily. He saw Frederic very seldom, and Annette very frequently, and Minna and Gertrude were regular correspondents. Serge had not for a very long time asked him for money, and for the first time for many, many years his expenses and income were on good terms with each other. Best of all, Mrs. Folyat had begun to see herself and her husband as a sort of Darby and Joan, and sweetened her conduct to fit the character. Everybody said you might go far before you could find a more delightful old couple. They achieved a sort of celebrity.

Mary too came in for her share of the general admiration, and her devotion to her mother was by more than one tyrannous old woman brandished over the head of a peevish and fading daughter. Mary recked nothing of it, and it would have made no impression on her if she had.

One Sunday, when her mother had rather explosively demanded her spectacles, and Serge without a word had gone down to the dining-room for them, and without a word had given them to her, a new idea came to Mary. She sat stupidly gazing at her mother and very slowly she began to think what would become of her if her father and mother were to die. There was a loud-ticking clock in the room, and it said with remorseless insistency:

"I-shall-be-alone."

This was a very dreadful idea to her. She strangled it.

There is no getting rid of thoughts. If they are strangled their corpses remain and rot in the mind, to its lasting detriment. This idea remained in Mary's mind, cold and dead, and gradually poisoned the sweetness of her nature.

A fixed idea is a dead idea.

Mary's temper suffered, and she vented her spleen on her pupils to such a degree that there came a time when she had only one left—the youngest daughter of the sausage-machine manufacturing widower, all of whose daughters she had instructed in turn in a polite mastery of the violin. Her bi-weekly visits to his house had become part of the routine of his household, and she was part and parcel of its furniture, being fitted into the heavy dinner-parties when there was a gap. At other entertainments she was never omitted and was as much part of their colour as the faded best chair-covers that were taken out for the occasion or the Japanese lanterns which illuminated them. She was useful, for she was always willing to play the piano for hours on end when the young people wanted to dance. To the widower, who never saw her on other occasions, she was always associated with gaiety.

One day he proposed marriage to her, and she refused him.

"Be sure," he said, "that I shall always be your friend. And I shall continue to hope."

He was really relieved at being rejected, and retired to cogitate the extraordinary impulse which had driven him to do such a thing. He felt very uncomfortable, for the fictions with which he had surrounded his dead wife had been shaken.

Mary left his house in a flutter. The man had always been kind to her, he was an admirable father, and she had always respected him as a solid man, though he was a little too Northernly solid to be taken altogether seriously. His house was very comfortable, though ugly and too reekingly prosperous, but the habit of years had made it a corner of the equilateral triangle of her life. Its atmosphere was altogether different from that of her home and delivered her from monotony.

Her only feeling about his proposal of marriage was one of surprise. She thought of it only materially and was not signally disturbed by it until he sent her an extraordinary letter in which he sought to explain away his behaviour. In the course of it he cut deeper in his contemplation of the marriage—having been married—and had, unwittingly, set his emotions stirring. Mary's emotions responded, but her modesty plucked them back. She did not, she told herself, "love" Mr. Hargreave, because, after all, he was only a common man who had begun life as a boy in a smithy. It had been easy enough when she thought of marriage as a mere translation from one house to another, but, quite clearly, he was asking for a personal relation, and from that she shrank, chiefly because it was a change from the custom of years. When she desired a concrete objection she fished out from the confusion in her mind the prejudiced idea that she would be a stepmother; worse than that, a stepmother to children to whom she had been a paid instructress, children moreover who had, upon occasion, been so cruel to her that she had been unable to retort upon them or to maintain discipline.

. . . She read Mr. Hargreave's letter once more and saw that she could not easily enter his house again, except it were to leave her home.

She left the matter for a day or two, did not reply, and failed to attend for Violet Hargreave's violin lesson. A day or two more and she received another letter from Mr. Hargreave in which he completely abased himself, and, in his desire to be kind and to palliate the affront he conceived himself to have put upon her, waxed tender and was almost lyrical in her praises.

She tried to write to him but could find nothing to say. Tears rolled down and plopped on to the paper, and she grew hot and impatient with herself. Clearly she must go to his house and reassure him. No sooner had she resolved on that, than she felt that she could not explain herself, that he would renew his proposal, and she would have to say either "Yes" or "No." If "Yes," then a thousand and one objections would rise in her mind. If "No," then it would become impossible for her ever to enter his house again.

She dried her eyes and resolved that she would go there and then and get it over. It was evening. She could ask for one of the Hargreave girls, leave a piece of music; she was familiar enough at the house; no one would suspect the undercurrent.

As she went downstairs her mother called to her. She could not find "Johnny Ludlow" anywhere, and what had Mary done with it, and why was she so careless?

"I am not careless," replied Mary. "You were reading it yourself. You must have left it in your room."

"Johnny Ludlow" was found behind the cushions of Mrs. Folyat's chair. Mary felt a gust of impatience as she gave the book to her mother. She sat down suddenly, and with a desperate gulp she said very quickly:

"Mr. Hargreave has asked me to marry him!"

"You, my dear . . . Mr. Hargreave! He must be nearly sixty!"

The word "sixty" chilled Mary.

"Fifty-one," she murmured.

"An old man like that . . . Really he ought to be ashamed of himself. He ought to be preparing himself for his eternal life instead of thinking of a wife. . . . And with all those children too."

Mary's sense of justice was offended.

"A great many widowers marry again for the sake of their children, don't they?"

"But Mr. Hargreave has two grown-up daughters."

Again there was a chilly catch at Mary's heart, and she had a lump in her throat. She said:

"No one else has ever asked me to marry."

It needed melodrama to move Mrs. Folyat; tragedy or tragi-comedy left her blank. She was in no mood for general consideration, for she was thinking with cold practicability of the need of the moment. When she thought of the house without Mary it was as a place of absolute silence. There were many evenings when Francis said never a word; many again when he sat alone in his study or working in his greenhouse, and only came up just before it was time to go to bed. Mrs. Folyat had a horror of silence. . . . Mary must not go, she thought, Mary must not go. She came swiftly to the point and asked:

"Have you accepted him?"

Unreasonably, in the face of experience, Mary had been expecting sympathy; she so craved it. For a flickering moment she desired almost viciously to lie, but she was hurt into truth.

"No," she said.

Mrs. Folyat sighed with relief and triumph.

"Of course you couldn't," she said. "He is such a common man. . . . Let us play Bézique."

Mary fetched the cards and they played until Francis came up at ten o'clock. She let him take her hand and went downstairs to the kitchen to brew her mother's chocolate. She had lost all interest in Mr. Hargreave, and she felt nothing at all.

In her bedroom that night she found it quite easy to write to him. She said that she trusted him to understand that she could not marry him, and that it would be best in the circumstances if he found another teacher for Violet. He had (she continued) always been very kind to her. She was very grateful to him, and would think well of him, but her duty lay towards her father and mother.

So, without any ill-feeling she slipped into the part designed for her by her mother.

As she was writing to Mr. Hargreave, her mother said to Francis:

"My dear, what do you think? That horrid old Hargreave has actually proposed to Mary. Of course she refused him."

"Poor Mary," said Francis.

XXIX
DISCUSSION

Will kein Gott auf Erde sein?
Sind wir selber Götter.

W. MÜLLER.

THROUGH the years Father Soledano had remained a fairly frequent visitor at the house of the Folyats. His was the only really constar.t intimacy that Francis enjoyed, and it was based on the kinship of their humour and their common taste for mental caricature. Both strangers to our town and dwelling outside its activity, they loved to foregather and burlesque its politics, its manners, and its worship of money. Father Soledano went further than Francis and poked his fun at English institutions, though then he became malicious and Francis could not see eye to eye with him. Francis had no politics save a dislike for Mr. Gladstone and a distrust of Benjamin Disraeli and Lord Salisbury, and he knew too little of modern English literature to be able to appreciate the priest's sarcasms at the expense of Carlyle, Ruskin, George Eliot, or Robert Browning. He had never heard of George Meredith, but he became almost angry when Soledano scoffed at Dickens and Thackeray. . . .

Their discussions used to take place on Sunday evenings in the study, and it often happened that Serge was present. One Sunday night when, as often happened, Soledano, harked back to the Manchester murders, he launched out upon a violent assault upon England, and quoted once more words that were often upon his lips, words of the mother of Charles Stewart Parnell:

"'The English are hated everywhere for their arrogance, greed, cant, and hypocrisy. They want us all to think they are so goody-goody. They are simply thieves.'"

"Oh! come, come," said Francis, "not so bad as that. After all we have given the world a good deal and showed the way to other nations in many things."

"You have shown the other nations how to steal."

"I don't think any nation, or any collective body of men who have pooled their sense of right and wrong need much instruction in that," said Serge. "It is simply a question of stealing from a body of men weaker than themselves. Men in the mass are abominable. There isn't anything to choose between England and France, or Italy, or the new German Empire or America. England has been more successful than the rest and has therefore had more opportunity of doing harm. . . ."

"Good as well," put in Francis. "Good as well."

"Only incidentally and by accident," retorted Soledano. "What I contend is that you cannot have collective villainy and individual virtue, collective bad action and individual good action."

"You can't indict a nation," said Serge.

"I can and I do."

"Then you are not so clever as I thought. There is no such thing as collective action, there is only the action of individuals. You herd men together so that they may carry out the will of individuals, and, as in the present condition of society, the most cunning and cold-blooded and unscrupulous men survive to exercise their wills over the herd. What is produced by the herd is almost always bad, because their efforts are directed only towards base ideals. . . . In the long run it may be a good thing to gather men together into huge masses for the easier and more expeditious creation of wealth and the means of subsistence. I don't know. I can't see into the future. But you and my father know—who better?—how the poor are being ground down in this town, and it must be the same in every other. What appals me is that there is no sort of corrective to the base ideal of success and accumulated wealth and what is called power except the blind revolt of nature in man and woman—especially woman. There is absolutely nothing. There are a certain number of artists in this town, men of my own trade, but they all seem to be doing their work from the dealer's point of view, to produce a saleable article, and not for the sheer delight of exercising a talent, without which the result cannot give delight. The theatres are even worse: they are fed from London with stupid replicas of pieces designed to give the illusion of pleasure rather than pleasure itself. The newspapers will soon be nothing but advertising sheets. It will soon be impossible for any man to do his work with any joy in it. It is bad enough when a man wastes himself in feeding his own vanity, but when he is used only to feed the vanity of another man then there is absolutely no hope for him. There might be something said for an arrangement by which a man gave a certain number of hours of his day to joyless work, so that during the rest he can take joy in other things. But all these men who are doing work in which there is no reward at all are paid so little that they are shattered by financial anxiety. They marry wives whom they cannot afford to keep and produce children whom it is impossible for them to feed and educate. . . . England is in a bad way, Father. It seems to me rather unfair to attack her when she is down."

"The greatest Empire the world has ever seen!" said Father Soledano mockingly.

Francis looked thoughtful. He lit his pipe and said:

"I wish I understood what you are talking about, Serge."

"I want a corrective," answered Serge. "All this material organisation may be a good thing in the long run, but spiritual health is every bit as important as physical health—more. They're organising education now, but towards no ideal save the base ideal of cunning unscrupulous men—self-help, and all that. A man's life consists of only two things, work and love. At present love is wiped out of consideration altogether, and work is regarded as a damned unpleasant thing that has to be stomached. At present a man must be either a slave or an employer of slaves, that is, a slave who is promoted. If you promote a slave to the condition of a free man he goes bad, because he has the soul of a slave and cannot live except under tyranny. If he escapes from the tyranny of a man he seeks that of his own vices. . . . If you educate men as slaves they will be slaves, just as your Loyola said, Father—every child who passed through the Jesuits' hands remained theirs for ever. . . . You get revolt every now and then as in the French Revolution and in 1848, but that is nothing but the desire of the slaves of poverty for the slavery of wealth."

"Christopher Sly," said Soledano, "will always be Christopher Sly. If you are stupid enough you can stand anything. Men are stupid. That is the whole story. When you have said that you have said everything."

Serge brought his fist down on the table.

"I don't believe it. If, inspired by a base ideal, they can do all that they have done, they can, when inspired by a noble ideal, the simplest and most beautiful of all, the ideal of a life of love and work, do better yet and gain material well-being in justice through spiritual health."

"Bah!" said Soledano. "That is your English idealism. Men can only understand a base ideal. They are impelled only by one instinct—hunger. They are terrified of hunger and fight only to protect themselves against it. All their other instincts, even the instinct of reproduction, have to take their chance—a very poor one. Also my friend, your idealism is just a joke to women. Life is too serious, too immediately appalling for them, for they are just as cruelly driven by their instinct of reproduction as they are by the instinct of hunger."

"Very well, then," said Serge, "drop the idealism and call it practical good sense. Concentrate on the instinct of hunger and the instinct of reproduction and organise for the satisfaction of both."

"It is impossible. You are asking men to be intelligent. The English will never be that."

Father Soledano said good-night to Francis and held out his hand to Serge.

"I'm coming with you," said Serge.

"Still unconvinced?"

"Absolutely convinced that I am right."

They drove back in a cab to the priest's house in the asphalted courtyard under the cathedral.

"Will you tell me," asked Serge, "how you reconcile what you have said this evening with what you say in your Church?"

"I don't."

"Can you go on?"

"Like the rest of the world, I do what I am told. If I examined and scrutinised everything that I was told to do I should do very little of it. . . . On the whole we do good. We save a certain number of men from sinking into brutality, and to a certain number of others we give an outlet for their emotions, which amounts to the same thing."

"How much do you believe of what you tell them?"

"I have never examined my belief. Like your father, I do what I am told to do. Suppose I renounced my faith and the priesthood. My place would be taken by another. There are too many men, my friend, too many women, and life moves both too slowly and too swiftly . . . What can you do? You say that the good life consists wholly of work and love. Then work, my friend, and love. There is nothing to prevent you. I also work, and I also love. Very lovingly I despise men, because I know them, as you, I think, do not."

"Quite candidly, it seems to me cowardly and rather despicable to teach men to believe in another life beyond the grave."

"Life, as it is, must be made supportable."

"From within, not from without."

"You seem to be levelling an accusation at my Church, but you must be just and observe that we do display, for the benefit of the men whose souls are our care, a certain faith in the next life by renouncing the pleasures of this."

"You stifle an instinct. That seems to me as great a sin as abusing it by excess of the pleasure derived from its satisfaction."

"I find your point of view interesting, but too naïve and simple. The idea of original sin may be fanciful, it may have its origin in Oriental myth, but there is contamination from some source or other."

"Simply from a wrong interpretation of life. I say it is possible for men to understand life."

"It is quite impossible. They can only live it."

"Then there is absolutely no meaning in all their activity, all their inventions, all their discoveries . . ."

"I can see none. They are still the slaves of hunger. When you appease the hunger of the body there remains the hunger of the spirit."

"Exactly, and I contend that in the hands of intelligent men the machinery in their power could satisfy the bodily hunger of all men, and set them free to find satisfaction for the hunger of the spirit. . . . As I see it, it is towards that that the world is tending. There will be a great deal of cruelty and oppression by the way, but there will come a time when man's mastery of the world will be so great that anything save the most elastic organisation will make life intolerable for rich and poor alike. As you say, if you are stupid enough you can endure anything. Men are more intelligent now than they were fifty years ago. They will be ten times as intelligent fifty years hence. . . ."

"Look at home, my friend. Look at home."

"I do. And it is just that absurdly pathetic tragi-comedy that makes me scan the world to see what hope there is for future generations. . . . You make the mistake of taking men as you find them. I take myself and discover what I might be, to what I might grow if I could get my fill of friendship, and affection, and love."

"Love is of God."

"God is in Man. I take myself, as I say. There is much in myself that I despise, even as you despise men, but there is in myself an essence which I know to be unconquerable and free. That you translate into another world and call God and eternal life. You postpone freedom, because to you the crust of slavery seems impenetrable. I want freedom for that essence in myself here and now. It is the fiercest instinct in me, stronger than hunger, stronger than reproduction, which are only by the way. What I find in myself I believe to exist in all other men."

"But then," said Father Soledano, "you have never done as you were told."

Serge laughed and took his leave.

XXX
FREDERIC IN THE TOILS

O, you shall have him give a number of those false faces ere he depart.

EVERY MAN OUT OF HIS HUMOUR.

SUPERSTITION will have it that marriage is a good thing, and, being one of the most powerful agents in human affairs, forbids discussion of its pseudo-axiom. Superstition uses marriage as a club with which to lay men and women low. Sincerity insists on examining marriage, and discovers that there is no such thing, as superstition interprets it. Society does not marry people, neither does the Church. Society and Church can only record what they are told. Men and women marry themselves by as much free will as they possess, and their marriage will be good or bad or both in the degree in which they are good or bad or both. If their marriage is good it will endure. If it is bad it will come to an end and it will none the less be at an end though superstition insist that the parties to it continue miserably to dwell under one roof and never seek outside it the love they have suffered to escape. Superstition refuses to countenance divorce—a dissolution of the bond as free as the making of it—and smiles blandly upon every hideous captivity so long as it comes not to public knowledge. . . Superstitious persons are perpetually setting their faces against Nature's subtle and ingenious provisions for every emergency, but, it is to be observed, that if you set your face against anything in Nature, it will simply go round the other way and hit you in the back of the neck, exactly at the moment when you are congratulating yourself on having made a comfortable provision for the mature years of your life and a ripe and venerable old age.

They were very superstitious persons who lived near Frederic and Jessie Folyat, and they smiled benignantly upon their young marriage. Every morning several old ladies and more than one old gentleman peeped out of their dining-room windows to see Jessie walk down the garden on Frederic's arm and kiss him at the little iron gate.

"Ah!" they said, "young love! Young love! There is nothing like it."

And this in the face of their own appalling experience and the fact that Frederic and Jessie were neither of them very young: but superstitious persons realise very little of all that happens to them and they see even less of what is presented to their eyes. It was enough for these people that Jessie and Frederic were newly married, and they kept them in their minds as newly married long after they had settled down and the exciting novelty ha 1 given way to day-to-day habit.

Frederic never saw the heads at the windows as he hurried away to his office, but Jessie saw them, and more for them than for any satisfaction of her own she maintained the practice of kissing her husband. In the evening she would go down to the little gate and kiss him again as he arrived.

"Ah! Lucky man!" the audience would sigh in their withered, sentimental old hearts.

When Frederic did not come Jessie would turn and visibly wilt under the gaze of the superstitious persons, who muttered to themselves:

"Poor little bride! Poor little bride!"

At length there came a time when on four evenings in succession Frederic did not come, and on the fourth evening Jessie could not bring herself to turn and walk up the path alone. She went out into the street, round the corner, and in at the kitchen door, and not again for a long time did she go down to the little iron gate in the evening.

Frederic was a liar of the common type, which indulges in absurd and useless exaggerations. When he bought a neck-tie at a cheap hosier's for half-a-crown he would say he got it at a more fashionable shop for seven-and-six, though the name of the maker was sewn inside it. When he borrowed money he would ask for three times as much as he wanted. When he walked three miles he always stretched them out to ten. His lying was for his own benefit first of all, and it was to help in deceiving himself that he extended it to other people. His income was always estimated at at least three times too high a figure, and his expenditure, which also he blew out to convince himself of the truth of his estimate, always exceeded it. Jessie had two hundred a year: he persuaded himself that she had five hundred, and forced many quarrels upon her because she came to him with bills for household expenses. . . . Time and again did Jessie find him out in his lying, but, as he always carried it into their intimate relation and multiplied the nothing that he gave her to the nth power, she was appeased; but imperceptibly she was contaminated, and in spite of her many anxious moments as to their solvency, contracted the habit of lying to her family as to her affairs and the state of Frederic's business. This was, in fact, unhealthy. Outside the management of the Bradby-Folyat estate there was very little work that could bring in any solid profit, though in his office there was an air of bustling activity due to the fairly constant stream of small county-court and police-court cases, which came to him as a tribute to his prowess as a liar. Being what is called a gentleman, he could lie from a coign of vantage, and a number of small shopkeepers and shady customers came to Lawyer Folyat, though, when there was any danger of a skilful cross-examination, they soon learned to avoid him. Still, there was enough business in the office to go to Frederic's head: he was one of those men who are perpetually intoxicated, though they never touch alcohol and may be, frequently are, ardent temperance reformers. Every case that came into his office became four or five in his mind, and he never doubted but that he was building up a large, solid, and flourishing business. He had all the air of a successful man, hoodwinked many innocent persons and very soon had two young men as articled clerks, whose premiums went to swell his banking account. He was what is called generous, gave for the pleasure of being thanked, and lavished presents on his wife, his mother, his mother-in-law, his sisters, and Jessie's sisters. He thought for a long time of paying his father back some of the money that had been disbursed for him, thought it over so long that at last he believed he had repaid it and patted himself on the back as a dutiful son. . . . When he had moments of doubt—and they were very awful when they came—he would go to his mother and she would cluck over him like an old hen, and tell him he was the most grateful, the most affectionate, the most generous, and truly thoughtful of her children. He would gulp down her flattery and win back to self-deception, without which it had become impossible for him to face his wife, whom he was for ever pestering with absurd questions like "Do you love me?" "How much do you love me?" "Would anything ever make you cease to love me?" And when she replied as best she could with exaggerated demonstrations he hardly listened to her. . . . Truly in their relationship it was he who played the feminine part.

When Jessie was with child he lied to himself about his son, saw himself building up a great firm for his inheritance, and from the very first moment being a hero to the little fellow. He began to feel irresistible and so tormented his wife with his swaggering that she protested by mentioning one or two awkward little facts. She brought down on herself such a storm of anger that her nerves gave way and she had a fit of hysteria. . . In a week she was brought to bed of a miscarriage.

She was not very ill, but she suffered terribly, for Frederic hardly spoke a word to her for ten days, and then he arranged for her to go and stay at the sea alone, unless she chose to take one of her sisters with her. She would not do that and she went alone. He promised to spend Saturdays and Sundays with her, but at the end of each week he declared that it was impossible for him to get away. . . . He was hardly responsible for his actions. The most glorious fiction he had ever created had come toppling down and he was not altogether to blame for the breach which gaped so wide between himself and his wife that he could not avoid seeing it. She, too, had missed her opportunity, for she was so oppressed by the physical ugliness of the calamity that she was frozen by it and could not give him the warmth that might have saved him from still further floundering in the morass. . . . As it was, he was savagely resentful against her and missed not the pettiest occasion of hurting her. Under this treatment her love died almost without a struggle, so painlessly indeed that she attributed all her hurt and her agony to the discovery that came to her by the sea, that Frederic had never loved her. She saw that clearly and was instantly filled with dread lest she should betray herself and let him feel that she knew. . . . Every letter she wrote to him was carefully framed to convey a picture of herself as loyal, tender, devoted, proud, and—with the most cunning falsity of all—admiring. These letters soothed Frederic. He had found it difficult to admire his own brutality, though, as he moved further away from it, it was distorted by the prism of his vanity into something very like strength. That accomplished, it became an easy task to cover over the unpleasant fact of the disaster so that it became as a pearl upon his shell.

He was loftily forgiving when Jessie returned, and she was softly, cushionly submissive. For the first time—love being dead—she let loose upon him the full force of her sex. He was still sensitive enough to feel repelled, even as he yielded.

Their house was filled with stealthy shadows. It grew darker and darker. Each sought to illuminate it with lies, lies, and yet more lies.

At first, as usual, his lies gave him the illusion of greater freedom, and he heightened the illusion by treating Jessie with less and less consideration. He gulped down the forced admiration she gave him and was always trying to squeeze more of it out of her. When he was in a mood of self-abasement she admired the loftiness which could stoop to acknowledge its defects, and quickly he was riding off again with his head full of himself as the kindest of husbands, the best of sons, the most irresistibly successful of men. Such glaring divergence presented itself to his mind as consistency.

Such a state of things imposed a heavy strain upon Jessie. She was not always quick enough to follow him in his snipe-like flights. Sometimes when he was accusing himself of neglect and thoughtlessness and lack of consideration for her, it seemed to her that it would be easiest and might afford both of them relief if she agreed with him. Then his vanity writhed and furiously he would cry:

"You are always finding fault with me. . . My mother thinks me perfect."

It is impossible to be wise where love is not, and Jessie could not learn discretion. He was so extraordinarily convincing in his self-reproach that she always forgot the lessons of caution she had set herself in his absence.

Still he would force endearing phrases upon her and caresses and demand to be told that she loved him. Her parrot-cries appeased him, and, feeling confident that she loved him, in stealthy small ways he began to betray her, indeed, where before he had only dared to be false to her in thought. He absented himself from his house to seek the company of flattering fools. He returned at longer and longer intervals to stoke up the furnace of his wife's love. . . . He was like a child who, having built a house of cards, removes first one card and then another from the base and leaves only enough to keep the edifice ominously swaying.

Do what he would, Frederic was slowly forced into retreat. It is impossible for life to stand still. If it cannot move forward it will plunge backward. Life is for ever seeking its channel, love. . . . Frederic was borne backward, and it was not long before he came to the thought of Annie Lipsett. Easily he persuaded himself that he had been treated with injustice, and thwarted by interference from doing what was right. Pitying himself, he began to pity her, and, in a tremendous orgy of self-righteousness, told himself that he ought to make amends, and at least, even if he could do nothing, let her know that he had not forgotten her. It did not occur to him that she might have forgotten him: impossible to conceive that she could wish to.

Though he was on a considerably more amiable footing with his father, he could not broach the subject with him. As far as Francis was concerned it was buried, and was not to be exhumed. Frederic turned to Serge, and by hints and semi-questions drew his own conclusion that Serge was still in touch with Annie. He left it at that and waited, and took to frequenting Serge's company enough to form a fairly accurate idea of his habitual movements. These still included frequent excursions into the country, for Serge found a good market for water-colour drawings of the semi-urbanised fells and dales of Lancashire, and the little towns so tucked away into a narrow valley that from one side of them you could see across the smoke to the hills and the green country beyond.

One day, when he knew that Serge was out on an expedition, Frederic visited his studio and ransacked it. He found two letters from Annie Lipsett and from them became possessed of her history. Serge's friend, the farmer, had married six months before and Annie had had to come to town again to earn her living as best she could. Serge had procured her a situation in a dressmaker's, and she was in lodgings in a suburb not very far away from Annette's little house.

Frederic wrote a very cautious little letter on his office paper, and, in a spasm of jealousy of Serge, enclosed a five-pound note. The money was returned two days later without any reply. He sent it back again, imploring her to take it if she had a single friendly thought of him or any wish for his happiness. (He heaved an enormous sigh as he wrote the word—happiness). The five-pound note was returned again. He guessed, rightly, that Serge was responsible, and he swore that he would not be ousted from his rightful position as benefactor to the woman he had wronged. Was not his own happiness wrecked? Could he not, by this means, restore it? . . . He was persuaded that he could.

He left his office early, and with a hectic sort of elation in the adventure—it was so much more exciting than the idea of returning home—set out to discover the house in which Annie Lipsett lived. He waited at the corner of the street until he saw her coming. She was with Serge. Furiously he turned and strode away.

The next evening he waited for her. She was alone. With Byronic gloom he stood in front of her and said:

"Annie!"

She caught her breath and stepped back a pace.

"Please," she said. "No! I thought you would understand."

"I understand nothing," said Frederic; "nothing except that my life is miserable, wrecked, a thing of captivity and torture."

"You mustn't come to see me. It isn't right. . . . Your . . ."

"It is right," said Frederic. "It has all been wrong, but this is right."

(He knew his language was stilted, but he could not give himself time to revise it.)

Annie said simply:

"Please, Mr. Frederic, it isn't any good. It was all over long ago. Your way and my way aren't the same."

Frederic walked with her down the street, and found it hard to keep up with her, she went so swiftly. He made one last effort and said:

"I want to see the child . . . Our own was . . ."

Annie had heard about that from Serge. She turned to him and held out her hands:

"I'm so sorry. . . . You shall see him just this once, if you'll promise me never to come again . . . and he is not to know who you are. He has never heard of you."

The unconscious cruelty of her words did not penetrate Frederic's mind. The situation appealed to him as a situation. He was becoming a connoisseur, and the ironically bitter savour of this tickled his palate. With offensive humility and gratitude he said:

"Thank you . . . Thank you."

The boy was in bed sleeping, with the clothes tumbled by his restlessness and his arms flung across his face.

"He is such a good boy," said Annie; "he has always been good and happy."

"He is like you," said Frederic. "I am glad I have seen him. I am glad to have found you again."

"Will you go now?"

Frederic was startled. Her simplicity and gentleness had sobered him. He had grown so used to swaggering from situation to situation that it was alarming to find this, which should have been the most touching and moving and the most honourable to himself, dissolved by the light touch of sincerity. It was all the more disconcerting, inasmuch as he had made no allowance for change in Annie. In their previous acquaintance she had been as adroit and as eager as he in the game of False Positions, which is the principal occupation of human beings all the world over. He had taken her rejection of his proffered assistance as another move in the game, and lo!— here she was simply ignoring the past and out of a purely general sort of friendliness allowing him to see her son, and when he had seen, requesting him to go! He was humiliated, but still so astonished that, though all his desire was to play upon her pity and so to drag her back to the old footing, he could not find words keen enough for his purpose. He heaved great sighs and fixed her with sorrowful and yearning eyes, but she gazed only at the child, busied herself with his bed, put up her hand to the gas jet and waited until Frederic was out of the room before she turned it low.

He waited for her in the passage.

"Tell me," he said, "how you are off for money. You shall not want. . . ."

"I make my living. I like my work."

"I couldn't bear to think of you suffering through me."

Annie looked at him with that disarming directness that was unfamiliar to him:

"I have suffered," she said.

Frederic went away.

It was not long before he had persuaded himself that she had deliberately plotted to humiliate him, by meeting his generosity—had he not been generous?—with what he called "beastly pride." Generosity, in his dual scheme of the world, should find its complement in a grovelling gratitude. Generosity was the prerogative of the male, gratitude the privilege of the female. That a woman should show self-reliance and fling back a man's generosity, suspect him most of all when he brought gifts, offended him as an indecency . . . After all if the woman does not take her cue from the man where is he? How can he continue to play his part? What becomes of the human drama?

Frederic's reflections of course were more particular than this, but, generalised, they would amount to the same thing. The world (*i.e.* Frederic) was so dishonest that honesty (*i.e.* an honest person, Annie) seemed to be offending against all the rules of the game, and, since the world is under the illusion that its whole existence depends on the game, it devotes its energy to the suppression of honesty. . . . Frederic told himself that he had a right to assist the woman, who was defiantly happy in the face of her sin, while he, her partner in that sin, was properly wretched and conscience-stricken and honestly desirous of making amends. He would obey his conscience—that must be right!—regain his self-respect and compel gratitude from Annie.

"We shall see!" he said, having partially restored his belief in his own rectitude and irresistibility.

He took to sending toys and little garments for the boy. They were returned to his office.

He went to Annie's rooms to find that she had flown. The devil of obstinacy was roused in him, and he bribed her landlady to procure her new address. He called but was refused admittance. . . . Then one morning he waited and followed her to her place of business and thereafter waylaid her several times. She was quite amiable but absolutely unyielding. One day as he was walking along by her side breathlessly pouring into her ear a tale of self-pity, self-accusation, self-abasement, entreaty for forgiveness, a word of kindness, extravagant out-pourings of love for the boy and his brave, splendid, true-hearted mother, all mixed together most adroitly with a complacent masculine belief in the softness and gullibility of the female heart, they met Serge. Annie called to him. Serge came at once.

"Take me home," she said.

Frederic caught hold of her arm and solemnly abjured her not to break his heart, to believe in him, to believe that he only was her friend. . . .

"Let her go, you swine," said Serge, and thrust Frederic away.

They were in a crowded thoroughfare. It had been raining and the streets were very muddy. It was evening and clerks and shop assistants were hurrying home. No one paid any attention to the little group. The stream of people parted, passed round them, closed again, and moved on. . . . The cold anger in Serge's tone infuriated Frederic. He saw it all now. It was Serge who was thwarting him. Serge who at every turn was thrusting humiliation upon him. He lost count of everything in hatred of Serge. He had a stick in his hand. He raised it and struck blindly. The stick was wrenched away, he received a terrific blow on the point of his chin, his feet slipped from under him, and he went down. . . . By the time he was up again Serge and Annie had disappeared. No one paid him any heed, only, a few yards away, grinning from ear to ear, he saw the boy from his office.

He hailed a cab and drove home. Jessie was alarmed at his condition, but her alarm gave way to pride as he told her how he had seen a man break a shop-window and run away with a handful of jewels—a huge, burly man, and how he had given chase, caught up with him, and after a tremendous struggle—the man knew a good deal about wrestling—held him until the arrival of the police. . . . What with the soothing influence of having his wounds tended, and the interest of his story, Frederic found it not at all difficult to recover from the degradation of the scene in the street and its outcome. He was so gentle and caressing, so apparently without thought beyond the moment, that Jessie began flutteringly to whisper to her heart that perhaps she had been wrong, perhaps, after all, Frederic had really loved her from the beginning. Both indulged in the luxury of forgiveness and fond indulgence, and they were like a shyly self-conscious couple on honeymoon.

Honeymoon folly is weakening, and next day Frederic had small power of resistance against his own miserable thoughts. His office-boy smirked when he saw him, and in the afternoon he grinned with a damnable familiarity as he announced Mr. Serge Folyat. Serge came in on his heels, caught the boy by the ear and thrust him out through the door. Frederic sank back into his chair, did his best to draw on his professional manner and sat with his fingertips pressed together and his lips pursed up.

Serge said:

"I've come to beg your pardon. I lost my temper."

Frederic could find nothing to say. Serge went on:

"Let us, if we can, discuss the matter on a friendly footing. You made a beast of yourself by pestering a woman. I made a beast of myself by hitting you. Now we know where we are. . . . We're likely to meet at home and other places where any obvious hostility would be embarrassing. . . ."

"I don't wish to meet you at home or anywhere else."

"It will be difficult to avoid. I think we had better settle the case out of court. Isn't that what you call it?"

Frederic tugged at his waistcoat and looked almost dignified as he said:

"I have no wish to interfere in your affairs. I will thank you not to meddle with mine."

"It happens, however," replied Serge, "that our affairs have overlapped. I must ask you to withdraw."

"And if I refuse?"

"Then it will become necessary for me to knock you down whenever I find you in my way. . . ."

"May I ask. . . ?"

"What I am getting out of it for myself? I was foolish enough to believe that you would not look for an interested motive. . . . The position is this. . . . You shirked a responsibility which I have had the pleasure and the privilege of assuming. Your beastly jealousy resents that, and you seem bent on taking up that old responsibility. There are two reasons why you should not do that—first, because it is too late; second, because your attempt to do so is an insult to your wife . . ."

"Keep my wife out of it."

"If you will tell your wife and ask her permission to make a settlement upon the boy . . ."

"You know I can't do that. I can't afford it."

"Then leave it alone."

"No."

"You'll take the consequences?"

"I'll take the consequences and be damned to you. . . . It's a fine thing to do, isn't it?—to take a woman when she's gone under?"

"My dear brother," said Serge, "you are the most childish little blackguard . . ."

"I'm man enough, any way, to stand up for my own rights . . ."

"When you learn that you have no rights you'll be a man . . . In a way you are right. My brother is not my keeper. I should prefer not to let the thing go any further, for your wife's sake. . . ."

"Keep my wife out of it!"

"Good-bye, then . . . You insist on being a fool?"

"I shall do as I think best."

The office-boy announced another client and Serge went away.

Frederic continued to waylay Annie Lipsett, but could never meet her without Serge, who called for her at her house in the morning and at her place of business in the evening. He wrote to her and implored her to give him an opportunity of explaining himself. (He had begun to believe, without reference to Jessie, whom he kept in a separate compartment of his mind, that he loved Annie, had never ceased to love her, and that a declaration of love would break down her resistance.) She did not reply and he wrote at great length explaining his desire to set her beyond anxiety, and hinting at the fires that were raging in his bosom, fires which he stoked with unceasing care.

At last he had a letter from her. She wrote:

"DEAR MR. FREDERIC,—Please, please believe that I want nothing from you, that I am happier as I am. I don't want my boy ever to know who his father was. He is mine by all the love I have given him. I could not share him with you, and to let you do anything for him would be sharing, wouldn't it? I have thought no ill of you for a long time now. I was to blame just as much as you. That is all over. You cannot take me into your life, therefore I cannot take you into mine . . ."

Frederic was interrupted in the reading of it and slipped it into the pocket of his coat.

His long absences had begun to stir jealousy in his wife. She was spying on him. She found the letter, her jealousy burst into flame, and thereafter was no peace in Frederic's house, nor any moment of sweetness and ease.

Once more, with horrible hypocrisy, Jessie resumed her habit of walking with her husband to the little iron gate in the morning, and meeting him there in the evening, and the old ladies and gentlemen, who had been a little anxious, peered through their windows and smiled their blessings.

Mrs. Folyat always said that Frederic's house reminded her of Eden before the Fall.

XXXI
NEWS FROM MINNA

"Sir" cries Adams, "I assure you she is as innocent as myself."

JOSEPH ANDREWS.

MRS. FOLYAT found the position of a grandmother entirely to her liking—the maximum of opportunity for beatific clucking with no responsibility. Annette had three children, Gertrude two, and Minna two, and Mrs. Folyat had already a large collection of their sayings for quotation in company, the most popular being an ode addressed by Annette's second boy to Mr. Gladstone, who had visited our town several times when its allegiance to the Liberal cause began to waver.

Minna brought her two children to stay in Burdley Park. They came for a fortnight and stayed four months. They would have stayed longer but that Francis began to be anxious and, after a good deal of cogitation, shyly questioned Minna as to her husband's doings.

"Basil is having a bad year," said Minna. "We're horribly poor sometimes. Rents in London are so dear."

"Even so," said Francis, "it seems hardly wise to leave him for so long."

"We have rows." Minna seemed to be quite cheerful about it. "Poor people always do have rows. They get so afraid, that they can't enjoy anything else."

"I was beginning to think that something serious might have happened."

"Oh, no. I'm still Basil's 'darling wife' when he writes to me, and he is my 'devoted husband.'"

"Marriage," said Francis, "is very difficult."

"Of course it is, to anybody who isn't an angel like you. . . . I'll go back and try again."

Francis sucked at his pipe thoughtfully.

"I oughtn't to tell you this," he said, "but Annette ran away once."

"Did she?"

"Yes, after breakfast. She was back again in time to give Bennett his tea."

Two days later Minna returned to London. The day after she had gone, Basil appeared with a drawn, miserable face. He asked Francis if he might speak to him, and Francis, quaking, led him into the study. Basil said he had been abroad. Minna had run away from him with the children.

"She came here," said Francis. "For all we know, she was writing to you every day and hearing from you. She said she was hearing from you. . . . Only just before she went she spoke about your letters. She went back to London yesterday. You ought to be with her. . . . In my opinion you ought to have fetched her back months ago."

Basil seemed to have a great deal to say, but he gulped it down and reached out for the railway guide.

"Yes," he said. "I suppose we must try again."

"If you want money," said Francis, "I would rather you came to me than were obliged to any one else."

"It isn't money. Thanks all the same."

Francis felt his heart sink, but he let it pass. It seemed all the more imperative to him that Basil should hurry back to London. He bustled him out of the house and saw him to the station.

Three weeks passed during which no word came from Minna or Basil. Francis did not write to them, hoping that they were settling their differences—whatever they might be.

One morning when he was up early he took in the letters and found one from Minna addressed to Mary. He watched Mary read it at breakfast. Without looking up she thrust it back into its envelope, her hand trembling so that the paper rustled, and slipped it into her pocket.

"Who's your letter from," asked Mrs. Folyat. Francis held his breath.

"It's from Fawcett's, the music-publishers. They haven't got the piece I wanted. Perhaps I didn't give the name right."

Francis breathed again.

Mary disappeared soon after breakfast. She went to Serge's studio. He was out. She waited for him all day and had nothing to eat. She did not even light the gas but sat thinking, thinking on no thought. Serge found her in the dark.

"Why, Mary!" he said.

She held out Minna's letter, and he sat and read it.

"Have you told anybody at home?"

"No. It's too awful."

"It isn't awful at all. It's very silly of them to be angry with each other."

"But divorce. . . . It's wicked."

"Nonsense. It may be necessary. It often is. . . . She'll want a good deal of sympathy."

"She doesn't deserve any."

"How absurd you screwed-up people are! You don't give sympathy because people deserve it, but because they need it."

Mary pondered that for a moment or two. Then she asked:

"What did you say I was?"

"Screwed-up."

Mary said nothing.

"We'd better burn this," said Serge. "We shall have to be discreet. Letters nearly always convey wrong impressions."

"Shall I write to Minna?"

"If you want to. Don't give her your opinion. She won't want it."

"Who is to tell them at home?"

"I will, if you like."

"That's what I wanted you to do. . . . I felt that something was happening all the time Minna was here."

"I'll go home with you now."

"I think the sooner the better. . . . Something awful might happen."

Serge found his father in the greenhouse and went straight to the point. Francis was in his shirt-sleeves. He laid down his trowel and very slowly put on his coat.

"I knew something was happening, but I never thought it could be as bad as that."

He sat down heavily and blinked through his spectacles.

"I seem," he said, "I seem to have brought my children into the world to very little happiness. I suppose Minna ought never to have married a poor man. . . . It's very queer, Serge, very queer. One reads of these things and the rights and wrongs of them appear to be very simple. They happen in one's own family and the rights and wrongs don't appear so simple. . . . If Minna were to come in now, I should be glad to see her. I should at least know that she was safe. . . ."

"The truth is," said Serge, "that the rights and wrongs don't matter. You either love people or you don't. If you love them, you help them. If you don't, some one else does."

"I think," said Francis, "I had better go to London. I always liked Basil. He always liked me. I might be able to make him see reason. . . . Minna says she is innocent. He ought to take her back."

"My dear father, that isn't reason. That is nonsense. . . . You're thinking of what people will say. Public opinion doesn't matter any more than my opinion or your opinion. If they have fallen so far apart as to wish to break the tie between them it will be quite impossible for them to live together without degradation— —"

"You go so fast. I can't follow you. I don't see . . ."

"It is always degrading for a man and a woman to live together when they have no love for each other."

"Dear me!" murmured Francis. "Dear me!" His face wore an expression of immense surprise. He went on muttering to himself in a puzzled way, and finally, with a sort of triumph, as though he had found the solution of his riddle:

"But if they are married?"

"My dear father, you must admit that love and marriage are two very different things. Love is divine, marriage is human."

"But— —"

"Marriage is not a divine ordinance. It is a respectable human institution contrived for the comfortable existence of society."

"I am thinking of Minna's children."

"So am I."

"She will lose them."

"That is her affair. Anything is better for them than being brought up in a house with a man and a woman who hate each other."

"I can't admit that."

"As a matter of principle, perhaps not; as a matter of practice, you will, just as you took over Frederic's mess. . . ."

"How did that turn out?"

"Splendidly."

Very slowly Francis turned that over in his mind and went back in memory to the day in Mrs. Entwistle's cottage. It did not bring him any great elucidation, but it gave him a feeling of confidence in Serge, and, clinging to him, he said:

"What are we to do?"

"If you'll agree to say nothing to my mother, to write nothing to Basil, and not to bother your head about the rights and wrongs of it, I'll go to London and see Minna. If there's a glimmer of hope I'll do everything I can. If there isn't, I'll see Minna through. . . . I don't think I shall come back. I can't stay in this place much longer. It gobbles men up and doesn't even have the decency to digest them properly. . . . It's a machine and has no conscience about the past, no concern for the future. It darkens men's minds so that they live hideously and their horrible sins are visited upon their children. No, I shan't come back. I can't. . . ."

"There is a great deal of wickedness in this place. It is God's will," said Francis.

"Men's will. The will of men cheated and cozened by their own rapacity. . . . But that is neither here nor there. Will you agree to say nothing to my mother until you hear from me?"

"I'll promise you that," said Francis with a little compunction, for he saw how dark would be the days of waiting with such a secret tugging at his heart and his wife babbling of her children's marriages. "How did you know? Did Mary tell you?"

"Yes, Mary told me. Mary has been rather a trump about it."

"I shall be able to talk to Mary," thought Francis, with a sigh of relief.

Serge spent the night packing and dismantling his studio. He destroyed a great many of his pictures, called up the porter and made him a present of his furniture and the clothes that were left after he had packed two bags.

In the morning he went to fetch Annie Lipsett. He found her just leaving, but made her go back with him to see the boy. Him he hugged and kissed, and then he gave Annie a cheque for fifty pounds for his education.

"And for God's sake," he said, "don't make him a gentleman. Put him to a trade. If he's any real good he'll get out of it. If he's only middling good he'll stay there and marry and die respectable. If he's bad—God help you; but he won't be that."

Annie said:

"You're going."

"Yes. I'm going."

She was very plucky and fought back her tears. Serge took her shoulders in his hands and said:

"You and I have had a queer sort of love, an impersonal sort of meeting in Heaven here on earth. I never understood before what it must feel like to be a seraph—just a head and wings. We've been so busy fighting our way up out of a slimy pit that we haven't had time to think much about each other—only the boy."

Annie's tears flowed freely and she clung to his hand and said:

"You don't know what you've been to me, but I can tell you now. It was so much to have you for my friend in that time when I had no one. I loved you. . . ."

"I know, I know."

"But all that sort of love went away afterwards when I had the boy. It has been a great thing for him too. . . ."

"I've learned a lot from him."

"That's so wonderful about you. You seem to be always learning. And now you're going. I used to dread your going, but now it doesn't hurt me at all. . . . You will always have me to think gladly of you."

"And I of you. . . . We've made the world richer by a friendship."

"I want to say thank you," she said, "but I can't, not enough."

"Of course you can't. . . . Come along."

In a few hours Serge was in the express for London. He had a portfolio of pictures and drawings, two bags, and one hundred and twenty pounds in notes. As the train passed out of the dingy murk and his eyes lighted on the green, undefiled country, he drew in great breaths and found it hard not to shout for joy in the new zest for adventure that had come to him.

"That seraph notion," he thought, "I wonder where it comes from? That curious hunger for the state of childhood, the pretence that it is superior to adult life. . . . Surely it all comes from their incompetence in managing their affairs as men and women. They seem to lose their simplicity. I wonder why? . . . Old Lawrie must be right. Mind, body, spirit. You can't poison the spirit. That's God, and He's beyond contamination. Body and mind are the instruments of the spirit. Poison the mind and the body suffers. . . . That's right. Yes: old Lawrie's right. Fear of love and fear of death; the mind hemmed in and losing its bright power of reflection, so that it shows only a distorted image of life. . . . No wonder they hate life when it looks like that. . . . It can't go on for ever. The spirit must break through it all in time . . . in time."

The train rushed along, and he began to think that perhaps the problem was being solved. When men had made it so easy to escape from their cities of captivity, would not their minds also be freed? Would there not be a gradual adjustment of mind to larger surroundings? Or were the minds of men so clothed with centuries of tyranny that swifter transportation also would be used as an instrument of slavery? . . .

"No," he thought, "there is a deeper faith in men than they know. They endure heroically because they are sure that in the end their efforts will lead to deliverance."

As an ironic comment upon his reflections the train ran into a real "old particular" London fog and was held up for half an hour outside the station. In that half-hour his thoughts ran swiftly. He had never been to London before, and he was moved by a boyish excitement at the prospect of entering it. That he found absurd. It would be hardly at all different from the place he had just left. That had held little for him: this could hold nothing at all. He had no ambition, and often ludicrously had learned the scorn a man can come by who prefers anything to his own advancement; often he had seen how profitable it was for a man to sacrifice his talent to his vanity, and how incredible to such a man that it could be possible to sacrifice vanity to talent. From all he had heard of London, the greatest city in the world, its subservience to ambitious men was as immense as its renown. In our town, Benskin and his school of little fishes had dubbed Serge "amateur" by way of killing him. He had liked the isolation that had followed, but now he thought that isolation could be of little use to a man, except he could spring from it to greater freedom and a purer joy in his work. "Amateur." . . . Being interpreted, that means one who loves his work, as its contrary, "professional," signifies one who works for gain. . . . These cities were professional. They rejected him, as they rejected all amateurs. . . . So be it. Serge felt no bitterness. He was a free man. He asked nothing: he had been given much, first of all the power to enjoy. . . . He chuckled to think that the only usefulness the suspicious world of professional men would allow him lay—apparently—in succouring females in distress. Knight-errantry, once the loftiest of professions, was descended into the hands of the contemned amateurs.

"At bottom," said Serge, "the difference between them and me is that I take women seriously and they don't."

His stay in London was shorter even than he had thought it would be. He visited Basil first, and found him working desperately, paintings, charcoal drawings, black-and-white, Christmas cards, book illustrations, designs for menus, chocolate boxes—all slipshod, formal, but just neatly and obviously charming. Through his teeth he asked Serge what the hell he had come for and went on working. Serge turned over a pile of drawings on the table by the window.

"Benskin would dote on you now. . . . How you must hate art to be able to do them so well!"

Basil grunted. "I hate everything."

"You always were extreme."

Basil laid down his pen.

"Did she send you?"

"No. She doesn't know I'm in London. I came to you first because I thought your point of view might be helpful when I come to tackle her. I've got nothing to go upon except her letter to Mary, which wasn't particularly illuminating."

"It wouldn't be. It's just funny to her—just funny, do you hear? I've implored her, on my knees I've begged her just to help me to understand her, to give me some clue as to what it is that she really wants, to keep us from going to smash, and she just sat and listened to me with that slow grin of hers. . . . I frightened her, I think, the last time, and the grin faded from her face, but she became as hard as a stone. . . . She didn't care. She didn't care. And I think she wanted to break me. . . . She hasn't done it. Do you hear? She hasn't done it!"

"Did you weep?"

"I . . . I broke down."

"Ah! Not a good way of convincing her of your capacity to give her what she wants."

Basil strode angrily about the studio, waving his arms and shouting.

"It's not a bit of good. It's done now. . . . It's all over. It's finished."

"It won't be finished until you've done thinking about it. There doesn't seem to be much prospect of that."

"I'm not going to discuss it with you."

"I don't want to. What are the facts? You've accused her of infidelity. Who's the man?"

"Fry. . . . His wife's divorcing him. That's evidence enough, isn't it?"

"I'm not concerned with the evidence. I only want to know whether it's necessary that there should be a divorce."

"She's left me."

"I might persuade her to return."

"Could you?"

"I might. . . ."

"I'll forgive her. . . . If she will come to me as a contrite woman. . . ."

"That's slush. If you are going to spend your lives in quarrelling as to which is really the magnanimous party, I shan't stir a finger. . . . Do you want her?"

"If she . . ."

"If you want her, there can be no conditions. . . ."

"But she . . ."

Serge saw that it was hopeless. Basil was clinging to his grievances, nursing them, cherishing them. They had become more precious to him than his own happiness, than his wife, than the well-being of his children. . . . Still there was hope that on Minna's side there might be magnanimity and generosity enough to uproot the thick-set hedge with which Basil had surrounded himself.

Minna was in rooms in the Marylebone Road, near Madame Tussaud's. She had a woman friend with her, a queer inanimate creature who looked as though she had stepped out of the waxworks—a model of Nell Gwynne. Minna seemed quite happy. She was lying on a sofa eating Turkish delight and reading "Jane Eyre." She dropped her book as Serge entered and her friend glided away.

"I *am* glad to see you," she said. "It's so dull. Isn't it a beastly business?"

"I've just been to see Basil."

"Is he still weeping?"

Serge ignored that question and asked her another.

"What's the trouble between you two?"

"Basil says I'm——"

"I know that, but that's only the outcome of the trouble."

Minna was interested. She sat up on the sofa with her hands between her knees.

"How clever you are, Serge! No one else has ever thought of that. Everybody else is quarrelling as to whether I did or did not."

"Did you?"

"No. That comes long after the mischief's done. The trouble between Basil and me is simply this. Basil wants me to be a mother to him and I can't. People are simply sickening about mothers. I'm a woman first and a mother afterwards. Being a mother grows out of being a woman. . . . Basil wants me to be a work of art in theory and a mother in practice. I simply couldn't do it. . . . It's my own fault. I knew Basil was like that before I married him. I had a sort of blind moment when I thought I could change him. You can't change people. I can't change myself. . . . I ought to have left him long ago, but Basil's the sort of man you can't leave. He clings. He plays on your nerves and makes you frightened. He looks at you with his big eyes and seems so helpless that you're afraid to leave him, and you don't like hurting him. He simply *makes* you be a mother to him and then takes advantage of it, and things go from bad to worse. . . . London seemed to frighten him, took away all his courage and his ambition. London's too big for him. He wants to be at the top of the tree all at once, simply because he's afraid of the climb. . . . We should have done better to stay at home."

"That wouldn't have made any difference."

"No, I suppose not. I am I and Basil is Basil and that's the whole story, and it's just like a man of that sort to turn round and try to kill you when you won't let him cling to you any longer."

Minna's voice became venomous.

"Grievances again!" thought Serge, and he saw then how impossible was his position. He could not tell Minna of Basil's willingness to take her back upon conditions. Either of them or both must surrender their grievances if anything were to be done. That seemed to be extremely improbable.

"You will not go back, then?"

"I'm quite willing to go back, if Basil——"

More conditions! Oh, the folly of insistence upon rights! . . . Serge dropped the subject, accepted the inevitable and asked:

"Then it is to go on?"

"That rests with Basil."

"If he does not withdraw the petition I suppose you will not defend."

"I shall defend my honour if I have to spend my last penny on it. I'm not going to have mud thrown at me and say 'Thank you' for it. I don't trust Basil. He's a vindictive little beast. He's sure to say our marriage was happy. . . . Besides, I must think of the children."

"I wish you would."

"I do. Their mother's honour is precious to them."

"Personally," said Serge, "I would sell my honour for twopence."

"Oh! you! . . . But then you don't care what anybody thinks of you."

"Not a straw."

"Then it isn't any good talking to you. You really are an immoral man. . . . If Basil goes for me, I shall go for him. You'd hold up the other cheek, I know, but then you're not human. I told my children once to think before they struck, and Benny said, 'I do think, and then I strike. . . .' I'm like that too. I'm not going to listen to you. I'm not going back to Basil, I'm not going to lie down and let him weep over my sins in public. He's a little beast and everybody shall know that he's a little beast. . . ."

Minna had worked herself up into a state of anger. She was hot and red in the face with it, and looked coarse and unpleasant.

Serge said to himself:

"No wonder knight-errantry is dead, since women have taken upon themselves to be as stupidly selfish as men."

He made one last effort, and suggested that she should take the more sensible course and leave it to Basil unopposed to set the cumbrous machinery of the law in motion, if only for the sake of her father and mother. To that Minna only replied with a brilliant but spiteful caricature of Mrs. Folyat's state of mind as slowly she digested the unpalatable truth that all marriages were not made in Heaven.

Serge wrote to Francis that night and told him that there was no hope, since both Minna and Basil were resolute to part. All that could be looked for was that they would injure each other as little as possible in the process. So far as he could see, the pain of uprooting was over. The pair were absolutely divorced. Unhappily, they seemed determined to call down on each other the disapprobation of the world, in their frenziedly childish desire to hurt each other. . . . Serge begged Francis to make his mother take a reasonable, human view of it, since Minna would need friendliness and assistance, and suggested that he should come to an arrangement with Basil's family for the maintenance of the children.

His letter ended thus:

"Good-bye, my dear father. I was your first disappointment, but in the end you and I recognised each other. That is permanent. It will be with me wherever I go, with you to the end of your life. You are of those who believe that understanding is not given to us. Your belief must be a bitter comfort to you. I believe that men are rapidly coming to an end of their material activity so that soon they will be forced to find understanding or perish. . . . Do you remember a night when you and I watched the rest acting an absurd play, and I said involuntarily, 'Round the corner'? Modern life is theatrical. Everybody is playing a part, because they are without understanding. Life for modern men and women is for ever round the corner because they attempt to tackle their affairs with the minds of children, children who believe everything they are told and examine nothing. They play with everything. They can do nothing else. Unhappily, life is a serious business which yields its reward of joy only to simplicity, sincerity, and purity, or, if you like the old trinity better—faith, hope, and charity. The old beliefs are true—nearly all that you preach, I mean; but from repetition they have become stale and meaningless. They need restatement. . . . I am going back to the sea, not because I believe that the 'great wide spaces of the earth'—

what a lot of twaddle is talked about them!—have a monopoly of truth, but because I must move and keep moving. It is in the air. Perhaps I feel it before other men. The salvation of human life lies in movement, circulation. . . . More simply and less philosophically I am going because it amuses me to go. I like passing through the world saluting the few men of courage and good heart whom one can find, and, of such men, my dear father, I count you not the least."

Francis kept this letter and through his hours of torment often read it. It let in air.

XXXII
THE CUTTING OF A KNOT

Fear, and the pit, and the snare, are upon thee, O inhabitant of the earth.

ISAIAH, xxiv. 17.

IT is one of the most disconcerting phenomena of existence that, when passionate love has answered its purpose, it simply disappears, leaving its instruments wedded by such truth as they have discovered in each other or divorced by the lies they have forged for each other's delight. Very rarely, however, is the issue so simple. The bone-and-shadow business comes into play here also, and most people marry with very little passionate love and a great deal of careful imitation of it, so that most marriages are strangled in their birth with a very tangled web of lies.

It was so with Frederic and Jessie Folyat in their marriage, and they were never so nearly united as when jealousy came between them. Their marriage feast did coldly furnish forth the funeral of love, and over love's dead body they quarrelled. They had scenes, hysterical skirmishes and almost as hysterical reconciliations. There was grim sport in it all, a sort of fascination in the stealthy prying and spying, each crouching and shrinking in readiness for the other's spring, the snarling bravado with which each dared the other to come on, a little further, a little further, inviting to a caress, repelling with a scratching blow; and all smooth-seeming, veiled, polite, with polished airs and graceful manners and feigned interest and inquiry: a pooling of the common stock only to wrangle over the division of it again. The gambling fever was in it. At any moment all might be lost upon a throw, a little gain, a little loss, more gain, more gain, a little more and the other might be beggared, the game won. But neither dared let the game come to an end. When one was near ruin, grey-faced, anxiously glaring for the turn of the card, the other cheated and the game went on. It absorbed both. Neither could do without it. It was a drug. Their craving for it was agony; its satisfaction a seeming delight.

They were very skilful and cunning to let no trace of it appear on the surface of their lives. Frederic abandoned all pursuit of Annie Lipsett, he deserted the company of his flattering fools, for these things trespassed upon the field of his fevered sport. It was very rarely that they went of their own accord to seek purchasable pleasures. Visits they paid, when politeness and discretion compelled, and everybody found them charming. They could be good company and their talents were useful. They became popular and were much in request to organise entertainments, bazaars, jumble sales, and such functions.

In his business Frederic became more cunning, quicker-witted, and his reputation gained. His practice increased. His whole life was concentrated on his home and his office. He grew lean and alert, but he was always tired.

In the early days of his management of the Bradby-Folyat estate he had borrowed large sums of money. These debts he was able considerably to reduce, and very soon there were no arrears of interest outstanding. As he began to feel himself on more solid ground his habit of exaggeration lost much of its hold upon him, and men who had previously avoided him began to seek his company. Many who had dismissed him as a bore now came to see qualities in him, and, as he gained the acquaintance of a better class of men, the quality of the work that passed through his hands improved.

Over Minna's disaster he behaved well. He explained the legal aspect of divorce to his father, and by telling him what he heard men saying about it—men who had known Basil Haslam, men of the world—helped him to understand that there was less malice than idle curiosity in gossip, that scandal was the thing of a day, and that sympathy was to a great extent on Minna's side and altogether with her parents. . . . Francis was not greatly comforted. He felt that the attitude of mind of Frederic's "men of the world" was rather dirty, but he appreciated the kindness, which was greater than he had looked for. He was not at all easy, remembering Serge's and his own attitude towards Frederic's imbroglio, when Frederic rushed up to town, pounced on Herbert Fry, and insisted on his marrying Minna. . . . As it happened, it was a fatal step. Minna complied only because she thought the marriage would infuriate Basil (the horrible ordeal through which she had passed had deprived her of all control), and Fry because he loved her and because his affairs were more complicated than any one knew save himself, and, having to leave the country, he preferred to pass into exile with a beloved companion. His life had come to ruin, and he thought that to have Minna for his wife would be a step towards reconstruction and would help to blot out the past. . . . Frederic came back glowing with virtue and manly pride, feeling that he had made an honest woman of his sister.

Frederic's interview with Herbert Fry had seemed to him a direct triumph of right over wrong. It was the first time he had ever found himself in the van of the big battalions, and it gave him a feeling of confidence that was almost exhilarating. He returned to his wife, to find that her suspicion of him was not abated, and convinced himself that she was cruel and unjust. He gambled in marriage more recklessly than ever, and if before she had been anxious, now she was filled with dread as she saw that she was playing a losing game. Sooner or later he would have cleared her out and the last tie between them would be broken. Her dread paralysed her. Only mechanically could she keep the cards fluttering and the pot a-boiling.

Frederic lost his drawn look. He was winning, and was sure that the luck would never turn again. Feeling immeasurably superior to Fry, who had committed the unpardonable folly of being found out, and morally on a different plane from Minna and the world of illicit love which had spewed her out to the scorn of all men (except men of the world, who could wink at these things), he fell back upon the cushion of middle-class prosperity, thrust aside happiness as a thing to be desired, and concentrated all his energies on money. He began to speculate—successfully at first, then unsuccessfully. In his early days of practice it had hardly been worth while to keep his accounts separate, and, as his business grew, he never troubled to reorganise his books.

Mrs. Bradby-Folyat died. She had taken a dislike to Gertrude and left Streeten Folyat only a thousand pounds. Frederic received twenty-five pounds to buy a mourning ring. That did not fret him. There was the estate to be wound up, and the pickings of the process would be rich.

The executors asked to see the accounts. Frederic made them up, but they were found so slovenly and unsatisfactory that further inquiry was instituted and an accountant was called in—a precise, mincing little man who spoke with a strong north-country accent, sniffed, and walked in and out of the office as though he were treading the aisle of a chapel. He exasperated Frederic so that he went out of his way to be rude to him. The accountant sniffed and smugly turned the other cheek. He was a week in the office and went away without saying a word.

Frederic received a letter from one of the executors requesting him to hand over all papers and securities to another larger firm of solicitors. Without comment a statement of account was enclosed, showing a deficit in the Bradby-Folyat estate of six thousand pounds. Every nerve in Frederic's body quivered and went hot and dry. He locked the statement away and gave orders for the Bradby-Folyat deed-box to be handed over to the representatives of the nominated solicitors upon their giving a receipt for it. Mechanically, with a fevered concentration upon the figures as an occupation to keep himself from thinking, he went into his banking account. He had three hundred pounds in cash. His shares, which would have to be sold at a loss, would realise another thousand. Outstanding debts amounted to not two hundred. . . . His wife's money was hers upon trust for her children, or, failing her children, for her nephews and nieces. All the Clibran-Bell money was trust money. His father had none, only enough to make a small provision for his old age and his wife and Mary.

The executor called. He was polite—a barrister by profession, with the most suave and urbane brow-beating manner. He supposed that the numerous mistakes could be rectified, and that where losses had occurred through incompetent investment the deficiency would be made good. Frederic said not a word. He twiddled a little piece of paper between his fingers and his face was as white as the paper. The executor drew his own conclusions and said:

"It is misappropriation and embezzlement. I have tried to persuade Batson's not to take proceedings, but they insist that it must go before the Law Society. . . . You will be lucky if you get no worse than being struck off the rolls."

The words bit into Frederic's brain and went trickling down his spine. The executor took his hat and left him sitting by his table still twiddling the little piece of paper, with his face as grey as a goose-feather. He sat very still for a long time staring at the piece of paper in his hand. Presently he let it fall, but still he sat staring. . . . He heard his clerks go. The cashier brought the key of the safe. He said good-night. Frederic said good-night, and was startled at the sound of his own voice. The silence had seemed to him so inevitable, so final, surely eternal.

One thought sprang to life in his brain: "No one must know." That gave him a purpose and brought him to the need of action. At home he forced an amiable mood upon his wife. In the evening they called at Burdley Park and took Mary to the theatre. They saw her home after a merry evening, and, in the highest spirits, they called on the Clibran-Bells and invited some of the family to come and play whist on the morrow. Frederic smoked a cigar with his father-in-law and discussed the new waterworks scheme and the police scandal which had lately set all the town by the ears, a whole division having been discovered to be drawing large profits from organised prostitution in a certain district. Many droll stories were in circulation of constables caught *in flagrante delicto*, and Frederic and his father-in-law laughed heartily over them. At certain moments Frederic had a crazy desire to pick his father-in-law up by the scruff of the neck and shake him: there was something in his manner so ridiculous and undignified, and his jocularity was so trivial and pointless. However, Frederic continued to laugh, and old Clibran-Bell patted him on the shoulder and told him he was a good fellow, a very good fellow.

In the office next day Frederic teased and pestered his clerks and kept them all bustling, finding errands for them to go, requiring books from the Law Library, discovering papers that were long overdue and had to be fetched. Seized with a wild, hilarious impulse, he made out a whole series of bogus writs and sent them to be stamped and delivered. . . . When all the clerks had gone he sat down and wrote to Batson's, saying that he had made further inquiries and had many papers and much information to lay before them which had previously been overlooked, and he added that such deficiency as might remain after final examination would be paid in full. This letter he posted himself. He returned to his office, wrote a cheque for each of his clerks, repaid his articled clerks their premiums, laid an envelope containing them on each desk, looked round to make sure he had forgotten nothing, locked the outer door, walked down to the bridge by the Collegiate church and threw the key into the river.

At night, after the whist-party had dispersed, he pretended that he had papers to look into and sent Jessie to bed. He sat by the fire staring into the glowing coals. It died down, but he made no effort to keep it alight. He was exhausted. The assumed hilarity of the evening had been too great a strain, and yet not strain enough. He was driving himself to a collapse, but was fearful lest it should come too soon.

It was very cold. He shivered and crouched over the black grate. He heard his wife's voice calling him:

"Aren't you coming up to-night?"

"Presently . . . presently."

When he judged that she would be asleep he crept upstairs, and in the dark, to avoid waking her and also to avoid seeing her, he slipped into the bed by her side. All night he lay awake, cold, throbbing, straining and starting at all the small noises of the house.

At breakfast he chattered gaily over the newspapers. There was a school board election toward, and a woman had offered herself as a candidate for their division. He chaffed Jessie and said he supposed she would soon be wanting to vote for Parliament. Jessie was to spend the day in town shopping with her mother. He asked her to make sundry small purchases for him, and they agreed that they would have a crab for supper.

He was rather a long time packing the little handbag he always took with him to town. She went to remind him that it was getting late and found him with his hand in a drawer. He shut it hastily and asked her to fetch his tobacco-pouch from upstairs. When she came down again he was waiting for her at the front door. She walked to the little iron gate with him and they kissed. As he reached the kerb he turned to look at her and saw the old ladies and gentlemen at their windows, and he felt with a twinge of shame that for years he had been a spectacle without knowing it. . . . He thought Jessie looked rather ill, tired, old, and bony. It was absurd for them to kiss in public. . . . Everything seemed absurd, fantastical, and unreal. The world was presented to his eyes in sharper outline than he had ever seen it before. It was bathed in a cold grey light. It had nothing to do with him. It was going on. He felt stationary. That his body was moving was nothing. His thoughts were not moving. Everything was absurd. The new sharply outlined world, with its curious interwoven activities (he saw how they were dovetailed), was moving on. The world with which he had been concerned—the world in which he had been miserable, elated, crestfallen, amused, disgusted—the world in which he had known affection and companionship and spite and jealousy—was moving backward, sinking from under his feet while he himself stood on the verge of a nonsensical dawn that had its light from a setting sun. Away from him, backward and forward, everything moved faster and faster, making him dizzy, intolerably dizzy, sick and cold with it.

He had intended to go to London, but at the station he saw a sign indicating a train for Plymouth. The name started out of the blurred past and relieved him, a little restored his balance, and he saw clearly the scenes of his boyhood—the grimy little office where he had been articled, the ships, the Hoe and the Sound. Then all that too slipped away from him.

He took the train for Plymouth, and had a carriage all to himself as far as Crewe. He sat stupidly staring out of the window. The train was going so fast. Why did everything move so fast? . . . He was very tired. At Crewe a man entered the carriage. He had not thought of that. He must change. He must be alone. The train moved on before he could bring himself to stir. . . . With the presence of the man at the other end of the carriage his mood changed. Out of the cold mists that were upon him a desire rose and took possession of him. He did not know what desire it was but it took the form of an itch to speak to the man. He stole glances at him but his lips would not obey him. The man said:

"It's a fine day."

Frederic agreed that it was a fine day, and the desire in him fell back into the void. The man was part of the absurd world that had nothing to do with him, the world that went on, the trivial, silly world. How trivial and silly everything was: the train was silly, movement was silly; absurd and grotesque was the man's voice and his idiotic comment on the day, and that was silly too. A day was but the passage out of night into night. The whole world was nothing, moving out of nothing into nothing. Some things were clear because they did not matter; other things were blurred because they had mattered to him, Frederic, who mattered no longer because he was standing still and everything else was moving. . . . His eyes mechanically read the legend—"To Stop the Train Pull Down the Cord Outside the Window. Penalty for Improper Use, £5."

"I could stop it," he thought, "but it would only move on again. Everything moves on again."

With that slight movement in his mind old habit reasserted itself and he began to crave for self-pity, but the unfamiliar presence of the man made that impossible. That habit of mind needed the co-operation of other habits. It was isolated and fell away again. . . . There had been so much clear-cut action in the last few hours, action for a purpose, action that could not be recalled and therefore drove him on to the fulfilment of the purpose.

"I must be alone," thumped Frederic's mind, and the train-wheels took it up, "alone, alone, alone."

He became exasperated with the presence of the other man. What right had he in the world where there was nothing but Frederic, nothing at all, an empty world where a man must at last make sure, make very sure, that he is nothing?

The man got out at Bristol. It seemed to Frederic that he had come and gone like a shadow. So little time, the emptiness of the world moving so swiftly, and through it Plymouth coming nearer and nearer to him. Plymouth appeared to him as a sort of monster, a dogging shadow that had run after him for a long time, terrifying him, to spring ahead and come to meet him. And yet it was still behind. Everything was two things, behind and in front; the contradiction made it nothing. . . .

He was frozen with terror. Back, back, this way; no, that; now the other. . . . "It will have me! It will have me! Why? I am nothing. I am nothing. It doesn't believe that I am nothing. . . . No, no. There is nothing but myself, myself, myself. . . ."

He drew the revolver from his pocket.

"No, no. I will go back. I will go back."

He sat absolutely numbed for a long time. Suddenly he thought of his wife, coldly, clearly. He saw himself in her. She was stronger than he. He must show her that he was the stronger.

He thought of his father and passed into a golden stream of peace. He would go to his father. . . "I will arise and go to my father and say unto him, 'Father, I have sinned against Heaven and before thee and am no more worthy to be called thy son.' . . ." His father would understand as he had understood before. . . . But then he knew that all that his mother had thought of him would be sponged away from her mind, and he remembered with what bitterness she had spoken of Minna.

"Too difficult," he thought. "Too many people."

The train gathered speed down an incline. Faster and faster. His terror lest the journey should come to an end clutched him back into the present. He must make haste. He must be the quicker.

He had dropped the revolver into his pocket again. Now he fumbled for it. It caught in the lining, and he tugged at it with feverish impatience. . . . His heart leaped on the report, which seemed to come from far away. . . . He felt nothing; less and less; out of the swiftly moving world he was sinking downward, downward, gathering speed, falling, falling into nothing.

In the small hours of the morning Mr. Clibran-Bell rang furiously at the bell of the house in Burdley Park. After many minutes Francis came down in his dressing-gown with a candle in his hand. Mr. Clibran-Bell stepped into the hall.

"Frederic," he said, "has not been home all night. Jessie is at my house. . . . My dear friend, my dear old friend . . ."

"Has . . . something happened?"

"He's . . . he's at Plymouth. Dead. They found him in the train, shot in the side."

Francis stood very still, his mind slowly grasping this new appalling fact. Tears trickled down his cheeks into his beard.

"I shall go to Plymouth by the first train," said Mr. Clibran-Bell, "I must get at the truth for Jessie's sake."

"Yes. It is very good of you."

It was a long time after Mr. Clibran-Bell had gone before Francis went upstairs again. The candle burnt itself out. His thoughts see-sawed up and down.

"Frederic—dead. Frederic—dead."

When he had groped his way back to his own existence, burdened with this new catastrophe, he said to himself:

"I can't go on. . . . I can't go on."

He saw Frederic lying huddled in the corner of a railway carriage, strangers to whom he was nothing finding him. . . . Then he thought of that other dead body that he had seen long, long ago, the woman lying in the little dark house, under the guttering light of the tallow candle and the clement light of the moon. Death violent, death insistent, death that would not be shrouded away or softened or made seeming blessed with words or tears. Tears! Death was too harsh. And yet it mattered nothing how it came about. It was always the same: bitter, the bitter end to bitterness. All life was salt with the savour of death. Vain, vain the endeavour to sweeten it. Sweetness and corruption, were they not yoke-fellows? . . . Words from the Bible passed through Francis Folyat's mind: "I am the resurrection and the Life," and again: "For behold, the days are coming in which they shall say, Blessed are the barren, and the wombs that never bare, and the paps which never gave suck," and again in his bitter grief he turned to the Book of Job:

"My days are past, my purposes are broken off, even the thoughts of my heart.

"They change the night into day: the light is short because of darkness.

"If I wait, the grave is mine house; I have made my bed in the darkness.

"I have said to corruption, Thou art my father: to the worm, Thou art my mother and my sister.

"And where is now my hope? As for my hope, who shall see it?

"They shall go down to the base of the pit where our rest together is in the dust."

XXXIII
THE CONCLUSION OF THE MATTER

The vision of Christ that thou dost see
Is my vision's greatest enemy.
Thine has a great hook nose like thine
Mine has a snub nose like to mine.

THE EVERLASTING GOSPEL.

TWELVE middle-class Englishmen and an official sat in inquest on the body of Frederic. They gazed shyly and uninterestedly upon it and then heard the evidence to the effect that he was most happily married and was without financial worry of any kind. . . . The verdict, in view of the fact that the revolver was in the deceased's overcoat pocket, was one of death by misadventure.

Francis learned the truth from Mr. Clibran-Bell. Mrs. Folyat was not told, neither was Jessie. Queer things were rumoured, however, and Mrs. Folyat began to feel—not absolutely without foundation—that she was looked upon askance. She went into deep mourning and raised Frederic to sainthood, and surrounded herself with relics from among his personal belongings. She brooded over the past and began to piece together her scattered memories. Nothing took clear shape except, what she had not seen at the time, the long coolness between her husband and her son, and she began to charge and reproach Francis with it. By vilifying Francis she had the illusion that she was exalting Frederic. She kept insisting that Francis must be sorry now that her poor angel was dead. Francis was remorseful. He was probing deeper and deeper into the unillumined past, groping his way through tortuous mole-galleries. The perpetual false deification of Frederic bothered him, his wife's voice, lachrymose and thin, dinning in his ears, was an exasperation. He was busy, frantically busy, forcing his way with all the strength of his nature out of the slough of despond into which he had fallen, and she seemed intent on thrusting him out of the slough into a sea of treacly mud. At length, one day, when she had raised Frederic a peg higher in her idolatrous beatification, suddenly the truth was wrenched from him:

"Can you not see that he meant to kill himself?"

"Oh! Frank . . . !"

He could despitefully have bitten his tongue out for having said it, but, having done so, he owed it to her to go on. It might prove her salvation. It might bring her back to him so that together they might perceive and win to the ways of brightness.

"He took the pistol with him in his pocket. He had no luggage with him. He had locked the door of his office and paid up his clerks' wages and the premiums of his pupils."

"Oh! Frank . . . Oh! Frank!"

And Francis hoped that she would turn to him and understand, but her very anguish of sorrow she must turn to self-indulgence, and she moved from the luxury of worship to the luxury of self-accusation:

"We drove him to it. All of us. We never understood him."

She told Jessie, who was prostrated by the knowledge, and Mr. Clibran-Bell refused ever to enter the Folyats' house again.

Francis passed through the very blackest hours of all after that. He prayed to his God but was not comforted; his mind would run only in the harshest channels of the faith he had spent his life in teaching. The God he found was a jealous God, a God of cruelty and vengeance and punishment. In vain he told himself that this was the just visitation of sins. He could not believe it. All his spirit craved for the belief in mercy, the living eternity, the life everlasting. He was hemmed in by the habit of years, and long familiarity with things sacred, all the vocabulary of paradox that had flowed so easily from his lips week in, week out, year after year. He wanted the truth of it, but it was all words, words, words, a rain of fine dust falling upon his intelligence, blinding his eyes. He needed that in his religion which could square with and illuminate the facts of his existence, but ever the darkness grew more impenetrable.

For three weeks he went on mechanically with his work, going blindly through the ritual which he had fought so hard to establish, but always when he came to the Benediction and commended the congregation to the Peace of God, he knew, could not away with the knowledge, that there was no peace in his own heart, and he rebuked himself and called himself Hypocrite.

He could not take refuge in self-torment. His need was too great. He told himself that he no longer believed, and prayed for help in his unbelief. But there had always been faith in him. Nothing had ever shaken it. His necessity lay in the fact that the symbols he had always used were cheapened, worn, debased. His mind could not change. It was definitely cast in the story of the Godhead in Man in the person of Jesus of Nazareth, born of the Virgin birth, persecuted and slain by the Jews to rise again in glory to the eternal salvation of souls. . . . The teaching of this gospel should, if it had any purpose, lead to noble life, a superb preparation for eternity. But whither had it led himself? To the smallest of small lives, to the ruin of two of his children, fallen into the very snares against which they had been warned with all the threats of eternal punishment and Hell fire at the command of an appointed minister of the Christian religion. . . . He tried to look beyond his own family, to see what effect the Gospel had had upon his parishioners and he could not disguise from himself the pitifulness of their condition. To consider the effect of the Christian religion upon the history of the world was too large an undertaking for him.

Serge had said that he was of those who believe that understanding is not vouchsafed to us. What did he mean? . . . Words haunted him:—"To justify the works of Man to God," or was it "To justify the works of God to Man"? Surely the last. The works of Man could not be justified. He felt himself to be near the clue he was seeking, but the effort to follow it was beyond him. For him the only tie between Man and God was Jesus Christ.

He read the Gospels, and soon gave up trying to unravel the hard sayings, but he read again and again every passage in which the words Love and Mercy occurred. They soothed him, and, reading over and over the gentleness of Jesus under persecution, he became softened and very tender, and sought the company of children, his grandchildren.

He rested for a fortnight and then took up his work, for one Sunday only. All the old business of threatening and hectoring and denouncing and holding the wrath of God back with prayer, and piling up mountains upon mountains of sin to teach the love and mercy of the Gospel through and after punishment, everlasting and relentless, was empty, all sound and fury.

His conclusion was, not that the Christian religion had become theatrical, rhetorical, mechanical, inhuman and unjust, but that he himself by his own life had become unworthy to administer it. Like many Christians, faced with the difficult, almost (in these days) impossible, task of distilling the essential truth from its accumulation of tainted lumber, he took refuge, without seeing any inconsistency, in the ascetic ideal, thinking that a life of absolute chastity and poverty and abstraction from the things of this world would give a man the right to hurl thunder and the lightnings of the Jewish Bible at his fellow men. And yet in his heart, as, latent in the hearts of all men, was the true faith in the ineffable love,

... che muove 'l Sole e l'altre stelle.

He could not disentangle this love, this spirit of man, from the superstition of the ages, and could not therefore let it freely move his own existence. He told himself that he had failed, that he ought never to have entered the priesthood, that he was an old man and could not change. No other course lay open to him than to retire.

He wrote to his Bishop to ask his leave, and, if it were granted, to apply for a pension from the Diocesan fund.

Never again did he conduct Divine service in any church.

He felt infinitely happier when he had done this, and a new brightness came to Mrs. Folyat and Mary when they knew they were to escape from the town where they had come by so much suffering, and the numbing monotony of a rather idle existence in drab surroundings. They set their faces southwards, for they had decided to live in Potsham, where Francis had held his first curacy. They were going to live in Crabtrees, where Francis Folyat and Martha Brett had met and loved each other so long ago, and all day long Francis would be busy in the garden running down to the river, and all day long Martha would sit in the gazebo and look out at the water, and see the tide coming in, and the herons fishing, and the boats go sailing by, all as it had been long ago, peaceful and beautiful. . . . Already, weeks before they could go, the peace of it began to fill the house in Burdley Park, and the dark past slipped away from them and Francis began to feel the richness of old age, when best and worst have been done, and the fruits of reflection can be gathered in.

Often as he sat working in the greenhouse, or in the study turning over his books—he had gone back to the loves of his early days, Fielding and Don Quixote—Francis would think of Serge, and the day when together they had walked away from Mrs. Entwistle's cottage. That memory preoccupied him more and more, and he felt a desire to see Annie Lipsett again before he went away. She wrote to him at long intervals to let him know that she had not forgotten. His feeling about the episode had always been spiced with the joy of forbidden things. It had been entirely separate from the rest of his life, and yet, unknown to him, it had informed the whole of it, and, in his most need, had given him the assurance of love and mercy which had upheld him in the face of the doctrine and dogma of his Church, even though he had seemed to himself to be upholding the Church by the sacrifice of himself.

He found Annie Lipsett busy and thoughtful. She was going to be married to an auctioneer who had been a lodger in her mother's house. She had just had a letter from Serge in Ceylon and its friendliness had removed her last anxieties.

"You see, sir," she said to Francis, "Mr. Serge found me when everything was as complicated as that piece of lace, and he made it all simple. And after that, being with him made one able to bear everything, because one felt that, whatever it was, it would go away. He used to say that being unhappy and dark in your mind was just the same as being unwell in your body, and if it was taken in time there was always a cure for it. So funny he used to be about it. He was always talking to me about the boy, and he used to say that I must teach him nothing, because children are always right by themselves until they begin to imitate grown-up people, and bad things are easier to imitate than good because they are grotesque, and grown-up people have always to be learning good things from children over and over again."

"I have never forgotten that day when I came to see you."

"Nor I, sir."

"We're going away, for ever. It is queer, but you are the only person whom I really wanted to see before I left. We have never seemed to belong to this place."

"I used to hate it too, but Mr. Serge made me laugh at it all. He said it was just an accident, though I didn't know what he meant by that. I often didn't really understand Mr. Serge, except about the boy, but then I could see that everything he said was true."

"I hope you will be very, very happy."

Annie surprised Francis by putting her arms round his neck and kissing him. He returned the kiss.

It was only some time after he had left her that it struck him that he had never once thought of Frederic in connection with her. When he called

Frederic to his mind it was always as a graceful, impudent, funny little boy. He had never known the man Frederic. Frederic had never been a man.

Even in our town the green of spring was showing and the zestful wind was blowing upon the blackened houses when Francis, his wife and Mary left upon their long journey to the south. Gleeful and glad they were, and the spring was in their hearts and the keen adventurousness of escape. After long captivity they were shaking from their shoes the dust of the hostile city, leaving in its toils the sole hostage of all their family, Annette, doomed to the life of drudgery to which that city condemns its women, for, except they be born in drudgery, the sons of its women could never endure its service, nor would they be fitted for it.

XXXIV
NUNC DIMITTIS SERVUM TUUM, DOMINE

For mine eyes have seen Thy salvation.
THE SONG OF SIMEON.

MANY wise men have laughed at the futility of thought and discarded an opinion as a worthless thing.

In the garden at Crabtrees Francis grew roses and delphiniums and tall hollyhocks and all homely flowers, and busily he tended his vegetables and herbs. He kept bees and grew skilled in their ways. Every day in summer Mrs. Folyat sat in the gazebo, and in the winter she had her own little drawing-room where the gossips would come in and take tea over a great fire.

Their living was very frugal, for their means were small. Only two houses besides Crabtrees were left of Mrs. Folyat's inheritance.

Outwardly Potsham was hardly at all changed since the day when Francis and his bride had set out on their honeymoon, but its glory was departed. Its fragrance and faint perfume of the high manners of an older day were gone. Little boys whom they remembered playing barefooted in the street called the Strand, down by the little dock and the mud flats, had made fortunes and dispossessed little by little the old gentlefolk. Their sons had gone to the universities and their daughters had visited London. No longer were the inhabitants of Potsham gently little in a little place, but in a little place aped the follies of great cities. People and place were no longer in harmony. Men and women seemed continually to be adjusting themselves to an outside standard. They were as sluggards who protest their wakefulness. . . . But for Francis and Martha, Potsham was as it had been in their youth, a place of sleep, of tranquil sleep attended by pleasant dreams of roses and blue water and warm figs ripening in the sunlight mellowed by the soft, moist air.

Their golden wedding came, their diamond-wedding, and between the two was but the drowsy humming of bells in a lofty tower. The hair of both was snow-white, and Francis had his brushed into two long ringlets that fell down on to his shoulders on either side of his head. His eyes were bright and young, often twinkling with merriment behind his spectacles, and people used to come and tell him funny things to see him enjoy the joke and chuckle down in his throat and shake all over with his inward mirth.

Gertrude often came to stay with her two children, and upon a day she arrived and never went away. Streeten had shed his capital bit by bit in one profession after another until he had not enough left to support his family. Then he disappeared without a word and no trace of him could be found.

Every two years Annette used to come and bring with her one or more of her children. Like her mother, she had eight. She could never stay long because Bennett would write every day and implore her to come back. . . . When any of her children had been ill she used to send them down, and they stayed until Francis judged them well enough to return, and that was never until their little pinched white faces were filled out and baked as brown as a bun. The second boy, Stephen, once spent five months at Crabtrees. He was a very queer, silent little creature, and he used to sit and stare at his grandparents and his aunts. Once, after dogging Francis for two days and scrutinising him in the most embarrassing way, he said:

"Grandpa, what is it makes your eyes so bright and blue, like the sky?"

Francis chuckled and replied:

"My dear, they're little mirrors and I polish them."

A great summer passed into a melancholy misty autumn, but on a rare fine day, the sun warming the first sighing breath of winter, Stephen Lawrie sat with a book in his lap under the Siberian crabtree on the lawn. His grandfather was digging in the vegetable garden near by, when, looking up, Stephen saw him pitch forward and fall flat on his face. It was as though he had been blown down.

The boy sat staring, stunned by the heaviness of the fall. Then he was seized by the terror of it and rushed screaming away.

It was a stroke, and Crabtrees became a house of the sick. Stephen was packed off home.

Before the winter was out Francis seemed to be quite well again, and he was out and about and busy preparing for the spring. February was hardly gone when he was laid low again, this time never to rise. He was partially paralysed and could not speak. For a long time his wits were gone. . . .

Slowly he crept back again into the existence of the house. His spirit would not yield up his body to the earth.

Gertrude was his nurse, and very gentle with him. She was creeping about his room, thinking him asleep, with her shadow swinging to and fro as she moved. In a sudden, strangled voice, she heard him say:

"I can speak."

She turned to him, but he lay very still, and his face looked pinched and whiter than it had done. She was alarmed and sat up with him all night. In the early morning he asked to see his wife. Gertrude fetched her, and she came huddled and bunched up in shawl and flannels and sat by his bedside. He moved his hand a little and she reached out and took it in hers. He said:

"It has been a long time, but it has been a good time. It has not all been good for you. I would be glad if you—if you could forgive me . . ."

"Oh! my dear, my dear. . . . The best . . ."

"I have always been afraid," he went on, and his voice gained in strength. "I have always been afraid of saying too much, and I have said too little. . . . It has been best when we were old. You have much to forgive."

Mrs. Folyat could only weep. Francis asked to be given his Bible and the amethyst cross he had worn on Sundays on his watchchain. They were laid by his side and he took the cross in his hand. He said that everything he left was to go to Mary, but she was to help the others when they needed help. . . . Then he told his wife she must go away and rest, for he desired to communicate for the last time and must have a space in which to prepare himself. Gertrude aided Mrs. Folyat out of the room.

It was All Fool's Day.

At nine o'clock Mary was having breakfast alone when Serge walked in. She told him, and he went up at once to his father's room. He stood by the bed for a long time before Francis opened his eyes and saw him. His eyes smiled and he said:

"My son."

"Father."

"I am not of those who believe that understanding is not given to us, for I came to understand. The beginning and the ending of all things is in God, and we may not question, nor idly interpret the beginning and the end. We pass from dust to dust, but the spirit endureth for ever, and in all things in our passage the spirit moves us. Is it not so?"

"It is so."

"And life is very good, to be rounded with a sleep."

"Life is very good."

"Surely I have not altogether failed my God, since I have known you."

"We have known each other. A man must die many times before his life be done."

"So be it. . . . I shall sleep now."

Serge stooped and kissed his father's brow, and in a few minutes he was dead.